come back
to me
SARA
FOSTER

**SIMON &
SCHUSTER**

London · New York · Sydney · Toronto · New Delhi

A CBS COMPANY

COME BACK TO ME
Published in Australia in 2017 by
Simon & Schuster (Australia) Pty Limited
Suite 19A, Level 1, Building C, 450 Miller Street, Cammeray, NSW 2062
First published by Bantam in 2010

10 9 8 7 6 5 4 3 2

A CBS Company
Sydney New York London Toronto New Delhi
Visit our website at www.simonandschuster.com.au

National Library of Australia Cataloguing-in-Publication entry
Creator: Foster, Sara, 1976– author.
Title: Come Back to Me / Sara Foster.
ISBN: 9781925456714 (paperback)
                  9781925456721 (ebook)
Subjects: Marriage – Fiction.
                  Man-woman relationships – Fiction.

Cover design: Christabella Designs
Cover image: Chris Prakoso / EyeEm
Typeset by Midland Typesetters, Australia
Printed and bound in Australia by Griffin Press

For Matt and Marian
Thank you for helping me touch my dreams

And for Hannah
My sunshine

part one
holding on

1

london
november 2009

It was already dark outside, the wind working itself up into a frenzy against the bedroom window. Chloe sat at her dresser, staring at the mirror while absently fingering the latest gift from her husband – a dainty row of black beads dotted with brilliant red stones that shimmered in the lamplight. Distantly she could hear Alex getting ready in the adjacent bathroom – the sound of the shower turning on and off, water running in the basin, electric toothbrush whirring, then feet shuffling, getting louder as he re-entered their bedroom and walked over to her.

In the mirror, her eyes met his reflected ones, and she smiled.

'You look distracted?' he commented, his voice rising with the question.

'Mmm,' she murmured, fingering the beads. She wanted

so much to tell him. To share the news that she herself had only just discovered. But now was not the time.

She lifted the beads. 'Would you?'

He came close behind her as she pulled her shoulder-length bobbed hair out of the way, and she felt his fingers softly brush her neck as he clumsily manoeuvred the clasp. She watched in the mirror and saw a frown flicker across his face as he fumbled for a moment with the delicate links. As he let go, she whirled around and kissed him.

Alex stood back and looked at her, shaking his head. 'Damn, you look gorgeous, Chloe. That dress is stunning on you.'

Chloe smiled as she ran her hands down the simple black wraparound dress she was wearing, as Alex added, 'Although, what I'd really love would be to push you back on that bed and ravish you – and get you all messed up again!' They grinned at one another, then Alex sighed. 'However, I guess it wouldn't be good to keep Mark waiting. I'm sure he'd happily get the evening off to a bad start given half a chance.'

Chloe smiled sympathetically. She knew Alex hated these get-togethers with her colleague Mark, not that there had been many of them. She went out of her way to avoid them too if possible, having realised that being with the two men together was akin to refereeing a verbal bout of boxing. Alex could probably just about have put up with the pompous, pontificating lawyer-Mark, but as he was also Chloe's ex-boyfriend this steered them into even more uncomfortable territory. And in front of Alex, rather than being unnerved by the situation, Mark seemed to revel in it, and would preface as many comments as he could with, 'When Chloe and I were together . . .'

She hoped that tonight would be different. Mark was bringing along a new girlfriend, and Chloe was optimistic that this dinner date might mark a fresh beginning for all of them; especially since Neil, one of the senior partners at work, had recently involved Chloe and Mark in one of the biggest cases the firm had ever had. It meant they would be working together quite a bit in the coming months.

Without thinking, she opened her mouth to tell Alex her news, despite her earlier good intentions, but as she did so he turned away, and something in the tense set of his back made her stop herself and suck in a breath instead. What if he didn't like what she had to say? Could she be sure his reaction would be the one she wanted? She stood there for a second, faltering, unaccountably nervous.

Alex sensed her watching and turned back around, grinning at her as his fingers flew deftly upwards fastening buttons. And there, as always, his eyes, with their utter familiarity and lack of guile, reached through her inexplicable nerves like a caress, shooing away all irrational thought.

She shook her head at herself as she slipped on her shoes. She would wait until later to tell him, when they weren't in such a rush, but she was sure it would be okay. Why, when life was on the up, was she worrying that it might slide away from her?

They ran along the pavement for the short distance between their parked car and the warm, welcoming lights of the restaurant, holding their jackets over their heads to try to shelter themselves from the sudden downpour. Chloe saw Mark as soon as they got inside Casa Bella. He was sitting in the corner opposite a brunette with her back to them, who appeared to be studying the menu intently while Mark gazed at her. The lighting around them was perfectly pitched to create romantic ambience, and something about the semi-darkness meant that everyone was talking in hushed and reverent tones. Mark looked like he had come straight from work – he was wearing the same suit Chloe had seen him in earlier, and she felt a moment of panic at the hours he put in compared to her. She imagined the senior partners' expressions as they walked past her dark, empty office at 5.05 p.m.

Mark looked towards the door and Chloe raised a hand in greeting. He didn't appear to see her, but ran his fingers through his short, thick brown hair, patting it to check it was in place before his gaze returned to the woman in front of him – who, Chloe assumed, must be Julia. From the entrance-way she could make out long, dark, slightly wavy hair with a small flower pinned behind one ear. The hair shone with health, and the shape of her head, neck and shoulders made Chloe instantly sure that Mark hadn't been lying when he'd said Julia was beautiful. She wished she'd done something more with her own hair, which had just been tucked neatly behind her ears and was now plastered messily against her head by the rain, but she seemed to have become more prac-tical about her appearance of late and dressing up had begun to feel unnatural to her. Now she felt instantly plain and underdressed, aware of the slight protrusion of her stomach and the oblique width of her thighs.

Chloe and Alex made their way over to their seats, directed by a waiter. 'There you are!' Chloe said brightly as they neared.

'Hi, Chloe.' Mark reluctantly turned his gaze from Julia and kissed Chloe's cheek formally as she sat down next to him. 'This is Julia.' He smiled proudly.

Julia half-turned in her seat and the two women exchanged handshakes and hellos. Chloe's impression had been right – Julia had high-set cheekbones and enormous dark eyes. She smiled and said, 'And this is my husband . . . Alex . . .'

Her voice trailed off.

She watched Alex's eyes widen as he went to shake Julia's hand. He took a tiny sharp breath and swayed slightly, then he quickly put his free hand on the back of his chair to steady himself, whilst the other one, although still held out, drooped like a flower in sudden wilt.

'Nice to meet you . . . Julia?' he said, in a broken, tremulous voice unlike anything Chloe had heard come from him before.

Mark looked up from his menu and he echoed Chloe's startled expression as they glanced from Alex to Julia. They both saw Julia's face – stricken and raw with pain for just a moment, still ashen as she reached out her hand.

'Alex.'

She said his name gently, and soft intonations of unknown meanings reverberated around the table like an aftershock.

Chloe had never experienced the notion of time standing still until now. For long, sludgy seconds they were all transfixed within a silent, painful tableau. No one moved.

Then Alex recovered himself, straightening his back, and

he and Julia shook hands. Chloe thought that the shake had looked more like a hold . . . that they'd held hands for a second.

As she watched, Alex folded himself into his seat, picked up his menu and hid his head behind it, but Julia's back remained rigid. 'Could you excuse me for a minute?' she said, turning to look at Chloe and twisting her mouth into a smile. Her eyes were vacant and glassy, her skin pale. She looked entirely different from the composed woman who'd shaken Chloe's hand a few moments earlier. She scraped her chair back jerkily, and the ugly noise echoed on the tiles. 'I just need to go to the bathroom.'

'Of course.'

They watched her go. Alex remained hidden behind his menu, pulling it as close to his face as he could. His shoulders rose and fell jerkily, as though he were breathing heavily, working on a ragged edge of self-control. Chloe and Mark made small-talk, mostly about work, and Mark regaled her with his frustrating meeting that evening, where his client seemed to be trying to put some kind of metaphorical arm-lock on him before they went to court.

After forty-five minutes they all finally admitted to themselves that Julia wouldn't be coming back.

2

Alex navigated the route home on automatic pilot, painfully aware of Chloe watching him. He was grateful that she hadn't asked any questions other than an 'Are you okay?', to which he'd nodded mutely with his eyes averted from hers. But he would need to explain, he knew that. Where the hell would he start?

Once home, they got ready for bed in silence, the ambience of their bedroom just a few hours before now replaced by an atmosphere tight-packed with tension. It felt like the room was holding its breath, ready for Alex to start talking.

He got into bed and felt the mattress give as Chloe got in beside him. He took a deep breath and turned to face her. 'Chloe . . . I . . .'

Their eyes locked for a moment, and then the phone rang.

He thought maybe, just this once, she would leave it. But no – she sighed, turned away and pulled herself out of bed, padding into the hallway where he heard her resigned response, 'Hello? Mum, are you okay?'

Alex sighed. They could always rely on Margaret to pick the most inopportune moment to call. He knew Chloe had been growing increasingly worried about her mother since her stepfather, Charlie, had died, but that was over a year ago now and the endless phone calls and regular trips up north were beginning to take their toll. If only Chloe's brother, Anthony, hadn't fallen out with the family and moved to America. It meant that Chloe was all Margaret had left.

Alex waited for a while, listening to his wife's soothing murmurs, presumably during those times that his mother-in-law couldn't help but pause for breath. Eventually he turned off the bedside light.

As he tried fruitlessly to summon sleep, he berated himself for not telling Chloe more from the beginning. There had been plenty of chances, and he had avoided them all with a determination to leave history behind him. But Chloe would have understood . . . wouldn't she?

Of course she would; she would have told him there was no need to be ashamed, to blame himself. And that was exactly why he had kept quiet: because he still didn't entirely believe he deserved to hear those words. Because if he could go back and have his chance again, then of course he would do it all differently.

Except, would he? At the start he had thought so, but now he had Chloe, and that meant everything had changed. He wanted to protect her from the miseries of the past. He had learned to live with it and come to accept that there was nothing he could do any more; never believing there would be a time when the whole nightmare would come full circle to fling itself at him again.

Eventually the bedroom door creaked open, and the mattress jolted as Chloe lay down. She kept her back to him, preventing him from touching her, from scooping her into the welcoming curve of his body, as he did most other nights.

As the hours dissolved, his mind began to race faster, the full realisation of what had happened hammering into him with every quickening beat of his pulse. *My god, she was there, in the restaurant; she is alive.* He kept replaying their brief hello until it became like listening to vinyl on half-speed, their voices chewed-up baritones. His thoughts churned over and over, more tumbled and chaotic each time, until he gave up on sleep and made his way downstairs. In the kitchen, he poured himself the first drink that came to hand – from a half-finished bottle of merlot – then went through to the lounge. He sat on the sofa in the darkness and slugged the wine back in two mouthfuls, feeling the bite of the liquid weaving its way down his throat.

The more he tried not to remember, the more his mind replayed the same scenes. The white van rounding the corner. The chaos at the roadside as their worlds, cut-glass prisms of possibilities, had shattered in the sunshine. His last view of her: just a shadow behind a window. Until the restaurant, that was.

How the hell was he going to live his life from this point forward, knowing that the woman who had meant the world to him, who he'd thought might be dead, was in fact alive and living somewhere nearby? That tonight, for a brief moment, he had held her hand and then let it go again – just as he had the last time.

Right then, surrounded by transfiguring darkness, he knew he desperately wanted to see her again. He needed to talk to her; to explain; to understand. And he had a thousand questions to ask, not least of all why she was calling herself Julia when that was not her real name.

3

Kara Abbott: fifteen years old; blonde; beautiful.
Dead.

Mark tried to focus on Kara as he walked towards the lifts, still in shorts and T-shirt from his early-morning squash game, but her blonde hair kept morphing into darker, more exotic locks, and her slightly chubby face kept thinning out to the beautiful, haunted one that seemed to be shadowing his thoughts.

He had been so mortified last night when Julia hadn't come back. When Alex had turned to greet them, Mark had had the strange sensation of all his optimism fleeing his body with each deflating exhalation of breath. Worse still had been watching Chloe ramble on for half an hour trying to ignore the empty chair next to her. Tiny particles of her pity had floated across the table with every word she'd uttered and he'd breathed it in until he felt he might choke. And

Alex, fucking Alex, who had so obviously upset Julia – who so obviously knew Julia, probably intimately – had said nothing. The least the man could have done was provide an explanation. Mark felt the muscles in his back constrict as he thought about it.

When they'd decided to call it a night – after one round of wine and no food, much to the chagrin of the waiter – Chloe had looked like she wanted to offer more crumbs of comfort, but by that time Mark had been so livid that he was having trouble keeping his voice down and staying civil. 'I'll get the bill,' he'd rasped at her. 'You two just go.'

She'd guided Alex quickly away and Mark had an absurd longing to head for the ladies' toilets to see if Julia was still hiding in there. But he wasn't going to be reduced to a laughing stock for any bloody woman.

Yesterday, as they'd walked into the restaurant he'd felt great, the best in a long time. He'd taken stock of his work, his recent promotion, his finances, and his impending date, and felt he was slowly building himself a concrete plinth. Every day he climbed a little higher. One day he would perch on top of it, looking down in contentment at all he had achieved. Now he felt as though he were halfway up that god-awful Jenga game his young nephews loved playing, and with one false move the whole thing could come tumbling down at any moment.

He had to stop thinking about her; if nothing else she didn't deserve his attention after she had humiliated him last night. He needed to get through some of the notes in his briefcase pronto, or he'd never get on top of the Kara Abbott case.

'Get a grip,' he muttered to himself as he strode along, causing the receptionist to look up in surprise, unused to any sign of a greeting from Mr Jameson.

He loved playing squash, but this morning had been less fun than usual because he was a lot better than Neil so had to hold back, while still playing well and casually enough to make his efforts look natural. It was a load of bull that events on the court wouldn't impact on working relationships, especially with someone like his boss, who was fiercely competitive and used to winning. Problem was, Mark was just the same, so he had left the court distinctly frustrated.

Neil had made reference to the Abbott case a few times, and each time Mark had felt a small jolt in his stomach at how much he still had to do. Neil was friends with Kip Abbott, Kara's father, but to Mark's way of thinking, friendship and business should be kept firmly separate at all times. Neil would never have got away with this if Mark's father had still been one of the helmsmen of the company. Now retired, Henry had got a whiff of the case on one of his frequent visits to Lewis & Marchant and had said nothing, but Mark could tell by his expression, eyebrows slightly up, jaw tight, that he thought it was a big mistake.

Kara Abbott was the sad end to the kind of bullying story Mark had heard umpteen times. It had started as cruel jibes about her supposed puppy fat. It escalated into pushes, trips, Chinese burns, on one occasion a pencil jabbed into her hand when she moved one of her tormentors' bags out of her way. There were threats and jeers, which went on and on. When she'd died, Kara had bruises and penknife cuts to her inner thighs, which three perpetrators had enacted on her at the bottom of the long school field, in front of more than half a dozen onlookers. The diary that had been Kara's only confidante, now tagged Exhibit D, was a slurry of scrawls about her desperation, her loathing of the girls in question, and her incomprehension at what she could have done to have brought all this on herself.

Kip Abbott had been the one to find her, when she wouldn't come out of the bath. She was fully dressed, blood pooling beneath the cuffs of the shirt of her school uniform. She'd used Kip's spare razor blades. She was just unconscious then, but by the time they got her to the hospital it was too late. The coroner thought it might have been a cry for help, but Kara didn't know how to calculate the difference in millimetres of severed skin that would turn her plea into a successful suicide attempt.

Kip had gone to the school the next day, and resigned from his position as the deputy head. Even the kids in classrooms far from the headmaster's office could hear his shouting from where they sat, taking mock Maths exams. The police had been called.

Kip and his wife, Sally, had initially decided to try to get the girls responsible on some kind of charge. But the school had closed ranks, and the case was deemed impossible to win. So now they were going after the school instead – Kip's former employers and one of the most sought-after private girls' schools in the country. And, just to make Lewis & Marchant that extra bit nervous, two of the girls involved in the bullying were children of well-known parents – a politician and his wife, and a TV newsreader and her husband. The media were going to be on them like hungry jackals.

Their chances of winning this high-profile case were deemed, in the legal world, not good, particularly as the inquest into Kara's death had absolved the school of wrong-doing; in fact, praising it for the steps it had taken to try to help the troubled girl. However, not only had Neil agreed to be subjected to this public mauling, but he'd involved almost everyone in the office in one way or another. Perhaps determined he wouldn't go down alone, Mark thought ruefully. While Mark specialised in litigation, Chloe had been drafted in to help because she was more used to dealing with passionate and emotive cases in her daily family law work, and they were both down to attend court with Neil when the trial began next month.

Mark was looking forward to working with Chloe, although when she gave that coy little smirk as she talked about Alex, he always wished he could dig up something – anything – to turn that smile into more of a grimace. And now, he realised, it looked like he'd stumbled on something that could do exactly that. In fact, maybe last night hadn't been a complete write-off, he consoled himself. He checked his watch. Yes, if he were quick, he had time. He headed past his office, and strode along to the one next door.

4

'What the hell was all that about last night?'

Chloe had just arrived at work and was doing her best to concentrate on her own notes for the day when the door opened. Having spent a sleepless night listening to the rain pounding against the roof while wondering exactly the same thing herself, she was in no mood to listen to a rant.

'Nice, Mark,' she began wearily as she saw a couple of colleagues in the corridor turn and look at them. 'What a great way to bring personal shit into the office.' She was surprised at the vehemence in her voice – she usually trod cautiously where Mark was concerned.

Mark opened his mouth to continue, then stopped abruptly. He obviously wanted a row, but didn't know how to get there if she wouldn't play along. He came into the office, shut the door, and threw himself into a chair that had hosted a whole array of wretched spouses and at least three bigamists.

'What did Alex say?' His eyes narrowed as he watched her.

'Nothing.'

'So what the hell do you think was going on last night? They obviously know each other.'

Mark's words were forcing Chloe to think about the exact issue she was trying to avoid dwelling on. Yes, they obviously knew each other. Which led on to How? When? Where?

'I don't know. And I really don't want to discuss it right now – not with you.'

'So do you think they're having an affair?'

Behind the desk, Chloe clenched her fists. 'No, I don't, but trust you to think that,' she said firmly, feeling shaken. She glared at Mark but he ignored her.

'Well, has Alex ever mentioned Julia before?'

Another question Chloe had been pondering hard. And there was only one answer she could come up with. 'No.' She'd asked Alex the basic questions one asked when the moment came for them to share the details of their lives before each other, but she hadn't pushed for information. Besides, she was sure he'd told her his old girlfriends' names, and she didn't remember a Julia.

That didn't matter. Alex's reaction last night wasn't one of being reunited with an old, casual fling, and she knew it. And, obviously, so did Mark.

Mark was still watching her, but then gave a frustrated sigh and stood up. 'Okay, I suppose I'd better get on, I'm due in court in an hour. Just let me know if you shed any light on this.'

Chloe bit back her irritation: he sounded like he was discussing missing paperwork. She had no intention of making this a joint problem.

'Mmm,' was the best she could do as he made for the door. She could see Jana, the secretary they were temporarily sharing, trying to peer through the gaps in the inner wall where the frosted glass became momentarily clear. Nosy cow, she thought, irritated.

Her fingers hovered over the phone. Normally if Mark was driving her crazy – as he had a tendency to at times with his infuriating way of speaking to her and his frequent incursions into her office – she'd call Alex, just to hear the sound of his mellow, calm voice on the other end of the line. She often pictured him at home, working meticulously on one of his design projects. However, today the only image she could conjure up as her fingers hesitated on the handset was the look on his face as he'd met Julia's gaze last night. She quickly moved her hand away from the phone, and bent to her work.

5

'So, Doctor Fielding, you're telling us you are certain that on two occasions, at five o'clock on the afternoon of the 29th January, and at one o'clock on the 31st January, Doctor Hazeltoft was with you in the Water's Edge restaurant?'

'Yes, that's right.'

Mark sighed as he listened to the barrister questioning this idiotic witness and resisted the urge to check his watch. It wasn't long until lunch and he hoped that this blithering liar would be dealt with before then. He had no problem with the Old Boys' Network, but when they covered up major fraud it was going a bit far. Mark watched the barrister work the room like he was in the Crown Court of the Old Bailey. Every time Mark took a trip to court he wondered if he really should have gone to the bar instead of opting for private practice.

The witness, dressed in a dapper suit and yellow silk tie, a matching pocket handkerchief peeking from his breast pocket, stared back at the barrister.

'Are you completely sure about that, Doctor Fielding?'

'I am,' the old gentleman nodded, but his hand strayed up towards his breast pocket as though about to take the handkerchief out of there and mop his brow.

In the silence that ensued, Mark looked at his notes on the table, knowing exactly what was coming next. He never lost the satisfaction of watching a barrister seizing just the right moment to execute a perfect ballestra, usually leaving their naïve opponent fatally exposed.

'Well, although your own practice records show no mention of any surgeries, Doctor Fielding, when we finally located the operating theatre records at the hospital they have you performing an emergency heart surgery from eleven o'clock on the 31st January. Here you are –' the barrister strode across the room and placed a document before the witness – 'So I put it to you now, is it likely that you have your dates muddled?'

The witness hesitated, then glanced at his friend, who stared intently back at him.

Mark quelled the smile that threatened to rise as he watched this apparent capitulation. Just as the witness seemed to be drawing breath to speak, the barrister nodded smartly at the judge and said, 'No further questions, Your Honour.' His eyes moved with Mark's to the defence, who looked ready to object on the grounds their client had had no chance to answer. Mark watched as David Lockhart, opposing counsel, studied the downturned head of the witness, and then the bewigged man bent his own head back to his notes. He had obviously decided to cut his losses for now.

Mark waited, praying the judge was about to call lunch, and flicked a covert glance at the seats behind him while fiddling with the papers in his briefcase. He saw no faces he recognised, but the habit of looking had become a nervous tic that he couldn't control. Early on in his career, he had cast his eyes behind him and happened to notice a figure sitting there quietly. While his heart had begun to race, his father showed no outward sign of acknowledgement, but the message was as clear as if Henry Jameson had stood up and yelled it at him. Even though Mark was now qualified in the law, and a lifetime of diligent work had realised Henry's ultimate dream of a son following him into the profession, it seemed that the highly respected retired solicitor had no intention of loosening the reins on his protégé. Mark's career was to be closely monitored.

Mark knew, just as Henry would know, that this one appearance had the desired effect. Mark never got lazy, never slackened, as there could always be someone watching, the one person whose praise and respect it was almost impossible to earn.

So it disturbed him that he felt so uninterested today. Maybe he did need his father watching over him like a hawk, because although Henry Jameson liked to drop in to his old firm regularly to keep up with the latest cases, he had been noticeably absent for the past week or so, coinciding nicely with Mark's apathy.

The judge had indeed called the lunch recess. Mark gave a sigh of relief, closed his briefcase and made his way from the room and along the hallway, nodding as Sheree, the legal assistant, reminded him of the order of the afternoon. He strode out of the front doors into a blustering breeze, heading back to the office a couple of streets away where he could look over his notes undisturbed. But it was no good, because now he could vividly picture Julia sitting opposite him, on the night she'd walked into his life out of the blue.

It had been late on Monday evening. Most people had gone home – he'd seen Chloe race out just after 'official hours' ended – her cheeks glowing, her face full of anticipation at seeing her boring hippy of a husband. The secretaries had begun chattering inanely about whatever pathetic reality TV programme they would be gawping at over their TV dinners, while they logged off their computers and collected their belongings. David and Neil had done their nightly prowl of the corridors on their way out an hour or so later – both of them raising a hand in greeting beyond the glass partition that separated the solicitors' offices from the corridors and central open-plan area, but not interrupting Mark, whose desk was littered with papers and case files.

Mark loved working in the office when everyone else had gone. He felt more at home in the empty surroundings – evidence of people was to him a more comforting thing than negotiating their presence. He sometimes had a disconcerting feeling that people in the office were laughing at him. The secretaries were the worst. They worked for him, yet only the temps seemed intimidated by him. Even if he raised his voice with displeasure when an important document was handed to him with incorrect details, or a crucial legal date was missed, they just stood in his doorway looking mildly irritated or faintly bored, waited patiently until his diatribe was over and then sorted out the muddle, usually relatively efficiently. It was infuriating.

So there was solace in bending over case files with only the hum of the heating unit invading his hearing, his desk light illuminating the papers in an otherwise shadowy room. That night he had been searching for a precedent for a case that was worrying him, when he'd glanced up and seen a gloomy face peering at his through the glass divide. His heart had ricocheted wildly in his chest. For one insane moment he thought it was a ghost, and his stomach contracted as the figure immediately disappeared. Then the door handle turned and the door creaked slowly open.

The head that appeared first was substantially beautiful, and while he quickly dismissed all notions of visiting spirits, there was still something ethereal about her face. She was almost as pale as alabaster, but with perfectly proportioned, delicate features, large, mournful dark eyes, and beautiful silky brown hair. She wore jeans on her thin frame, along with a crumpled lightweight jacket and a pink scarf, and a satchel across one shoulder.

Mark was momentarily lost for words.

'Are you a lawyer?' she asked, in a hesitant, husky hot-chocolate voice.

'Yes,' he spluttered. 'Can I help you? It's after hours . . .'

'I know, I know,' she said. 'I took a chance. I saw the light, and I'm a bit desperate. I need some papers signed. Your receptionist is still here and she said you might help.'

'Oh, did she,' Mark replied, inwardly cursing the new receptionist and making a mental note to have a word. His voice was tainted with disappointment at the mundanity of her request. 'Well, it's not something I'd . . .'

'Please?' she interrupted softly. 'I just need a witness for my tenancy agreement. I really need it tonight or I won't get the place.'

Exasperated now, Mark raised his hand impatiently and gestured for her to hand him the papers. He took a quick glance at the tenancy agreement – a pretty standard affair from what he could see – flicked to the back, picked up his fountain pen and impatiently scrawled his signature. 'You know, anyone can sign this,' he told her rudely. 'It doesn't have to be a lawyer.'

'Oh,' she said softly, her voice so bereft that it made him look up at her. God, she really was beautiful. He had an urge to wrap his arms around her protectively, which surprised him – it wasn't the first urge he usually had in the company of attractive females.

'Sit down,' he commanded, and pointed to the chair opposite him.

She looked worried, but reluctantly perched on the edge of the chair he had motioned to. 'May I?' She gestured at the papers still sitting in front of him. 'How . . . how much do I owe you?'

Mark studied her as she watched him. His signature was worth an insane amount of money really. What had it taken him – a few seconds?

'Nothing,' he said, watching her face relax a moment before it instantly switched to high alert as he said impulsively, 'Just come on a date with me.'

He had shocked her. She paused for a moment. 'I don't date,' she replied flatly. 'I'm sorry.'

'Not that kind of date,' he said quickly, not sure himself where he was heading but mortified at being rejected so out of hand. 'I just need a companion for a dinner – there'll be others there. It's just making up the numbers.' He smiled in a way he hoped was reassuring to her. 'You'd be doing me a real favour . . . in just the same way as this . . .' He gestured at the papers between them.

She still looked guarded. 'When?'

Mark's mind was racing as to how he could organise this quickly. 'Hang on.' He got up and hurried through the door of his office into Chloe's adjacent room, almost running, worried that she'd make a dash for it while he was gone. He grabbed Chloe's diary and brought it back with him.

'Next Thursday,' he said, watching her.

'I'll try,' she replied noncommittally, staring at him as though trying to determine something.

'What's your mobile number?' He moved to his desk and picked up a pen.

'I don't have one.'

'Really?' He was intrigued. 'Wow, I thought everyone had a mobile. How do you cope?'

She shrugged. 'It's not that hard.' She made to get up. 'I should go.'

'What about a home phone?' he asked, watching her lithe movements as she turned away from him.

'The rental's not connected.' She was nearly at the door now.

'Meet me at Covent Garden Station – the Long Acre

entrance – at six thirty on Thursday,' he said desperately, aware she hadn't given him any commitment, and wanting to prolong her stay. He picked up the papers in front of him as she held out her hand. 'Flat 2, Delaware Court,' he announced, then scribbled it down on his legal pad. 'At least I know where to find you.'

In response she looked so frightened that Mark laughed. 'Don't worry,' he said, 'I just meant in case I need to change the arrangements.'

She nodded mutely. For a moment Mark thought she was on the verge of tears.

Alarmed, he added, 'I'll let my friends know, they'll be pleased you're coming.' He began to regret the offer, and nearly took it back, on the verge of saying, 'Never mind, forget it,' but some obscure notion of courtesy meant he felt that was simply too rude.

She grabbed the papers, and said 'Thanks' as their hands briefly touched. Then she turned and almost bolted for the door.

'Hang on,' he said, half-laughing at the absurdity of it all.

She turned around.

'I'm Mark,' he told her, lifting his hand in a mock-wave and smiling in what he hoped was a placating and friendly manner. He was intrigued, he realised. Intensely so.

'Julia,' she replied, not meeting his eyes, but replicating his smile with a smaller, pinched version of her own. Then she turned on her heel, and was gone.

6

The reverberations from the previous evening almost made Chloe forget the tremendously important task she had planned for that day. However, at lunchtime she went and bought another test.

Might as well be absolutely sure, she thought, returning from the pharmacy with her small paper bag. Yesterday she'd leaned against the wall of the toilet cubicle, stick in hand, hardly able to contain her delight as the blue plus symbol appeared. The instructions told her she'd know after a minute. She'd waited ten, checking her watch, just in case it disappeared again.

She tried to shake the excess water off her umbrella as she took it down, and then walked quickly through the communal corridors of the offices – wondering why she felt so shifty when no one had ever stopped her before and asked to see the contents of the brown paper bag she grasped. She went straight into the toilets, relieved to see the grey cubicles empty, and took out the test.

Today the blue symbol appeared again, and remained resolutely present.

Yesterday she had felt ready. It was perfect. The perfect time in her career, now she felt well-established in the practice. The perfect time in her marriage, with everything happy and settled, but probably not averse to an exciting shake-up.

However, today the thought of being pregnant scared the hell out of her.

It would be a shake-up all right. Chloe had never had any illusions about the challenges of motherhood, and that was before she had found out that her husband was keeping secrets from her.

Thinking of this while still sitting on the toilet, holding the white stick in her unsteady hand, Chloe wondered if there were other things she should have paid attention to of the tidbits she'd been fed from Alex's mother. Catherine Markham was a thoughtful and reserved lady with solemn, soulful eyes, who didn't automatically volunteer advice and information – which had been a blessed relief for Chloe, given her own mother's habit of dropping wildly indiscreet or inappropriate remarks into general conversation. When Chloe visited Alex's family home she loved spending time with his mother as she cooked a big meal in the kitchen. As they peeled sprouts and grated carrots they would sometimes chat, and at other times remained silent. Although sometimes she thought the peace was hemmed with sadness, still, Chloe had had an insight into a different kind of upbringing – one without the manic edge that her mother seemed to bring to any situation along with her inability to shut up, even for a few seconds.

Now, as she stared at the thin white plastic stick that foretold the biggest life-change she could imagine, she realised that she'd never thought that Catherine Markham might be privy to secrets about Alex that she, his own wife, didn't know. She wondered if she should ring Catherine up and ask her directly what she knew about Julia, but then, if Alex were in the middle of a steamy affair he would hardly confide in his mother.

Chloe had always thought of affairs as the worst kind of betrayal, but now she felt that if she discovered Alex and Julia were just having a fling, she might almost be relieved – at least for a few moments before the anger arrived. Whatever that look had been between them, it had seemed much more potent than acknowledgement of an affair, and that frightened her.

She didn't know what to think about last night. The whole scenario had been so unreal, and so unlike anything she'd ever encountered with Alex, that now she could hardly believe it had occurred. And Julia was Mark's girlfriend. How awkward would that make things in the future, if secrets weren't laid out in the open. She imagined them all at the dinners and law balls and charity events and Christmas parties that would have to be faced together, and once again she saw Alex and Julia's faces freezing as they looked at one another, and her stomach twisted.

She stayed seated on the toilet, staring at the stick. Five minutes passed, then ten, and that positive blue symbol wouldn't go away.

Yep, she was pregnant all right. But the joy of yesterday had entirely disappeared.

After Chloe had wrapped up all the evidence and pushed it to the bottom of the toilet bin underneath a variety of detritus, she called the local surgery and made an appointment for Monday morning. She needed to hear she was pregnant from a doctor, not just a little white stick. Then she tried to concentrate on her work for a while, but it was pointless. Eventually, she took a deep breath and went to talk to Mark.

At his open door she saw he was reading while eating a sandwich. Small pieces of lettuce were scattered over his papers, and as she watched he brushed them absently onto the floor.

She knocked. 'Mark?'

'I'm busy, Chloe.'

God, you can be a self-important prick at times, Mark, she thought to herself. But she bit her lip and said instead, 'I just need a second.'

He sighed and looked up. 'What is it?'

'About Julia . . .' She had so many questions she didn't know where to start.

Mark was alert at once when he realised she was ready to talk. 'What did Alex say to you?'

'Nothing as yet,' she admitted reluctantly.

'Nothing? Didn't you ask him?'

'Not really. He was upset, then my mother called, with her usual impeccable timing . . .'

'I couldn't care less how upset he is. What I want to know is What Did He Do to Julia?'

'Why do you think he did something to her?' Chloe defended, alarmed now. The thought had never crossed her mind. Alex wouldn't, couldn't harm anyone or anything, surely. 'What if she did something to him?'

'I somehow doubt it.'

'This is ridiculous.' Chloe's patience was suddenly worn paper-thin. 'Why don't you just ask her? I certainly don't intend to interrogate Alex for you. I trust him, Mark – not that I expect you to know about that, of course.' She couldn't help the bitterness creeping in and she was infuriated with herself.

'I can't ask her, Chloe!' Mark's voice was oddly pitched. 'I've only got a bloody address, and after last night I hardly feel welcome to pop round. So I expect I'll never see her again, thanks to your fucking husband. Now, can I eat my lunch in peace?'

Silently, Chloe headed for the door. She passed Jana on the way back to her office, which was next door to Mark's, divided only by a small stationery cupboard. The partition walls were useless – you could hear any noise above normal speaking tone, and she knew that the gaggle of secretaries that formed the centre pool in the nucleus of surrounding offices had probably heard that last line, as she was unceremoniously thrown out. Her cheeks burned, and she avoided looking at them. When she'd closed her own office door, she sat down and took deep breaths.

Despite the confrontation, Mark's last words had comforted her. What a fool she was. Why hadn't she realised that

Julia and Mark weren't necessarily in the kind of relationship he'd made it out to be? If he only had an address and had never been there, things with Julia obviously hadn't progressed very far. Just because he'd prattled on about her in the few days before their dinner date didn't mean anything.

Julia had certainly raced off like a frightened rabbit last night. Maybe she'd taken off completely. If she would just vanish, then maybe they could pretend that last night had never happened.

Perhaps this should have been a comfort to her, but it wasn't.

7

When Julia opened her eyes it was to cold white light streaming in through the uncurtained window. She'd slept fitfully through the night and for most of the morning, but even in her semi-conscious slumber she couldn't forget what had happened last night. She could barely remember the journey home. When she had run out of the restaurant and looked at the faces of those around her, she was surprised no one was staring. It was unbelievable that she was convincing amongst them, these strangers – just one of them – so ordinary that they hardly noticed her.

She kept trying to replay the time she had seen him from start to finish, breaking the few seconds down into milliseconds so she could savour each micro-moment. His head turning to look at her; his expression opening in recognition, then closing a moment later before he lost control and let something out of himself that wasn't meant to be revealed.

His hand automatically reaching towards hers. The warmth of his touch against her fingers, his grip lingering, testing out this new reality, involuntarily preserving the link between them for a short, extended fraction of time. Even before he had released the grip she had wanted him to hold on – it was real to her in a way she had forgotten a touch could be. But he had broken the small tie their fingers had forged, and watching him turn away had been more than she could bear. She was surprised that she managed to excuse herself; that she hadn't just evaporated next to the others. Her heart had pounded so hard she'd been sure it was about to break through her chest cavity. It had felt like she was shrinking suddenly, tunnelling down a hole that only she could see, away from everyone and everything.

It was so unbearably ironic. She hadn't been back to England for more than a few months in the past ten years, and she and Alex were both from the Midlands, so why he was living here in London she didn't know.

Except there was one big reason, wasn't there.

His wife. Alex was married.

She had always imagined that seeing Alex again would be more painful than anything else she could experience. But she had been wrong, because stupidly, stupidly, she had never added Alex's wife into that equation. It had never occurred to her that Alex could have, would have married. Because Alex already had a soul mate, and he had lost her.

The thought of him having such incredible intimacy with another woman made it difficult to breathe.

Chloe. She tried to think back to what Mark had briefly told her about Chloe and Alex before they arrived for dinner.

Not much. He had mentioned Chloe's husband by name, she recalled, but she had never dreamed that it could be her Alex.

Except it wasn't 'her Alex' any more.

She grabbed her coat and headed for the door, making her way down the tiny narrow stairway that led from the cramped flat. The carpet was worn and rucked in places, there was no banister and she had already nearly tripped once or twice, so now she rested her hand on the wall as she went. At the bottom she pushed open the half-rotten door of peeling white paint, which opened into a small courtyard, and hurried through, not glancing at the doors to the left and right, which, she'd concluded, from the amount of loud music, shopping trolleys and the smell of pot around the place, must be largely inhabited by students. The little alley-way was a dark oasis of calm, despite its sinister shadows, before she suddenly merged onto a busy street, a teeming multicolour of bicycles, people, umbrellas, buses and taxis all heading in their own directions.

Head down against the crowds and the rain and the cold, she walked briskly along the road until she saw the orange strip of an internet café. She went in, exchanged coins for a ticket, and took her place at a computer.

Once logged on she wasted no time in finding a search engine and typing in 'Alex Markham'.

The very first page that came up was his website. Her damp cheeks were still stinging from the sudden transition from the cool air outside to the warmth indoors, as she held her breath and went straight to it, looking through the pages, fascinated by the designs she found in front of her. It was like reading a storybook and suddenly skipping forward one hundred pages in an instant. At the last juncture she had known about, Alex had been one of a promising mass of recently graduated graphic artists, but now she suddenly zipped forward so many years to see that he had fulfilled his talent, or at least had begun to. He was doing what he had always wanted to do.

Anger rose up in her. She had had a passion for journalism a long time ago. She had wanted to do a post-grad course and then throw herself headlong into the profession, making a name for herself on a paper or magazine. Instead, she had spent the past ten years drifting round the world doing odd jobs, not wanting or daring to go home, sending off the occasional travel log from somewhere remote and beautiful, and even more occasionally being contacted by an editor – once or twice even being paid, only to find that most of her articles were simply kept on file and never actually appeared.

And here was Alex, living his life as though he had never veered from the straight path he intended for himself.

She clicked on the Biography page.

Alex lives with his wife in South London. When not designing he likes to indulge himself in travelling, modern-art galleries and fine wine.

She read the blurb a few times, trying to take it in. The Alex of old did indeed like travelling and art galleries, but she couldn't remember seeing him drink wine at all.

And then there was 'his wife'. She thought back to the pretty-featured girl at the restaurant with her light brown hair tucked casually behind her ears. Chloe had immediately made her feel stiff and formal, with her wide, welcoming smile and easy manner. Not that her relaxed posture had lasted long, once Alex had appeared.

There was an address on the website and she scribbled it on the back of her internet ticket. Then she clicked back to the search page and typed in 'Chloe Markham'. There were a few links that were obviously irrelevant, but then one came up under lewisandmarchant.com. Going to that, she found a page containing a picture of the girl she had just conjured up in her memory. Yet in this portrait Chloe's smile wasn't the natural one she'd had at the restaurant, and she wore a suit jacket with a white shirt underneath as she sat straight-backed and gazed into the camera lens.

Julia read the blurb next to the photo:

Chloe Markham, solicitor, is one of Lewis & Marchant's rising stars. Qualified for eight years, her specialty is family law, alongside general litigation.

This wasn't the kind of information she wanted to know about Chloe. She wanted to find something that could tell her what it was about Chloe that made Alex smile. How they'd met. Where their wedding had taken place. And a million other things.

Why did he love her?

She pressed the 'back' button, stupidly surprised to see Mark's face appearing before her. She clicked on his name and idly read the details set out there, noticing that he looked disdainfully handsome in his photo, but not really taking the words in.

Back at the search page, she typed in 'Chloe and Alex Markham' again, just in case, but there was nothing new. She flicked through pages impatiently, wanting more. On the third page that came up there were a couple of quotes from Chloe about legal cases, but nothing interesting.

While she was there, she plucked up her courage and typed in another name. She held her breath. But, as always, there was nothing.

She picked up her bag and the ticket she had scribbled on, and marched towards the door of the café, eyeing the address, trying to decide what to do. She passed a phone box and took a lingering look at it, just as she always did. Her father might be dead because of her, but she knew exactly where her mother was. She tempted herself with the uncertain promise of resolution, of redemption even, though the last time they had spoken her mother had been hysterical, threatening to disown her if she didn't come home. She reminded herself that now her mother might have answers she couldn't bear to know. Yet each day the desire to pick up the phone increased a little more, in proportion with the conviction that she didn't want to be found.

So why, then, had she written down that address on Alex's website? Was she finally admitting to herself that she needed someone who knew her Before to be in her life – a tenuous link both to who she had been and who she might have become? Or was it simply because she still loved him, despite what had happened in the end?

She had no idea. She turned away from the phone box, shook her head and moved on. She couldn't make the call.

Back at her flat, before she was fully aware of what she

was doing, she was kneeling by her rucksack – the only bag she'd arrived with a few weeks ago. She unclipped the top of it and pushed it back, to reveal a zipper hidden on the inside. She unzipped it quickly and pushed her hand into the secret compartment, groping around, pulling out one item at a time until they were all laid pitifully before her on the bedcovers.

Here were the only three things that really mattered to her.

The first was a charm on a necklace chain, like those you'd usually find on a bracelet. It was a tiny wishing well, the detail on it astounding: the gabled canopy; the tiny spindle; the coiled rope. A lot of wishes had been cast fruitlessly into the small hollow, far too many for its tiny size.

The second was a fluorescent patchwork lizard-gecko hybrid about the size of her palm, with splayed fingers and big googly eyes. Sometimes Julia would sit it on her pillow, and each protruding iris seemed to follow her round the room, until she would have to put the duvet over its head for a while just to escape the sense of being watched.

Lastly, there was a small silver box containing a cutting of short brown hair.

Although, she realised, there was a fourth item back there too. Something she hadn't looked at for a long time. Her hand delved into the pocket again, and pulled out a crumpled piece of white paper. There were a few black smudges on there now, where the ink had run since getting wet, but most of it was still legible. She looked over it quickly – was it really ten years since she had first read these words? In the light of the past twenty-four hours it was too painful to dwell on them for long.

She placed the piece of paper next to the other items and cast her eye over them all as they lay forlornly on the bed. Each one was a reminder of who she had been, which was why there was always an inevitable pang of pain and longing whenever she looked at them. It hadn't been as difficult as she'd thought to discard the bloodied entrails of her old life – but she didn't seem to be able to let go of these last things. They seemed so little, but they stood for so much.

Or perhaps it was that they wouldn't let go of her, she thought now, fingering each item tenderly, willing with everything she had for the tears to come, to show her that she could still feel something. In fact, surely seeing Alex again like that, out of the blue, had to be a sign.

That even made her smile slightly. She hadn't realised she still believed in signs. As she looked down at her nail-bitten fingers, a thought struck her with such velocity that she heard herself gasp.

What if there had been signs all along, and she had just missed them?

8

The car in which Chloe and Alex sat in silence formed one tiny scale of the huge glittering snake that coiled around the M25 and slithered ever so slowly forwards.

They hadn't spoken since Alex picked Chloe up from the station after work. Chloe was regretting that they had promised the weekend to her mother. On a non-travelling Friday evening they would meet at the station and spend a couple of hours in the local pub, indulging in idle chitchat with friends and neighbours they encountered there, and then head home for either a takeaway or an easy meal – pasta and salad, or something similar. They'd crack open a bottle of wine, sit companionably on the sofa, shuffling positions every now and again, limbs draped comfortably over each other's bodies. She would perhaps put her hand up his shirt and rub the flat circle of hair on his stomach, and he would slide his hand up her blouse and cup her breasts and stroke her nipples.

They'd stay that way until one of them couldn't take it any more and made a definite move . . .

Had they really done that only last Friday? Just one week ago everything was normal. Just one night ago she'd sat at her dresser and stared at herself in the mirror, feeling so wonderfully thrilled with the way things were going. Twenty-four small hours later and here they were, wrapped within a leaden silence punctuated only by honking horns.

She looked across at Alex. He was grim-faced, one hand over the top of the steering wheel, the other resting on the gear stick. She had practised the first sentence – 'Alex, about last night . . .' – but she was still unsure how to follow it up.

Did she want to know? Yes, of course, but she was praying that the price she would pay for knowing wouldn't be too dear. She was disconcerted to find she wasn't sure she wanted her marriage shattered for one tiny item of knowledge. Men and women came into her office all the time to begin divorce proceedings, and the misery etched plain on their faces often brought her to the conclusion that secrets only became malignant when they stopped being secrets. A secret in itself was just a silent benign fact – unless it was released upon some unsuspecting person . . . wasn't it? More likely she was just being a coward, she decided grimly.

She wished Alex would come out with an explanation himself. The fact that he hadn't, and that he was so obviously affected by seeing Julia – still, a day later! – was terrifying her more than anything, more even than those horribly uncomfortable moments at the restaurant last night, which made her cringe when she relived them.

But even if they never saw Julia again, she had to ask. Otherwise, if Alex didn't say anything, then this incident would rip the tiniest corner off their happy marriage, and she'd vowed to herself that she wouldn't let little cuts become big holes. She saw the result of that every day at work – the smallest nuances in her clients' voices, even the way they took a breath before beginning to talk, betraying all their anger and desperation and sadness.

'Alex . . .' she began, at the same moment as he leaned across and flicked up the volume dial on the radio.

He turned it down again when he heard Chloe's voice.

'Sorry. Yep?'

'About last night . . .' she began.

Alex stared straight ahead and said nothing.

'Are you having an affair?' she asked. She held her breath while waiting for the answer to come.

'Bloody hell, Chloe,' Alex spluttered, turning sharply to look at her, then swivelling back to the road when the cars started to slow. His knuckles clenched, blanched, against the steering wheel. A muscle twitched near his jaw-line. 'No, of course not.' His voice softened to become earnest and his face was pained.

'Then how do you know Julia?'

'Chlo, I really want to talk to you, but not like this . . . it's a long story . . . She . . . Julia . . . I never thought that I'd see her again.' Alex's jaw was set tense and firm and his mouth was a thin line.

Chloe digested this, but persisted, 'So were you in a relationship with her?'

Alex hesitated. He looked across at Chloe, then back at

the road. 'Yes, we were.' He paused before adding, 'But it seems like another lifetime now.'

Neither of them spoke. The cars in front of them sped up and Alex put his foot down hard on the accelerator. They raced forward, gaining momentum quickly, before realising the same cars were stopping again. Chloe thrust a hand out to steady herself for possible impact while Alex cursed and slammed his foot onto the brake.

The car lurched to a stop.

Chloe bit her lip and rubbed her stomach protectively under the coarse strip of seatbelt.

'Chloe . . .' Alex's voice was gentle and he moved his hand across to caress the nape of her neck. It made her shiver and she looked up at him. 'I'm so sorry. It's nothing for you to worry about, but I want to talk about this properly, not in the sodding car, or in front of your mother. It gave me one hell of a shock, seeing her like that. Can we just wait till we're alone?' He waved his hand angrily at the traffic.

His words were something of a balm to her nerves. She looked at his face and saw his expression, guileless and caring, but still, she was wary.

'I want to know everything,' she told him. 'I don't see why you need to be so cloak and dagger about it.'

'Because,' Alex said slowly, his eyes fixed on the road, 'what happened to her was beyond terrible.' His voice cracked on the final words. He cleared his throat but the raw emotion was still present as he added, 'I can hardly . . .' He trailed off.

Chloe cursed herself for making them come up to her mother's. They should have stayed at home where they could have talked. She almost told Alex to turn around, but as she thought of her mother's sorrow-filled face the traffic began to speed up and Alex indicated for the next exit.

'Okay,' she said when he was no more forthcoming, alarmed at how quickly he'd got upset. 'You can tell me later.'

'Thank you,' Alex replied, and Chloe heard the heartfelt timbre of his voice and leaned back against her chair, suddenly very, very tired.

9

The memories came in droves in the night.

Screaming – her own.

Shouting – everybody else.

As Julia half-dozed fitfully her remembrances held her down and whispered cruel things into her ears.

She saw her father's face in the hospital, the light gone from his eyes. She saw him before that, at home when she had been a child, his strong, solid arms, a face full of lines that deepened into great crags when he laughed, his hands shaking slightly as he went about day-to-day tasks, his crafts-man's fingers thick and gnarled. Tinkering away in his shed, while her mother cooked for them all. The miniature garden in the wicker basket that he had made for her so that fairies might visit them, which had been a constant feature of her childhood, and which they had both continued to tend long after she stopped believing in magical creatures at the bottom of the garden. That miniature bucolic idyll had come to represent all the fundamental feelings that lay between them, shared without words.

She sat bolt upright with a pounding heart and tried to recover her breathing. Blearily, she wondered if the basket was still there in the garden; hoped fervently that it was. If it had gone, then, irrevocably, so had one more small part of her. But there was no way to find out without making that dreaded call home.

Gradually, she succumbed to a half-sleep again, until she was gliding through a Turkish beach resort, accosted by an old lady who spoke bad English but had kind eyes, who grabbed her hand, saying, 'Wait, lady. I see man, he walk with you. Wait! Lady, wait!' When she turned around the woman was frowning as though some invisible being were whispering something in her ear that was hard to understand. 'He say you are lost soul.' The woman turned big, heavily pencilled mournful eyes towards her, as if a hundred things suddenly made sense. Julia wanted to run from that knowing gaze, but it seemed the message wasn't finished, and her legs were unaccountably heavy. 'He say you lost somebody, but they will come back to you. So it okay,' the woman smiled, tears in her eyes, bouncing Julia's hand up and down in her own cold, gnarled grip. 'They will come back to you.'

She came to again with a start, her whole body trembling. Was this a memory or a dream? She wasn't sure – and that in itself frightened her. If it was more than a dream, then who was the message from? Her father? Who else would it be? And who did it refer to? Was it Alex, who had just come back to her in such an unforeseen and painful fashion?

She pictured her father's face. Maybe he had forgiven her, now he could see everything up in heaven, and was paying the puppetmaster who dangled everyone's lives beneath him so ruthlessly to do him this one big favour, to make the fates turn just once in the right direction. That way his daughter might become a truly earthbound person again, instead of just a wandering lost soul.

But then perhaps it was only a dream, came a cloudy thought, as her head grew heavier once more against the pillow.

Later on, in the hazy time between sleeping and waking, sleeping and waking, more things came back to her; things she had pushed away for years. She had separated her life into two halves – Before and After – although she knew the line was really a lot more blurred than that.

One image replayed itself over and over: of Alex's twisted face as he walked away from her. That had been After.

But, now and then, there was also Alex's kind face, peering down at her.

Before.

10

Chloe was already exasperated after a few hours with her mother. After Margaret had woken her at what felt like dawn, they had raced into town and spent twenty minutes driving around the multi-storey searching for the perfect spot, before Margaret phoned Alex in a panic to remind him to lock the house up when he went out. They made it into the shopping centre, only for Chloe's mother to realise she'd left a voucher for Marks & Spencer in the car's glove box, so they trudged all the way back again to find the voucher wasn't in there at all – she had in fact carefully added it to the zip pocket of her shopping bag. Once they were inside M&S, Margaret headed straight for the accessories section, and spent half an hour wondering about a scarf there, before deciding she needed to come back when she was wearing her other coat to see if they matched properly.

And so it went on. All the time, Margaret wittered away,

Chloe hardly getting a word in. Her mother hadn't always been like this, she thought. She could recall a much more confident and self-contained woman, although it was only through the fog of childhood memory. But then something had happened, their grandmother had looked after Chloe and Anthony for a while, and it was after that that her mother had changed. But after what? The shadows of a memory began to float into the edges of her mind, and she felt her heart begin to race and pushed it back quickly. However, now its presence had been felt she couldn't wipe it completely.

As they sat down for elevenses, Chloe's mother took a good look at her.

'You look a bit peaky, dear. Are you okay?'

'I'm fine, Mum.' Chloe set down their tray of steaming coffees and muffins.

'Working too hard again? You must be careful. You know what they say – "all work and no play . . .".' Margaret chuckled to herself as she placed her plastic bags carefully on the seat next to her, and then fussed over which one lay on the bottom.

I'd have a damn sight more time to play if I weren't driving up to the Lake District on a regular basis, Chloe thought. But she smiled back benignly.

They sat in silence for a few moments, before Chloe took a deep breath and announced without preamble, 'I'm pregnant', startling herself with her own bluntness. She hadn't realised the secret had been crouched on her tongue, waiting to jump. As she immediately picked up her muffin and took a bite, she wished she could put her words on top and gobble them back up.

Her mother's jaw had dropped.

I've done it, Chloe thought. I have finally shut her up.

No sooner had she thought this than Margaret rallied with a torrent of exclamations. 'Oh my darling, I'm so thrilled . . . I'm so delighted. I can't believe I'm going to be a grandmother . . . this is fantastic, wait till I tell June tonight –'

Chloe cut her off abruptly. 'You can't tell them yet . . .' She paused and took a deep breath as she watched the confusion on her mother's face, before adding, 'Alex doesn't know.'

'Alex doesn't . . . ?' Her mother tapered off and once again seemed lost for words.

Unbelievable, Chloe thought. Now she'd silenced her mother twice in five minutes. Alex would love this.

Immediately she felt miserable.

11

The rain didn't seem to have stopped since Thursday, and it matched Alex's mood perfectly. Wrapped up warmly, he was on his way to the village pub, a trip he'd taken regularly with Charlie on previous visits to the Lake District. It still felt strange to be heading there alone. Today he had intended to drown his sorrows while watching the football scores come up, but when he opened the door and the warmth of lights, laughter and air all hit him at once, he knew straight away he couldn't stomach it. He let the door swing shut again, leaving him on the outside hunched against the cold as a couple of people stepped around him to get in. As a wave of noise and heat assaulted him for the second time, he strode quickly away, not really sure where he was going. He just knew he needed to try to clear his head, and the ice-cold air would help him more than the fug of the bar.

It wasn't difficult to find a walking trail. A couple of minutes later he had hopped over a dilapidated wooden stile set into a fence, and was following a small stony path around the bottom of a hill. The rain splattered his face persistently, but it was welcome – cool and cleansing. His trainers were quickly soaked; he could already feel water creeping between his toes. He was breathing hard with the exertion of keeping pace with his feet, which seemed to have independently decided upon a brisk trot.

There was so much to think about that he didn't know where to start. His mind was running around wildly in circles leaving chaotic footprints everywhere that he had no hope of following.

He'd thought he had it all figured out, but when it came down to it he had just been living on circumstance. He was angry and upset – with himself most of all, but little sparks flew off towards others. How could she just turn up after almost ten years without a word? And what wicked circumstance had allowed Chloe to lead him innocently into that restaurant, both of them unwitting victims of the hand of fate?

And Mark – in his wildest thoughts since Thursday, a lot of Alex's anger had been directed towards him. They had never liked one another. He imagined Mark somehow finding out about what had happened back then, and bringing his new girlfriend, Julia, along just to spite him – but how the hell could he know?

The general consensus about the path of life was that it usually took time – days, months, maybe years – to effect change. Yet the twists and turns Alex's world had taken boiled down to a few short moments. A missed underground train one afternoon. The police knocking on his family's door in Leicester with news of his brother. Letting go of a hand just a fraction too soon. In fact, letting go at all.

He thought about his family: how much Jamie's sudden illness had straitened the atmosphere of his home. His mother, Catherine, had become increasingly hesitant and nervous, while his father's emotions were held carefully in check, but, like a leaky vessel, seeped out at odd moments. Geoff Markham had lost both parents while Alex was in his teens, then his sister had died of cancer a few years later, and he had remained sadly stoic but dry-faced throughout, yet Alex had once seen his dad cry in exasperation after he tried some DIY car repair and managed to damage the wheel's axle. Once, when Alex's frustration with his dad's reticence had become apparent, his mother had told him that it was just the way he was made, and that it was what she loved the most about him – that it was refreshing when so many people were full of pandering, self-serving platitudes. This had made Alex take a look at his dad afresh, and for a while his lack of communication hadn't mattered so much – until Jamie was found wandering along a motorway in his underwear on a cool summer's night when he'd been missing for two days, and was subsequently diagnosed with schizophrenia. Because, at the time, Alex had responded in exactly the same way as his father: comforting his mother but unable to share the depths of his emotions with anyone.

Now, as he strode along the muddy path, he wondered if this thing the male Markhams had got – this inability to express themselves outwardly at appropriate moments – was some kind of curse. Perhaps it was a worse condition than his brother Jamie's, as there was nothing they could take for it.

He began to pound the track so furiously that he could hear the quicktime thump of his heart. He was soaked – raindrops were everywhere, dripping off his nose, cascading over his eyelids, breaching flimsy barriers of hems and lining. But he didn't care. He was thinking that the only time he had taken charge of his direction in life was with Chloe. But even that meeting had not been the chance accident she imagined it was.

He thought of Chloe, of her lovely selfless nature and her funny self-conscious habits – how his life had changed once he met her, from its endless dullish hues into a release of fresh colour. It had no longer seemed as if his soul mate had disappeared years ago, but rather that she had been waiting patiently all this time for him to relinquish the past and catch up to her. And until now, he thought he had moved on.

But in the past forty-eight hours everything had changed. It seemed you couldn't just shrug off your past. It was attached to you like a shadow – travelling with you everywhere, catching up with you whenever you faltered. The only real option was to turn and face it; deal with it; be rid of it in such a way that you could be certain it wouldn't reappear.

And that was why he had to find Julia. To talk to her. To understand. And to tell her just how utterly, utterly sorry he was. Yet he had an unshakeable feeling in the pit of his being that, whatever he did now, someone was going to get hurt. More than anything he wanted to protect Chloe, but he had made a promise, hadn't he, and now that Julia was back in his life, he couldn't just forget about that.

No matter which way he turned, he couldn't see the right way forward.

It was only when he reached the end of the track, with densely packed trees blocking his progress in every direction, that he realised he must have strayed off course without even noticing. At the same time it dawned on him that to have any chance of finding Julia he was going to have to talk to one of the few people he disliked intensely. He only hoped Mark didn't feel as strongly about him, or he was already in trouble and he hadn't even started yet.

With a heavy heart he stopped walking and turned around to retrace his steps, hoping it wouldn't take him too long to find the pathway again.

12

The sun was low in the sky as they drove the few miles to June and George's. Chloe grimaced as it bored brightly into her eyes, and tried to keep her concentration on the road.

Alex was sitting beside her, silent, smartly groomed in a white shirt with a light blue check and dark blue jeans. Chloe's mother was behind them in the back seat, chattering away inconsequentially. Alex and Chloe had stopped replying to her a good ten minutes ago and she didn't seem to have noticed. It was like supermarket muzak – they tuned in now and again and the rest of the time it washed over them subliminally. The sweet stink of her mother's perfume – had she bathed in the stuff? – had overwhelmed Chloe when they'd first got in the car. She wondered if it was the pregnancy – she didn't normally get queasy from her mother's Elizabeth Arden.

After Chloe had made her verbal slip that morning, her mother had continually tried to talk to her about the pregnancy as they progressed through town, until Chloe had had to say quite rudely, 'Can we just stop,' at which point Margaret had taken umbrage and stopped talking about anything at all, which meant the rest of the shopping trip had passed in a rather blissful silence. They hadn't got back until late afternoon, and so it had seemed a rush to turn around and get ready for their trip out this evening. Chloe just prayed that her mother would be able to keep quiet. Why had she entrusted her with something so important?

June and George's house suddenly rose to greet them as they topped a hill, and Chloe slowed and pulled into the driveway. The huge farmhouse door was open within milliseconds – June must have been watching for them through the letterbox, Chloe mused, as she got out of the car, waving and smiling.

June and Margaret greeted each other as though they were two old Dames reunited at the BAFTAs, and everyone watched and waited from the wings till the performance had finished. Then Chloe spotted George in the doorway and walked over to him.

'How are you, Chloe?' he greeted her warmly, kissing her cheek. 'And Alex.' He extended his hand and they shook firmly. George looked across at his wife and rolled his eyes. 'You wouldn't think those two saw each other every Wednesday at the gardening club. Come on in.'

George led the way and they followed, Alex gently placing a hand on the small of Chloe's back as she moved forward. She was immediately aware of his touch and turned to him.

He was watching her, an odd intense look on his face, but as she smiled so did he.

This is unbearable, Chloe thought as she turned away. Why am I trying to read his every expression? This is my husband: we're best friends, soul mates – we instinctively know the other. How on earth has this suddenly become so hard?

Two hours later, after a feast of roast lamb and veggies and conversation dominated by gardening-club gossip from June and Margaret, they had all retired to the lounge. The men were swirling whisky around their glasses, listening as the older women held court. Chloe was exhausted. She kept watching Alex to see if he exhibited signs of tiredness, but he appeared fine. Mind you, she thought grumpily, he'd had a lie in, while it felt like she'd been up shopping since dawn. She'd managed to abstain from alcohol over dinner by saying she was driving. Normally she would still have had a glass, but she'd said she was tired so didn't dare indulge, and everyone had accepted that.

'So, Chloe –' Chloe snapped out of her daydreaming as she heard her name – 'getting clucky yet?'

Damn you, June, Chloe thought, noticing that her mother was watching intently. She glared at her, wondering if Margaret had been unable to keep her mouth shut for even half a day, but the woman gave an almost imperceptibly small shake of her head in reply.

'A little . . .' she said hesitantly.

Alex came to life immediately. 'Are you?' He leaned forward, leather chair creaking as he did so. 'That's news to me.'

'Happens to us all, Alex, sooner or later,' Margaret chipped in breezily.

'Well, maybe, but we're not ready for that yet, are we, Chloe?'

'Aren't we?' Chloe, stunned, looked at Alex.

'Well, no. I need to establish my business more – and you've got stuff you want to do in the practice – there's no need to rush it.'

'I suppose –'

Margaret cut in. 'But there's never a perfect time, Alex. Remember that.'

'I know.' Alex sounded irritated. 'But Chlo and I need to feel solid and secure in our lives before we complicate everything with a kid. I'm just not interested at the moment.'

Margaret, her jaw slack, looked at Chloe. And Chloe, horrifyingly, felt tears spring to her eyes. She stared down at her tepid mug of tea. 'Well, then,' she said, fighting her tears and the hot blush she could feel staining her cheeks.

When she glanced up, Alex was watching her in surprise, and she was sure he'd guessed. There had been an awkward silence for a number of excruciating seconds now, and he opened his mouth to fill it just as June said, 'Well, poor Jeanna can't have any children. It breaks my heart that our son won't ever be a father.'

'June!' George scolded crossly. 'It's actually none of our business, and besides, our girls have produced enough between them to keep a primary school from going under.'

Alex's attention was still on Chloe, but he didn't seem shocked now so much as intrigued. Maybe he hadn't guessed at all.

Chloe avoided meeting his gaze, then sat back and closed her eyes. June was still talking about how Jeanna and Michael were planning to travel for six months next year, now that they'd come to terms with the news. Lucky old Jeanna, Chloe thought to herself, then immediately rubbed her tummy superstitiously and said silently, *I didn't mean it, baby. I didn't mean it.*

13

Mark arrived at the house in a foul mood. An hour's journey on a winter's night had taken him more than twice as long as it should have done. Had he not felt so tired, he would have been furious and vowing to write to somebody important over this disgrace of a transport system. Leaves on the line, snow on the line – even bloody bodies on the line, according to one whispered remark behind him. There was something utterly repulsive about the mindset of a commuter, that now, every time he heard of a body on the line his only thought was, 'Well, get it off the bloody line, then, and let's be on our way.'

In actual fact a train had broken down ahead of the one Mark was on, so he had to get off and board a bus between Orpington and Sevenoaks. At that point he'd tried to call his parents to collect him rather than suffer the indignity of bus travel with a plague of hyperactive adolescents, the boys' low-slung waistbands beginning on roughly the same portion of their bodies as the girls' tiny skirts ended. However, the house phone at The Willows rang out without even the answering machine clicking on, so Mark endured the bumpy, windy bus ride with his head stuck determinedly behind his paper, not reading a word, but checking his watch every two seconds until the bus pulled up outside Sevenoaks Station.

Thank god there was a cab there. He pushed his way through the throngs on the platform and raced along the walkway with his arm outstretched and a silent plea that no one would claim it first. The cabbie nodded as he got in and said, 'Barnfield Drive, please', then they were off. Mercifully, the driver was a silent let's-get-you-there type rather than one of the let's-get-it-all-off-my-chest-on-the-way cabbies Mark dreaded. Cab time was vital court-prepping time, and you didn't need someone asking your advice about importing their underage Thai girlfriend.

When he finally arrived he was somewhat disconcerted to find the house in total darkness. It wasn't a major problem, he had a key, but still – as they had invited him over, they should at least be home.

He let himself in and switched on a few lights. The answering machine on the Edwardian rosewood table in the hallway showed a resolute 0 messages. The curtains to the front rooms were still open, so he went around closing them, wondering where on earth his parents could be. The house seemed so quiet now, since the dog had died a few years before.

He peeked into his father's study, feeling like a trespassing child, hearing his father saying to his ten-year-old self, 'The law is the foundation upon which society stands, and also upon which it falls. Ergo, to uphold the law is the most important job that one can do,' as Mark was allowed to handle legal books reverently as though they were lost covenants. But the room was absolutely still.

He went back to the lounge, poured himself some Glenmorangie and sat down on one of the leather armchairs, idly picking up a nearby *National Geographic* and flicking through it with no real interest in the content. His mind kept drifting towards shiny dark hair and mesmerising brown eyes. Bloody hell, why on earth couldn't he just let it go; even thinking about her made him feel like an idiot.

Two hours and a few more glasses of whisky later, he was exhausted. He had tried both parents' mobiles, but they were off. He briefly thought about ringing hospitals or checking the news for car accidents, but he couldn't imagine his father rushing into a panic in the same situation – in fact, Henry would just have been enraged at the inconsideration – and his resolve stiffened. He would go to bed, sleep on it, and if they weren't home by morning he would be sure something was up. He'd grown up with a father promising to be places and turning up hours late, if at all, due to some kind of emergency court session/meeting/law function. Perhaps his mother had been dragged into some such thing and they'd forgotten he was coming – they'd arranged it a couple of weeks ago, after all.

He pulled at his loose tie, brought it over his head and folded it into a small neat oblong. Then he made his way wearily up the stairs, grateful now for the sandwich he'd grabbed on the train, which at the time he'd thought of as a stale appetiser for the decent meal he would be getting at home.

He had just crawled beneath the sheets when he heard the front door open, and footsteps echo through the hallway then up the stairs. They paused on the landing outside his door, but Mark froze, annoyed at his parents now for being so tardy. Not long after they moved on, he was asleep.

When Mark woke up, light was marauding through the gap between the curtains. He knew something was wrong. He couldn't believe that he *hadn't* known it the night before. A quick check of his mobile told him it was ten past eight, and he pulled on some clothes before rushing downstairs.

His mother sat at the kitchen table, one hand pressed to her forehead as she brooded over a cup of tea.

'Where were you last night?' he asked tersely.

'I needed to go out.'

'Well, that's nice. You invite me over for dinner then neither of you can be bothered to turn up. Thanks a lot.'

'Oh, Mark,' his mother turned on him with a glare. 'Stop being such a pouty little boy. That's the last thing I need right now, seeing as your father's run off in a sulk.'

'What? What do you mean? Why didn't you wake me?' Mark replied, more angrily than he intended.

'There's nothing you can do,' his mother said, not looking up.

'Why . . . what . . . ?' Mark asked, uncomprehending. 'Where's Dad gone?'

Finally, his mother looked at him. Her face had lost some of its usual composure. Her cheeks sagged, her eyes were red.

'I don't know,' she sighed. 'He just left.'

'Left?' Mark was mystified. 'What? What do you mean left?'

'He packed a bag, and left.' His mother shrugged her shoulders. 'He didn't tell me where he was going. When I asked him, he told me to fuck off.'

Mark couldn't help it, the laugh was out before he could stop it. 'Don't be silly,' was all he said. At which point his mother rose slowly and imperiously from her seat. She put her hands on the table, leaned forward, and, with such vehemence that Mark took a step back, hissed, 'Don't you *ever* say that to me. *Ever.*' She waved a finger at him then paused, eyeing him mirthlessly, before she sighed and said coldly, 'Stop trying to make yourself into an identical version of your father.' She gave a rasping laugh, warped and humourless. '*That* is not such a great thing to be, Mark. I'd aim a bit higher, if I were you.'

Mark held up his hands in surrender, though anger began to course through him at her words. 'Well then, Mum, why don't you explain this to me properly, and then I might have more chance of understanding exactly what's going on.'

Emily Jameson turned her empty eyes towards him. 'He's been in one hell of a mood for a while, then he came home yesterday, wouldn't say two words to me, packed a bag and told me he was leaving. When I'd ranted enough he grabbed me by the shoulders and told me it was for my own good! Hah!' She turned around abruptly so he couldn't see her face, and stared out of the kitchen window. 'I always knew he was a condescending, supercilious bastard – I knew there'd be a few floosies somewhere, a few tarts lurking on the side – but I *never* thought he'd actually leave.' Her voice broke on the 'never'.

Mark was rendered speechless by this outburst. *Floosies? Tarts?* Eventually, to break the awkward deadlock, he moved forward and clumsily put his arm around her shoulders. 'Mum . . .'

She shook off his arm. 'Don't patronise me. I know how much you idolise that man – just leave me alone.'

Mark remained where he was, still staggered by what he was hearing.

'GO!' she shouted, her hands pushing against his chest in a surge of strength before she seemed to succumb to an intense tiredness, collapsing back on to her chair, whispering, 'Please, just leave me alone.'

Mark moved into the hallway in a daze. He walked calmly upstairs, finished getting dressed, and grabbed the rest of his things. He heard his mother's brisk movements in the kitchen, and various crashes of china, pots and pans. Suddenly he was infuriated. He felt his heart harden, and he marched downstairs, banging the front door shut loudly without looking back.

As he walked down the drive he used his mobile to phone a taxi. Ten minutes, the man said. Mark leaned against the gate, trying to shut out his parents' troubles. He couldn't remember the last time he'd waited here – probably not since the school bus collected him en route to the high school, when he'd hope that Stuart Gaskell and David Tamworth were in a good mood and might give him a day off the constant goading and ear flicking and skin pinching that was their forte. Now, at the memory of them, he almost smiled. He hadn't thought about them for such a long time – yet their pettiness had once been the sum of his concerns.

His mobile phone began to trill. Mark looked at the phone but didn't recognise the number.

'Mark Jameson,' he announced as he answered it.

'Mark, it's Alex,' came the voice. 'Sorry to ring you on a Sunday . . .'

Mark felt irritation well up in him at the same time as disappointment crushed against his chest. He hadn't realised how much he'd hoped it would be his dad, calling to explain what the hell was going on.

'. . . I just wondered if you have a number for . . . Julia,' Alex was saying as Mark tried to refocus on the voice in his ear. '. . . I need . . . I would like to contact her.'

I just bet you would, Mark thought. Alex's tone might have been polite, but it came across as condescension marked with disdain. The smug bastard already had Chloe, and now he was muscling in on the one woman whose recent presence had pierced through Mark's general lethargy towards the opposite sex.

'Alex . . .' he cut in.

'Yes?'

'Go to hell,' Mark growled as he snapped the phone shut.

14

'**W**hy were you so upset last night, Chlo?'

That's what Chloe had been waiting to hear – in the car on the way home from June and George's; in her mother's guest bedroom surrounded by primrose wallpaper; at breakfast the next morning when her mother left the room. She was still waiting, and they were in the car only half an hour from home. If he could only have asked the question she would have blurted out exactly why. She was desperate to talk, but as Alex commented on petrol prices, roadworks, her mother's back garden ('very overgrown, considering she's in the gardening club – it could be so nice') her growing anger began to form knots in her stomach. She put a protective hand on her abdomen.

She winced every time she remembered Alex's dismissive comments last night. How could she tell him about the baby now, knowing that he would be disappointed and upset – so far from the overjoyed reaction she had previously pictured. Okay, so it wasn't planned, as such, but they had talked about children and always agreed they would love to have them someday.

The Alex that Chloe had seen in the past few days was becoming less and less recognisable. She could have sworn she knew her husband inside out, but now doubts had begun to plague her. *How many secrets does he have? Do I know him at all?* She tried to think about the skeletons in her closet – not that there were many – the things she'd deliberately never told Alex. Like the time Mark had tried to kiss her after a work evening out a few months before her wedding. She hadn't told Alex as she thought it would just cause trouble, and she'd handled it. And Mark had been steaming drunk. Besides, all people have such secrets, she consoled herself. And Alex must have them too.

Julia was simply one of them.

Isn't it fair enough that he never told me about her if he had not foreseen her intruding into our lives?

Perhaps, she said to herself. But the point was that now she had, and for that reason Chloe felt she deserved an explanation.

She thought of all the things they'd shared. Alex's frustrations with his parents and brother. Chloe's confusion about her own early life – her mother always changed the subject when she asked about her real father, saying the divorce was messy and he'd cut off contact with the children soon afterwards. When her brother had moved to America, Chloe knew he had hopes of finding their dad, but so far she'd heard nothing, and now Anthony seemed to avoid the subject as well. She didn't want to live like that, tiptoeing through life as though it were a minefield of secrets.

I'll talk to Alex when I get home, she decided. Once we've had a chance to get showered and changed and we're sitting down for the evening. Then we can have a nice long talk, and I can try to get to the bottom of what's bothering him before I tell him about the baby. After all, she reassured herself, delaying that announcement for a day or so was of little consequence if it meant the difference between it bringing them closer together or pushing them further apart.

For the rest of the journey Chloe struggled to sleep with the radio blaring. Alex's eyes never wavered from the road. When their house finally came into view, she breathed heavily with relief. Not long now, and it would all come out. She wasn't letting him put her off any more.

She rushed to get changed when they came in. She turned the shower taps on and stood inert as warmth poured onto her, restoring some desperately needed vitality. She pressed her hands against her stomach, trying to picture a microscopic baby in there. Trying to imagine herself standing there in seven or eight months' time, hands over the same skin, vastly distended by a growing baby. It was impossible to believe she would be a mother soon. What kind of mother was she going to make? Would her child grow up as she did, feeling mainly sadness when it thought of its family, or feeling duty-bound to drive 500 miles over a weekend to see a parent it couldn't really relate to in any way, shape or form?

Could she raise a happy child?

Would she raise it with Alex, or was that doomed too, just like her own parents' relationship? Perhaps her mother had once stood in the shower, drowning in her own fears while the water poured over.

Doubts began to flood over Chloe. Briefly, she thought of abortion. Then Alex would never need to know. Possibilities streamed through her brain, but she knew that, regardless of what happened with Alex, she wanted this baby. It's just this wasn't how she'd imagined feeling on finding out her first child was on its way.

It was no good. She needed to talk to Alex now, and put this thing behind them before her fears gained too firm a grip on her.

As Chloe grabbed a towel, she heard the telephone ring and Alex pick up. His voice downstairs was muffled, and she thought there was an edge to it.

She had dried herself and was beginning to towel her hair when he walked into the bedroom. She looked up and caught his eye, then he turned and grabbed his keys from the dresser.

'I'm really sorry, Chlo, it was Mum – I need to go and check on Jamie, he's not answering his phone and she's worried.'

'Now?' she asked. It wasn't the first time this had happened, but her heart sank at the timing. She knew that Jamie's parents were pleased their two sons were living close to one another, so that Alex could keep an eye on his taciturn and solitary younger brother, but it meant Alex often had to deal with the fallout from Jamie's unpredictability.

Alex's face was dark with what looked like anger. He sighed. 'I know, it's not ideal, but what can I do?'

It was Chloe's turn to sigh. She looked at her feet and

nodded. After a weekend spent indulging her mother she had little right to complain if Alex's family needed him.

He made for the door, and shouted from beyond it, 'I'll be as quick as I can.'

The front door banged shut behind him seconds later. Chloe was left frozen, one hand holding the hairbrush, the other tightly gripping a soggy towel. Now he had gone she struggled to stay rational. What if that had been an excuse? What if he were avoiding her? Avoiding any extra time with her when she might ask him questions he didn't want to answer? Perhaps he was really going to see Julia . . .

She dashed to the phone and called Jamie's mobile. No answer. Then his home number. Nothing. She slowly straightened, making sure she didn't catch her own eye in the bedroom mirror, and picked out her comfy tracksuit bottoms and a fleecy top, throwing them on rapidly and running downstairs. She then chopped a mountain of vegetables and threw them one by one into a hissing and spitting wok, stirring the mixture and making sure that the sizzling noise was the only thing she let past the perimeters of her thoughts. Once she had a bowl of steaming food, she turned the telly on, volume high, and munched and stared, munched and stared. Every now and again she let her gaze wander to the clock on the wall, and small calculations would flutter through her head.

She remained rooted to the spot for the rest of the evening, not daring to move lest the protective spell she'd woven around herself be broken.

15

Mark had spent all Sunday trying to concentrate on work, reading through notes so he'd be ready for court tomorrow. His mind kept wandering to the inordinate number of people who had annoyed him lately. He was fed up with the lot of them.

However, as the evening went on he'd felt his anger towards his mother softening, and he'd picked up the phone.

'No,' she had sniped upon hearing his query, 'there's no word, Mark. I'll tell him to call you if he returns any time this century. He'll be needing a good divorce lawyer.'

'I don't do family litigation,' Mark snapped back.

'I was thinking of Chloe, not you,' his mother retorted.

'Look, Mum, I know you're angry –'

'Oh, you do, do you, Mark? Well, as your father always says, you are extremely intelligent, since you take after him.

And perhaps you're even a little bit psychic too, if you know just how I'm feeling right now.'

'Mum, for god's sake, I'm just trying to help.'

'Just leave me alone then,' Emily Jameson had shrieked, and the line had gone dead, leaving Mark bristling with pent-up fury.

He gave up on reading his case notes and went out to buy something to eat, musing over another case coming up this week, where he had mixed feelings about the middle-aged policeman they were representing. Returning to his apartment block, he cursed the maintenance man who had stuck an orange cone in front of the ground-level lift. It was getting late and he just about had time to eat the takeaway he'd bought before he'd need to get to bed in order to be on top form for work tomorrow.

When he reached his front door he fumbled around for his key, dropping it twice before he made it inside. He flung the takeaway box onto the kitchen top then decided to have a quick shower before eating. He marched through his bedroom into the ensuite bathroom and turned on the taps.

It was amazing how a spell in his high-pressure shower with the taps turned up as hot as he could stand could lift his mood and reinvigorate him. He emerged back into his bedroom from within a cloud of steam, towel wrapped around his waist, and went to the kitchen to re-heat his Thai meal. His mind was clearing, beginning to focus on what he needed to get ready for tomorrow. For starters, he had to talk to Chloe about the Abbott case before Neil got to them both, as he was completely out of touch and was praying that Chloe had got around to doing more than he had so far. Neil had warned them that the media would be all over them when the time came, and Mark had not had the experience of fending off a whole tribe of journalists during a case – the odd court reporter didn't quite compare with what was threatening to develop here.

Perhaps he should read the papers in his bag now, he thought, as the microwave announced with a ping that dinner was ready. He collected his meal and, still clad only in a towel, got his papers out of his briefcase and began to read.

He was at the bottom of the first page when the doorbell rang. He cursed loudly – it was the last thing he needed, and who the hell was it anyway at this time? – then stalked across and flung the door open, to find the concierge had let a sodding tramp upstairs. 'Jesus,' he said to the sight that greeted him, eyeing the unbrushed, unwashed grey hair, the patchy stubble of silver beard, the untucked, half-open shirt, dirty trousers and only socks where shoes should be. And it wasn't just his vision getting assaulted – his nostrils were on high alert as well.

Then he looked at the face again, closer. His disdain turned to horror as he found himself staring at a twilight-world version of his esteemed father, Henry Jameson.

Mark would have liked longer to gather himself, as his head was spinning, but after a few seconds' delay his dad lurched to the door and over the threshold, falling towards him. Mark instinctively put out his arms to help him upright, but instead found himself unexpectedly required to support most of the weight of a sixteen-stone man and, unable to do so, staggered back inside the apartment where they fell in a heavy, painful heap to the floor. Mark felt his wrist jar awkwardly as he hit the ground with it trapped underneath his father's chest.

They both lay there in silence, until the ting of the now functioning lift alerted Mark to the fact they were in full view of the corridor. As fast as he could he pushed his dad off him and was at the front door, slamming it shut. He looked down and saw he was naked; his towel still half-trapped under his father.

Mark had never been required to reverse roles with Henry before. Surveying the crashed-out heap of parenthood at his feet, he found himself thinking of cases he'd come across where children would come home to find parents passed out from some kind of excess. He suddenly understood as never before the burden of responsibility such children were forced into. Some of them were still babies themselves, and he'd read about them dutifully providing comfort to a needful father or mother. Now here he was, in his thirties, faced with the same predicament, and he had absolutely no idea what to do.

After a few moments, with his father out cold on the hallway floor but quite obviously breathing, Mark stepped over him, threw on some clothes, and then went back to his cooling microwave meal while he tried to figure out what to do next.

16

Four a.m., and Chloe was wide awake.

Alex had got home an hour ago and slipped into bed silently beside her. Neither of them had tried to talk or even to touch one another. Now a soft yellow glow from the streetlight filtered in through the curtains, making his sleeping face just visible to her. She could still remember lying in bed awake like this before, newly married, enthralled by the sleeping person by her side who she could now call 'husband'. She'd traced the contours of his face with her eyes: his soft skin; the dark stubble that appeared almost immediately after he shaved. It drove him mad, but she loved the tousled look he took on with the shadow of a beard forming. It was the informality of it – the contrast to the men she met at work with fresh red nicks on their faces daily, and ties strangling their bulging Adam's apples. Alex never did up the top button of a shirt unless he absolutely had to.

Now, as she looked at his face, she had the urge to slap him. It seemed that all the solidity they had built; the foundations of their relationship, their marriage, which they had painstakingly erected and climbed up together, could be brought down in an instant by nothing more than a short, sharp pull from a third party.

Chloe's mind was hastily replaying scenes from the past, re-evaluating them in the light of the last few days and hating what she saw there afresh.

They'd met on the underground during that strange time during Christmas and New Year when everyone seemed to move in a dream, suspended in the twilight of the year, waiting for the turn of the calendar. She had come back from the Lake District early, thankful for the excuse that she had to go into work to finish some case notes, and had perched on one of the uncomfortable metal seats at Holborn to read while she waited, the platform thronged with red-nosed people, wool scarves wound tightly around necks, everyone desperate to jump on a train and make their way home. Chloe had gone past the point of jostling with other people and standing staring at sweaty foreheads, struggling to find a hand-hold to steady herself. She preferred to wait until there was a comfortable amount of space, and always walked to the ends of platforms, knowing the carriages were emptier there. Then, that day, Alex had come up to her.

'Excuse me?'

She'd looked up to see an attractive man with wavy brown hair and a slight frown watching her.

He paused for a moment, seeming to release a frosty

breath, looking at her curiously, then asked, 'May I sit down?'

'Of course.' She moved slightly, not that it was necessary as there was plenty of space. She wondered where he was from – not London if he felt the need to ask to sit; when you travelled the tube every day such politeness disappeared quickly.

He sat down, and she tried to resume her book, though she was still aware of him next to her. She felt like she should say something, but didn't know what, then he'd got there before her.

'Good, isn't it,' he'd said to her. 'I could hardly put it down.'

She'd looked up from her book. She was reading *One Hundred Years of Solitude*, and every time she took the book from her bag she grimaced at the irony of the title. She was so busy with caseloads she barely went out any more. Startled, she said, 'Yes, it's a beautiful book.' She looked down at the cover, then at the packed platform, just as someone trod on her toes in their effort to find a pocket of space in which to wait. She winced, and added, 'Sometimes one hundred years of seclusion sounds quite tempting.'

He'd laughed. 'Indeed. Well, don't let me stop you!' He'd gestured to the open pages.

So Chloe had turned back to the book, but had failed to read another sentence, now acutely aware of him perched next to her. Although she was no longer looking at his face, it had imprinted itself on her mind – his laughing brown eyes, and the kind smile.

Each time a train came they'd both leapt up. Each time

they were at the back of a queue of people, who all pushed and fought their way on. Each time the doors closed before they could make it on themselves she had felt relief that they were both still there.

The first few times they didn't acknowledge one another. But as they sat back down for the fourth time, they finally caught each other's eyes, and laughed.

'I hate fighting my way on when it's packed,' Alex said. 'Do you fancy getting a coffee while it thins out a bit?'

He'd asked it in a leisurely manner – too leisurely really; Chloe could hear the nervousness in his voice. The last thing she'd wanted at the time was a man in her life: not only was she always manically busy at work, but she was having a lot of fun with her girlfriends and enjoying the freedom of it all. Yet Alex had a smile that drew you to him, and she found herself saying yes, and not only going to a coffee house but to a restaurant and then a wine bar, before finally heading home as the first wisps of midnight snow floated around her, with a smile on her face and the faint impression of a first kiss still hovering on her lips.

He had phoned her often from that point – not too much or too little, but enough to make sure she knew he was keen. And she responded in kind, loving the laughter that seemed to come easily when they were together; their enjoyment of simple things, such as a walk in the park; feeling that she didn't need to be something other than herself to make an impression on him – that he saw past suits and makeup and job titles and salary, straight into the core of her.

As Chloe lay awake, she wondered whether she had ever seen into the core of him, or if she had been so wrapped up in being appreciated herself that she had forgotten to look properly at Alex, to see if she could penetrate his own outer shell and glimpse his heart. She thought she had, but now . . .

She swung her legs over the side of the bed and crept quietly downstairs. In the kitchen the table was covered with newspapers, coins, a Blockbuster card . . . and Alex's mobile phone.

She snuck over to it, feeling like a criminal. They had never felt the need to check each other's texts or emails, or open each other's post. They voluntarily shared all the details of their lives without the other having to go over them beforehand.

However, all that had changed in the past few days, Chloe thought grimly. And it had not been of her doing.

She pressed the tiny buttons and the screen lit up. As she went to text messages and scrolled through, she breathed a sigh of relief. There was nothing in there apart from various short messages from friends – mostly about football. There were no hidden love-notes or secret expressions of rediscovered longing.

Yet she still couldn't stop. She went into the phone book stored on the SIM and scrolled through the numbers. There was nothing in J except for 'Jamie' – Alex's brother.

Her mind was already beginning to succumb to tiredness, soothed by the knowledge that her fears were unfounded. The buttons bleeped quietly under her fingers as she tried to get back to the screensaver picture of her and Alex. She found herself looking at his call log, and quickly scanned the numbers. Apart from calls to her, most were to clients, and there were a couple to Jamie. But there was one number that stood out. It was not converted from digits to a name, therefore obviously not a regular contact. He'd called it less than twenty-four hours ago.

Chloe's heart fluttered as she stared at it. There was something familiar about it. She checked her own phone, and moments later, knew who it was.

Mark.

Why on earth was Alex calling Mark?

She flung the phone back onto the table, hating it for reaffirming her fears, and crept up to bed, rubbing her stomach gently. She opened the bedroom door as quietly as she could. It gave a tiny wail as it was pushed aside, then another one as she held the handle firmly and re-latched it.

Chloe tiptoed towards the bed, guided by the light of the streetlamp outside, and looked at Alex's still form, then his face, to check she wasn't disturbing him. She found his eyes – coal-dark in the dim light, but wide open, staring at her. She jumped slightly and took a quick breath, blinked and refocused. Now his eyes were shut and his breathing seemed even. She shook her head, wondering if she'd imagined it after all. But her heart was racing.

17

Mark was in the office early, keen to get a headstart on work this week, but his thoughts kept returning to his dad. He wondered if his father were still snoring his unshaven head off in Mark's bed. By the time Mark had finished his dinner last night, Henry had shown no sign of moving. Mark had watched him for a while from his chair, and the longer he stared at the inert form, the more irritated he felt. Eventually he'd got up and given Henry a sharp poke in the ribs, which seemed to have no effect on his consciousness, but did cause him to curl up into a foetal ball.

At the movement, Mark had decided he'd had enough. He'd yanked hard on Henry's arm, bending at the knees, his muscles straining as he pulled with all his strength to get his dad's arm around his shoulder and heave him up into a sitting position. 'Come on, Dad,' he yelled. 'For fuck's sake.'

Henry had responded with a load of mumbled slurs, which Mark could make nothing intelligible of, but he seemed to have got through, as his father moved obligingly, and Mark managed to get him to his feet and propel him towards the bedroom. Once Mark had Henry sitting on the bed, he had let go of him, and his dad had immediately fallen smack back against the mattress like a dead weight. If Mark hadn't been so cross and out of breath he would have laughed at the sight. It was too surreal. Henry's mouth had opened upon impact and he began to inhale in gurgling snores.

Mark had taken his pillows from the bed and a spare blanket from the walk-in wardrobe, and dumped them in the lounge. He'd returned with a pint glass of water and the washing-up bowl – in case his dad felt like throwing up. To make sure Henry would see it, Mark left it on his father's stomach, the bowl moving up and down gently with Henry's breathing like a boat bobbing in the breeze.

Then he'd gone into the lounge, turned the TV up higher than was necessary, and nestled under the blanket, half-watching the screen while he flicked through his papers until he fell asleep.

When he'd woken up he'd had to go into his bedroom for clothes. Henry had moved in the night. The bowl was on the floor, unused, and the water glass was only a quarter full now. Henry was on his side, back to the room, breathing evenly, but Mark had the feeling his dad was awake. He was grateful for the pretence. He couldn't even begin to frame a suitable conversation with his father since they had been thrust into such uncharted territory.

As he doodled on a legal pad, he wondered whether to phone his mother and tell her that her wayward husband had made an appearance, but he had no particular desire to talk to her either, since she seemed somehow to be holding Mark accountable for Henry's actions.

He hadn't got much done by the time everyone started arriving around nine. Half an hour later he got a phone call telling him one of his clients had decided to settle, which meant he didn't have to go to court that afternoon, but also that quite a lot of the work he had been doing for the past week, not to mention that morning, had been a waste of time. Mark secretly loathed parties who chose last-minute settlements – they lacked the gumption to call proceedings to a halt early and save themselves money and their legal team time; and they also lacked the integrity to follow through on their cause. He was especially curt to the opposing party's solicitor on the phone, and she ended the call having barely got out her final sentence.

A few hours later, he had just sent the temp running out of the office near to tears after he'd berated her for bringing the wrong case file, when David Marchant stuck his head round the door, glanced briefly at the secretary's hunched, departing back, and said, 'Everything okay, Mark?'

'Fine, fine,' Mark replied, leaning back in his chair nonchalantly, hoping he could replicate a confident, relaxed manner, which was in reality eluding him right now. 'And you?'

'All good.' David came in and sank onto the chair opposite Mark's desk. 'I heard Dawson and Hamish settled.'

'Yes,' Mark said, smiling. 'Eleventh hour.'

'Oh well.' David leaned forward. 'At least you can shift

that one along now, it seems to have been dragging on for an eternity.'

Mark had the feeling David was making small talk, and was intrigued. It wasn't characteristic of his boss. He smiled and waited.

'So,' David continued, settling back into his chair again after a pause. 'How's Henry? We haven't seen him round here lately.'

A-ha. Mark felt his shoulders stiffen and froze in an attempt to appear relaxed, then realised that was a dead giveaway. He began to shift a little in his seat. Neil and David seemed to accept his father's frequent office visits, although Mark had managed to glean a few signs of irritation over the years when Henry overstepped the mark in company matters that really no longer concerned him. He usually dropped in to the offices once a week, and did the rounds, meeting and greeting people whose doors were open, offering advice where he felt it needed to be dispensed. When Mark heard his father talking to Neil and David, he was usually bragging about the heaven of retirement – long lunches after rounds of golf, afternoons at his club, where he dined and supped with former judges and barristers. It was obvious to Mark and, he presumed, others too, that his dad was struggling with an excess of spare time and a recess of status far more than he was admitting.

'He's fine,' Mark smiled pleasantly, thinking of his father's inert form in his bed a few hours earlier. 'Just . . . busy, I think.'

One of David's eyebrows twitched slightly. 'Well, give him our regards, won't you,' he said, getting up.

Mark sighed impatiently once David had gone. His desk was cluttered with case files, but now he had nothing urgent he didn't have any desire to look at them.

He thought of Alex's phone call yesterday morning, and the piece of paper stuffed in his top right-hand drawer. He needed a distraction.

He looked at his watch. It was one o'clock. Her flat wasn't all that far away. And he could drop off the Blythe documents to the barrister en route.

Don't be an idiot, he berated himself. You're not a love-sick teenager with bad acne any more. It was bad enough last time. You'll just look like a stalker now.

Yet as he got up, his legs didn't seem to be following his brain's commands.

18

'Mrs Markham to Doctor Chen's office, please.'

Chloe got up and walked quickly to a bright blue door, knocking once and then opening it when she heard the doctor call, 'Come in'.

Juliet Chen swivelled round in her chair and gave Chloe a smile. Chloe had only seen Dr Chen a couple of times, mostly for repeat prescriptions, but she was instantly put at ease by the other woman's sympathetic bedside manner.

'Hello, Chloe,' Dr Chen began. 'What can I do for you today?'

'Well,' Chloe paused, 'I think I'm pregnant.'

'How wonderful!' The doctor's smile broadened, then she noticed the lack of excitement from Chloe and asked, 'And are you happy about this?'

'Yes, yes I am.' Chloe tried to animate her face but her

features were like stiff dough. 'It's just . . .' She felt tears prickle her eyelids. 'It's a difficult time.'

'Okay.' Dr Chen nodded as though she understood everything. 'Let's start from the beginning. When was your last period?'

'About six weeks ago, I think.'

'You think?'

'I'm never very regular, and it's always pretty light, so I find it hard to keep track.'

'Well, I'll take a urine sample in a second.' The doctor moved to glance at her notes, then looked back at Chloe. 'But I'd just like to do an exam. Is that okay?'

Chloe nodded, and wished away the ensuing five minutes as she lay on the bed while the doctor poked and prodded her. Once she was sitting back down, Doctor Chen turned to her and paused, looking at Chloe intently.

'You certainly are pregnant, Chloe, but I would say you're quite a bit further on than six weeks.'

'Really?'

'I'd say more like nearly four months, judging by the size and shape of your uterus.'

Chloe sat up, incredulous. 'But I can't be. I've had periods.'

Dr Chen smiled. 'Don't worry, Chloe. As you say, they've been light, and it does happen with some women. I'm going to get you organised for a scan straightaway, to make sure. But I'd prepare for a baby in about five months, not seven, if I were you. Didn't you notice your stomach changing?'

'Well, yes, I suppose.' She had noticed the roundness to

her stomach recently. 'But only in the last week or so, since I've known. I just thought that was what happened.'

'It does, but normally a little further on than six weeks,' Dr Chen said kindly.

'But I haven't felt sick at all.'

'That's a good thing.' Dr Chen smiled, then paused again on seeing Chloe's unhappy face. 'Is something wrong, Chloe?' She sat patiently, hands in her lap. Chloe wondered if the pose had been taught to her at medical school.

'It's my husband . . .' Chloe started, but trailed off, unsure how to explain.

The doctor looked briefly at her notes. 'Is he unhappy about the baby?' she asked.

Chloe shook her head. 'He doesn't know.'

If the doctor was surprised she didn't show it, but laid a hand on Chloe's arm. 'Tell him,' she encouraged. 'He needs to know, and you need to be taken care of right now.'

Chloe nodded. It wasn't as simple as that, but doctors' sessions usually lasted ten minutes, and if Chloe started pouring her heart out she would be here a lot longer than that. So she just took her referral for the ultrasound and left with a quiet 'thank you'.

When she got outside she suddenly felt nauseous, as though all the morning sickness she had avoided so far had been stacking up inside her to come in one enormous wave at that moment. She got halfway along the surgery path, then had to lean into some bushes and deposit most of her lunch, thankful that there was no one around to see her.

This was no good. She had to tell Alex about the baby. In fact, it now seemed stupid she hadn't done so already.

Whatever his thoughts about Julia, the idea of being a father would distract him so much that this little hiccup would pale in comparison. Wouldn't it?

Before her thoughts could take hold of her she tried Alex's mobile, but there was no answer. That was weird. He normally picked up when he was working at home.

A jolt went through her as she remembered looking at his phone the night before, and before she could question what she was doing, she was dialling Mark.

19

Mark was walking out of the office when his phone rang. He reached inside his jacket pocket, pulled it out and flipped it open.

'Mark, did Alex call you at the weekend?'

Mark heard the sharpness in Chloe's tone and was surprised. 'Er, yes, he did,' he said, then paused, not knowing how to follow it up.

'Oh, okay. What did he want?'

She asked it as casually as she could, but the pause that followed was packed with tension, as though she were holding herself still in readiness for his answer. A strange wave of emotion came across Mark, and with some surprise he found himself saying, 'He dialled me by mistake, it was a five-second call. I don't think Alex and I have all that much to talk about.'

'No, I don't suppose you do,' Chloe answered, but the

suspicion was still clear in her voice. 'Okay, then. Thanks.' And she was gone.

Mark made his way out, thinking of the restaurant last Thursday: Julia's obvious distress, Chloe's blatant innocence as to what was going on; and Alex's shocked face. Then he remembered the man's haughty voice on the phone at the weekend.

Why should he bloody well get away with it? Anger rose in him, crushing every other thought, and he turned back. He pushed open his office door, pulled out the rumpled piece of paper from his desk drawer, and marched into Chloe's room, flinging the miserable scrap on to the table. He borrowed a biro to annotate it.

'*I think this was what Alex wanted,*' he wrote, the pen scratching out every word. '*I'll leave it up to you whether he gets it or not.*'

20

Alex was exhausted. As he tussled with each waking minute, a dark-haired wraith-woman paced the corners of his mind, darting out before him then back to the shadows again before he could stop her. In his dreams the night before she had been there too, wearing a vest top and a short skirt with thick ugg boots, her back to him, walking fast. Although he was running, lungs stinging with gasped oxygen, he could not close the gap. He had cried her name, but she gave no sign she had heard him. Then fog descended around them and she disappeared.

By the time he had got up, Chloe was gone, just a note from her on the table telling him she had an early meeting at work and signed with a 'C' – love and kisses conspicuously absent. He had tried not to read anything into that, but who was he kidding?

He thought about ringing her. At work she was invariably

with clients or colleagues, however, so she would hardly want him to start pouring his heart out. He felt terrible that he hadn't come home until the early hours. He'd ended up finding a panicked Jamie at his local police station, his brother having locked himself out of the house. Not only had they and a helpful constable had to break into Jamie's flat, but then he'd had to stay with his brother until he'd calmed down enough for Alex to be sure he'd be safe on his own. Looking out for Jamie could be a thankless and depressing task at times, but his parents relied heavily on him to do so. It was they who had decided to buy Jamie a flat close to Alex when their younger son had insisted on moving out. Thinking back, Alex couldn't ever remember a conversation where he'd agreed to this responsibility, but it seemed to have been handed to him anyway.

Frustrated, he tried to turn his mind to his work, relieved he didn't have anything urgent today. Making his way through the house, he simultaneously began to effect the mental transition from home to work mode. It was a relief to get down to the cellar, which also functioned as his office and was one of his favourite places. Everything there was set up and streamlined so he could get through the maximum amount of work in a day – working for himself, time really was money. He'd put strip lighting in there, but it rarely went on; instead, spotlights and desk lights illuminated his work space, as well as his top-of-the-range Apple Mac, the machine he spent most of his days in communion with. The walls were peppered with the works of some of his favourite artists – including plenty of Dali and Magritte, a couple of Rousseau's jungle scenes, and a particularly large print of

L'Ange du Foyer by Max Ernst – the latter always causing him to smile when he remembered Chloe's expression the time he'd suggested putting it up in the lounge. As the house was an old-fashioned one, there was a tiny strip of window at the very front of the room, which allowed a snippet of a view of the front pathway. It was quite grimy on the inside, and Alex had decided that, since cleaning it would involve moving Apple Mac, desk and god knew how many wires to allow access, it would stay that way for quite some time.

As he switched on the computer, the whir of it coming to life was drowned out by the buzz of his fractious mind. He needed to talk to Chloe . . . and to Julia . . . He was still fuming from his conversation with Mark yesterday morning, when the arrogant wanker had not only been utterly unhelpful, but had sworn at him and hung up.

Wearily, he turned to his work. There were about half a dozen emails waiting, two of which involved current jobs. When he had quit his in-house job at ArtSpace he had anticipated some time out, and then going back into the fray – never this. It had been Chloe who encouraged him to resign, seeing how unhappy he was with the office politics and backstabbing, which for most people seemed to take up a far larger part of the day than design work. There had been constant frayed nerves and speculation over the next round of redundancies; and an endless succession of 'bright young things' coming in, impetuous and overconfident in their abilities to transform the company, quickly becoming bitter and twisted as they morphed unwillingly into the status quo.

Then one of his clients from ArtSpace – Jed Morenzo, who he would thank forever – had put Alex in touch with an associate. Although Jed's company was tied to ArtSpace and they were disappointed that Alex was no longer working on their account, they had loved his designs enough to show them around, and from that one recommendation things had snowballed. Every now and again he put an ad in one of the trade presses, but for the most part his work evolved through word of mouth – the very best form of advertising there was, and, best of all, the only one that was free. He did some posters, bits of marketing material, but enjoyed logo design the most. He loved getting to grips with the essence of a company and trying to sum it up so that their vision shouted out from a small, often abstract motif. One of his proudest moments had been having his work featured in *HOW* magazine – at that point he'd finally begun to think he was getting places.

Now, he replied to those emails he could deal with straight away, and checked his schedule for the week. He had only two meetings with clients, both on Wednesday, so the rest was design time. Yet he had a feeling that the week wasn't going to go very well. As he flicked open his web browser he started typing a name in, hoping against all odds that something would come up.

He spent twenty minutes on this. There was nothing new.

There was only one more thing to try. He picked up his phone and dialled the number, hoping he'd still got the right one.

'Kelly, it's Alex,' he said when a female voice answered.

'Alex? Alex! Bloody hell, mate, long time no see!'

He immediately felt guilty that he was ringing her after all this time with a purpose other than one related to their old friendship. He asked her how she was and they chatted for a while, and he was just wondering how to ask the question when she said, 'Do you want me to do another search on Amy?'

He felt a surge of warmth for Kelly for making this so easy for him, as well as guilty that he hadn't kept up contact. But it had been too painful, when he had returned from Australia on his own, to talk to joint friends from their carefree uni days about what had happened. Contact had drifted off until it became Christmas cards, if anything.

'Can you?' he asked.

'Al, it'll take me one sec. Hang on.' There was a short pause, then, 'Nothing new, I'm afraid. Still listed as missing. Hold on a sec, there's a note on her file, though. Let me check it.' Another pause, longer. 'Jeez, Al, it seems there is something new on here, after all.'

He listened to what Kelly had to say, his heart pounding harder with every word she uttered, clenching his fists as the old memories and the anger returned.

'And Amy doesn't know this?'

'I wouldn't know, Al, but we don't often get missing persons ringing up asking after themselves.'

'Of course,' he said, feeling stupid.

'It's all over the Australian news,' Kelly continued. 'Just look on the Net.'

'Yes, but even if she's seen it she might not realise it's possibly connected to her,' Alex said, thinking aloud.

There was a pause on the line. 'Al, has something happened? You know, if you've heard from her then we need to know. Her family will still be suffering.'

'I haven't,' he told her quickly, hating himself for lying. 'I was just reminded of her the other day, and I realised I haven't called for a while, and felt a bit guilty, I guess. I still hope . . .' He trailed off. He didn't want to weave himself into a growing lie any more than he had to.

'We all do, Al,' Kelly said gently. 'We all do.'

As soon as he had hung up, Alex logged on to the web and began flicking through news articles with growing shock, printing out everything he could find. The need to locate Amy and tell her the news became more pressing with every article he read. Eventually his work head and his emotions had a gentleman's handshake that he would concentrate for a couple of hours and get lots done, and then he would think about how to find her. Since it looked like Mark would rather actively hinder him than help, he would have to do it another way.

Having made a short-term decision he began to get into his work. Before he knew it his stomach was growling, and a quick glance at the clock told him it was after eleven.

He was leaning back in his chair, studying the design he was currently manipulating on screen, when he heard a noise outside. Footsteps. He glanced up at the long, thin, rectangular window, and saw a pair of scruffy suede boots, the kind with no heel and a thick woollen lining, pass by.

He didn't recognise the boots, but his heart did a bungee dive inside his ribcage as he understood for certain just who they belonged to.

He jumped up and moved quickly to the window to get the best glimpse he could, even then doubting his own conclusion, wanting to double check. The boots were outside the front door, and he waited for the sound of the doorbell, but it didn't come.

He was holding his breath, watching this pair of feet, half-joyous, half-terrified that she had found him.

And then the boots moved. Past the window, quickly, as though their owner had had serious second thoughts about where she was. And that movement catapulted him into action.

'Fuck!' he yelled, and rushed to the stairs, taking them two at a time, fumbling with the catch of the cellar door at the top, rounding the doorpost, down the long hallway, grabbing his keys off the hall table – every movement taking forever – and unlocking the front door. Even though it was still wet outside from the intermittent rain, he raced down the path in his T-shirt and slippers, feeling the water seeping through his flimsy footwear, but not caring. He ran into the road in a panic.

They lived on a street of large terraced houses set back from the wide road, with old horse chestnut trees standing guard at periodic intervals either side. The paving stones were uneven, and most people had some kind of hedgerow built up at the front to discourage intruders or busybodies. Alex took all this in, all those places to hide, all those places she might be. Surely she was close. He looked around wildly for anything that might betray where she was, but it was quiet. He was about to shout her name, when he heard a woman's voice.

'Are you okay?'

It was Esther, from the house opposite. On her way to collect her son from nursery. Wrapped up for the weather, in long coat and gloves, and doing a swift appraising top-to-toe of him, her face clouding with worry as she did so.

Alex gulped back the cry in his throat, and ran his fingers through his hair, attempting to intimate some level of composure. But he couldn't. 'Did you see a woman, just now, in the street?' he jabbered. 'Wearing boots, suede boots?'

He could see Esther trying not to look disturbed at this strange question. She and Chloe were quite friendly when they saw one another, and she was obviously mentally computing that he wasn't referring to his wife.

'I didn't, I'm sorry,' she said politely, but with a little more restraint in her voice. She looked unsure of him now. 'Sorry, Alex,' she said, moving to her car. 'I've got to dash, Nathan will be waiting.'

'No problem,' he replied, trying to smile normally but feeling his face crease up oddly. Esther gave him a quick, tight smile back, confirming to him that he was looking more like a lunatic than a friendly neighbour, and got in the car, firing the engine quickly and waving without looking as she drove down the street.

Once she was gone he took a few more glances left and right. Nothing.

'FOR GOD'S SAKE,' he bellowed, not giving a shit any more if the whole neighbourhood decided to watch. 'COME OUT IF YOU'RE THERE. PLEASE!'

Silence. The only things moving in the street were flimsy branches on the skeletal trees.

She had been so close for a few moments, and now she was gone again, and for how long he didn't know. Maybe forever.

As he trudged back inside, frustration making his head throb, he heard his phone ringing downstairs. He reached it just in time to see 'Chloe' on the small screen, and was frozen in indecision until it went silent.

21

Chloe made her way hurriedly to Bar 38, thanking god that she was meeting her cousin for lunch. In her opinion Mikaela was capable of lightening the foulest mood, though not many of her relatives would have said the same. It was well known that, in the family, Mikaela could be found under any of the more downbeat euphemisms – she was everything from the problem middle child to the black sheep of the family to the skeleton in the closet – although they all had great trouble actually keeping her in the proverbial closet as Mikaela tended to spring out over and over again like a demented jack-in-the-box.

At the doorway to the pub, her mobile rang. It was her mother, who barked, 'Have you told him yet?' and was outraged when Chloe said no. Chloe was sure this meant that Margaret had either phoned the entire gardening club already and was now waiting for her daughter to get her act together so Margaret wouldn't look bad, or that she was suffering great pains in keeping the confidence. She was fervently wishing she hadn't let her mother in on such a precious secret.

When she had finished the call, she walked through the door and spotted Mikaela as her cousin rose with an excited wave and gestured to two goblet-sized wines already waiting on the table. They made small talk for a while. Chloe was enjoying the ease of female company: seeing her friends seemed to have become a frustratingly rare thing since her mother had begun competing with her job for her spare time.

'Okay, spill the beans,' Mikaela said suddenly, startling Chloe from her reverie.

'What? There are no beans.'

'Of course there are. You look like you've got something you're dying to tell me.'

'What makes you think that?'

'The way you're acting, like, all quiet and brooding. I know you of old, Chlo. Spit it out.'

'Well,' she hesitated for just a second, then to her chagrin found herself blurting, 'I'm pregnant.'

'What?' Mikaela looked gobsmacked. 'Really?'

'Yes, really.' Chloe attempted a feeble smile. It didn't quite work.

'So, you've got a great job, you're happily married, and you're having a baby. Is that why you're looking so miserable?' Mikaela put a hand on Chloe's arm and stroked it softly. 'C'mon, Chloe, aren't you pleased?'

Chloe was taken aback by the way her life had just been described to her, as though it were some textbook example of how to move steadily through adulthood. 'Of course I am,' she said, somewhat defensively, 'it's just . . . oh, god, it's just I can't believe I'm telling you before I've even told the father.'

Mikaela's grip tightened on her arm and she leaned forward. 'Why? Who's the father?'

'What? Mikaela! It's Alex, of course.'

'Oh.' Mikaela looked a bit disappointed. 'Okay, why haven't you told Alex?'

'It's . . . complicated.' Chloe began to fill Mikaela in on the scene in the restaurant the week before, Julia there looking gorgeous, and Alex's strange behaviour since.

When she paused, Mikaela sat back looking thoughtful. 'Hmmm. Well, it's always the quiet ones.'

Chloe was rapidly wishing she'd never started this. Mikaela was anything but reassuring. '*What's* always the quiet ones?' She sighed. 'He isn't having an affair, Mik. It's just made me feel a bit weird, that's all, and I wanted it to be . . . happy, when I told him about the baby, not strained. Besides, Alex isn't quiet.'

'What? Of course he is, Chloe. He's not silent-quiet, but you couldn't get much more reserved and brooding – in that mysterious, sexy way he's got. Like, like . . . Mr Darcy!'

Chloe was stunned. She'd never seen Alex as approaching anything Mr-Darcyish by nature. He wasn't a chatterbox, but . . .

How many people thought like this? She felt giddy, and put down her wineglass. How many people had an entirely different perspective of her own husband? And – most importantly – who the hell was right?

'What do you think I should do?' she asked.

'You're asking me . . . !' Mikaela began. 'Haven't you noticed I never get past the third date?'

'Well, perhaps you should wait longer before putting out,' Chloe retorted, before biting her lip, but Mikaela just laughed. Then, seeing her cousin sitting there looking crest-fallen, Mikaela rubbed her finger against her chin while she thought.

Finally, she leaned in and said, 'Don't take it from him, hon. Demand to know what's going on. And, for god's sake, tell him you're pregnant. Then he'll have to treat you right – nothing like a bun in the oven to be able to add in some emotional blackmail.'

'I don't want to have to "blackmail" him to get him to do the right thing, Mik,' Chloe snapped, then added, 'but you're right, we need to have it out.' She sighed. 'I just want things to get back to normal.'

'I know you do, babe.'

Chloe had had enough of this discussion; it was making everything seem worse. Her mind searched for a new topic to cause a diversion, and came up trumps. 'Have you spoken to your mum yet?' Mikaela and her family had been on dif-ficult terms since Mikaela had discussed some of the wilder aspects of her sex life on a late-night television show.

'Nope.' Mikaela knocked back the last of her wine. 'Waiting for her now.'

'Mik, she doesn't even know where you are.'

'I know, I know. But I'll leave it a while longer, I think.'

'Mik –'

Mikaela held up her hand. The devilish glint in her eyes

was extinguished for a moment, and Chloe realised that her cousin looked tired.

'Things can't always go back, Chlo. However much you want them to. You have to work with where you are right now, and go forward. Wishing things could be what they once were just sends you dotty, believe you me.'

'Do you wish you hadn't done it?' They both knew Chloe was referring to Mikaela's five minutes of television fame.

'Of course not!' Mikaela lifted the carafe and poured herself some more wine. Then she looked up and raised her glass, and the mischievous glint was back in her eyes. 'I just wish that it hadn't been broadcast to the nation on a rare night that my family stayed up past ten!'

Chloe couldn't help but smile.

Chloe made her way back to the office feeling much brighter after an hour with Mikaela. The freezing wind swirled around her, nipping her legs and biting her cheeks as she pulled her coat close. It was time to get out hats and gloves, something she put off as long as possible, knowing that it always seemed such a long time before she could put them away again. She hated the frozen winter months of slippery pavements and dirty splashes down her tights.

As she walked through the office corridors, David Marchant approached her. One half of the two senior partners in the practice, David was usually the bad cop to Neil Lewis's good cop as far as their employees were concerned, and Chloe immediately stiffened.

'Neil and I would like a status meeting with you, please,

Chloe,' David said to her as he neared, looking at her from under bushy grey eyebrows. 'We're feeling out of touch with your caseloads, particularly your progress with the Abbott case. Get Jana to set something up with Marie.'

'No problem, David,' Chloe replied, hoping that was it. But David followed her towards her office.

'Do you know where Mark Jameson is, Chloe?' There was only one Mark in the office, yet David nearly always referred to him by his full name.

'No.' Chloe looked startled. 'Why?'

David grimaced and she swallowed a frustrated sigh at the ill-conceived insinuation that her relationship with Mark still went beyond office hours. Their involvement had been treated as an infidelity towards the firm. It had never been quite forgiven. Even though they had ended it long ago, and Chloe had since married, David Marchant regularly treated them both to looks of suspicion and distaste.

'Well, he seems to have disappeared.'

'Has he?' Chloe had almost reached her own door as, surprised, she looked over to Mark's office, which stood empty as if in silent agreement. She wondered, uncomfortably, how often the partners noticed these things.

David Marchant raised an eyebrow and lowered his voice to a discreet hum. 'Neil played squash with him last night and said he seemed quite out of sorts – apparently, for the past week he's been letting Neil win far more easily than he usually does.' Chloe thought she saw the briefest trace of a smile cross David's lips, before he cleared his throat and added, 'Chloe, if anything is going on that we should know about, then – this time – tell us, won't you, and avoid another embarrassing episode.'

He gave Chloe a curt nod, before striding off like a military general – casting glances left and right along the corridor as though checking his troops were all in order.

Chloe watched him go. Then she turned to look back at Mark's office. She thought over David's words, grimacing at the 'embarrassing episode' comment. She thought he was referring to the Christmas law ball, but that was nearly ten bloody years ago, for god's sake.

She walked round to her desk, and sat down. It took her a moment to register the note waiting for her, and another moment to read it. Then she gave a strangled cry, jumped up, grabbed her coat and bag and rushed out again, no longer caring whether David saw her go or not.

22

Mark was frustrated as he got out of the taxi. The barrister's clerk on the Blythe case had been in his office and only too happy to witter on about next week's court appearance.

It took him a while to find the passageway, and once he was through it, he looked around, startled. It wasn't what he had expected. He'd been thinking quaint, but these were grimy tenements arranged around a squalid, overgrown courtyard, with graffiti tags scrawled on the walls of the passage that led to them. He checked the crumpled paper in his hand, trying to ignore his befuddled brain, which was still puzzling over why he'd left work during the middle of the day to come here. There was a scruffy door, red paint flaking badly, with numbers 2 and 3 in brass on the front.

He couldn't find a doorbell, so he pushed gingerly against

the smooth brass plate to one side, and felt the door swing open.

There was a narrow staircase, and a door leading off to the right with number 3 on it. An empty McDonald's wrapper and a discarded cigarette packet lay next to a shabby footmat. He debated for the thousandth time just what exactly he thought he was doing, then looked up the stairs, took a deep breath, and began to climb.

At the top a doorway was positioned on the uppermost step. Before he could change his mind, Mark knocked.

He heard a flurry of activity behind, which then fell silent. Anger and embarrassment suffused him. He shouldn't have come. Nevertheless, he rapped smartly again, and waited.

'Who is it?' an unsteady voice called.

'Mark,' he shouted back.

'Mark?' There was more movement from inside. A bolt drawn back. A key turned. Then she was there, in front of him, like everything and nothing he'd imagined. Her hair was loose and tucked casually behind her ears, and she had a long black coat on, as though she were about to go out. 'What are you doing here?' she said. She looked worried.

He paused. The truth was, he didn't know.

If he had been told this story by a third party and asked for his reaction, he would have said run! Get away from her, she sounds like big trouble. But in actual fact it wasn't having that effect on him at all. There was something about these bleak surroundings and her lovely pale face that was bringing out the *chevalier* in him, making him stand up straighter, self-conscious of every movement, wanting to find the right juxtaposition of limbs and expression that would reach out to her.

The only thing that threatened this feeling was that Julia didn't seem too keen on fulfilling the required role of distressed but willing damsel. She was fidgeting with the key in the lock behind the door now, and she hadn't invited him in.

He looked straight at her and said, 'I wanted to make sure you were okay, after . . . last week.'

She sighed. Her face relaxed slightly as she said, 'That is very kind of you. I'm afraid I owe you a big apology.'

Mark waved his hand automatically. 'No, don't worry. It's just . . . well, it was obviously . . .' Why was he finding it so hard to pick the right words when in his job he was put on the spot all the time, and could always come up with a snappy retort? '. . . You obviously had a shock – seeing Alex like that.'

She looked distinctly uncomfortable now. 'Yes,' she said. 'It was a surprise.'

She wouldn't be drawn out so easily, he realised. Undeterred, he pressed on, guessing his way. 'An amazing coincidence, wasn't it, you two meeting again like that.'

Julia lifted her head and looked at him intently. Mark held her gaze, searching her eyes, her face, for small cracks he might plunder for information. She looked nervous and weary and confused, but there was still enough composure about her to make him feel that to ask her anything outright would be judged as impertinent, and he didn't want to watch her lovely face close against him.

Then she surprised him by seizing an initiative of her own. 'There's a coffee shop around the corner,' she announced. 'Do you want one?'

'Great,' Mark replied, taken aback.

'Okay then.' Without looking at him she removed her keys from the interior lock. 'Let's go.'

It had begun to rain heavily in the few minutes since Mark had arrived, so they ran, Julia with her hands in her pockets, pulling her coat close to her; Mark following, having nothing to shield himself with, praying that this place was close.

A few doors down from the alleyway, Julia yanked open a door in undignified haste. Mark rushed in behind her and collided with her when she came to a sudden stop by the cashier's desk as she scanned the interior for a table.

'Sorry,' he said, as he automatically put a hand on her shoulder to steady himself. He felt her quickly pull away, but when she turned to look at him he was surprised to see she was laughing. Her face was alive with merriment for just a few precious seconds, before her expression faded into sombre composure once more.

'It's stupid,' she said, with a small smile. 'Getting caught in the rain always makes me feel so alive.'

Then she turned and made her way to an empty table at one side of the room; and Mark, entranced, followed.

23

They sat opposite one another, Julia watching the window behind Mark, where runnels of rain cascaded down the glass. She knew he was smiling at her, but a small tic in his cheek beat crazily, undermining his forced expression.

She had been at Alex's door only an hour or so ago. She had been so close to him . . . but it had been too much, that street full of beautiful redbrick two-storey Georgian-style houses with parapets and sash windows, like something out of a BBC drama. She had thought that if she moved quickly enough she would go through with knocking on the door, but her brain caught up with her as she stood there with her hand raised, and her mind had been flooded with all the parasitical doubts and fears that had hitchhiked everywhere with her for ten long years.

She had realised as she stood at the door that his office

address was also his home, which meant that Chloe lived there too.

She had run for two streets, then hidden behind a huge tree trunk, looking up at the sky, her blood rushing noisily through her ears, her heart smacking hard in her chest cavity, breathing quickly while feeling as if she were not getting any oxygen at all. She was terrified he would suddenly appear from around the tree, close up and angry, and that had sent her fleeing all the way to the tube station.

Now, Mark looked like he was waiting for her to speak.

'I'm so sorry . . .' She paused, pretending to scan the laminated menu while she mentally rehearsed her speech. 'I knew Alex a long time ago, but we parted on difficult terms. My fault as much as his, but I couldn't bear the thought of sitting next to him for the entire duration of a meal, and I didn't want to make a fuss in front of you all either. So I asked the waiter to tell you I had to leave urgently, and to pass on my apologies.'

The last part was a lie, but it worked. Mark rolled his eyes. 'Well, I never got the message. Charming. Won't be going back there again in a hurry, that's for sure.'

His face relaxed. She hadn't run out on him – she'd left word. It made a difference.

He leaned forward, open curiosity now dominating his face. 'So what happened with Alex?'

Julia had been expecting that one too. 'Oh, you know, uni students always doing everything to excess, drinking and partying – you shouldn't expect to try and maintain a relationship with all that merry abandon going on around you – you're doomed from the start.'

In fact, neither of them had ever been ones for the more reckless excesses of university, although they had enjoyed their share of carefree fun. When she thought back to those times it was like remembering disjointed scenes of a movie she once watched. She barely recognised the characters portrayed there.

'But,' she continued quickly, before Mark could interrupt with more questions, trying hard to keep her tone neutral and measured, 'despite the shock of seeing him, it's nice to know he's happy and settled now.'

'Well, yeah.' Mark gazed up into the distance for a moment. 'Bit of a surprise, Chloe and Alex – bit of a whirlwind. When she announced they were getting married, everyone in the office thought she must be pregnant. Chloe's so – so strait-laced, normally, that to jump into marriage without a second thought was so unlike her – far too daring . . .'

'So how long have they been together then?' She felt certain Mark would notice the high pitch of her voice, so hard was she trying to appear normal, casual.

'Oh, they must have been married a couple of years now,' Mark replied. 'And they were together for a few months before that. So two and a half years, maybe three, I guess.' He looked down at the table.

'And are they . . . happy?' Her voice was barely a whisper.

Mark looked up, his vision clouding for a second before he replied. 'Yes, I suppose so.'

She was glad he couldn't see the stab of pain that ripped through her chest. 'Well, that's good then.'

They fell silent. Mark kept his head down, and she suddenly realised that he wasn't paying attention to her reactions at all. He seemed lost in contemplation, his finger absently rubbing a mark on the tablecloth and spreading the stain further into the weave of the cotton.

'Are you okay?' she ventured.

He looked up, surprised. 'Of course,' he said, smiling. 'It's lovely to see you again.' His gaze softened, then his eyes dropped to her breasts for just a fraction of a second.

She felt her mouth fall open in surprise and quickly snapped it shut again. She had a sudden desire to get up and throw his water over him and then to kick him as hard as she could. She wanted to get out of there. In the sprawling metropolis of London she doubted she'd see him again once they went their separate ways.

Although he knew where she lived.

She felt a shudder ripple through her. She would have to play this out carefully, and tactfully. So she smiled and they ordered coffee, and she asked Mark as much as she could about his work, his life, his interests. She was ready to deflect any questions about herself, but Mark seemed to enjoy answering her enquiries so much that he didn't make many of his own.

When they finally paid and got up to leave, she let Mark open the door for her and stepped outside.

It felt like she had been sleepwalking for years, and seeing Alex had finally woken her up. Even in the dusky light, everything seemed brighter: colours were so vivid it hurt her eyes to look at them; people talked so loudly she wanted to clamp her hands to her ears; everyone and everything seemed to move so fast that she had to stand still and look at her feet just to stop feeling dizzy . . . Yet she had been drifting through such places for years, preferring big cities to small towns, as it was easier to get lost amongst the people. She felt more claustrophobic in open spaces than pressed against sour-smelling bodies on a bus, train or pavement, yet enjoyed neither. She would have stayed home as much as possible, but that required a certain stillness she could only manage in short bursts. She had to keep moving. If she stopped, if she gave herself too much time alone with her thoughts, she began to feel that something terrible would happen.

'It was nice to see you again,' she said politely to Mark as he stood next to her, watching her expression.

'You too,' he said, 'I –'

'– and I'm so sorry about the other night,' she continued quickly, knowing she wouldn't like what he planned to say next. 'I'm very embarrassed. It was nice to meet you, though.' She held out her hand.

Mark looked at her outstretched arm with a blank expression, then extended his own and completed the handshake, his grip firm and assertive. She refused to meet his eyes and turned to go, then her heart sank as he immediately said, 'Julia.'

She turned around slowly, reluctantly.

His hand was inside his jacket, then he pulled out a card. 'Take this,' he said. 'If I can do anything for you at all, just give me a call.' He paused. 'And I would love to buy you a proper dinner, if you ever fancy it,' he added, his armour of controlled charm deserting him for a moment and leaving just a frustrated, eager, wishful man in its stead. It was the first time she had felt a real surge of warmth towards him, perhaps because she knew he was letting her go.

'Thank you,' she said graciously, taking the card. Again, she turned to leave.

'Alex called me,' he blurted to her back.

It was as though a huge serpent had just uncoiled and reared in front of her on the wet, grey London pavement. She was deadly still, listening. Waiting.

'He wanted to contact you . . . But I haven't told him anything, as I wasn't sure . . . Do you want me to, if he asks again?'

'Yes,' she called out, not trusting herself to turn around. Hoping he could catch her voice above the rumble of traffic and people. Feeling desperate, frustration and longing breaking over her in waves, she capitulated and turned. 'Yes please.'

She glanced quickly at his surprised face, added 'Thank you' and swung around again, walking briskly away.

She was so choked up she could hardly breathe. Her head filled with white noise. She hurried along the path, keeping close to the grimy cement facades of buildings, her eyes blurring with tears as they watched the grey pavements flash by. She bumped into a few people and ignored the tutting or cursing that followed.

Alex wanted to talk to her. But for good or ill, she had no way of knowing.

At the passageway to her flat, she paused, then moved on towards the station.

24

Mark saw Julia stop at the passageway to her courtyard, then watched as she hurried on. She was heading away from her home, and he was drawn to follow, to find out something about her everyday life. He didn't know whether he would have kept tailing her had she gone grocery shopping, but she didn't. Instead she headed for the station, and so did Mark.

He began to enjoy this impromptu sleuthing, an activity that was definitely not on his list of priorities for today. He got into the carriage one along from hers, but could still see her through the small window of the train as it rocked its way along in the usual stop-start fashion of the underground.

The first time Julia looked over her shoulder was when they had both just alighted from the train, and Mark swung round and bent down to fiddle with his shoelace, cheeks reddening. When she dared look back she had gone, but he jogged to the exit and could see her walking away up the street. He was pretty sure of where she was going. But still he followed. Knowing the way, he could keep a bit more distance now, but he made sure he was watching from behind a wall as she went up to the door. His face was grim. He could well imagine what he was going to see next.

25

This time it felt different, because now he was looking for her too, and so she was standing at his door, her feet together, her head down, and her impetuous hand in a world of its own, lifting, lifting, and then knocking.

She waited. Behind her, the last of the autumn leaves on the dead-looking trees held fixed, tense positions, determined not to take their final plunge to earth until it was beyond their control.

As she heard footfalls coming closer, their rapid pace suddenly in time with her heartbeat, there was no space for thought or memory. Her head was filled to the brim with these few stretched seconds. She dared not even breathe. She had longed for this, yet was immeasurably frightened as well. Not of seeing him, as much as of what this confrontation might do to her. It could remould her, but it could just as easily be her final undoing.

The sound reached the door and it opened in front of her. She raised her head.

He stood in the doorway.

She stared at him for just a moment, before he strode forward and wrapped his arms around her.

She almost collapsed within them, letting him take the sagging weight of her as he buried his head against her neck, her thick wavy hair falling around his face.

He was breathing hard, and crying too. Every now and again a noisy sob or intake of breath shocked her from her own stupor. She had never seen him like this, not even when things had gone so dreadfully wrong for them back then. He whispered 'Amy, Amy' as though he were pleading for something.

Eventually, coming to, she realised that they were still by the open front door. There was no one within sight, but she could hear voices, not far away.

At that moment Alex gently pulled her inside and pushed the door closed.

He guided her along a hallway and into a lounge room. The first things she saw were photos of Alex on the shelves, with his arms around his wife. She averted her eyes.

They were silent for what seemed an eternity, not looking at one another. Julia didn't want to be the one to break it. She felt they were wrapped within a small gift of suspended time within which they had found one another, and once they unwrapped it, everything would move forward again, and she couldn't be certain they would ever recapture it.

Then Alex began to speak. 'I can't believe it,' he said, over and over. Reaching out to stroke her face. Lifting her chin. 'You look just the same,' he added, although she could see he was lying, for she still startled herself when she stared into the mirror and a pair of small, dark, deadened eyes peered back. Alex immediately looked down, as though knowing she could read him.

'So do you,' she said. And meant it. 'Apart from the hair, of course.' His once long surfer's hair was now cropped short at the back and sides, and showed the first signs of receding. 'You have a grown-up's haircut now.'

He smiled. 'I suppose I do,' he murmured, running a hand over his head. Then he said, 'Amy, what's this "Julia"?'

'*I* am Julia,' she said harshly. 'Amy hasn't been around for a long time.'

They were silent, and in that time it appeared the spell was broken. Awkwardness surged over them like a rushing wave. They had gone from long-lost soul mates to strangers in just a few seconds.

'Would you like a drink?' Alex asked with stiff formality.

They exchanged small smiles at this politeness, which released a torrent of questions from Alex. 'Where have you been? How long have you been in London? I keep thinking I've been walking around the streets just missing you or passing you and not even recognising you . . . It makes me feel terrible . . .' He trailed off.

'I haven't been here long,' she assured him. 'About a month.'

'How on earth did you get together with Mark?' She sensed from his tone that he wasn't Mark's biggest fan.

'I went into the solicitors' office late one evening to ask

about getting some documents witnessed . . . He said he'd sign the papers for free if I went to dinner with him . . .'

Alex's lips pursed. 'That sounds like Mark.'

'Not your favourite person?' she asked.

'Nope.' His face clouded, then he changed the subject. 'My god, Amy, where have you been? Does your mother know where you are? Why didn't you come back for the funeral?'

Their eyes met. She looked away first.

'I've travelled,' she told him, gaze down. 'I've been getting work here and there. Paying my way. Teaching scuba diving. Doing short articles for magazines. Coming back to England once or twice to sort out visas and other bits and pieces.' She looked up defiantly, although she knew he would see right through her. 'I've seen so many places, so many wonderful things, like I always wanted to.'

'It sounds great,' he said, playing along with her, nodding, smiling.

There was a pause. 'Look, I'm so . . .' Alex began.

'Don't,' she said sharply. 'Don't, Al.'

Alex stared at his shoes. 'I'll get you that drink,' he muttered.

A few minutes later he returned with a cup of milky tea. She debated whether to tell him she drank it black nowadays, but decided against it. In the minutes they had been apart they seemed to have become ever more shy around each other, so they sat subduedly and made showy displays of drinking their tea.

'Anyway,' Julia said eventually. 'What about you? So you're married?'

Alex looked up, pain etched on his face. 'Yes. I am.'

'And what's she like?' She concentrated on maintaining a forced jollity.

'Chloe?' Alex spoke in a rush. 'She's . . .' His face took on a faraway aspect for a moment and she didn't like what she saw in his eyes. 'Look, I didn't, I mean I can't . . .' He threw his hands up in the air. 'Why didn't you come back?' he said suddenly, sharply. 'I know you needed space – but it's been *ten years*, Amy . . . What the hell –'

'Any children?' she interrupted relentlessly, looking around as though small people might jump out from behind the stiff leather sofas, even though she knew the answer. A hard edge crept into her voice that she hadn't meant to plant there.

Alex looked at her. 'No,' he said.

'I see.'

Alex put his mug on the table and looked down between his knees, banging the flat of his hands softly against his forehead. She recognised the frustrated gesture of old and her body moved before her mind could slingshot questions at it. She reached out to pat his knee. 'I know what the score is, Alex . . . I just can't believe you're really sitting here.'

Alex lifted his face to hers. His gaze was pained, full of guilt and uncertainty and torment. She held it steadily, letting all else wash away from her except the fact that he was there.

In response she watched his eyes change as they deepened with emotion. He reached up with both hands and stroked her face, looking into her eyes all the time. An incredible current passed between them at his touch – as if all the feelings they had once shared and then buried were being reignited by his hands on her skin.

Without breaking eye contact, he moved his fingers to pull loose the thin scarf tied around her neck, uncoiling the soft material slowly and steadily. He laid it aside, and then, as though in a trance, he leaned forward towards the hollow between her collarbones, and touched the long, narrow scar there.

'Amy,' he said, 'there's something I need to tell you.'

Just then they heard the front door open, and both turned sharply towards the sound.

26

As Chloe had raced home, cold rage had begun to course through her, first a trickle, then a stream, then a torrent so fierce that her whole body seemed to be caught within the swelling, rolling gathering of it. She was glad she had opted for the privacy of the taxi as she tried to calm her breathing, to still her swirling thoughts, to steady herself so she didn't explode before she got through the door.

Once home, she didn't get two paces along the hallway before she saw Alex. He was closing the living-room door.

'Hey.' He gave her a strained smile. 'What are you doing home so early?' He began to walk towards her, saw her stricken face, and stopped. 'Chlo, what's wrong?'

'I've had enough, Al, that's what.' She pushed past him and went into the kitchen, put her bags and coat on the countertop and ran herself a glass of water, draining it in one go. She turned round to find Alex watching her from a distance, a strange expression on his face. 'Mark told me you called him. I want you to tell me what's going on . . .'

Her voice trailed off as she realised Alex was hovering by the closed living-room door. A jumble of thoughts tumbled over her, none of them good.

'. . . Right now,' she finished, slowly.

'Okay,' Alex answered, his lips still drawn back in that spooked half-smile. 'Let's just go out for a walk, shall we?' He moved towards her, picked up her coat and held it out to her.

And she knew.

She looked Alex in the eye for a long, drawn-out moment, then took a deep breath, walked down the corridor, towards the living-room door, and stopped. She turned back to Alex, who had followed, and took another long look at him, drinking in the sight of the man she loved, wondering how she would look at him after this.

Then she said, 'I think I left my scarf in here, I'll just get it,' and had the briefest impression of Alex's shoulders slumping as she pushed open the door.

27

Chloe was smaller than Julia remembered, her face paler and more pinched. She stood holding the door handle, looking at Julia with pure contempt. Julia didn't know what to say, but still tried to speak, in a quavering voice.

'Hello.'

Chloe just continued to stare in silence. They were frozen until Alex came up behind Chloe.

'It's not what you think,' he said.

Julia stood there uncomfortably as Chloe whirled around to him. 'What are you, Alex? A walking cliché? In fact, who the hell are you? You're certainly not the man I thought you were. How – how dare you!'

Then Julia watched in horror as Chloe slapped his cheek and started banging her fists on his chest as she shrieked at him. Alex was trying to grab her wrists while dodging blows, telling her to calm down.

The explosion didn't last long but it seemed to have consumed Chloe. She stepped back from Alex, took one last look at Julia, her face crumpled with pain, then stormed out through the doorway.

Alex was motionless for a second. When the front door banged shut, he jumped, but it seemed to start him into action. He turned around without a glance back and raced after his wife, leaving Julia standing there in shock, wondering what on earth she should do now.

28

Mark had waited. He'd seen the embrace between Julia and Alex from a distance before they closed the door. Then, as he'd been about to head towards the station, he'd seen the taxi turn into the opposite end of the street and watched in horror as Chloe alighted from it. What an absolute bastard he was for leaving that note on her desk, he berated himself.

Before his train of thought was even completed she was coming out the door again, and he could see how stricken she was. She stopped for a second on the steps to the house, clutching at the railing, her body heaving, and he was heading towards her before he'd even thought about it, calling her name.

She looked up, startled and angry. He could see the snail-trails of tear tracks on her cheeks. As he reached her, she just had time to say, 'I don't know what the hell you think you're doing here,' before the front door banged open and Alex was there.

Mark saw straight away the storm brewing on Alex's face, but it was too late to do anything. Alex didn't even seem to see Chloe, as he marched past her, pulled his arm back, and sent the force of his fist crashing towards Mark's nose.

As Mark instinctively turned, the fist caught his cheek instead, which instantly began to throb.

'That's assault,' he spat at Alex as he righted himself, touching his cheek gingerly.

Alex still towered over him, hands on hips, taking short breaths through his nostrils, looking as if he'd like to do the same thing again. 'Well, I guess I'll see you in court then,' he retorted, glaring.

The two men stared at each other for a moment, jaws tensed, the atmosphere a lit fuse burning slowly towards explosion.

Chloe's petite form suddenly appeared between them. She pushed Alex away, her small hands against his heaving chest. 'What the hell are you doing, Alex?'

Alex looked startled. He took a step back. 'Chloe, I –'

'Just go away,' she screamed at him. 'Isn't there someone waiting for you in there – in *our* house,' she added, her hand gesturing towards their front door.

Alex looked from Chloe to their front door, then again, as though trying to make an impossible decision. 'Fuck!', he growled, and charged back up the steps to the house, slamming the front door behind him.

Mark and Chloe were glued to the spot.

'Chloe, I'm sorry . . .' Mark began feebly.

'I hope it hurt,' she replied, and strode off down the road.

Mark hurried after her, still wincing as he touched his cheek. 'Where are you going?' he asked as he caught up with her.

She whirled round. 'I don't know, Mark, okay?'

'Let me buy you a drink.'

The bitter laugh caught in her throat. 'You have got to be kidding.'

'Chloe, it feels like minus twenty out here, plus you need to calm down, and I want to apologise. Come on.' He gave her a push towards the pub, half-expecting her to turn on her heel, but she went grudgingly with him.

Once inside they found a booth tucked away in a corner, and Chloe slid into it, aware that her hands were trembling, while Mark went to get drinks. Only when he came back with two gin and tonics did she remember that she wasn't meant to be drinking. One won't hurt, she said to herself; however, after the first sip she felt sick and pushed it away.

Mark was watching her but she couldn't think of anything to say, so she let him, and swirled the liquid in her glass, staring at it.

Eventually he said, 'It might not be what you think.'

She looked up at Mark and rolled her eyes. 'I'm not that dumb, Mark. And since when did you give a shit about my marriage?'

'Okay, sorry. Just trying to help.'

Chloe gave a brief snort. 'Yes, that poisonous note on my desk was very helpful.'

Mark hung his head for a moment then looked up at her again. 'I was a complete shit for doing that, I'm sorry.'

'So what did Alex say to you on the phone?' As she waited she could feel the tension within her rising to boiling point.

Mark shrugged. 'He just asked for Julia's number.'

'How did he sound?'

'Honestly? Pretty stressed out.'

'Stressed out with all the lying, I'd imagine.' Chloe thought of all the duped wives she'd seen traipsing through her office. She couldn't believe she was one of them now. 'I'd never in a million years have believed that Alex could do this to me.'

Mark sighed. 'Chloe, you know I can't stand the guy, and that was before he punched me, so I don't know why I'm saying this – but what exactly has Alex done to you? Because if he needed to phone me to get Julia's number, I doubt he's having an affair with her.'

'It could have been an old affair,' she replied, but his comment had penetrated the fug of her thoughts.

'True,' Mark agreed. 'But at the end of the day, you won't know until you ask him, will you?'

29

When Alex stormed back into the lounge again, his expression was thunderous.

'I'm sorry . . .' Julia began, unsure of what else to say.

He tried a smile. It didn't come off. 'Not your fault.'

'You really love her,' she said quietly, feeling a fresh pang of pain, as though she hadn't quite believed this could be true.

'Yes.' He moved across to her, holding her shoulders, watching her until she looked back up at him. She thought he was going to shake her, but instead he just said, 'Oh, Amy, why the hell didn't you come back?'

She swung away from him so he couldn't see her expression. 'It was complicated,' she said. 'After Dad died.'

He ignored her, his voice becoming strident. 'I saw your mum, Amy – at the funeral. She was a wreck. She had no one.' She felt herself flinch but if he noticed he didn't care, his anger was leading the way now. 'She said she thought you blamed yourself – that was why you stayed away – but how could you –'

Julia swung around, her voice rising to a shout. 'You think it was easy for me, staying away? Do you think I was sitting someplace sipping a cocktail, painting my nails; that I couldn't be bothered to go home? It *broke* me, Alex. I thought I'd been broken before that, but no – it changed everything . . . So don't you *dare* insinuate that you know what it was like for me . . .'

'And do you know what it was like for *me*, Amy?' He barked every word at her. 'I made a promise to you. I kept it for *years*. I heard nothing. Your mother didn't want to talk to me after the funeral. I was in limbo. I tried everything. I even thought you were dead. It took *years*, Amy, before I moved on, and it was a slow and painful decision . . . and now you walk back into my life, and I'm the one who has to feel guilty as all hell that I broke that promise – but where were *you*, Amy? Tell me that.'

His words had drained the fight from her. She sat down on his sofa and put her head in her hands. Then took them away in surprise. They were wet. She was crying.

Alex seemed drained too, and slumped next to her. He put his hand on her shoulder, and rubbed it as she sobbed.

Eventually, she whispered into the silence, 'So, what do we do now?'

She heard Alex take a deep breath. 'I have no idea,' he said. 'But before anything else, there's something I really have to tell you.'

30

She looked at the printouts he'd got from the internet. As he talked to her, he took hold of her hands, stroking them. In response her memories slowly began to unlock themselves. Long-buried images poured out like unstoppable sand, filling her head with fresh pain. His voice became distant.

She was in the darkness again, with voices overhead. She could hear them plainly, as if it were still happening. She could see them looking down at her; blurry faces with blackened eyes. Noxious breath as they leaned in, staring. She was disorientated at the suddenness of it all, but as the panic kicked in and hands came towards her she had to get away . . .

She suddenly jolted. She had to move, right now. She pushed the hands away, all her focus on the door.

'AMY! AMY!'

The hands were still there. She flailed and kicked desperately until she realised she was just fighting the air.

She blinked, trying to focus.

Alex was watching her, horrified. She was so embarrassed that now her tears came in a torrent of release, and she heaved herself over to a chair and folded into it, sucking in oxygen.

She felt a glass pushed into her hand, and took sips of cool water, beginning to feel calmer.

'Amy, Jesus . . .' Alex was saying.

'Sorry,' she mumbled.

'It's okay.' He crouched near her but he didn't touch her again.

She thought back to what he'd told her. 'You mean it's happening now?'

'Yes, I've checked it all out. It's almost over, I think. It's quite high profile over there.'

And then she realised what had to be done.

'I have to go back,' she told him, shocked at herself as she heard her own words.

Alex turned his face away from her, towards the door, saying nothing. For some reason his silence only strengthened her resolve. 'I have to, Al. I need to. Confronting this could be a way for me to get a grip on my life again,' she told him fiercely. 'It might be the only way.'

Still Alex was silent. Still he kept his face turned away.

She paused, bit her lip, then murmured, 'I don't know if I can do it alone.'

She kept watching the back of his head, and saw it beginning to shake. 'This is crazy,' he murmured, and then swung around towards her, so she could clearly see his pain and confusion. 'I'm sorry, I can't just –'

'Okay.' She got up quickly. 'I understand.' She shoved the water back at him and he grabbed it as it sloshed over onto his hand. 'You've done enough.'

She ran into the passageway and pulled open his front door, then moved as fast as she could away from him. But she could hear him behind her, keeping pace, and he was saying her name – her real name – again and again, until it was a chant keeping time with her footsteps. Each time she heard 'Amy' it was as though another piece of her re-emerged, twisting and writhing.

Eventually, she couldn't run any more. She sank down onto the road, spent.

A second later, Alex crouched down in front of her. He took a deep breath.

'Amy, this is important to me too. So if you *really* want to do this . . .' He paused and took a long look at the sky, drawing in a deep breath that she echoed, holding on to the air in her lungs, feeling it swelling, burning, eager to be gone.

'. . . I will find a way to come with you,' he said eventually, looking back down at her.

And he put his hand over hers.

It was as though she had been drowning for ten years, and at last there was a hand outstretched within sight.

part two
millennium

australia
december 1999

Despite the dusk's warmth, the day's sun was almost spent. It flooded the sky with fiery colour in a last blaze of defiance as it sank towards the horizon. Except for the small motel, every turn revealed bushland, stretching on and on until it ran beyond sight.

Amy had thought such vast emptiness would make her nervous, and yet she was entranced by the fullness of this unspoiled land. They were going from east to west, taking the highway that had riven a harsh grey line in the red-brown sand, like a rogue thread within the great cloth of scrubby grass and bush that cloaked the southern reaches of Australia.

As she stood on a patch of dirt watching the sky change colour, she felt Alex's arms envelop her, and leaned into him. He rested his chin on her head and his breath was warm in her hair. She reached her hand up to stroke his stubbled cheek, and he lightly kissed her palm. Then his arm shot out, and he held a camera in front of them, and pressed the button as she laughed.

'You've just taken a photo of my tonsils,' she said, swinging around to see that there was a carrier bag by his feet. She peered inside and groaned. 'Not again.' It was the third night running that their evening meal had consisted of pre-packaged pies and soggy chips. But she guessed it was harder to come by fruit and veg in these isolated, barren parts.

They sat down on the veranda step in front of their small room, and took unenthusiastic bites of their dinner.

'Are you sad?' Alex asked between mouthfuls, his shaggy sun-bleached hair quivering as he turned to look at her.

She smiled, knowing what he meant. Their time away had gone so fast, in a couple of weeks they would be back home – in bustling, dark, frosty England, neon-lit with Christmas cheer – the complete antithesis to the hushed, sparse place they were part of right now.

'Not really,' she murmured. 'I mean, we're coming back, aren't we – well, at least away again.' They had spent most of the past five months discussing where else they would like to travel, having fallen in love with being on the road, and would have been tempted to stay if they hadn't promised families and friends that they'd be back for Christmas and the frenetic Millennium celebrations.

'Of course,' he said, running a hand down her bare thigh, leaving a few crumbs on her skin that he then lightly swept off. 'Although I don't think I'll be around when you tell your dad, if you don't mind.'

Amy smiled, but he was right. Her dad had become a

complete nightmare when they'd announced they were going away, first trying to dissuade them, and then, when he couldn't, attempting to organise them to within an inch of their life. He'd spent a fortnight buying them all sorts of gadgets and gismos that they'd hardly ever used, and made them both get complete medical records from the doctor, just in case they happened to need a blood transfusion or three. Then, at the airport, he had given Alex a lecture about his responsibilities in front of Amy and her mother, while Alex looked petrified. Her father had ended the talk by shaking Alex's hand and saying, 'Take good care of her for me,' to which Alex had replied, 'Yes, sir,' as though they were in some midday melodrama. Amy and her mother had laughed, but neither man had seemed to find it amusing.

Now, she shook her head despite her smile. 'Poor Dad, he finds it hard letting me be grown up. He's got no one to be a kid with any more.'

They sat in silence for a moment. In the time it had taken them to eat their meagre meal, the sun had vanished, the bold colours thrown out in its descent now fading to pastels as the sky darkened.

Amy was remembering everything they had packed into the past few months. Riding tuk-tuks in Thailand and visiting temples teeming with people in Bangkok; then the rickety, laborious train ride to the north, to find themselves on the backs of elephants or sitting skimming the water on bamboo rafts as they floated through small rapids. Their skin had become bronzed, making their teeth glow whiter. They had lost weight on a diet of rice, fish and chicken, and their hair and nails had seemed to grow faster than they did at home.

Then Sydney. Alex had found a few weeks' casual work in a pub, while Amy waitressed in a café nearby, on the strip at Manly where tourists ventured through night after night, traces of sand and salt lingering around their hairlines.

And then had come this whistle-stop road trip – first to Melbourne and then along the Great Ocean Road towards Adelaide, before this final journey over the deserted, tree-less plains of the Nullarbor, the hire car churning steadily through the endless kilometres.

'Come on.' Alex jumped up and held out his hand, and they headed into their room. He went over to the esky and dug around in it, pulling out a couple of stubbies of beer. 'Here you go.' The ice they had poured in there that morn-ing had done its job of cooling them, although the rest of the grocery stores were now floating in melted water.

Amy set about pulling things out and drying them as Alex spread a map on the bed. He studied it for a while and then said, 'I reckon we can make Perth in two or three days. What do you think?'

'Let's take our time,' she replied. 'It's bound to cost more when we get into the city. And we'll still have a week there.'

'It's such a shame we didn't plan this better.' Alex shook his head in frustration. 'There's so much cool stuff on this side when you start looking – we'd need at least a month to explore the coastline, for a start.'

'We've made the most of the time we've had,' Amy reminded him. 'We can come back, you know.'

'I know.' He looked up at her and grinned. 'I'm just hav-ing so much fun.'

'Me too.' She smiled back at him, and headed across to

the bedside table where her washbag was propped, rummaging in it. As she did so she felt Alex's presence behind her, then his lips on her neck, and a blissful shiver ran through her. She turned to face him and he pressed against her, sending them both back onto the bed.

Once the motel closed for the evening, the outback darkness became absolute except for the pinpoint lights of stars billions of miles away. Amy couldn't sleep. Around her it was so black that it was better to keep her eyes closed, for if she tried to open them the lack of anything to focus on caused her brain to invent strange wispy whirls of colour within the darkness that pulsated into being and away again.

'Alex?' she whispered, wanting to hear his reassuring voice.

'Hmm?' he replied, but he sounded sleepy, too close to his dreams to want to begin a conversation.

Amy sighed and turned over onto her side. As her body shifted so did something in her, and their happiness suddenly became a trepidatious thing – precariously balanced on these small moments in time. She wondered what it would be like when they got home, and wished she could see the bigger picture. But for now she pushed her body towards Alex's, grateful for his arm coming mechanically across her, unnerved by the sudden, compelling urge she had to hide from the dark.

32

As Chloe negotiated the bustle of Oxford Street she wondered again about how her life was unfolding. It was as though she were being carried by a rip-tide and had no choice about where she was heading. Even the throngs of people now pressing against her seemed to be trying to submerge her within their smooth current.

She didn't enjoy the crowds, but this was by far the most obvious place to find a dress to wear at the law ball. She really wanted something hot, bright and sexy that would enslave Mark to her for the evening, but since it was a work function she was thinking black and minimalist might be more the way to go.

She wasn't enjoying her vocational training as much as she had thought she would, which meant she spent every other day wondering if she was really cut out for a legal career. If it wasn't for Mark's encouragement she would have felt even more adrift, but his enthusiasm was palpable, and although he could be a little patronising he was helping a lot; particularly by shielding her from some of his father's stinging sarcasm, which someone seemed to bear the brunt of every day.

She had been almost surprised to find that she and Mark were an item, but more and more she was growing to like the feeling of it. They had gone out with a group from work one Friday night, and the numbers at the bar had gradually dwindled until Mark and Chloe had tipsily called a cab to his place. Although she had felt mortified – not to mention ill – when she had woken up on his sofa the next morning, Mark had breezed in with filtered coffee and an easy smile. Since then they had gone out a few times – although without it resulting in such wicked hangovers, for which Chloe was extremely grateful.

She walked out of the biting cold and into a brightly lit shop with an array of party dresses in the window. Browsing the racks, a slip of black satin caught her eye. That might serve as a compromise, she thought. She found her size, made her way to the changing rooms and slid the dress on. It slunk over her skin, nestling against the curve of her hips, although as she turned sideways she realised she might need to breathe in for most of the event to really minimise her stomach. But she thought she could get away with it. She beamed at herself in the mirror. The woman smiling back had a face flushed pink with cold, and looked excited.

Back in the crisp, cold night, Chloe made her way home, thankful that the shopping trip hadn't turned out to be too arduous. She was sharing a poky flat with two friends, both of whom had one of their numerous Christmas events on that night, so Chloe would have the television to herself. She smiled, thought briefly about the paperwork in her bag, and dismissed it. She was determined to relax this evening.

At the flat she fiddled with the awkward lock, and finally fell through the door as it gave way with a jerk. She shook her head; she'd been living there for three months and it still happened every time she tried to unlock the door. They really needed to ask someone who knew about DIY.

In the hallway Post-it notes adorned the small telephone table. She glanced over them. Most were old ones that no one had got around to throwing away, but there was a new message in Sandra's handwriting. '*Mark phoned, says call him about tonight. Keen or what?!*'

Chloe sighed. She liked that Mark was calling her, but she had tonight planned. She was about to get changed out of her suit, when there was a knock at the door.

Her heart sank. She really wished Mark would wait for the invitation before actually coming around. Wearily, she went to the front door and pulled it open.

'Anthony!'

'Sis!' Her brother gave her a hug, his bristle of close-clipped hair shining in the hallway light.

It was a nice surprise to see him but Chloe was still thinking a little wistfully of her alone-time.

'What are you doing here?'

'Well, I'm going to a party tomorrow night, and it's so much cheaper to get the train down on a Thursday, so I made a last-minute decision to see if I could bunk with you.'

Chloe folded her arms and smiled. 'And if you can't?'

'Then I'm on the streets, sis,' Anthony said, strolling past her and throwing his bag into her room. 'But I know you'd never do that to your little brother. Mum would kill you!' He walked into the lounge and sat down on a sofa. 'Have you got a takeaway near here? I'm starving. Unless you haven't made dinner yet, of course?' He grinned cheekily.

Chloe gave him a sarcastic smile back, went over to the table and chucked a sheaf of takeout menus at him. 'Be my guest.'

They munched on pizza while half paying attention to the television. Despite her thwarted plans, Chloe was enjoying this rare time with her brother. It was strange getting used to one another as independent adults after living in close proximity for all those years – knowing someone inside out and yet hardly at all.

'I think I'm full,' Anthony announced, throwing down a chewed crust and sitting back in his chair.

'Me too,' Chloe agreed.

Anthony was watching her, an indiscernible expression making his features more intense than usual. 'Chlo?'

Something in his voice made her senses become alert. 'Yes?'

He paused for a moment, then said, 'I'm going to tell Mum I want to find Dad.'

Chloe closed her eyes for a second as tension rippled through her body. She sat up.

'Ant, I really don't know . . .'

Anthony leaned forward. 'Chlo, I don't feel this is a choice any more. It's eating me up. It's on my mind all the time – if not in the forefront then always at the back. I have to know.'

'But what makes you think Mum will react any differently this time?' Chloe asked, thinking back to the arguments Anthony had had with their mother while he was a teenager, when he was disillusioned with Charlie's lack of get up and go, and desperate to believe that his real father was an action hero of some sort. She had thought that Anthony was past all that.

Margaret had always been elusive about their dad. They hadn't even been sure of his name until Anthony had found it written on some old photos. Chloe vaguely remembered Charlie coming into their lives, but for a while when he was quite young Anthony had thought Charlie was his father. When they had approached their mother, Margaret had told them, 'You have to trust me – we're all better off without him.' The high level of mystery only intrigued them both further, until in the aftermath of one particularly virulent row sixteen-year-old Chloe had overheard Charlie comforting Margaret, saying, 'Wouldn't it be better to tell them than to have them blaming you like this?' And Margaret had replied, 'Oh god, Charlie, how can you say that? Absolutely not. You know they're better off this way.'

The conviction and desperation in her mother's voice had sent a tremble through Chloe. What if her father were a criminal? Or a wife-beater? Perhaps he was in prison. She was glad to be sheltered from the truth. But even though she had repeated the conversation to Anthony, he had not taken the same view. Perhaps it was because he was that much younger, or because he needed to keep the myth of his father alive more than she did. All these years later he still couldn't let it drop.

'Look, Chloe,' Anthony began, his hands working frantically as he tried to explain. 'She doesn't need to even talk about it. All she needs to do is to write down the facts she knows on a piece of paper, and I can take it from there.'

'I don't know,' Chloe said, as the phone started ringing. She got up to answer it.

'You didn't call me back?' Mark said without preamble.

'I know, sorry,' Chloe answered. 'My brother turned up unannounced.'

'Oh. Well, I was going to see if you were up to anything but I guess that means you are?'

'You can come over,' Chloe offered half-heartedly, not relishing the thought of introducing Mark and Anthony right then.

'No, it's okay, I'll see you tomorrow. Sleep well,' Mark said, and hung up.

Chloe returned to the lounge feeling disgruntled at how the evening was turning out. While she'd been gone Anthony had switched chairs, found football on another channel and turned the sound up. She thought about starting another difficult conversation, then decided against it, and went to run a hot bath instead, thinking that surely there she would get some time to herself.

33

As Mark threaded his way through the logjammed traffic towards work, he felt the same vaguely churning stomach and dizziness that he'd had for weeks. He'd contemplated seeing a doctor, but his symptoms were too vague, and besides, he had an uncomfortable suspicion about them.

It had come to him last night as he had lain in bed and tried to stop thinking about her. Could he be *in love*?

The prospect didn't excite him much, particularly if this was how it made him feel. Love was awkward, vulnerable and emotional, and Mark felt he was the antithesis of all those things. And yet when he thought of Chloe, well, maybe he was more of a suppliant fool than he cared to admit.

He reached the kerb just as the cars and buses began their slow crawl forward, and tried to gain control of his feelings before he reached the office.

Chloe's personality was what Mark thought of as understated, and that in itself spoke volumes to him. Everyone seemed to like her; she was working on cases without antagonising people, yet was unafraid to assert her opinion, because she had the knack of making it sound like a point of view rather than the imposing assertion of fact that Mark went for, and it seemed to serve her just as well.

And she was very pretty, no one could deny that. He couldn't wait to see the glamorous side of her at the ball tomorrow night. It would make a change from an array of suits in dull navy, black and grey, however well they fitted her slim frame.

He reached the double doors of the office building and tried to compose his thoughts into sharp focus on what lay ahead of him at work. No contact with Chloe, that was for sure. She'd been taken under the wing of one of the senior solicitors who worked in the family-law area that Chloe was keen on, whereas Mark was learning fast about the genteel cut and thrust of the English litigation system.

'Morning, Mark.'

'Oh, hi Dad.' Mark resisted the urge to look down at his watch, hoping he was in at an acceptably early hour. Despite still living at home, Mark resisted coming to work with his father. He didn't want to remind others that Henry was the primary reason he worked for this firm, as he felt it devalued his own standing and hard work in having got this far.

'Busy day ahead?' Henry Jameson peered at his son from underneath bushy eyebrows as he strode alongside him.

'Is there any other type?' Mark tried to joke, and watched

his father smile, but without comment, making Mark feel slightly foolish for being so flippant.

They walked on in silence until they reached Mark's office. Henry followed his son in, while Mark took off his coat and laid his briefcase down.

'Mr Jameson?'

They turned as one to see Charlotte, the new secretary, standing by the door. She was looking at Mark but flicked a nervous smile towards Mr Jameson Senior as well on seeing him there.

'Mr Zanuski has been on the phone already, wanting to discuss the Connell case – apparently they are missing some documentation.'

'Okay,' Mark said, 'let me have the number and I'll get onto it.'

Charlotte walked across the office and handed Mark a memo slip, then turned on her heel and left, seemingly unaware that Henry Jameson's eyes were affixed to her shapely bottom.

Henry turned around with eyebrows once more aloft, and said, 'What a looker.'

Mark smiled. There was no denying Charlotte was stunning, and by now he was used to his father's comments on the aesthetic merits of the opposite sex.

'Taking Chloe on Saturday?' Henry asked.

'Sorry? Oh, yes,' Mark replied, looking down at the memo slip, already running through the forthcoming phone conversation in his head.

Henry nodded, looked like he was about to say something, then changed his mind. 'Okay, well, I'll see you later,' he said. 'I'm in meetings all day today.'

Mark nodded absent-mindedly, and when he looked up a moment later Henry had already gone.

When Chloe peeped around the door of his office at lunchtime, Mark's head was still buried in his work.

'Want me to bring you anything?' she asked.

Mark looked up and smiled, trying to quell the surge of pleasure in his chest at seeing her.

'If you've got time?' he asked.

'Of course, what would you like?'

She was back with sandwiches fifteen minutes later, and came and sat opposite him without being invited, opening her own paper bag and pulling out a roll. Mark normally didn't like unagreed-to interruptions, but he couldn't be annoyed at her when she smiled at him like that.

'How are you getting on?' she asked between bites, nodding towards his desk.

Mark blew out his breath and looked briefly at the ceiling then back at Chloe. 'There's a lot to do.'

'Sorry,' she said, wrapping the paper bag around the roll and making to get up, 'I should let you get on.'

'No, no,' Mark found himself saying, even though two minutes ago he'd thought exactly that. 'Ten minutes doesn't matter.' He unwrapped his own sandwich, and said, 'How's your brother then?' before taking a bite.

'Okay, I think,' Chloe answered, 'though he's about to cause a few ructions in the family. He wants to push Mum into giving him information about our father.'

Mark swallowed his mouthful, then said, 'Really? And what do you think?'

'I still think it's best left alone, but there's no reasoning with him – besides, who am I to stop him if it's important to him?'

'You might get dragged into it, though.'

'I might well,' she agreed, looking resigned.

They ate silently for a few moments, then Chloe said, 'Actually, I was wondering . . . if you think it's too soon just say, but my family always have a party of some kind the weekend before Christmas, and I thought maybe you might like to come . . . if you haven't got any other plans.'

Mark beamed. 'That would be great.'

'Okay.' Chloe smiled. 'It's a long drive, though, so we might have to stay a couple of nights for it to be worth it . . .'

'Fine by me,' Mark agreed. 'However, before that we need to think about tomorrow night. Shall I pick you up?'

'No, don't do that,' Chloe demurred, knowing her place was far out of his way. 'I'll meet you there.' She finished the last mouthful of sandwich and scrunched the paper bag into a ball. 'I found a dress. I hope you'll like it.'

Mark smiled. 'I'm sure I will.'

They grinned at one another for a moment, and Mark avoided dwelling on the sensation in his stomach as it began to churn once more.

34

Despite being the height of summer it was raining as they drove into Perth, the city's skyline forming an elegant iridescent backdrop to the wide Swan River. They found parkland on the southern bank of the river and got out of their vehicle to stretch their legs, revelling in the freshness of the rain, and laughing as water trickled into their eyes and ran off their noses.

Although the weather wasn't ideal, they couldn't resist driving a little further to the beach – neither of them had dipped their toes into the Indian Ocean before, and they were both keen to. It didn't take long to find Cottesloe, and they parked and ran down to the water in their shorts and T-shirts. By the time they reached the surf they were both laughing like maniacs. Alex's fringe was pipetting drops of water into his eyes, while Amy's long dark hair was plastered messily against her skull. Amy enthusiastically pushed

Alex as though she were going to propel him right into the sea. Her face was flushed and her nose was smattered with freckles. She looked beautiful, Alex thought as he watched her. She had no hope of beating him, though, and in one swift movement he had caught her up into his arms and run into the water until it was past his knees, and she was half-pretending to scream as he did a count to three, bobbing her up and down as though getting ready to release her. 'No, Alex!' she cried, squeaking, laughing, looking down at the foamy sea. On the last lift he brought her up higher, and instead of letting her go, he leaned forward and went in for a long kiss. She wrapped her arms tighter around his neck as she responded.

He waded back out of the sea, with Amy light in his arms, and couldn't imagine feeling any happier than at that moment.

'Life is just about perfect right now,' she said, grinning.

'Bloody perfect,' he agreed, in his best Australian accent, pronouncing bloody as *bladdy*, making Amy's smile widen.

Back at the car they dried off as best they could with their beach towels. Alex wished they could stay and relax in the cafés along the beachfront road, but they still had some practical matters to attend to. The car needed to be returned to the hire company by mid-afternoon, so they worked their way through the traffic, with Amy directing and a fair few wrong turns in the city one-way system, before they reached the depot.

By the time they had made their way to the hostel and checked in to a familiar-looking featureless room with chipped-paint walls and drab bedding, the day had turned dusky. They made themselves some dinner and chatted to fellow travellers, before falling into bed full of advice about places they should see, both aware that yet another precious day had slipped away, and longing to pack as much as possible into the short time they had left.

The next morning Alex was awake before Amy, and for a while he watched her sleeping face, the embodiment of peaceful contentment. He wondered what life would be like when they went home. Even though they were young, he loved her and could not imagine a day without her. Maybe he ought to propose, he thought, feeling an inordinate urge to wake her up and ask her right that minute. Perhaps he should find somewhere irresistibly romantic, go back to the beach where they had been yesterday and just do it. He smiled at himself for taking things so seriously. There would be plenty of time for all that later. He didn't know why he had this sudden desire to rush things.

He headed for the shower, and by the time he returned, Amy was not only awake but dressed in a vest top and short skirt, looking ready to go out.

'Good morning,' he said, smiling at her then searching his belongings for something at least half-clean that he could wear. He picked out some shorts and a vest top, and grabbed a crumpled shirt to go over it.

'Morning,' she smiled, planting a kiss on his lips. 'Shall we go and find breakfast? I'm starving.'

***

They found a café along the main backpacker strip in Northbridge, and settled in for a morning feast. Now that they were going home in a week Alex felt freer to spend his remaining money, so he ordered the biggest breakfast on the menu and ate like a king. Amy managed to put away a similar amount, which always amazed him since she was half his size.

'What do you want to do today?' he asked her as they stood at the counter waiting to pay for their meals. 'The art gallery is just up there.' He made a hopeful gesture, but suspected he'd pushed his luck too far since he'd dragged Amy to numerous exhibitions already.

She rolled her eyes then smiled at him, and put her arms around his waist. 'I don't know about that. Maybe something relaxing, like the beach – or perhaps we should do something active since we've been stuck in a car for the past week. That French guy last night mentioned those steps at Kings Park, though that sounds quite strenuous.' She paused, thinking. 'Or maybe we should take one of those boats out, that sounded great fun – or the ferry and the zoo, that would be quite nice as well, though I'm never sure about zoos, but the Dutch couple said it was good, didn't they?'

He took his change from the waitress. 'Blimey,' he said, stuffing it into his pocket. 'Anything else?'

'Probably,' Amy laughed, not letting go of his waist, her hands locked around him. 'What do you think?' She rested her chin on his chest and peered up at him.

'Maybe we should just go back to the hostel,' he grinned, stroking the small of her back, then propelling her in front of him towards the door of the café.

'Well, we could, but that won't take all day!' she replied, laughing over her shoulder.

'Oh really?' he said, grinning at her. 'That's charming.'

She shook her head and rolled her eyes at him again, and they made their way along the pavement. Alex took her hand and it felt soft in his. He listened happily as she discussed plans and possibilities, making him laugh as she flitted from one idea to another. He played along, teasing her, watching her smile, until there was the sudden loud noise of a car engine, racing towards them at speed.

35

Chloe was nervous as she dressed for the evening. The dress looked good, but she felt like an impostor in it. She tried to view herself from the outside, as others might see her, but couldn't do it.

What was this block within her; this ever-present divide she felt between herself and everyone else, barely discernible, perhaps not obvious at all if you weren't Chloe, yet always there, impregnable, cutting her off? Where did it stem from?

She had felt more like this since Anthony's visit. He'd unsettled her. She ought to speak to her mother about him, but she still hoped she might quietly persuade him not to go to America. If Anthony found their father, then she might be forced to as well, and she didn't want to. Why was she so sure of that? What did she know that she couldn't remember?

She thought back to when she was young, scanning for

early memories. Her mother had, on a number of occasions, told a story about her husband Charlie and six-year-old Chloe at dinner parties, as part of her general repartee. It was about how when Charlie had first met Margaret he'd offered to pick Chloe up from school one day, had driven there, met an old friend in the car park, chatted, then driven home again, put his feet up and cracked open a beer or two, and it wasn't until Margaret got back with Anthony four hours later that she had questioned Charlie about Chloe's whereabouts.

Chloe was still at school. In the playground. In the dark. Uncollected. Unnoticed by teachers, as they drove off one by one. Staying hidden in the shadows rather than bringing herself to an adult's attention. Her mother told the story while shaking her head fondly at 'hopeless' Charlie, and the implication was that Chloe was rather strange for allowing herself to remain abandoned like that. But although Chloe smiled along with it, she found various parts disconcerting – not least because she couldn't remember a bit of it. As a small child she'd sat alone in a darkening, empty yard for hours, quite possibly scared out of her wits, and yet her mind was a firm blank when she tried to recall it. But her mother swore the story was true; and Charlie had shamefacedly admitted it as well. So why had she stayed silent? Why had she been so scared of being found?

It was the same when she tried to think back on other things – in fact, much of her early life was just a haze. Was that how it was for everyone? Surely no one remembered that much of their formative years anyway. So why did Chloe feel as though she were missing something; some critical piece of the jigsaw of her life, which when put into position would form a picture she could recognise?

She took a deep breath, looked at her watch, then checked herself in the mirror. Her appearance was good; and that was all she needed for today's big event.

She headed downstairs to wait for the taxi to arrive.

36

Time slowed right down.

To almost a pause.

To a fractured sequence of movements.

To the split second when all things would change.

Alex turned around to look for the source of the noise, and as he did so he went to grab Amy's hand, although she was not in the path of the vehicle bearing down. It was just a reflex, to grab on, but she had turned to look as well, and he missed her, by which time the van was right next to them, screeching to a halt.

A side door was flung open, metal grating as it sped along its runners, and a chubby, unshaven man jumped out. Alex had the vague impression of another man inside the van.

He didn't understand. He didn't get it until it was too late. Until Amy was locked in the other man's meaty arms as he lifted her and flung her into the van's maw as though she were an inanimate parcel.

But when he got it, he moved, lightning fast. He rushed towards the van, towards Amy, who was screaming, her terrified eyes finding Alex's, her look beseeching him to save her from whatever this was. He reached out at the same time as she lunged forward, and their fingertips missed one another by millimetres, and then the chubby man sent a knee into Alex's groin so that he instinctively doubled-up, eyes watering, wanting to retch as pain shot through him, and in the time he had to recover before he could react again, the other man had leapt into the shadows of the van's interior, from which Alex could hear Amy screaming in terror, and the vehicle sped off before they had even closed the door.

There was a pause, like a missed heartbeat, when the world seemed to be frozen in an ethereal silence.

Then people converged on Alex. Hands helped him up and over to a chair. There was shouting. Someone was dialling triple 0 and relaying what had just happened in a breathless, excited voice.

Even if they had been able to crawl under Alex's skin right then, no one could have touched him. He was somewhere else, far beyond them, stupefied, watching Amy's small discarded flower-patterned bag lying on the pavement, unnoticed.

Then the urge to move came over him as fast as a reflex. He shrugged off his comforters and ran along the road in the direction the van had gone only seconds before, roaring. A man tried to hang on to him, but Alex swatted him off easily.

It took two of them to bring him down, and he fought all the way, crying out in his impotent fury.

A woman came up, her face white with shock, and knelt down to talk to him. All his energy seemed to have been consumed by that one pointless charge. 'The police will be here any second,' she said. 'They will get her back, I'm sure they will.' But she looked stricken and her expression belied her words.

She put Amy's small bag into his hands, and he gripped it tightly. 'Just hang on,' she urged him as he stared at her uncomprehendingly. 'Hang on.'

37

Amy's leg throbbed from the pain. It was all she was aware of for a while after she stopped screaming. Her shoulder hurt too, she realised, as she tried to move her arm to steady herself. She cried out when she leaned on it to stop herself rocking violently.

She could hear frantic voices issuing directions, but they were muted as though there were a wall between them and where she lay. She registered breathing close to her before she felt his presence, but once she had she couldn't escape it. A bulky form next to her, crouching, leaning into her as if it were looking at her, but not touching.

Her eyes travelled upwards across the slats of light that streamed in from badly covered windows until she reached a face. It was chubby and creased, rising above a thickness of tattooed shoulders. When she stared at it she saw glassy, drug-disorientated eyes looking back at her.

She began to scream again and he fell on her, immediately covering her mouth with a meaty hand. She tried to bite down but he gave no sign of feeling it, and she quickly opened her mouth to gasp in pain as they rolled around on the metal surface of the floor, her shoulder jarring into the unforgiving surface.

There was a sudden noise and light poured in above her as some kind of divide was pulled back. She tried to look up, but could only make out a hand with dirt-blackened nails resting on the seat-back.

'What yer doin back thir?' said another reedier voice. 'Ey, Dregs, wait for us.'

A deeper voice near her face grunted back, 'Just hurry up.' His breath reeked of spicy meat. 'Where we goin'?' he shouted towards his buddy.

'The falls,' the man answered, then the window slammed shut again and the darkness was back.

Amy tried to blank out their words, but she couldn't. Each time the monster holding her removed his hand from her mouth she screamed as loud and hard as she could.

Suddenly the man moved and she was freer still to roll and scream. She felt a surge of triumph at this victory, but it was short-lived. Hands tried to grab her wrists and she flailed madly, her nails finding flesh, until a stinging slap across her face knocked her breathless for a second. While she was still stunned, her wrists were held tightly together above her head, and heavy knees pressed painfully into her thighs. Her mouth was pulled open by probing fingers and a cloth stuffed in. She could smell petrol fumes emanating from it and it tasted vile. Thick black tape was wound roughly around her head, catching and pulling her hair. She kept on screaming, but the noise now stuck in the back of her throat and became an unearthly guttural moan. After a while she couldn't bear the sound she was making any longer and fell silent, concentrating on the effort of breathing enough oxygen through her nose.

She tried to think clearly, but waves of panic washed over the coherent strands of thought, breaking them down into fractured phrases – '*away*', '*hurt*', '*die*'. She thought of all the things she still wanted to do with her life, then of Alex – it was beyond surreal that only seconds ago he had been there smiling at her – and her mum and dad. Great tears found their way through her closed eyelids and rolled down her face. Her breath came more jerkily and she tried to breathe through her mouth, but gagged on the cloth again and for a moment she thought she was going to vomit and choke, until her body took over and forced the breath back through her nose.

Finally, the motion stopped and a whole new realm of panic swept through her as the back doors were wrenched open.

She was pulled out roughly by the legs from the blackness of the van's interior, and her head hit a platform as she fell a few feet onto dry spiky grass below. She moaned as she landed hard on her wounded leg.

Two men stood over her, their eyes dilated and vacant, their movements twitchy like demented dogs. The fat one she had seen in the back and another man she recognised as the man who'd opened the window. It was this man who spoke.

'I'll go first,' he said.

The chubby man moved around behind her, and she felt her clothes begin to be yanked off. She tried to scream again, and thrashed and struggled. Her T-shirt came up over her face, and she found her hands free, so fought to grab it and pull it down, twisting and writhing to get away.

'Hold her,' she heard someone say, and her top was left alone, pulled up to the neck. Hands instead found her own and yanked them both behind her head once more, crushing her wrists. More hands then grabbed and pinched at her skin, her breasts, worked their way along her thighs. The pain in her shoulder was unbearable.

Something cold was at her throat. She could feel it slicing into her skin.

She knew she was beaten.

Then there was a weight on top of her. A moment later, rhythmic grunting.

Pain everywhere.

She closed her eyes against it all, tears still pushing their way through. Her body went limp, just waiting for the end, whatever it might be. She could hear the constant rush of water somewhere near, a gentle *shussssssh* that never stopped. The fight deserted her and a part of her mind flew away, higher and higher into the cloudless sky. It left her behind as it reached the vast blue void, up and up it went, searching for what lay beyond. Vowing never to come back down.

When the weight lifted she automatically opened her eyes a fraction. Another man was striding over. This one wore a sleeveless lumberjack's shirt, his arms muscular and strong and patched with tattoos, his face grim and determined, his eyes black holes like the others', but his right cheek scythed vertically with a puckering scar.

She quickly closed her eyes again as he fell on to her roughly, the rancid stench of alcohol mixed with sweat washing over her. She didn't make a sound; pain annihilated any thought she tried to form. She still had her eyes closed when she heard a spitting noise and felt something wet land on her cheek. As the weight lifted off her, the man uttered the word 'Bitch' in a rasping whisper as he moved away.

She heard sounds of movement coming closer once more, but there was another noise now, a whirring getting louder.

'Shit,' a voice said close to her ear. 'What do we do now?'

'Back in the fucking van,' shouted another voice. 'Get rid of her, quickly.'

Cold metal was back against her throat, pressing hard. Her eyes closed in preparation for the end, and she dipped into an endless black void.

38

Alex didn't know how long he'd been sitting there, but at least three cups of tea were in front of him, all now cold. The room was bright and freshly painted, bare except for a chair and a beech-coloured table.

His mind was a blurry carousel of thoughts.

She was next to me.

She was taken right out of my arms.

And I didn't stop it.

I was too slow.

I just let them take her.

What if I never see her again?

What if . . .

What if . . .

His throat felt constricted. His stomach burned. His chest was on fire.

He looked up each time someone walked past the small

window set into the door, willing them to come in and tell him something. Faces had peered in when he had first arrived, but now he had finished his witness statement they obviously had other things to attend to. He felt so impotent, sitting on his hands, waiting. He was ashamed of his inaction.

He rocked on the chair, looking down at his clenched fists, his tight knuckles. He still didn't understand it. How could he have just let them take her like that? He banged one fist on the table, feeling the tears threaten to unman him again. If only she'd been on the other side of him. If only he had caught hold of her hand for just that one moment he would have stood more of a chance.

He could still hear the thud and scrape of her body against the van as she was pulled inside. He could see the thick hand grasping her arm, the face with vacant eyes. Passers-by had provided pieces of the number plate but when the police had looked it up nothing had registered. Number plates were easy to disguise, the sergeant had told Alex. Apart from that, all the witnesses could describe was a white van and a scruffy man inside. Hardly a great starting point for a lead to follow.

He debated whether to call his parents for some support; but was stopped by the thought of how worried they would be. He still remembered the unbearable atmosphere in his home when Jamie had gone missing – his dad retreating into a stoic silence belied only by fingers that fumbled over everything, while his mother repeatedly collapsed in tears. He couldn't bear the thought of putting them through anything like that again. He knew he should call Amy's parents, but he kept picturing her father's expression at the airport as he entrusted Amy into Alex's care, and he couldn't face the conversation. In the first hour he had been hoping there would quickly be news; that they would find Amy fast. Then he could call once the crisis had passed, and relay the story in the past tense, assuring them that she was just shaken, but otherwise fine. That they'd be home soon. But now, with each minute that ticked by, he lost a little bit more self-possession, and a little bit more hope.

39

Amy heard screaming as she came to. It sounded dislocated. She could feel the grass, wet and slimy, against her back, cool air on her face, and her tongue bone-dry and swollen against the oily cloth in her mouth.

'Chris,' a voice was shrieking above her head. 'Chris, quickly. Oh my god, QUICKLY.'

Then there was another voice, a deeper one. 'Oh Jesus, Jesus, Jesus,' it said over and over.

Amy tried to turn onto her side to curl up, but she couldn't move. It felt as though there were a slab of concrete on top of her, pinning her down.

'Fuck, she's moving. She's alive.' It was the deep voice.

'Chris, give me the picnic blanket now. NOW!' the female one shouted shakily. 'AND GO AND PHONE THE FUCK-ING POLICE.'

Amy felt coarse material covering her, rubbing painfully

against her leg. The woman's voice kept repeating words: 'You're all right, love, you're all right, you'll be all right now, you're all right.' Amy could hear the woman crying over her as she spoke. A warm hand stroked her brow and hair, and she tried to pull away but couldn't move. She felt some tugs as the woman attempted to break the thick black tape wound around her head, pulling her hair, and then she stopped and left it alone.

Amy kept her eyes closed.

More voices.

'Grab the stretcher, Brett,' someone said.

A radio crackled.

'Caucasian female, young,' someone else said.

The radio crackled again.

'Could well be,' the voice replied.

'Hello there, hello?' A finger pressed against Amy's eyelid and lifted it up, shining a bright light into it. She winced involuntarily. 'We've got you, you're safe now.'

'She's conscious,' someone called, and it seemed as though more people crowded around her.

Something soft was pressed gently against her neck. Then she heard the snip snip of scissors next to each ear, and the cloth was pulled from her mouth. She gasped one, two great lungfuls of air, her whole body contorting upwards at the sudden freedom, vomit coming from her mouth and running over her chin, and then she heard an almighty wailing begin. This time she knew it came from her own body, because she felt the quaking tremor of it as it filled her ears.

Her eyes flicked open and there was a snapshot of shocked and stricken faces. A uniformed policeman gaping at her with his mouth a slack O. A middle-aged woman's back heaving as she sobbed into the chest of a man in shorts and T-shirt, who had his arms round the lady and was looking away from the scene and into the distance, his face grim. And then a green uniform, a face close to Amy's, leaning in, saying 'for the pain', which she heard, although it sounded like one of the records her dad used to play where he would slow the speed right down to make her laugh at the sound of deep, treacly voices. She stared upwards, beyond the few trees that peered over the scene, up into the clear void that still beckoned her, where a part of her already lurked, looking down. She felt the inconsequential stab of a needle and her mind moved off again and up into the air towards the endless blue of the sky.

40

Alex looked up at the sound of the door opening. The detective in charge – Thompson, he thought his name was – came in, grim-faced.

Alex clenched his fists hard under the table as the policeman began to speak.

'We've found the van. It was abandoned in a remote parking spot – and originally stolen. We think they switched to another car, as there are tyre tracks leading away from the scene.'

His heart skittered. 'Amy?'

'No sign, I'm afraid . . . We're searching the area now.' The man paused. 'You know, you don't have to be here if you don't want to, Mr Markham.'

'What? What do you mean?'

'You're free to leave the police station whenever you like. It's been almost five hours and there are no developments yet. It might . . . take a while. Of course, you're welcome to stay, but if you give me your mobile number I'll keep you fully informed. Maybe you'd rather find somewhere more comfortable to wait?'

Alex couldn't keep the sarcasm from his tone as he jumped up in agitation. 'Well, that's great. We did have some sightseeing planned today, after all. I suppose although Amy's been kidnapped there's nothing to stop *me* . . . Then I'll go back to our shabby little room and just set up camp till you find her. God, I can't believe this.'

'I do understand your distress, Mr Markham . . .'

A woman opened the door and leaned in. 'Sir.' Her tone commanded his attention immediately.

'Excuse me for a sec.' Thompson got up and followed her out, closing the door behind him.

Alex immediately headed over to the door and peered through the small window. They were talking outside, the woman animated and serious, the detective nodding with his lips a grim line, asking short questions and then nodding again. Not knowing was more unbearable than anything else. Alex was on the point of opening the door and demanding to be included in the conversation when the detective gave some instructions and the woman hurried off. Alex turned away from the door as the policeman came back in, but immediately swung around as the man announced, 'They've found her . . .'

When Alex saw Thompson's stony expression his insides turned to ice. He began to hold his hand up, to ask him not to say any more, as the not knowing had instantly transformed itself into a blessing, but the policeman continued too quickly.

'. . . and she's alive, but she's been badly hurt. We need to get to the hospital.'

Alex's knees gave way for a moment and he had to lean against the wall. *Amy, Amy . . .*

While they raced to the hospital, image after sickening image strobed through Alex's mind, but nothing could prepare him for the shock of seeing Amy in that hospital bed. He had to focus all his energy into pushing down the queasiness rising like a bubble of air inside him, before he threw up on those pristine white covers.

She was asleep – sedated, they told him. They wouldn't collect specimens for forensics until she woke up, and they asked him not to touch her until they had done so. However, much of the evidence of what had occurred was clear for all to see. On her face and the unbandaged portions of her arms – the only parts of her visible – purple bruises flared in patches. Even the uninjured skin was raw, red and blistered from where the sun had had its own cruel way with her.

There were thick bandages on her left shoulder and wrist, but they were not as appalling as the large plaster stretched across her neck, covering the place where they had tried to slice her throat. Alex realised with a jolt that she was still there only because of poor execution on her attackers' part.

Less than six hours ago she had been walking next to him, laughing, intact and unscathed. God, how he wished he could have a moment alone with the animals that had done this to her. A moment would be all he would need.

His legs felt unsteady and he stood with both palms on the edge of the mattress, letting his arms take his weight.

'Hello?'

He turned slowly, to find a woman by the door, dressed in a navy suit. She walked towards him. 'I'm Isla Bardello.' Held out a hand, which he shook silently. 'I'm your family liaison officer. You must be Alex?'

He nodded.

She looked at Amy for a moment, and then said, 'You know, if you need to let yourself go, that's okay. While she's asleep is a good time for you to cry or be angry. When she wakes up she'll need you to be strong.'

He didn't know how to respond to this. Markham men did not emote on command, they found it difficult enough to do so at all. Especially in front of strangers. He couldn't trust himself to have a conversation without losing control. He was not ready to be grateful for Amy's life, as though he were thanking the bastards who had done this for the smallest of mercies. He was ready to punch flesh until he heard the bones splinter, to set fire to all the white transit vans he saw.

She was waiting and he was flustered, so he tried out a smile. 'Thanks. I'm okay.'

She watched his face, and he wondered if she was disappointed in him. Then she straightened up, becoming more businesslike.

'Have you spoken to Amy's family?'

'No. Have you?'

She ignored the snippiness of his reply. 'They need to be told. It would be more reassuring coming from someone they know.'

Alex choked back an ugly laugh. There would be nothing reassuring to them in this news, whoever told them. He had already mentally gone over the dreaded conversation with

Amy's father a hundred times, trying to imagine what Raymond Duvalis would do when he heard about this.

However, she was right. There was no choice: he needed to let Amy's parents know.

'You can use my mobile,' she said, handing him the phone.

'Thanks,' he replied, taking it and wandering out of Amy's room after a glance back.

He searched the maze of linear corridors for somewhere private enough, ending up in the car park, on the far side by some eucalypts, their scent wafting over him as he dialled.

It was breakfast time in the UK. He imagined Ray and Tess sitting in companionable silence in their small kitchen, unaware of the devastating news about to reach them.

'Hello?' It was Amy's mother.

'Tess, it's Alex. There's been an accident,' he began, trying to sound calm. 'But Amy's alive.'

'Oh my god.' Her voice broke immediately as he cursed his wording – by telling her that Amy was alive he had reduced her daughter's present condition in the world to one of mere survival – but he couldn't think what else to say. He was about to add more when he heard rustling at the other end. Then a gruff voice said, 'Who is this?'

'Ray, it's Alex.'

'What's happened?' Ray demanded.

'Amy was grabbed off the street earlier today . . . and kidnapped. They found her a few hours later, but she's been badly hurt. She's in hospital; under sedation.'

'*What*? Oh, Jesus, *Jesus*.' There was a short pause, then, 'Alex, tell me straight, how badly hurt? Will she be okay?'

Unless Raymond Duvalis asked him directly, Alex knew

he could not bear to explain what they had done to the man's daughter.

'I . . . I don't know. Physically, yes, I think so. Mentally, I don't know. She's still sedated.'

'They didn't . . . Was it . . . ?'

Alex sucked in a breath. 'Yes. And they meant to kill her.' His voice cracked into a roughened croak. 'They tried to cut her throat.'

He could hear the other man's breath rasping as this was taken in. 'We're coming,' Ray growled down the phone. 'We'll be there as soon as possible. I'll sort the flights out. How do I contact you?'

'Er . . . I . . .' Alex looked around. He realised he wasn't even sure of the name of the hospital. 'I'm not sure where we are, to be honest.' He felt pathetic.

'Get me a phone number, and the hospital details,' Ray barked. 'As quickly as you can.'

'Okay,' Alex replied, and heard the click as Ray hung up.

He walked slowly back towards the ward, his legs dragging, his body feeling impossibly heavy, like he'd been drugged. He suddenly wanted to sleep, to sink into oblivion, where he could discard this day, the past six hours, at least for a while. He gave back Isla's phone, and she told him she would return in an hour to check on Amy.

Finally, they were left alone.

Alex moved over to Amy's face. The image he had of her sleeping just that morning overlaid the bruised, beaten face before him now. He went to stroke her hand, then remembered he couldn't even touch her. The dam inside him crumbled and he finally broke down.

41

Mark waited at the bottom of the steps of one of Surrey's grandest stately homes, fiddling with the hem of his dinner jacket.

He had been looking forward to the Christmas ball all week. It was hosted sequentially by a number of top London law firms that fell just outside the Silver Circle, inviting barristers, solicitors and their aides to put aside their quarrelling for one evening in the spirit of Christmas festivity. It was a night of good-hearted camaraderie, but with an underbelly of point scoring that saw everyone on their guard. The occasion had also become a mock awards ceremony to publicly congratulate and commiserate with the year's successes and failures of those gathered. Mark, as a rising star, had thus far only been mentioned favourably on the two previous occasions he'd attended, while this was Chloe's maiden voyage into the jurisprudent atmosphere, so neither of them felt the same level of trepidation with which others from their office approached the event.

'Looking for me?'

Chloe was suddenly right in front of him. No wonder he had missed her, he thought, inhaling sharply at the sight of her. She had metamorphosised from besuited trainee lawyer to sexy and sophisticated debutante. Gleaming black satin hugged her body, accentuating her curves, the split skirt revealed flashes of tanned calves, and strappy black sandals sparkled as she moved.

'Wow,' he said. 'Chloe, you look superb.'

'Thank you,' she replied, beaming.

Mark held his arm out and she slipped her hand through it. Then they turned and made their way up towards the light and noise.

The dinner, awards and speechmaking were uneventful, though by the time they had finished, Mark's head was humming from the champagne he'd slugged back with each toast. As the tables broke up to become informal groups of animated conversation, a swing band struck up and people began to dance. Mark followed Chloe over to the bar, and with freshly topped-up glasses they stood in front of a red and gold strewn Christmas tree, the tip of which stroked the high-vaulted ceiling, and watched the festivities around them.

There was a lot Mark wanted to say to Chloe as he watched her sip her drink and gaze about her. Yet he couldn't find the words to begin, nor could he work out the phrasing in his head.

As they stood there in silence he saw his father approaching, with another man in tow.

'Mark! Chloe!' said his father in his usual booming voice. 'This is Risto Kiesi, he's taking over from Pamela in family law when she goes on maternity leave. You'll be having a lot to do with him, Chloe.'

Mark sized up Risto as the other man proffered his hand. He had a mop of curly brown hair and deep-etched laughter lines. Mark reached out and they shook hands, brisk and businesslike.

Risto then turned and said, 'Chloe', and again offered his hand, but as she took it he held on to it as he said, 'It's very nice to meet you,' in a tone that was almost *too* genuine. Mark studied the grip of Risto's hand on Chloe's, until it was broken.

'Likewise,' Chloe said. 'I'm looking forward to working with you.'

Risto smiled. 'Oh, me too.'

'Chloe!' Henry butted in, watching them, the proud benefactor of these exchanges. 'You look wonderful tonight, my dear.'

'Thank you,' Chloe said mildly, then there was a pause. Mark knew Chloe was awed and a little frightened by Henry. He had no doubt that Henry was aware of that too, but his father seemed to bask in the fact like a cat in sunshine, lingering longer than was strictly necessary.

'Would you like to dance, Chloe?' Risto interjected easily.

Mark's heart sank. Chloe looked at the packed dance floor then laughed and said, 'Yes, okay.' And Mark could only watch as she followed Risto and they joined the jostling crowd. He caught glimpses of her now and again as Risto moved easily around the dance floor, whirling Chloe with him.

Henry stayed by Mark's side, but his gaze was in the same direction as his son's. 'Those two have taken a shine to one another,' he said. 'Risto is a brilliant lawyer, I've long admired him. We've had to promise we'll keep him on if Pamela comes back, but I doubt there'll be a problem, hardly any of them can hack it once they've started down the family road. His curriculum vitae shows he's worked with some impressive names; no doubt he'll be filling the coffers a bit as well.'

Mark said nothing.

'Better circulate, then,' Henry said. 'Wouldn't do you any harm either, Mark.'

Mark cast a quick glance towards his father, who was waiting expectantly, portly stomach protruding over a burgundy cummerbund.

'I'll just grab another drink,' Mark said, indicating his glass, which to his surprise he'd emptied in the last five minutes.

Henry nodded and strode away.

Mark took his time at the bar, keeping an eye on the dance floor as he downed two quick whisky chasers, and he had only just returned to his position near the Christmas tree as Chloe walked towards him alone, face flushed, smiling.

Mark held out a glass. 'I got you another one.'

She took the drink. 'Thanks, Mark. I'd better be careful,

though, I'm feeling all light and floaty already.' Still, she immediately took a sip.

Mark felt the same way, curiously disconnected from his body. His focus on the glass in his hand wasn't as clear as it might be, but then again, the lighting had dimmed now, and the softness was relaxing him. He tipped a huge slug of liquid into his mouth, enjoying the flare of it against his throat as he summoned up courage.

'Chloe, you do look absolutely gorgeous tonight.'

Chloe gave Mark a curious sidelong glance. 'Well, thanks, Mark.'

'I just wanted to tell you, you know . . .'

'Okay.' She looked amused now.

'Look, do you want to dance?' Mark asked, regretting it as soon as he said it. He wasn't a dancer, but the music was slow enough that he might get through it by simply swaying, which, now he thought of it, he seemed to be doing already.

He grabbed Chloe's hand and pushed his way towards the dance floor. It had been packed earlier, as he watched, but now it had thinned out. However, it was too late to back out, and he wrapped his arms around Chloe's waist and pulled her tightly to him, beginning to move to the music.

He pressed his mouth against her neck, then put his hand up to cup the back of her head as he leant towards her for a passionate liplock. He felt her tense, then relax into it, and he let himself go, covering her mouth with his own, running his hands up and down her satin-clad back, over her bottom, back up to her waist again.

When the song finished, the next one began at a much faster tempo. Mark had a momentary bizarre urge to break into some silly kind of jig, but as Chloe finally pulled back from him he saw the look on her face. She was flushed and smiling, but also seemed a bit embarrassed. Was she laughing at him? Was he a joke to her?

'Are you laughing at me?'

She shook her head. 'Mark, you're drunk. Come on.' She grabbed his hand and tried to pull him off the dance floor, but Mark wanted to feel her in his arms again. He said, 'Chloe, come here,' and pulled her back, harder than he meant to, and her body met his with a hefty bump, sending them both reeling a few steps, with Chloe trying to regain her balance by clutching onto Mark, and Mark staggering with the weight of trying to right both of them. They only stopped when Mark met the ledge of the stage, fell backwards over it, and landed with a great crash against the band's drum kit, which let out a simultaneous bang and cymbal clap.

As Mark lay sprawled, with Chloe now recovered and standing over him looking mortified, to their credit the band played on after only the slightest of blips, the drummer and a few nearby people with quick hands managing to steady the kit. But everyone on that side of the room had noticed, and was either staring, laughing, or looking away in awkward embarrassment.

'Come on, Mark,' Chloe hissed, pulling him up. He followed her lead, and they made their way over to the entrance hall, Chloe's head down. Mark saw faces he recognised among the onlookers but didn't really care, as his head was both pounding and spinning from the combined effects of alcohol and a whack from the drums.

Chloe pulled him all the way outside to the front steps

of the building. 'Sit down,' she said. He sank onto the cold stone. 'Do you want me to get you some water?'

'No, just kiss me,' he replied, his speech slightly slurred.

'Mark! I don't think –'

'What the HELL do you two think you're playing at?'

Mark looked around towards the source of the noise. He saw his father bearing down on them, towering over them as they sat on the steps. His face was bright red.

'Do you think you're at some kind of school disco?' he demanded. 'Where you can grope each other in front of everyone, and people will just smile fondly at you? David and Neil are outraged. You've disgraced the company, both of you.'

Mark couldn't take it in. He looked from his father to Chloe, whose eyes were brimming with tears.

'Dad, hang on . . .'

But Henry was already hailing one of the waiting taxis, which promptly drew up in front of them.

Chloe dashed up the steps without a word, and returned a moment later with her coat and Mark's jacket. Henry leaned into the darkened interior of the cab.

'Take them anywhere,' he growled. 'As long as it's right away from here.'

42

The first night had passed in a blur. Alex had refused to leave Amy's side, despite a number of voices imploring him to rest. At some points he dozed in the hard-backed armchair in the corner, at others he tried to stay awake on the upright chair by Amy's bed. His dreams felt more like hallucinations, where he chased Amy but lost her; or was confronted by groups of faceless men who he would attack without hesitation, breaking bones and ignoring screams until his hands were covered in their warm blood. Eventually he dragged the larger chair across to the bedside, and fell asleep for an hour slumped forward, his face buried in the hospital mattress.

During the first twenty-four hours Amy opened her eyes a few times, but she was groggy from the shock and the painkillers, not really registering her surroundings much, blinking wearily, then closing her eyes again.

Alex waited outside while the doctors examined her and collected evidence. When they had finished they gave him encouraging reports. There was some internal bruising and a small amount of bleeding, they said, looking down at their notes as they did so, and they would need to keep an eye on her, but there shouldn't be any permanent damage. The rest of her wounds were not as severe as they looked. Her shoulder was sprained, and her shin had taken a bad knock but there was no bone break. The cut across her throat looked shocking and would probably leave a scar, but it would fade. The CT scan showed no internal swelling or bleeding to the head, and while the bruises looked nasty they would disappear eventually. The list went on, each item increasing Alex's burning need for vengeance – but all her physical injuries would heal, and without the need for too much medical intervention.

The psychological prognosis had not been delivered with as much reassurance. The effects of such an experience would be wide-ranging and long-lasting, Alex was warned by Isla and others. Amy would need time and space to react in the way she needed to, and unobtrusive, consistent support over the next days, weeks, months and years. He nodded, trying to take it all in, doing his best to understand what was needed from him; but even then he was not prepared for the first thing Amy said when she opened her eyes properly the following day.

'I'm so sorry, Alex.'

Her voice took him by surprise, as he had been staring at her hand, stroking it while she rested, feeling groggy and disorientated through lack of sleep, and he hadn't sensed her waking.

He looked up, trying not to be overcome with emotion at the sound of the familiar sweet voice he had been longing to hear. He tried to smile reassuringly. 'Hey,' he cooed in an almost-whisper, his heart constricting in love and pain to see his lovely Amy finally awake. 'Don't say sorry, you've got nothing to be sorry about.'

Tears began to seep down the sides of her face. 'I tried to fight them, I promise I did. But I couldn't . . . I should have tried harder, I should have done whatever it took, I should have . . .'

Alex stood up quickly while she was talking. 'No, Amy,' he interrupted, trying to stroke her cheek and catch the tears as they fell. He was so stricken by her words that his voice came out much harsher than he intended. She winced at the sound and again at his touch. 'Don't say that, please,' he begged more softly, as her sobs became louder. He looked around desperately for help; he wasn't sure how to calm her.

A nurse came bustling in. 'Ssh,' she said to Amy, reaching across to quickly pour some water into a plastic cup. 'You're safe now, my love. Don't fret. Nothing can hurt you. Here, take these pills, they'll help with your pain.'

The nurse assisted Amy with the water and the pills while Alex looked on, standing back, feeling useless and pathetic that this stranger could comfort her so easily when he couldn't.

By the time the nurse left, Amy had closed her eyes again.

She woke up a couple of hours later, and this time she was silent, staring across towards the window as though in a daydream. Again, Alex didn't know what to say to her, so he tried to fuss to make up for his earlier ineptitude.

'Amy, I'm so sorry . . .'

She shook her head. 'Don't, Al. Not right now, okay?'

He paused, searching for something to say.

'Do you want some water?'

'No thanks.'

'Can I get you anything else?'

'No, it's fine.'

'Shall I put the TV on?'

'If you want.'

He switched it on and flicked through the channels.

'Any preference?'

'You choose something.'

The news? Too gloomy, he thought. Sport? Not Amy's thing. So he left it on *The Simpsons* and they listened to inane squeaky chatter that usually made them giggle, as Amy continued to stare out of the window. Alex felt silly and selfish, as though in the middle of this crisis all he could think to do was to put the telly on. When the nurse came in to help Amy to the toilet, he left, embarrassed, even though when Amy had been ill in Thailand he hadn't even blinked at keeping her company in the bathroom.

Detective Thompson called in twice to see how Amy was doing. Finding her awake in the afternoon, Alex watched as he asked her questions, quizzing her relentlessly, reminding Alex that speedy progress was essential, when he tried to jump in upon seeing Amy's distress. Every word the policeman uttered, each question he posed, repeatedly slammed the reality of all this into Alex's mind, that it was not just some horrible twilight nightmare they could escape from.

Finally, the detective left them alone, and before long the day receded into evening. Alex spent another uncomfortable night in the chair, still unwilling to leave, but less sure of his purpose in being there, unnerved by how ineffective his actions and presence had been in the past twenty-four hours. He resolved to talk to Isla in the morning, to ask her more about what he should do, and how he should be.

At nine o'clock the next morning, Amy's parents arrived, dishevelled and tired-looking, cases in hand, having come straight from the flight. When Amy first saw them she broke down, howling her pain to them, a rag doll in her mother's arms, sagging against her. Alex's intense awkwardness returned. He hardly looked at Amy's father as he rose to shake hands, but when he did he realised that Ray hadn't even registered Alex's presence yet, staring horrified at his distressed and injured daughter.

When Ray finally saw him, Alex imagined for a moment that Amy's father was going to hit him. This slightly stooped old man with watery eyes, half a foot smaller than Alex, sprang forward as though possessed, and Alex instinctively backed away. Just in time, Ray seemed to rein himself in and gave a curt nod instead, just saying, 'Alex.'

Tess looked round when she heard Alex's name, her daughter still buried in the cradle of her arms, and put a hand out briefly to rub Alex's arm. The gesture made him think of his own mother, and for a moment he longed for that familiar comfort. But after Jamie's troubles had begun Alex had stopped leaning on her, not wanting to cause her any additional worries. Now, he reminded himself that since there was little she could really do, it would be unfair to burden her with this. And the thought of his dad's unease in the presence of others' emotions was enough to put a stop to any notion of confidences there.

Amy drifted in and out of sleep over the following excruciating hours. Her mum and dad had taken the seats so Alex was propped against the wall staring out of the window, or offering to fetch them drinks, which they declined.

Detective Thompson returned around lunchtime. He asked them all to leave, as he thought Amy would find it easier without an audience. As they made their way out, Alex saw the policeman sit on Amy's bed and speak softly and solemnly to her, and that she nodded in understanding.

Ray wandered off without a backwards glance, his shoulders hunched, while Tess walked over to Alex. 'Ray just needs some space,' she said. 'He's taken it very hard. Do you want to get some air?'

Alex nodded and they walked outside and stood in the shade of a large melaleuca tree.

Tess took Alex's arm and rubbed his forearm with her other hand. 'Alex,' she said, 'it's okay –'

She hesitated. Alex was silent, unsure what she meant.

'– I don't know if . . . if you are thinking along these lines, but it's not . . . it's not your fault, what happened. There was nothing . . .'

Even though he had berated himself a million times in the past forty-eight hours – *if only, if only* – he was shocked to hear her say this, and turned to look at her, searching her face to see if she meant it. He wanted to shake her off, to tell her of course it wasn't his fault, he had done everything he could to keep Amy safe.

'Thanks,' he said instead, standing stiffly, looking at the floor.

'It's okay,' she replied sadly, dropping his arm.

43

When Mark had woken up the morning after the law ball he had had that blissful momentary void as he moved between states of consciousness before his memory kicked in, along with a particularly aggressive hangover.

With rising indignation he remembered Chloe supporting him up the stairs to her flat, and rolled over, realising he was in Chloe's room, with Chloe next to him, snoring softly. He reached over to the floor and grabbed his jacket, pulling out his mobile and seeing that it was only six forty-five. The movement made his head groan with pain, so he rolled back and lay staring at the ceiling for a moment, trying to collect his thoughts.

There was no avoiding it. He kept replaying the moment he'd overbalanced; the crash of the drum kit behind him; Chloe's surprised, shocked face as she almost came with him but managed to right herself, as he'd used both his hands to try to break his fall and keep any percussion from falling on top of him.

Then the walk of shame to the entrance, the replay now accompanied by the slow clapping of his throbbing head. Seeing Risto Kiesi, the new guy, smirking at them both, and passing David and Neil, who both had heavy scowls on their faces. Being glad he hadn't spotted his father as Chloe dragged him outside, then hearing Henry's voice, the rage in it, the humiliation.

He pulled himself up again. His mouth was dry and disgusting, he needed water. He made his way slowly down the poky hallway of Chloe's flat, body aching, to the kitchen, ran the tap and pushed his mouth straight under the flow, not even bothering to look for a glass.

He wiped his mouth and sighed, looking out of the kitchen window, straight at someone else's curtains on the opposite side of the road. What should he do?

Wearily, he made his way back down the hallway, grabbed his clothes from the floor and started putting them on. Chloe didn't stir. Her arms were flung out from her sides like she had fallen onto the bed and straight into a deep sleep. Her long brown hair fanned out across her pillow, a section of it across her face, the rest of it framing her neck and graceful shoulders. His gaze continued down over the soft mounds of her breasts under her T-shirt, the rest of her enveloped in a duvet.

He had an urge to ease himself down onto her, hug her tightly into the softness of her covers, kiss her lips, her neck and that sweet button nose. But he was dressed now, a dishevelled version of the previous night, bow tie in his pocket, and ready to leave.

He moved towards the door, then turned back to look at Chloe once more, so peaceful and still; hesitating, feeling that somehow this one decision of leaving was a defining moment in his life.

He walked back over to the bed, sat on the edge of it, and kissed Chloe lightly on the lips.

She didn't stir, even though he willed her to. He needed her to wake up and see him there with his mussed-up hair and his stinking breath and his bloodshot eyes, even though he wasn't quite sure why.

'Chloe,' he whispered.

She murmured something unintelligible, and he began to smile, anticipating her eyes opening, but she rolled away from him and half-buried her head under the pillow he'd used.

Mark remained where he was for a moment. He ran a hand lightly down her arm. He tried to think, though his sore head made it difficult. He pushed away the edginess that jostled with his hangover for attention, and slowly got up, turned away from Chloe, and made for the door.

44

Each time Amy opened her eyes there were a million fluorescent pin pricks dancing upon the dirty white ceiling. At first she had thought they'd strapped her down, but apparently it was the bruises on her stomach that felt like a dead weight. Her shoulder was swathed in bandages and when she moved it produced a sharp shooting pain. The whole of her ached and ached, inside and out.

It was surprisingly easy not to think. Just to stare in front of her and let all conscious thought drift into the misty recesses of her brain. Now and then the fog cleared a little and then she cried, wretched, gasping sobs beyond her control.

Alex sometimes looked at her with a strange expression on his face. At one stage she had met his gaze to find him studying her like something that had dropped out of the sky and landed at his feet. She was searching for disgust in his eyes, but he was hiding it well.

She needed him. But not like this – him mute and staring out of the window. She needed him to find the right words, the ones she so desperately needed to hear, even though she herself had no idea what they were. She wanted to tell her mum and dad to go away half the time, but also to cling to them and try to disappear inside the cavern their arms made.

She needed them all. But not like this.

Her mother was soothing, helpful, but persistent, like those outback flies that wouldn't give up until they had attached themselves to you. And Alex . . . Alex was distant and tense, full of latent rage that might only be assuaged by inflicting pain on someone. She could sense him trying to mentally move away from these surroundings, this reality. She couldn't blame him for that; she was doing the same.

Her father, on the other hand, was quiet, anguish written on his face; and a growing frustration in his movements and his sharp words for anyone other than his child. His distress was like an invisible cord stretching across the room, drawing her to him. When he'd arrived, for the first time since it happened she had been comforted. She had realised with a shock that what she had been waiting to see on someone else's face was not empathy but the companionship of unmitigated suffering.

He had refused to leave the hospital since they'd got there, though he told her mum to get rest. He'd barely said a word to Alex, who usually left when her mother did. A lot of the time when Amy was awake in the amber-lit hours her father was folded over in the chair beside her bed, snoring softly. But if she caught his eyes watching her, she didn't know what to say. She didn't think he did either.

When she thought of the person she had been just a few days ago, she felt like she was watching a film of another girl with plans and hopes and dreams. She spent most of the time now trying *not* to think, not to conjure up images she didn't want to see, not to dwell on the future, when she couldn't possibly imagine how she would ever get beyond this point. For the rest of her life she would be a girl who had been raped. She didn't want to be that girl. She wanted to tear off her skin and climb out from beneath the bloodied mess of it and run away. She didn't want Alex to see her like this. Defiled. She wanted him to tell her it was all a lie, all just a nightmare, but every time he looked at her she saw in his eyes that the nightmare was real.

45

When Chloe had opened her eyes on the Sunday morning it was to a feeling of lightness: the events of the evening before suddenly looked a lot funnier. Sure, it was extremely embarrassing – and despite her desire not to replay it, it seemed her mind had a will of its own and kept doing so anyway – but it wasn't the end of the world.

When she'd turned over she was surprised to find an empty space beside her. She'd hurried into the corridor and checked the bathroom, lounge and kitchen, but Mark, it seemed, had gone.

She hadn't heard from him for the rest of the day, but felt it was really up to him to make the first move after sneaking off like that.

When she'd got to the office the following day, she'd seen that Mark was in his room, his head bent over his work. She went and put her things down and tried to get on with her own tasks, but it was no good. Eventually she gave in and went to see him.

'Hello?' she said, standing in the doorway.

Mark looked up. 'Hello,' he replied with a formal smile.

'Are you okay?'

'Of course.'

'You left pretty quietly yesterday.'

'I know. I had things to do.'

'Oh, I see.'

Silence.

Chloe felt a bit light-headed. 'Are you still on for Saturday?' she asked.

Mark looked up quizzically.

'The family do,' she reminded him. 'I've told everyone you're coming,' she added, although it was untrue, but she felt she needed to use some coercion.

'Oh, that. Sure.' Mark gave her a quick smile. 'Just let me know when we need to leave. I'm quite busy this week, so I might not see you much before then.'

'Okay,' Chloe said. She knew a brush-off when she heard one. She went back to her own room, trying to dispel the tears that threatened. He was treating her as if she'd been the one who'd disgraced them, whereas they both knew he'd been the main culprit.

The rest of the week had dragged interminably. With the Christmas party over, everyone just wanted to get to the Christmas break. Ordinarily they would have shirked as much work as possible, but there was simply too much to do.

On the Thursday, Risto appeared at her office door, and asked if she could spare him some time. He sat down and they chatted about what they'd be working on in the New Year, about their Christmas plans, and the need for comfier furniture in the offices. By the time he left, Chloe felt considerably lighter in spirits. She was looking forward to having him around more, she decided, and there was no question that he'd been flirting with her quite openly throughout their conversation. Her mind went to Mark working hard in the next-door office, then she pushed the thought away. Mark had hardly spoken to her since the weekend, and a little flirting was hardly a crime, was it?

As she shrugged off her niggling anxiety, Mark appeared at the door, as if she'd conjured him up. He didn't bother to knock.

'David wants to see us,' he said, his face grim.

'Oh?' Chloe's stomach sank but she tried not to show it.

'Now,' Mark added, indicating with a flick of his head that she should come with him.

Chloe jumped up, smoothed her suit down, and felt her hair to check it was in place. Her mouth was dry. Surely this wasn't about the weekend – they couldn't sack her for watching Mark topple into a drum kit, could they?

As they reached David's office her alarm grew. She saw Neil was in there as well, and that neither man looked happy.

'Come in, you two, and close the door,' David said, indicating that they should both sit down.

Chloe glanced at Mark. He sat rigidly on the chair next to her, looking grimly past David towards the window.

'Neil and I thought we should discuss the events of last Saturday,' David began, forgoing preamble.

Chloe's insides began to curl up in shame.

Mark cleared his throat. 'Before you go on, I would like to say that it wasn't Chloe's fault in any way. I accept responsibility entirely. I'd had too much to drink and I behaved like an idiot. It will never happen again.'

'Mark –' Chloe began, thinking that she should at least support him, take some culpability onto her own shoulders, but Mark turned and glared at her so fiercely that she couldn't think of what to say next.

David held up his hand. 'I don't wish to start apportioning blame,' he said. 'All Neil and I would like to say is that if either of you *ever* do anything like this again while you are representing Lewis, Jameson & Marchant, there will be *very* serious consequences. We have discussed this with Henry – though he felt it better not to be in this meeting for obvious reasons – and we are all in full agreement that we are willing to let it go *this once*, but this is the last time, and you should still both be on your best behaviour while you make amends. If you do wish to conduct a relationship, then you will leave it at the doors to these offices; this is not some kind of libidinous stomping ground, and whenever you are representing this firm we demand the very best from you. That's why we hired you. Are we clear?'

Chloe nodded.

'Okay, then,' David said. He got up and opened his office door, showing them out. 'That will be all.'

Neil hadn't said anything throughout the entire meeting, just stared at them both as though they were emitting some unpleasant odour he was forced to sit in. At David's dismissal, Chloe jumped up and exited the room, finding she could breathe easier once she'd crossed the threshold. She felt indignant at being spoken to like a four-year-old, still unable to see why there was such a fuss being made, and no evidence of at least a portion of humour amongst all the stern words. Considering the array of shocking behaviour they came across every day in cases, what had happened was surely a little bit laughable.

She walked a few paces then automatically looked back for Mark, to see he was still in the office, saying something further to David and Neil, and then shaking both men's hands. She paused, wondering what was going on, but thought it better not to hang around too obviously in the light of what had been said. So she made her way back to her office deliberately slowly, hearing Mark's footfalls catching up behind her.

She turned around. 'Jesus!' she said to Mark, smiling, 'you'd think we'd shot the drummer, not just wobbled into his kit.'

Mark looked at her solemnly. 'Don't, Chloe,' he replied, sounding irritated. He walked past her towards his room, and she followed, unnerved.

'Mark, it'll blow over. And thanks for trying to get me off the hook,' she said, coming towards his desk.

'For Christ's sake, Chloe,' he hissed, throwing himself onto his chair, 'get out of here, will you. It's hardly the best start if they come round and find us gossiping two seconds after they told us to cool it.'

Chloe was taken aback at his tone. 'Okay,' she said, holding her hands up. 'I'm going.'

'Good,' Mark retorted grumpily, looking at his computer screen.

Back in her office, Chloe was unsettled by Mark's demeanour. Surely this was a storm in a teacup, and would be forgotten by next week.

But now she couldn't stop dwelling on it, and found herself typing an email to Mark, thinking that he couldn't berate her for double-checking after what had just happened.

'*Are you still coming on Saturday?*' she wrote nervously. '*For the family do?*'

Her inbox bleeped a moment later.

'*Yes.*'

Chloe let out a sigh, feeling a little better. They could talk about everything then, away from the office, and by next week it would all be back to normal.

46

It was only eight a.m., but the sun was already merciless as Alex made his way to the hospital, forcing his feet to move in the direction he dreaded going. It was a long walk, but his funds were seriously low and he couldn't afford a taxi. There had been a small amount of coverage from the local press in the week since Amy had been kidnapped, and Alex was notorious in the hostel now. Most people tried to stare without him noticing, but wouldn't catch his eye. One or two had attempted to confront the situation head on, offering their condolences – they appeared earnest, but Alex couldn't believe they wanted anything more than gossip, so he had been surly enough to stop them in their tracks. Since he had taken all Amy's things to the hospital the room was just a dark place to rest his head. He rarely saw it in daylight.

The police were encouraging the media interest, hoping for leads. Alex felt they were useless; they had got nowhere so far. He thought they were probably keeping their fingers crossed that the publicity would outrage the friends and relatives of the perpetrators and thus do their job for them.

Each day this journey was getting more and more difficult to make. He didn't know what to say to Amy, or to Amy's parents, or especially to Amy in front of her parents. Ray seemed to avoid looking at him; Amy too sometimes, and even when she did, he couldn't read her expression. Was it a plea? For what? Action? Compassion? Something he needed to do . . . ?

When he arrived, Amy was resting, her skin grey against the white sheets. He took up his position in this excruciating daily tableau – on another hard plastic chair brought in for the extra visitor, which he moved to the window. He was sick of these four walls and their minimal furnishings, the beige linoleum.

Amy's parents were either side of her bed: her mother sewing; her father dozing. Each time Amy woke up they all jumped to attention, and Alex could see in her eyes how awful she found it. What else should they do? he thought. Ignore her? Sing and dance for her? He had no fucking idea at all. He wished someone would give him some kind of clue.

In the past couple of days, Amy had not been as sedated, and so when she was awake they all watched TV. Heaps of it. Hours and hours of shitty TV, so they didn't have to talk – Alex couldn't tell whether that little box in the corner was a blessing or a curse.

As Amy was asleep this morning, he flicked idly through an old magazine that was on her bedside table, presumably left by a hospital worker. It was full of pretty dresses and anxious headlines: model can't cope; actress can't have a baby; alcoholic sports star shames his wife again. He didn't feel a jot of sympathy for any of them.

He had returned to gazing out the window when a doctor poked his head in, saw Amy was asleep and said 'A word?', looking at each of them. Amy's parents quickly jumped up and headed out, not looking back. The door swung shut behind them. Alex took it that he was not welcome.

They were alone. He went over to the bed, pulled up a chair and leaned forward, peering at Amy's face. He reached out his hand and, as softly as he could, stroked her hair, her brow, then her cheek. Her eyes remained closed, but a single tear escaped from beneath one of them and quickly ran towards his hand. He stopped it, held his fingers still, and Amy opened her eyes.

'Hello.' He smiled at her.

'Hello,' she whispered, watching him.

Quickly, not knowing how much of this precious time he had, he reached into his bag and pulled out Bug-Eye, the weird gecko toy he'd bought Amy as a joke in Thailand, knowing how cute she found the tiny real-life counterparts that stuck themselves to the hostel walls in the evenings. He tried not to remember how her eyes had lit up with laughter when he had given it to her, for now she could barely raise a smile, let alone one that reached her eyes.

'This little guy got left behind,' he told her, waving the toy at her as though she were a child, not telling her that he'd gone to sleep holding it on a few occasions to try to feel close to her.

She took the toy and looked at it for a moment, managing a weak smile, then said, 'Alex . . .'

'What is it?' He leaned towards her.

Her gaze moved to meet his. 'You don't have to stay.'

'What?' He recoiled as though she had just spat in his face. 'What do you mean?'

'This . . .' A weak arm came up and gestured around the room. 'It must be awful for you.'

'Well, not as awful as it is for you.'

'Use your plane ticket tomorrow – go home. I'll be home soon. Don't miss out on Christmas with your family.'

'Amy, I . . .'

'Al, go home. Mum and Dad are here now . . . I don't need . . .'

She cut the sentence short, but he had no doubt about which word she had faltered at.

'Okay,' he said, getting up, heading over to grab his things. 'I see.'

He could hear her ragged breathing, and, just for a moment, he looked at her face. The appeal in it was plain.

'This is silly, Amy. Do you want me to stay?'

She shook her head, still crying silently.

He couldn't bear this. 'For *CHRIST*'s –'

The door opened and Amy's parents were back. Amy's mother looked alarmed to find Alex yelling at her daughter. Amy's father's face instantly clouded with anger. Before either of them could do any more, Alex grabbed his things, and without a word or a look at anybody, he walked out the door.

47

Amy was in turmoil. She loved Alex so desperately, but now she was not the same. He hadn't changed; but she had transformed. She was ugly and scarred. He didn't love this girl – how could he, he didn't even know her. At the moment he was just holding out, hoping that the woman he knew was still there somewhere. But Amy was certain that person was gone for good.

So she had thought, perhaps I should let him go for good too. Better he leaves and I can make our happiness into a dearly held dream, than he stays and I watch his love for me gradually wither and die.

She had thought all this, and yet watching him leave, upset and angry, sent a fresh pain through her, overwhelming her aching body. She would have called out, but the appearance of her parents made her pause, and then he was gone.

Her father smiled at her as though he hadn't noticed

Alex's swift departure. 'I have good news,' he said, coming across to her bedside and taking her hand.

'What is it?' she asked. She couldn't imagine what it might be, but she longed to hear it.

'They say you're healing well. You can be discharged in a couple of days.'

'Oh.'

She hadn't really contemplated leaving the hospital – her thoughts had been focused on all she had lost, her past life and her future one, her dimorphic existence, not the progression of the current days and hours, which seemed unbearably long and pointless.

Noting her lack of enthusiasm, her father said, 'I've spoken to Thompson. They're at a standstill. He says there's no point us waiting here in case of arrest. We can always come back.'

Amy nodded, looking at Bug-Eye.

'Where's Alex gone?' her mother asked.

'I don't know,' she said, and burst into another interminable round of tears, feeling quite revolted at the sound of herself.

48

Mark had been silent for most of the drive so far. Chloe watched him as he concentrated on the road, and sighed inwardly. She couldn't help but think that he was making it worse, for himself most of all. She was desperate to ease the atmosphere.

'Mark, last weekend . . .'

'I don't want to talk about it,' he snapped.

'But –'

'Chloe, DON'T.' She almost jumped in her seat. 'What makes you think I want to relive any part of it?'

'But it wasn't that bad,' she said meekly. 'It was only –'

'Bloody hell, Chloe!' Mark roared. 'Just leave it, will you.'

'Okay, okay,' Chloe capitulated. Then added snippily, 'Just stop sulking then.'

But Mark didn't respond to this, and the silence continued to pollute the car.

By the time they arrived, Chloe didn't know whether to fume or get upset. She was regretting inviting Mark now, seeing as he barely seemed able to hold a conversation with her.

As they pulled into the driveway her mother came rushing out to the car. 'My darling, it's so great to see you. You look so well. Have you put on a bit of weight? It suits you. And you must be Mark. Lovely to meet you. Another lawyer, eh? How exciting. Come on, then, everyone's inside . . .' And she headed off still talking over her shoulder. At that moment Chloe was very grateful for the distraction of her mother's effusive greetings, and they both followed her inside.

By the time Mark had been introduced to Chloe's aunt and uncle from the Lakes, her aunt and uncle from Ireland, her brother Anthony, her stepfather Charlie, her seven cousins, and their various young offspring, as well as Great Uncle Bill in the corner and a number of family friends, the party was in full swing. Mark immediately got talking to some of the men, and Chloe was distracted by her cousins, particularly Mikaela, who was showing off her new navel piercing and hinting in far too loud a voice that she'd had something else pierced as well, but she'd better not get THAT out or her mother would have a fit.

'Is it your nipple?' Tom, the fourteen-year-old Irish cousin, yelled.

'That would be telling, and you're too young,' Mikaela replied, to which Tom squirmed and blushed but looked excited.

'You're disgusting, Mikaela,' said Danielle, Tom's nineteen-year-old sister, but she still looked intrigued.

Mikaela just smiled at them. 'Come on, Chlo, let's leave these kids to it,' she said, ushering Chloe over to the food table.

'So are you having them on?' Chloe asked, loading her plate and taking a bite of a chicken wing.

'No,' Mikaela said, heading straight for the desserts at the other end of the table, 'it's my . . . you know.' She indicated downwards with her eyes.

Chloe choked and spat a disgusting blob of half-chewed chicken out onto her plate. 'Oh my god. Why would you do that?'

Mikaela laughed. 'It's pretty good actually. You only have to move and it sets things off. You should try it.'

'Bloody hell, no thanks. I can't believe you let someone do that to you.'

'Well now, I must admit that bit wasn't so fun.'

'What wasn't so fun?'

Chloe turned to see Mark standing behind them. She felt herself blushing and couldn't think of what to say. However, Mikaela, while spooning jelly onto her plate, said, 'I've had my labia pierced. I was just telling Chloe about it.'

Chloe was unsurprised to see that Mark reddened at this. 'I see,' was all he said, then stood there seeming lost for words. Mikaela turned around, looked at both of them, laughed and said, 'My god, you two are hilarious,' then sauntered off, doing a little shudder as though an electric pulse had run through her as she disappeared, which her cousin was sure was solely for effect.

Chloe was uncertain what to say next. 'Do you want some food?' she asked, gesturing at the plates.

'No, I'm okay. Look, Chloe, do you mind if . . . if I head off?'

Chloe laughed. 'Head off where? We're in the middle of nowhere.'

'Back to London.'

She stopped laughing. 'You're not serious. We've only been here a few hours. It took us five bloody hours to get here!'

'It's just I've got a lot of work on, and I need to get through it before Christmas.'

'I see.'

'Sorry.'

'No, don't be . . . Okay, well, I suppose I can get a lift back with Iris. I'll walk you to your car.'

They made their way out to the front of the house in silence. As Mark opened the driver's door, Chloe said, 'Mark?'

He turned and looked at her.

'Us . . . this . . . is it . . . are we . . . ?' She didn't seem to be able to add the final word.

'No . . . I don't know . . . Look, right now I just need to get a bit of space, get my act together, you know. But I'll see you on Monday.'

'Oh, okay. Right.' She stood with her arms folded, and watched Mark get into the car, start the engine and drive away, all without looking at her.

Once he had gone she turned to walk back towards the party, but then sank down on the front step of the house and dissolved into tears. As she sat there she felt a pair of comforting arms around her, and heard Mikaela's voice whispering in her ear.

'They're all idiots, babe, every single one of them.'

49

The flight was proving unendurable. Alex was caught up in a revolving succession of emotions – feeling fractious, irritated, enraged and upset by turn, leaving him unable to sleep, to eat, or to numb his mind with any of the entertainment on offer.

In the past twenty-four hours his anger had been cataclysmic, without an outlet of any kind, so much so that he wouldn't have been surprised if he had worked himself up into spontaneous combustion.

He had been trying to do the right thing all bloody week. How had he got it so horribly wrong that she had wanted him to leave? And who did Ray think he was, treating Alex like some distant relative who had no place with them through all this, discarding his efforts, hogging Amy's care, not even allowing Tess in. And Tess, so compliant, so understanding, so selfless and giving in the wake of everyone else's struggle to cope with the fallout from this horrendous, vile event. And the doctors, deferring to Ray and Tess as soon as they arrived, when they had been filling *him* in for the first thirty-six hours, treating *him* as someone important, then simply ignoring him. And Detective Thompson, with his platitudes and his excuses for having absolutely no leads whatsoever. Alex hated the lot of them, although not with half as much vehemence as he'd reserved for Amy's attackers.

He shifted miserably in his seat, aware of the space next to him – Amy's space. They should have been coming back together today, excited about the next chapter. Now what was there to look forward to?

And yet . . . within the restlessness that pushed and poked at him, causing him to be unable to sit still, let alone sleep, there was something else nagging at him, worrying away like a dog with a bone, trying to break free. He wanted to ignore it, to remain stubbornly livid, but it was too persistent. It came at him again and again through the interminable hours as he sat and stared blankly at the small screen above his head.

A short time before he arrived at Heathrow, he finally couldn't take it any more. He let the realisation descend on him. There was a distinct possibility that Amy had never wanted him to leave at all, that she had given him a get-out; she had made it easier for him to do what, secretly, he'd been wanting to do all along, ever since the moment he knew she'd been hurt. And, without comprehending what he was doing, he had taken the chance, and run away, without even thinking of what this meant for them long term. He had deserted her, and now all he wanted to do was to take it all back, to start again, and just to be there for her whether he got it right or wrong.

But he had an awful, gnawing feeling that ate away at him as the plane began to descend. It was the understanding that now he couldn't go back. It was too late.

50

Mark's heart was heavy as he headed back towards London through the drizzling gloom, peering hard through the windscreen at endless tail-lights, trying not to let tiredness overtake him too much.

Chloe didn't deserve this. Whenever he thought of her he recalled her woebegone face of just a few hours ago. She'd been trying hard to talk to him all week, and he had been avoiding her, as he didn't want to come right out with it.

Because Henry's words had not stopped booming in his ears.

He had made his way home from Chloe's the previous Sunday with a heavy heart, to a cataclysm of repercussions before he even had a chance to get changed out of his tux. Henry had collared him the moment he walked in the door, and then ranted and raved about his behaviour, shouting so loud that Mark's mother had taken the dog on a long walk just to get away from them.

'You will never be a great lawyer if you can behave like that . . .'

'You have disgraced yourself, and the firm . . .'

'You have made a laughing stock of me . . .'

'You need to pull your socks up quick smart, my boy, or you'll be out on your ear.'

At first Mark said, 'It was one silly lapse in judgement, Dad, not the end of the world. Just one drink too many.' But his father had continued.

'Your work has been going downhill lately . . .'

'Everyone has noticed. I've had to excuse you . . .'

'You can't keep up . . .'

'This isn't what we took you on for. Everyone has expectations of you . . .'

And then:

'Ever since you and Chloe began this little *affair* . . .'

'What?' Mark was appalled. 'I barely see Chloe at work, and she hardly forced the drink down me last night. It was my error.' A brief image of Risto and Chloe dancing flashed before him and he grimaced.

'I've seen you,' Henry shouted. 'Eating together in the office, always at each other's door. It's a distraction. It's leading you down the wrong path.'

Mark was floundering in the unremitting torrent of antagonism coming from his father. 'That's ridiculous, Dad,' he said without really thinking.

'How dare you,' Henry had replied, further incensed. 'Let me tell you, Mark, you need to choose – Chloe or your career. You're young, only just starting – there's plenty of time for all that later. If you let yourself get distracted now, you'll never make the top grade, never have a chance of going for the big jobs, never fulfil your potential – and all because of some little romance that probably won't even last the distance.'

Mark couldn't help himself. He began to listen. And Henry pressed on, with points about how it was best for both of them, Chloe too, as they could always pick things up later if they still felt the same. How Chloe didn't seem that serious anyway – just look at the way she'd flirted with Risto last night, without even a care for Mark. How Chloe wasn't right for Mark; he needed a stronger, less emotional woman. How Chloe's work was suffering – the partners were voicing concerns – if she didn't knuckle down, there might be serious repercussions for her too.

'Finish it now,' he urged. 'Before either of you gets too involved.'

We're already too involved, Mark had wanted to say at first, thinking of Chloe's sweet sleeping form of just a few hours before. But the image had wavered in the face of his father's onslaught, and by the time Henry had finished making his case, Mark had been utterly swayed. Only much later, too much later, would he look back at it as a supreme display of persuasive talent from the most wily of legal minds.

51

Amy was discharged from the hospital the day after Alex had stormed out of her room. He hadn't come back.

He will come back, she thought, as the nurses helped her dress, manoeuvring her aching limbs into her clothes; as they put her things together; as her dad hefted her backpack over his shoulder, and her mum linked arms with her; as they thanked the medical staff and headed slowly towards the exit. She looked around for him in the car park, at the sides of the road as the taxi journeyed along, in the cavernous airport check-in area, before the milling people made her feel faint and she had to sit down. But it seemed he had abandoned her. And by the time the plane lifted into the air her upset had turned to numb dismay, and she wasn't sure if she had ever really known him at all.

52

Christmas had been going so well. Chloe's mother had put out the turkey and a raft of vegetables with a flourish, and the four of them had delved in.

Charlie poured them all sparkling wine.

'Cheers,' Chloe said, lifting her glass and looking round at them.

They all echoed her, and then Anthony had given Chloe a searching look. With a sinking heart she realised what was coming, but before she could do more than give a swift shake of her head, he had continued, 'I have an announcement to make.'

'Oh?' Margaret spoke for them all, sounding intrigued.

'I've put my course on hold, and I'm moving to America!' Anthony grinned.

There was silence.

Then, 'How nice for you,' Margaret murmured, stabbing her fork into a sprout and jabbing it into her mouth.

'What?' Anthony said, half-laughing, looking round at them all.

Charlie looked irritated, even though he had made it a rule never to get involved in disputes with Margaret's children. Life was easier that way.

Chloe kept her head down.

Margaret was not to be mollified, however, and after a pause said, 'Anthony, do you think we don't know why you're going to America?'

'Mum, I really regret not having a gap year, and Tommy is over there at the moment working, so it's free digs – the chance of a lifetime. I'm so lucky having a US passport, and I want to see the world while I'm young.'

'I don't believe you,' Margaret retorted.

'What?'

'You're going to find your father.'

'Well, I might make some enquiries while I'm over there. What's the harm, Mum, honestly? You've had me completely to yourself so far, you can hardly begrudge sharing a bit now.'

And then, to everyone's surprise, Charlie stood up, knocking his chair back as he did so.

'You ungrateful little tyke,' he said. 'Your mum had bloody good reasons for leaving that man, and you should be thanking her every day, not making her life a bloody misery –'

'Charlie . . .' Margaret put out a hand to try to calm him.

'No, Mum, it's okay,' Anthony said, glaring at Charlie. 'I think I should leave.' And he pushed back his chair roughly, scraping it against the floor tiles, then stormed out of the room, slamming the door behind him.

Margaret immediately burst into tears and went into a torrent of speech, with Charlie trying to soothe her. Chloe sighed, looked at her still-full plate of delicious food, and slowly got up to find her brother.

Anthony was in his room, angrily throwing things into a bag.

'I can't believe you,' he hissed when he saw her at the door.

'What?!'

'Just sitting there. Can't you have an opinion? He's your dad too.'

Chloe was incensed. 'I do have an opinion. I agree with Mum. I TRUST Mum.'

Anthony gave a bitter laugh and shook his head. 'Well, thanks a lot. I see that becoming a lawyer has made you able to see only one side of the story.'

'Ant, you're behaving like a little boy.'

'Oh, and you're so grown up, aren't you, you snooty bitch.'

'Ant! For god's sake.'

Anthony pushed past her. 'Don't worry, I'm leaving.' He ran down the stairs, calling out a sarcastic 'Happy Christmas' behind him, then was out the front door. Chloe heard his car rev up and spin away down the drive a moment later.

She went downstairs to find Charlie and Margaret eating silently, Margaret's face streaked with tears. Chloe tucked mechanically into her own meal, now tepid and unappetising. She didn't know what to say to either of them, and so the only sound to accompany their Christmas lunch was the ticking of the cuckoo clock on the wall, and the distant sounds of carols coming from Charlie's permanently playing TV in the next room.

53

It had been a long week since Alex had got home. Christmas had passed excruciatingly slowly, his parents and Jamie tiptoeing around him, realising something was wrong but not knowing exactly what. Until tonight.

His mother found him alone in the kitchen, snacking on biscuits after the others had gone to bed. She sat down next to him.

'Alex?' she began, reaching for his hand.

He wanted to snatch it back, but didn't want to hurt her, and although his hand felt uncomfortable on the table he focused his energies on keeping it there.

'What's happened?' she asked gently.

The indefinable soothing quality in his mother's voice broke him, and he began to sob softly into his hands.

'Oh my darling,' his mother crooned, moving her chair next to his, and pulling him into her body to cradle his head against her as though he were just a small child.

The whole story tumbled out. By the end of it, Alex was pacing the kitchen, and his mother was watching him, horrified, tears in her own eyes.

'Oh, Alex, why on earth have you kept this to yourself for so long?'

'I didn't want to burden you.'

As he said it he found that was partly it, but perhaps it was also that he had thought he could hide from it by not telling people. How ridiculous that suddenly seemed.

'Alex, that's crazy, we're your family. We're here to share your load; to help you.'

It was as though she knew what he was thinking – that he never wanted to see her crushed again like she was after the onset of Jamie's schizophrenia. He wanted to protect her.

'We go through good and bad *together*,' she added firmly. 'That's the most important thing. Oh Amy, the poor thing. It's just beyond words.'

'I know.' Alex sat down, feeling an enormous sense of relief at finally being able to talk things through with someone. He ran his hands across his face to try to stave off the exhaustion that seemed to hit him like a blow. He looked at his mother. 'So, what should I do?'

Alex's father was waiting by the door the next morning. He had told his mother he would get the train, but she'd insisted that his dad drive him, and wouldn't brook any argument. He had given in, even though he wasn't sure what he and his father would find to talk about on the long drive.

But, of course, this was his dad. He patted Alex's back as they headed out the door, then for the entire journey proceeded to talk about whether he should sell his shares, whether they should unplug everything in the house before midnight on New Year's Eve in case the Millennium bug struck . . . and that they should make sure all their files were backed up . . . and they should know exactly what was in their accounts . . . He was like a droning mosquito in Alex's ear as he stared out the window, biting down the impulse to tell him to shut up – because they were never that impolite in their family.

It was less than an hour from their door to Amy's. Geoff parked the car on the road, and said, 'I'll wait here for you. Doesn't matter how long,' and nodded towards the Sunday paper in the back.

'Thanks,' Alex replied, then got out and headed up the path.

At the door, he took a deep breath, lifted his hand and knocked.

It didn't take long for Ray to answer.

'Hello, Ray. I'm sorry just to turn up like this, but I wondered how Amy is doing.'

Alex was immediately encouraged as he spoke. He had expected Ray's face to be dark with anger, but he seemed almost friendly.

'Alex, hello. Amy's doing . . . okay. She's getting a little better every day.'

He made no move to invite Alex in, so Alex had to ask, 'May I see her?'

Ray paused, stared down, took a breath, and looked up

240

steadfastly into Alex's eyes. 'She's asked me to let you know that she doesn't want to see you at the moment. I'm sorry, pal. Just give her a bit of time, eh.'

Frustration expanded in Alex's chest. 'Look, Ray, I don't want to be shut out. I want to support her.'

'I know,' he said, coming outside and closing the door behind him. 'But I think the best way to do that at the moment is to give her some space.'

And then Alex lost it. 'AMY,' he yelled up towards the windows. 'AMY, PLEASE, LET ME IN.'

'Alex,' Ray barked, his eyes going to the neighbours' houses, 'there's no need . . .'

Alex ignored him. 'AMY,' he shouted, wandering across their front garden, shouting up to blank-faced windows. 'I'LL KEEP ON SHOUTING TILL YOU LET ME IN.'

Ray lost his patience and marched up to Alex, grabbing his arm. 'Listen, son,' he hissed, 'if you won't go away and keep making a scene, I'll call the police.'

Alex vaguely heard a car door slam as he pushed Ray away harshly and watched him stumble. Barely registering how shocked and angry Amy's dad looked, he marched towards the front door, but before he could get there a pair of strong arms grabbed him from behind, hauling him back and holding him still.

'Just stop and think for a minute, Al,' his dad said. 'Don't make it any worse.'

Alex shrugged him off, but his words were registering, and the anger was passing into upset before he could hold on to it. Distress weakened him, and he put his hand up to his face as his eyes blurred, trying to stifle the sob.

'Come on,' his father said. Geoff turned around to Ray, who was still standing in the garden, looking grim. 'I'm so sorry about everything, it's just that Alex is very upset. I'm sure he and Amy can get in touch when a bit of time has passed.'

'Why won't you just let me see her?' Alex implored Ray as his dad tried to drag him back to the car.

Ray looked at him sadly. 'She doesn't want to see you, mate,' he said softly. And his face was guileless.

Alex closed his eyes, trying to get a grip on himself. He opened them and took one last beseeching look at the door and windows. They all stared back, impassive, empty, then he thought he saw a shadow pass behind one at the front and his heart gave a painful throb.

She must have heard him, he thought. If she wanted to, she would come out. Ray must be telling the truth.

He was glad he had written the letter now, though he'd hoped it wouldn't be needed. He reached into his pocket and passed it to Ray. '*Please*,' he said, 'give her this.'

Ray looked at it, then at Alex, and nodded.

54

When her father had gone out through the door, Amy had walked quietly into the front room and listened; although she could have stood in the back garden and still heard Alex's pleading voice.

But her father was right. She couldn't face him.

When she had been in hospital, she'd thought it might be different when she left. When they had come home, she thought she might feel comforted by her childhood surrounds. She was sure her mother and father had been hoping this too.

But every day was getting a little worse. Each time she went to sleep she hoped that during the night she would be able somehow to escape what had happened, and wake up feeling a little better – and every time she woke up, as she came to consciousness a black cloud floated quickly down to smother her, so she had to leap out of bed and away from it just to avoid screaming.

She didn't want to see anyone. She didn't want to go any-where. She didn't want to eat. She didn't want to wake up in the mornings.

A counsellor had been around to the house twice since they had got home. Both times she had talked to Amy through her locked bedroom door.

Her Christmas presents were still unopened. She had told her mum she'd open them when she felt a bit better. She knew she wouldn't be able to summon up the effort to look thankful at the moment, however lovely they were.

Every day she stood in the shower for what seemed like hours. Although her shoulder was still strapped up, most of her bruises had evolved from garish purple to pastel greens and yellows. She was amazed at her body's capacity to heal despite the predations of her mind.

She looked at the letter on her bed, and even though each time she read it she felt more lost, she picked it up again.

Amy,

I'm so sorry. I wish so much that I had stayed with you in the hospital that day, and come home with you. I want to support you, and if that means giving you space then so be it. But be sure of this, Amy: you are the one for me, and I promise I will wait for you, however long it takes. And I also promise that I will support you in any and every way to help you through this; to help you be happy again.

There's so much more to say, but I'll wait till I can do that in person.

I love you.

Al

This time, reading Alex's words gave her courage. For she had made a decision.

First, she needed to talk to her dad.

She picked her moment, when her mother had gone to bed.

'Dad?' she began.

He quickly put down his book. It had been rare for her to initiate conversation in the past few weeks, and each time she did people jumped to attention.

'I need to go away,' she told him.

'Well, we can take a holiday . . .' he began immediately, but she held her hand up.

'Alone, Dad.'

Her dad opened his mouth straight away to protest, but was then lost for words, so Amy continued.

'I just need to get away for a little while, on my own. I know you're all trying to help, but it's making it worse. I need to sort myself out with some space away from everyone, or I'm going to go mad.'

'Amy, I know you might feel like that, but you can't. You're not thinking rationally at the moment, love. Just let us look after you.'

'No, Dad,' she cried, trying to keep her voice low enough that her mother wouldn't hear. 'You don't get it. How can you? You've never been in this position, for god's sake. You have no idea.' And then she played her trump card. 'If you don't let me go, you might well come in one morning and find me hanging from the ceiling.'

'Amy!' Her father looked horrified at her words. 'Don't

say that, love. Look, it's early days, we'll sort something out. Tomorrow we'll get that lady round again, you need to talk to her . . .'

'Dad, you're not listening,' she told him. 'Unless you tie me up and lock me in, I'm going. This is what I have to do.'

'No, Amy, you're not,' he said.

She stormed out, and headed up the stairs, and a few seconds later he was behind her. 'Look, get a good night's rest, and we'll talk about this in the morning.'

'Okay,' she said, knowing all conversation was pointless.

She waited till four a.m. She figured that after what she had said her dad would be paranoid about her leaving, so he wouldn't get to sleep for a while. She wasn't wrong. Even though the house was quiet and dark, the keys to the front and back doors were all missing, even the ones she'd put in her bag in the hall.

She left two notes on the kitchen table. Then she climbed out of the kitchen window, her shoulder throbbing, pulling her small bag through with her. Just a few clothes, her passport and bank cards, Alex's letter and Bug-Eye. She had no idea where she was going; but she knew she needed to go – her sanity depended on it.

As she moved through the back garden she hesitated, then diverted her course for a moment. Her eyes were adjusting to the dark, and the moon was three-quarters full, so she could recognise the outline of the little garden quite clearly. She could still remember the first time she had seen it, when she was six years old, on a night like this. Her dad had brought her here in her pyjamas, and as they had drawn close, she could see a few tiny lights near the ground. She had blinked sleepily, trying to make out where they were coming from, though the light only served to cast all about it in shadow. It was only when they'd been less than a metre away from treading upon those little beacons in the darkness that the wondrous moment of clarity had occurred. There, within an enormous willow-woven basket, was a tiny, exquisitely crafted garden, perfect in every detail, from its minute thicket of trees in one corner, to its flower-lined paths and a small wishing well in the very centre. On another grassy knoll was a tiny bird table and bird bath, each less than the size of a postage stamp. 'So the fairies can come and visit,' her father had told her.

As she thought back to the joy she had felt then, she wanted to sit down and weep, but instead she pulled the little wishing well out of the centre, and put it in her bag. A talisman to ensure that she was linked to home. To her parents. To her dad. She didn't know why she felt as if she needed it. She didn't imagine that she was going away for long, just for a short time while she got herself together.

Then she headed up the side path, taking care that the gate clicked softly, and soon she was walking along the road, away from home. She had made her escape.

55

The pub was dark, and full of nooks and crannies that made it hard to find people. Mark was hoping he'd done the right thing in coming. He was never all that enthusiastic about socialising with work colleagues, but Susan was nice enough, and her husband, Terry, was a banker who was often prepared to pass on invaluable advice on shares, and talked of little else, so Mark knew at least there would be someone to listen to. He felt he should make an effort to be sociable for such a significant New Year's Eve.

It looked like half the office had turned up – minus David and Neil and his father, of course, who he knew for a fact were all attending a well-known barrister's dinner party tonight and toasting the Millennium with sherries and glasses of Cristal. He was a bit dismayed to see that some of the secretaries were also here. Mark didn't think it was a great idea to fraternise with subordinates, it made it more difficult at work, but Susan had always been a soft touch with everyone, bosses and cleaners alike.

He waved his hellos to people and got a drink. By the time he sat down, the only space available was next to Charlotte, who seemed quite tipsy already as she leaned over him and slurred hello, giving him an expansive view of her considerable cleavage in a low-cut sparkly top. Then Risto joined him by pulling a chair up to his crowded booth, and they tried to make small talk over the din of chatter.

Mark had half an eye out for Chloe, but didn't think she was coming – he had heard her mention to Susan that her brother had invited her to a party, so she probably wouldn't make it. Yet part of him was hoping she would turn up.

He did feel badly about avoiding her. He could tell she was confused, but he didn't know what to say; and he felt that if he spent too long in her company, he might succumb to her sweet charm and end up back at square one. And his father was right. They were still young; there was so much time ahead for all that; but only one chance to send his career hurtling skywards and set himself up for life. He didn't just want to be a run-of-the-mill solicitor – he wanted accolades, mentions in parliament, everything. That's why he'd stayed behind in the office to offer sincere apologies to both David and Neil, and to promise that he would never let them down again.

Yet, he missed her. He'd wanted to contact her on Christmas Day, at least, but he knew that any gesture he made might be seen as reconciliatory, which would start them down the wrong path once more.

Charlotte was patting him on the knee and trying to

tell him something. He smiled and played along, though he couldn't really make out what she was saying. She leaned closer to him, and her hand slid a little higher up his leg. Mark turned to look at Risto, but he'd moved off to the bar and become embroiled in a discussion there. Everyone else in their booth was in deep conversation.

Mark thought about moving her hand off his leg, but was momentarily stunned by the vast cleavage positioned right under his nose, pushing against his chest. As her hand reached almost up to his groin, which was stirring despite his best intentions, he finally heard her as she slurred 'handsome' against his cheek, and then her face was blurrily in front of his, her breath saturated with wine, and to his surprise she leaned forward and kissed him.

56

Chloe was not having a good New Year's. She had popped in to see some friends earlier on during the night, then headed to Anthony's Millennium bash, which he'd been going on about for at least six months, and which she'd originally planned to invite Mark to, before he had stopped speaking to her. Over Christmas she had decided she needed to forget about Mark, but even having come to this decision she couldn't dispel the hurt she was feeling at things ending so abruptly, and without Mark having the good grace at least to explain where they stood.

On arriving at the party she'd found out Mark wasn't the only one blanking her. After a cursory hello, Anthony had proceeded purposefully to ignore her, which had become quite embarrassing in front of his friends, who tried to make small talk with her for a while, their eyes glancing over her shoulders as other people came into the room, unsubtly looking for their getaway. She was put out, to say the least. If anything, she shouldn't be speaking to Anthony after what he'd done.

After an hour of this, Chloe had had enough and stalked out. But she didn't want to be at home alone for the Millennium, particularly as both her housemates had paid to go to swanky dos, and would be full of it when they got in. She decided she might as well show her face at Susan's bash, as she was now much closer to that than anywhere else. It began to rain as she made her way there, so she ran along the pavement in the gloom, trying to dodge all the swaying, merry people calling out their New Year's greetings to anyone around, and pushed her way into the packed pub. It was hard to see anyone, but she finally spotted Risto in conversation at the bar. He raised his eyebrows and smiled at her, using his thumb to point behind him as he carried on his discussion.

She made her way over and then stopped in her tracks.

She'd thought New Year's Eve couldn't get any worse, but this topped it off.

Right in front of her was Mark, his lips locked with Charlotte's.

In a daze, Chloe turned away immediately, but before she could make her escape she heard someone say, 'Hey, Chloe!' from behind her.

She swung round again awkwardly and waved hello to the people at the table, now looking at her, then at Mark and Charlotte, who were both staring at her. Charlotte was smiling like she hadn't a clue, and Mark looked as shocked as she'd ever seen him.

'Chloe,' said a voice behind her. She turned. It was Risto.

'Can I get you a drink?' he asked.

She nodded, trying not to show him how upset she was, and he ushered her towards the bar. She moved automatically as he said, 'I saw what just happened. Do you want me to take you home?'

She just nodded again and let him lead her outside.

57

Alex was just about to go out the front door with Jamie when he saw Ray coming up the drive.

'Come on, Al, let's go,' Jamie said. He had decided he didn't like Ray after hearing snippets of what had been going on.

'No, Jamie, I'll just be a minute,' Alex answered, alarmed.

'But, Al, I really want to –'

'Just wait inside for a sec,' Alex said, shoving his brother back through the door.

His heart thudded as he saw Ray's stricken face. 'Oh my god, what is it?' he asked.

'She's okay . . . I think,' the older man said sadly. 'It's just I've made a terrible mistake.'

Alex let him in, and he came into the lounge, said a subdued hello to Alex's mother and father, and told the whole family the story.

Amy had snuck out. She was gone. Tess was furious with him for not taking Amy more seriously when she had confided in him, for allowing it to happen.

Alex's mother pointed out that there was little he could have done other than physically restraining her, and Ray nodded sadly. 'I know, but still . . . looking back, I should have realised how determined she was. I just never thought she'd go that night . . .'

He looked at Alex. 'I came to see if you've heard anything from her.'

'I'm sorry.' Alex shook his head. *Oh, Amy*, he thought, *why haven't you been in touch? Why are you pushing us all away?*

'Have you talked to the police?' Alex's father asked.

'Yes,' Ray nodded. 'They're sympathetic, but say that often there's nothing much they can do. She's an adult, entitled to exercise her own free will; she's never had any mental health issues before, even though she's obviously been through something truly terrible . . . They can do some checking, but once we said we thought Amy might have gone overseas they weren't very optimistic about locating her.'

He got up to leave. He looked broken. 'Anyway, I won't keep you. You've probably got things to be doing tonight. I just wanted to give you this.' He held a piece of paper out to Alex, who took it, his heart thumping. 'Just let me know, will you, if she . . .' Ray added, looking at Alex. 'Keep in touch.'

Alex nodded. 'Of course.' He watched as his mum and dad said polite goodbyes, the paper scratchy in his hand, then saw Ray out to the door.

Ray turned at the doorway. 'Alex,' he said. 'I'm sorry if I was a bit harsh on you . . . in the hospital. I wasn't thinking very clearly, and I . . .'

Alex didn't know what came over him, but as Ray stood there on the doorstep he moved forward and patted him on the shoulders in an awkward semi-hug. 'I understand,' he said, pulling back quickly for fear of overstepping the mark, but Ray was smiling sadly at him.

Amy's father turned to go. 'Ray,' Alex called.

Ray swung around.

'Did she really not want to see me last week, or was that just you?' he asked.

Ray shook his head. 'I'm sorry, Alex. She said she didn't, but we know she's not thinking straight, don't we?'

Alex nodded, and Ray turned to go.

Jamie appeared behind him. 'Happy New Year,' he called to Ray's retreating back.

Ray raised a hand in acknowledgement, but didn't turn round.

'Come on, Al,' Jamie said once Ray had gone. 'Let's go. I'm desperate for a pint.'

58

The little street was dark, though there were lights shining intermittently from the few restaurants dotted about the place. Behind the street, the sea lapped gently at the narrow shoreline, a rhythmic watery lullaby you could only hear between gaps in traffic noise and voices.

This seaside Caribbean village felt incredibly peaceful. And that's why Amy was here.

She did feel calmer, being away. And she felt sad about that, but it was so much easier, saying hello to strangers who knew nothing of her; being around people who didn't care a jot, rather than the slow, constricting, suffocating love from those she had left behind. She wasn't thinking long term, just trying to put one foot in front of another, get through the next hour, the next day. Seeing if she could heal from the inside as well as out, now the bruises had faded.

Yet she couldn't help but make the phone calls earlier. It was New Year's Eve, the Millennium, after all.

'Amy, thank god,' her mother had cried down the phone. 'Where are you?'

'I'm okay, Mum. I'm just letting you know I'm okay.'

'Come home, Amy, it's better for you here.'

'No, it's not.'

'Your dad will be so sorry he's missed you. He's just popped out.'

'That's okay. Tell him I love him. I love you both.'

Her mother was sobbing down the phone. It was frightening. She rarely lost control like this.

'Amy, you have to promise me one thing *right now*.'

'Mum, I –'

'PROMISE ME you'll do no harm to yourself. If anything happened to you . . . well, your father and I, we would die too – do you UNDERSTAND, Amy?' she said fiercely.

'Yes,' she replied.

'Say you promise.'

'Okay, I promise,' Amy agreed, as yet unclear about the implications of this.

'Right.' Her mother sounded a bit calmer. 'I want you to check in with us every day.'

'Mum, that's not realistic.'

'Every day,' she asserted.

'Mum, I can't,' Amy said. 'Look, I'll do it every week, okay? Even then, my money . . .'

'Do you have your bank card?' her mother asked.

'Yes.'

'Then we'll put money in your account, okay?'

'Mum, I –'

'Amy, the money will be there. Now, please tell me where you are.'

But she knew she couldn't. Her father would be on the next plane, looking for her. 'I'm sorry, Mum. I can't. Please understand. I just called to say Happy New Year.'

Her mother had begun to cry again. 'We love you, Amy.'

'I love you too, both of you,' Amy told her. She couldn't take any more, though. 'I have to go,' she said. And hung up.

Then she dialled the other number, quickly, before she could think too much.

His mum answered.

'Is Alex there, please?' she whispered.

There was a weighty pause. 'I'm so sorry, Amy love, he isn't,' his mum said in a tremulous voice that told Amy she knew everything. 'I can go and get him, though – can you ring back in twenty minutes? Or he can ring you?'

'No, no, it's okay,' she said quickly. She knew where Alex was. She had been with him last year, in his local, where all his mates gathered to see in the New Year. She felt glad he was following the routine. It meant he was getting on with things. He was okay without her. He really was. 'Please don't tell him I called. Happy New Year,' she said, then hung up before his mother had a chance to say more.

59

Mark had stormed out of the pub to try to find Chloe. But she'd already gone. With Risto, by the look of it. He was about to go inside again when Charlotte came flying through the door.

'Mark, there you are!' she cried happily.

He smiled reluctantly and made a move to step around her.

'Where are you going?' she pouted. 'I thought you might take me home, for a little Millennium celebration of our own,' she intoned, as seductively as she could while obviously trying hard to balance.

He looked her up and down. She was wearing a low-cut dark blue sparkly top with tight jeans and high heels. She looked fantastic.

She was asking him to take her home.

He had a choice. Find Chloe. Continue down that

path, which made him feel so alarmed as his mind oscil-
lated between Chloe's confused face and his father's furious
expression. Find Chloe. Who, after all, had gone with Risto.

Or he could give it up and take Charlotte home. And,
undoubtedly, other girls like Charlotte in the future.

'Come on, then,' he said. 'Where do you live?'

As they moved off, there was a chorus of voices as the
countdown began in the pub behind them.

60

Risto dragged Chloe through the crowds in the small square near her flat. As they moved along, people began to chant. 'Ten . . . nine . . .'

They stopped instinctively and joined in.

'. . . two . . . one . . . HAPPY NEW YEAR!'

'Happy Millennium.' Risto smiled at Chloe as people hugged and kissed and danced around them. He leaned forward and kissed her quickly and softly on the mouth, politely but with a definite promise. And to Chloe's surprise as he caught her off-guard, for just a moment the churning thoughts of Mark disappeared as she leaned into him.

61

The pub was a seething, rolling mass of drunken, sweaty bodies overbalancing as they revelled in the first seconds of a new year. A new century. A new millennium.

Alex was trying his best to pretend to join in as his mates danced round him, whooping and cheering. He could feel the note in his pocket; he'd memorised it already:

Al,
Thank you for your message. I understand this is difficult for everybody, not just me, but I need to get away for a while, to sort myself out. When I get back I will come to you.

I love you.
Amy

Where was she? he wondered. He wholeheartedly wished he were with her, not here in this claustrophobic press of people.

He forced himself out of his distraction as his mum and dad arrived, and he watched them make their way over.

'Happy New Year, love,' Alex's mum said, hugging him. She pulled away from him, and looked at him with a strange expression, as though debating something.

'What?' He attempted a quizzical smile.

She paused, then the moment passed. 'Nothing. Never mind.' She smiled too and hugged Alex again, and his father leaned over and handed him another pint as the party went on.

62

The only way to tell the New Year had come was a truck with lots of young boys leaning over the sides, swinging their shirts and yelling, 'Happy New Year'.

There were a few other people in the restaurant, mostly couples or groups, and everyone was pretty quiet. However, there was one woman on her own with a shock of curly hair and kind eyes, wearing the baggy shirt and trousers combo that was almost a traveller's uniform. As the van full of screeching lads went past, followed by a car with a waving Santa perched on top, she came over.

'May I?' She indicated the empty seat.

Amy recoiled at first, but then suddenly craved company. She glanced at the other people in the bar. They weren't going anywhere. And this woman didn't look like she'd follow her, or attack her once she'd befriended her. Besides, Amy decided, she didn't want to be watching over her shoulder all the time. And she could always move on. Now she was free to run away whenever she chose.

She wished she could be someone else; someone completely different.

Maybe that was the answer.

Immediately a person floated into her mind. The sunniest person at school. The girl everyone loved, who didn't seem to have a care in the world. Who floated through life, smiling. What was her name?

The woman was looking at her curiously, still waiting for an answer.

'Sorry.' Amy shook her head and gave a small smile. 'Of course.' She gestured to the seat. 'Happy New Year.'

'Same to you.' The woman sat down. 'Amazing, isn't it – the Millennium's arrived in most parts of the world now, and so far nothing terrible seems to have happened. So much time spent putting the fear of god into people, and it nearly always amounts to nothing.' She leaned across the table and held out her hand to shake. 'I'm Sophie.'

Slowly, Amy lifted her arm and tentatively grasped the other woman's fingers.

'Julia,' she replied.

part three
letting go

63

london
november 2009

Chloe walked through the front door and down the hall-way, peering into the living room on her way to the kitchen. Everything was neat and tidy, and very still. It felt as though the house were holding its breath.

She was unnerved by the quiet. Hearing a small noise behind her, she swung around.

Alex was standing there. 'We need to talk, Chlo.'

'Has she gone?' Her voice came out quiet and hoarse, and sinisterly calm.

'Yes.'

'For good?'

Alex paused a fraction too long. And Chloe's frayed temper finally snapped.

'Alex, you'd better start talking, and fast,' she shouted at him.

Alex came towards her and tried to put his hand on her arm. 'Chloe . . .'

She shook him off, walked a few paces, turned back and yelled, 'Just *tell* me, for god's sake – I can't bear all . . . this.' She threw her hands in the air. 'If you're having some kind of affair, just bloody well admit it.'

'No! Chloe, look at me. Look at me, please! I'm not having an affair. *I'm not having an affair* . . .' He strode across and grabbed her by the shoulders, shaking her slightly, trying to force the truth into her. She looked in his eyes and saw nothing except an entreaty for her to believe him. She felt a little calmer.

'So then, what's going on?' she asked.

'We were together for a couple of years, a long time ago,' Alex answered, not slackening his grip. She could feel the warmth of his breath on her face with each word he spoke. 'We met at university, and then went travelling. And while we were in Australia she got attacked and raped and nearly killed. And after that, we fell apart.'

'What?' Chloe couldn't take it in. She watched as Alex spoke; every muscle of his body seemed taut with tension.

'When we came home, she disappeared. She said she was only going away for a little while, but she never came back. I never saw her again until Thursday night – that's why I was so shocked. That's why this is all so awful and weird.'

Chloe just looked at him, her mind a jumble of incoherent, half-formed thoughts. How could she have ever prepared for this?

In a few days it felt as if her whole world had changed.

'Chloe?' Alex's voice was alarmed.

She stared at him blankly, then was jolted out of her

stupor on seeing the tears in his eyes. They were still so close, his hands on her arms, his face inches from hers.

'So you were a couple for how long?'

'Two years.'

Two years, Chloe thought. She and Alex had been together only a little longer than that.

'And you loved her?'

Alex sighed and closed his eyes for a moment as he said, 'Yes, I did.' She watched his face as he looked at her again, his intense dark eyes boring into hers. 'But it was a long time ago now, Chloe. Way before you and I ever met.'

'So you don't love her any more?'

Why had she asked that, when she was so close to his face she couldn't fail to gauge his reaction. He looked as though she had struck him.

There wasn't much of a pause before he tried to speak, but it was enough. She let out a cry and pushed him away, running out of the kitchen, down the hallway and up the stairs. She could hear him chasing her.

'No, Chloe, no, you've got it wrong. Don't do this, please . . .'

She swung around at the top of the stairs as he took them two at a time to try to reach her. '*Me* do this?' she screamed. She turned on her heel before he could touch her and strode into the bedroom, pulling open the closet and beginning to throw random items of clothing onto the bed.

'Chloe,' Alex cried as he came into the room. 'What are you doing? Come on, we need to keep talking about this.'

'I can't, Alex,' she said, as tears began to stream down her face. 'I just need some space.'

Alex came around the bed fast, and tried to pull her to him. He caught her arm but she wrenched herself away, her free hand groping along the dresser and grabbing things, hurling them onto the bed.

'Don't go, Chloe,' he said, his voice low and husky with emotion. 'Please. This thing happened so long ago – and I'm so sorry you've been caught up in it like this. But it doesn't change you and me at all. I love you, Chloe. Don't go.' He stood there watching her sadly, his eyes moist.

'Alex, I think the only way I can cope with this is if I know that it's over, that you're never going to see her again. Can you do that?'

Alex shook his head. 'Chloe, please try to understand. I don't want a relationship with her, of course I don't – I'm not in love with her like that any more, I'm in love with *you*. But there's a history, and a long time ago I made promises, to her and to myself –'

'You made promises?' Chloe interrupted, her voice rising again. 'What about the promises you made to me, Alex?'

'Chloe –'

She marched out of the bedroom and along the landing, grabbing a suitcase from a cupboard there. She carried it back to the room and began to throw things into it, not making any attempt to pack them properly.

Alex watched her for a minute, then came forward, and said, 'Chloe, stop.'

She paused and looked at him. His face was wretched.

'You don't have to go. I'll go, until we've both calmed down enough to talk,' he said, gently taking her things out of the case and laying them on the bed.

She watched him, but suddenly felt too tired to argue. She didn't have a clue where she would have gone anyway.

'I'll wait downstairs,' she said, and walked out.

She stood by the table in the kitchen for ten minutes, hardly aware of her surroundings. She heard a noise in the hallway and mechanically walked out to look.

Alex was there with a suitcase next to him. He picked up a bag and turned back to her.

Beyond all reason, she was suddenly desperate for him to stay. But as they looked at one another, in that moment she couldn't find her voice.

And then he was through the doorway, and as he turned back again, before he could say anything she had jumped forward and slammed it behind him.

She slid down the wooden panel of the door into a heap on the floor, crying and crying, as if she would never be rid of the tears that poured from her. She hugged her stomach, half-glad of the secret she still carried and half-imagining dramatic scenes that might make Alex rush back to her – blood pouring from her traumatised body, an ambulance taking her to hospital, Alex's guilt-ridden face as he sat by the bed and learned of the baby he'd almost had. That would serve him right.

When her tears eventually subsided, she sat still for a while, sniffing and rubbing her eyes. Eventually she turned around and pushed the letterbox open with her fingers, peering through the slit, praying he would still be there; but the rain-soaked path was empty and dark.

Is this it? she wondered. Is this the end of my marriage – sitting here in the hallway with mascara running down my face? Or is this just the beginning of something else – a difficult period, sure, but perhaps not an ending. She would give anything for someone to explain to her whereabouts down the proverbial line she and Alex were right now.

What had she been thinking of, that secrets could ever be benign? They were nothing of the kind – they were poisonous shards of glass that were trapped just below the skin, twisting and turning with every movement a person made, threatening to break through the surface.

Some dark thing began to rear up in her then, towards the surface of her consciousness. It was her mother, sitting like this against a doorway, and sobbing like she would never stop.

What had happened? It seemed she had pushed the memory down – although now something came to her – a darkened room she didn't want to look into. She forced the image away, fought it off until she was sure it was vanquished, made herself focus on Alex's ugly, buried secrets as she curled up on the floor.

There came a beeping sound from her pocket. She fumbled with the phone as she lifted it out, and looked at the screen. There was a text message.

> I WILL CALL YOU TOMORROW.
> TRUST IN ME. I LOVE YOU.
> I WILL COME BACK TO YOU.

64

For the rest of the week, Chloe's world seemed to revolve around one question:

'Have you told him yet?'

Mikaela had asked first, when she'd rung Chloe to see how she was and got more than she'd bargained for. Her mother had then outdone herself by ringing at least four times in one day, the same question bursting continuously from her lips. Chloe had almost ranted at her after a while, wanting to shout, 'How can I tell him about the baby if he isn't even bloody here?' but she didn't. While no one knew Alex had gone, she could still pretend this wasn't real, and avoid the awkward silences and pitying stares.

She'd made an exception for Mikaela. Her cousin had heard the quaver in her voice immediately, and once Chloe had started crying down the phone she couldn't seem to stop, so Mikaela had immediately insisted that Chloe came to stay. They had been holed up together for the past few days. Chloe brought home bad food for them both after work, and to start with they talked, then progressed to watching sitcom reruns while slating the perfect-looking actresses that swanned on and off the screen. It was an odd throwback to their teenage years, and initially Chloe had found comfort in that; then gradually it had begun to disturb her. She didn't want to go back to being one of the girls, sharing her broken heart and letting others help her to mend it. Her despair was something she couldn't even articulate, let alone allow others to pick over.

Tonight she would be going home. For a few days it had been a relief not to have to face the empty house, now devoid of its loving atmosphere; but Mikaela was away with work from today and Chloe had begun to miss some of her home comforts, not to mention clean clothes.

Alex had been persistently ringing her mobile, but she was still too hurt and confused to talk to him. When he'd tried her at the office, she had hung up as soon as Jana transferred the calls. She needed to clear her head first; she was scared she wouldn't be able to stop her mouth from spitting vile accusations and insults at him right now. He had left voicemails too, but she hadn't replayed them. She didn't want to hear his voice, so she deleted them instead.

This morning she'd already spoken briefly to her mother, who had been most affronted when Chloe had cancelled the next trip to the Lakes. As Chloe spoke she was aware of the irony – this was what Alex had been begging her to do for weeks, and it had taken his leaving to push her to it. Her mother spent the rest of the call making snide comments about how she hadn't realised she was such a burden to them. In response, Chloe had told her that now she was pregnant it might be more difficult to come quite as often, to which her mother had laughed and said, 'Don't be so dramatic, Chloe. It's not an illness, you know.'

As she tried to shake off that particular conversation, Chloe walked through the office doors in a daze, still absorbing the fact that she was further on in her pregnancy than she'd known, rubbing her stomach, unable to comprehend that a new life had taken a firm shape of its own in there before she'd even been aware of it, and that her husband still didn't know that he was going to be a dad.

As she walked out of the lift and past reception, she saw David Marchant striding towards her. With no time to avoid him, she turned and attempted a smile.

'Morning, Chloe.' David made no effort to hide the long look he took at his watch as he approached. 'Good to see you this morning. Don't forget you have a meeting with Neil at eleven. The Abbott case is looming large for us now. If you see Mark popping in at any stage this morning, be sure to pass the message on to him as well, won't you?'

'Yes, David.' Chloe sighed as she made her way towards her office. She tried to imagine the look on David's face when she told him she was four months pregnant. Normally it would have terrified her, but right then it made her almost laugh out loud. Great, she was becoming hysterical.

As she walked past the secretaries' pool, Jana noticed the smile on her face and gave her a shy, friendly hello. It took Chloe aback. Jana didn't often talk to her; in fact, Chloe didn't think the secretary liked her much. It hadn't bothered her overly, as she'd made a rule that her relationship with her secretary would be strictly business after what had happened with Charlotte. Spending a few years working with her former boyfriend's one-night stand hadn't been much fun.

She noticed Mark's office was dark, and the door was shut. She turned back to Jana.

'Where's Mark this morning?'

Jana shrugged. 'I don't know.'

'Has he got anything on?'

'Well, his diary's clear,' Jana replied.

'He hasn't phoned in?'

'No,' Jana said.

Mark was never later in for work than she was. What the hell was going on with everyone? Chloe wondered with tired exasperation. She usually felt she was a good judge of character, but she didn't seem to know anyone at all at the moment.

In her office she lifted her bag onto her desk and took out the number of the ultrasound unit at the hospital. She rang it and asked for an appointment, having to repeat herself when the lady couldn't hear her whispers. She watched the glass wall of her office closely, waiting to see either David or Neil appear there looking cross, but nothing happened.

They could fit her in tomorrow. Tomorrow she'd see their baby for the very first time. Alone.

As she sat down, she reluctantly looked at the in-trays piling up behind her with legal documents waiting to be drafted and letters needing to be written. The court applications to be made. Half-heartedly, she pulled a case file towards her, but instead of opening it she tried to re-examine just why she hadn't told Alex about the baby. If she had, surely he wouldn't have left. She thought back to the Lakes, and that fateful conversation when she'd only just found out herself. '*We're not ready for that yet*,' he'd said dismissively. If he hadn't said those words, would she have told him by now?

Possibly, as since then she had certainly been worried about how he would react. When the baby had been on the tip of her tongue so many times, one question kept recurring in her mind.

What if it changed *nothing*?

That was the core of it. And so their poor baby had become the trump card in its parents' marital problems before it was even born. She pushed away the thought that they would make terrible parents. But really, what chance did their child have when its mother was being torn apart by worry just as the very cells of its tiny, amorphous body were furiously dividing and multiplying and trying to get the act of creation right?

She tried to distract herself by going to Mark's office. The lights were still off. She frowned: it was past ten o'clock. She didn't think Mark had been late since the time they'd broken up. Her brief affair with Risto flitted through her head. Mark hadn't spoken to her much for quite a while back then, even though that relationship had fizzled out as quickly as it had started when Risto had had an unrefusable offer from a head-hunter.

She went back to her office and tried Mark's mobile. He answered straight away.

'You do know we've got a meeting about Abbott at

eleven, don't you? I saw David this morning and he didn't look too happy.'

Mark sighed. 'Fine, I'll try and get in. Jesus, Chloe, I'm hardly ever late like this, and now David is on my case.'

'Why are you late?'

Mark paused, then said, 'Look, you worry about your problems, and I'll look after mine. How is Alex, by the way?'

Chloe bristled. God he was infuriating. She took a deep breath. 'He's fine. I'll see you at eleven, then.' And she hung up before he could reply.

65

It had taken Alex three days of sleeping on his friend Justin's sofa to decide whether to go to see Amy again. It felt like betraying Chloe, but right now he couldn't find his wife to talk to her about it. She wasn't at the house, and she wouldn't take his calls. He had thought about going to her office, but it was such a public space that he knew this was a bad idea.

In the meantime he kept rereading the internet printouts he'd shown to Amy. Each time he did so he could feel his blood heating up rapidly.

Three men go on trial today accused of the kidnap, rape and murder of a Swanbourne waitress.

Michael Evan, 31, George Constantine, 34, and Clay Tate, 29, are accused of luring Vanessa Gordy, 24, from the Indian Ocean Bar in North Cottesloe. Her body was found two months later in bushland near Yanchep by a family walking their dog.

The case has attracted huge media attention in Perth, as Tate is a member of the prominent Tate Mining family.

All three men have pleaded not guilty.

The report was already weeks old. Each day it seemed more and more pressing that he come to a decision. If they didn't hurry, they might miss the trial altogether. This was their chance.

He had spent years after Amy had disappeared thinking of what those bastards had done to her, to him, to them. Not only that, but the more he remembered the time they had spent at the hospital, the more he felt he had let Amy down, unable to discern, much less offer her, the support she needed, and the stronger his urge had become to redeem himself and make it up to her. Time hadn't faded his feelings much; it was only upon meeting Chloe that he had been able to gradually lay them aside.

So many times he had dreamt of seeing those men caught and punished. Not quite as often as he had imagined the retribution he would inflict himself were he allowed, but this was certainly the next best thing. Amy's return had brought back all the old torments: the inadequacies he still felt; the rage he thought he'd quietened; and more and more his thoughts were consumed with at least seeing that justice was done.

Eventually, he left Chloe a long message on their home answering machine, explaining as much as he could think of, and then made his way to see Amy, still hoping beyond hope that this was the right thing to do.

Amy was overwhelmed when she saw Alex at her door. She had almost given up on him. The last few days had seemed to exist separately in time, as though there were nothing imaginable either before or after: past and future were on an entirely different plane of existence. She had been in a bubble, scared almost to breathe in case it should burst.

She invited him in, and watched as he cast his eye over her surroundings for the first time. She saw his gaze run across the bare white walls scarred with dirty marks, and the damp spot on the ceiling, then on to the scuffed wooden floors and over to the sofa bed in the corner at one end, the kitchenette at the other.

'This is . . . is . . .' He threw up his hands as if lost for words.

'Horrible,' she finished for him, moving to the kettle that perched on a tiny sill of the kitchenette. 'It's only temporary, though.'

Which was true, but the way she'd said it made it sound like she was about to buy a huge three-bedroomed semi-detached in the suburbs, whereas all her places in the past ten years had looked very similar to this, and she had no doubt the next one would too.

She looked up with a wry smile on her face as she said it, to let him know that she wasn't feeling sorry for herself, and he smiled back.

They stood there awkwardly for a moment. Eventually,

Alex walked across and put his arms around her, his cheek pressing against the top of her head. She kept her arms by her sides, but didn't want to push him away.

'Look,' he said, holding on to her. She could smell his skin – aftershave mixed with something earthier and more natural. She breathed deeply, listening as he continued, 'I don't know how much longer the trial will last . . .'

She moved away from him and walked over to the window. 'You don't have to come, you know,' she said softly, looking at the grey sky outside.

There was anger in Alex's tone as he said from behind her, 'Oh, really? For god's sake, have we really just picked up from where we left off ten years ago, Amy?' His voice became louder as he added, 'Have you come back into my life, turned everything I know upside down, just so you can continue to shut me out?'

She turned and stared at him. 'My name is *Julia*,' she replied, enunciating the name slowly as though he were a child.

'No, it's not,' he said. He stomped over to the door, grabbing the handle before he came marching back across the room, cupped her face firmly between his palms, making her look at him, and said, 'Amy – *Julia* – whoever you are – I am NOT leaving. This time, I am NOT going. I want to help you. You are GOING to let me help you.'

The force of his words terrified her for a moment – even though it was Alex, perhaps the one man she still trusted – and she burst into tears. And then he lifted her bodily, carried her to the sofa and sat her on his lap, shushing her as though she were an infant, holding her, letting her weep and weep. And when she was done, she realised she didn't want him to leave ever again.

That afternoon she told him the story of the past ten years, all her adventures – as bold a narrator as some returning conquistador. She described climbing mountains, rappelling off cliff faces, rafting through white-water gorges, snorkelling in coral seas. And he stared at her in open amazement.

Yet in between each word she spoke there was the void of everything she left out. She held his attention with the solidity of her words, distracting him from the great white sea of absence around them. What would he see, she wondered, if he could peer into this ocean of things held back? And what would he think of the terrible thing she hadn't yet told him? Would he understand that she had tried to live the life they had dreamed of having together? Or would he see that when she went rappelling she had been praying the rope would have an undetected fray; that halfway through her descent it would snap, leaving her plummeting to earth. Or that her life jacket would deflate, her scuba tank be empty of oxygen, her foot brush against a deadly creature that would not hesitate to bite. That she had spent the years since death first took a long, appraising look at her, actively seeking it out once more. But because of the promise she had made to her mother – and perhaps also the prospect of facing her father in the afterlife – she couldn't empower herself to take charge of her destiny. How galling it was that as much as she had become a victim of life, she was still forced to wait to be the victim of death – it was out of her hands, there was nothing she could do.

When she had finished talking, they both said little. The atmosphere in the cramped flat was dense.

After a while, he whispered to her:

'It wasn't easy for me, Amy. I was miserable for a long, long time. I even went back, you know – to Perth – a couple of years later. I thought I could play detective somehow, that if I found the men who attacked you, I might somehow karmically bring you back to me. But it was a waste of time, of course. There were no unsolved precedents to your attack; nothing new to uncover, however long I wandered around for. I didn't really know what I was looking for anyway, and the police didn't have time for me. I gave up after a few weeks and came home. Then I drank for a while . . . but pulled myself through that eventually when I realised how much I was upsetting my folks. And I tried to support your mum, until she cut me off. I checked in with missing persons regularly. I saw you everywhere, on the street, waiting for buses. I thought about you all the time, every minute . . .' His voice trailed off. Silence reigned again.

After an age, Alex lifted his head and said softly: 'I haven't changed my mind, Amy. I'll come with you . . . to Australia.'

'Alex, you really don't have to . . . there's no point,' she replied, hardened against his emotion.

'Yes, I do,' he answered, reaching across to tilt her chin up so she could look him in the eye. 'And there is a point, of course there is. I'm sorry, it's just that Chloe . . .' His voice cracked on her name and he shook his head as he added, 'God knows what she's thinking, I can't even find her to talk to right now. It's not an easy situation all round,' he finished.

Spite ran through her like an electric current. 'I'm not asking you to risk your perfect marriage,' she spat at him. 'I haven't asked you for anything.'

286

'I know,' he said, studying her face. 'But if you want to go back, then I will go with you,' he added, and there was fire in his eyes.

The bitterness ebbed in her as fast as it flowed. She looked down. 'Thank you.'

Alex reached across and stroked her cheek with the back of his hand. She had to stop herself from leaning into the pressure of his fingers. 'It will be okay, Amy. You can do this. I think maybe you should do this. I think perhaps I've come back into your life for this.'

She nodded, looking down at his chest. 'I know,' she said as he pulled her close. She wanted so much to believe in his words. She was praying that now he was back with her, Alex could make it all right.

An avalanche of decisions and deliberations came crashing over her, and she realised she couldn't do it. She wasn't strong enough. What was she thinking? But she had no choice now. She had to go to Australia. If she backed out, then Alex would disappear from her life again.

Alex began to tell her that he was trying to reshuffle his client commitments for the next few weeks, and some were being more cooperative than others. He spoke anecdotally, but she felt guilty. It hadn't really registered or concerned her at all that he was risking his marriage for her, as a large part of her thought that he shouldn't be married in the first place. But causing his business to go on the slide suddenly felt like too much to ask.

'Alex, you don't have to –' she began.

'Amy, stop it. I'm coming.' His voice was firm. Then he paused, and she could tell he had something more he wanted to say to her by the stiffness of his shoulders and the set of his jaw. He took a deep breath. 'Amy . . . your dad . . .'

'Is dead,' she said in a monotone. She put down a biscuit she had been nibbling on, which seemed suddenly dry and stale.

Alex nodded. 'I went to his funeral,' he murmured. 'I was hoping you would be there.'

'I couldn't . . .' she said, staring at the wall behind his head.

'I know. I spoke to your mum. She was very upset.'

Her gaze moved to meet his. 'Al, what is this? Are you trying to give me a guilt trip? You don't need to, okay? I already feel responsible. If it hadn't happened, if I hadn't run away, caused him so much stress . . .'

Alex looked alarmed, and she saw the knife edge he was on, trying to talk to her yet worried she might snap at any second.

'No, no, that wasn't what I meant. I just –'

She held her hand up. 'I just couldn't, okay? I hope perhaps Mum understands now – now it was so long ago. At the time it was too . . . difficult for me.'

'Of course,' Alex nodded, and his hand moved to cover hers. She let it, but her eyes slid away from his, down to her lap. Because she couldn't deny it any longer – she was still lying to him. He thought he knew everything now but he had barely scratched the surface. And what would he think of her when he did?

66

'Sit down, Mark,' Neil said from behind the desk as Mark appeared at his office door. He waved a hand in the direction of a vacant chair.

Mark sat.

'Now then,' Neil began, leaning forward. 'You two give me a rundown of exactly how far you've got with the Abbott research.'

Mark stared at his yellow legal pad uncomfortably, waiting to see if Chloe would speak first, but she appeared to be deferring to him.

'Anytime now would be good,' Neil said, leaning back and steepling his fingers.

Mark looked up. 'I've been going over everything,' he said. 'And I've found a few interesting and relevant precedents. When I've finished I'll draw up a memo –'

Neil held up a hand. 'The time for memos has long passed,

Mark.' He leaned forward again, and this time there was menace in it. 'Do you realise,' he growled, looking between the two of them, 'that we begin in two weeks? It is undoubtedly the biggest case we have ever had in this office and we are woefully – WOEFULLY – under-prepared.'

Mark surreptitiously looked at Chloe, wishing she would join in. She glanced at both of them, then back to the files on her lap. Mark was alarmed to see her eyes were moist. *Oh god, Chloe, don't cry. Not in the office.*

Mark's gaze moved back to Neil, unsure of what to do next, but to his surprise found that Neil was distracted, staring over Mark's head, his face alarmed. Mark barely had time to turn around before he registered, with dismay, a booming voice.

'Not disturbing anything, am I?' it said, and then there was a showy and rather irrelevant rat-a-tat on the office door.

There stood Henry, last seen semicomatose on Mark's bed, where he'd left him an hour earlier.

At first glance, Mark thought it might have been worse. Henry was decked out in what appeared to be one of Mark's pinstriped suits, with a navy tie neatly tucked in. But his father hadn't shaved. And the waft of alcohol hit Mark and disturbed his recently breakfast-lined stomach at the same time that he registered Henry hadn't done up the button of his trousers, which were straining badly at the extra bulk of him, plus he was only wearing one shoe.

Mark had a horrible flashback to the only time his father had come to school sports day, when he had run second in the egg-and-spoon race and caused a huge fuss afterwards, saying that the winner had made a false start and demanding a rematch. That had been excruciating, and it was about one hundred times less embarrassing than this.

He turned briefly back to the others, as if looking for help, but Neil appeared dumbstruck, and Chloe's mouth was slightly open, though her face showed both concern and surprise.

There was nothing else for it. Mark sprang into action, jumping out of his chair and heading towards the door. 'Dad . . .'

'Not now, Mark,' Henry said grumpily, and sidestepped him. 'What are you fellows discussing?' He glanced at the contents of Neil's desk. 'Ah, Abbott. Tricky one. Maybe I can help?' And he sat down with a thump in the chair Mark had just vacated.

Mark looked at Neil, who was slowly recovering himself. 'Henry,' Neil said. 'Would you like some water?'

'I'll get it,' Chloe interjected, and rushed out before anyone could say anything.

Henry looked between Mark and Neil. 'Good god, what's wrong with you two? You look like a pair of imbeciles.' He guffawed, with no apparent awareness that the other two men remained stony-faced.

'Excuse me a second, Henry,' Neil said. He gave Mark a studied look as he walked past him, and Mark watched through the open door as Neil bent and murmured into his secretary's ear, her glance behind confirming the topic of their discussion.

Mark looked at his father. 'Dad, where's your shoe?'

Henry peered down at his feet. 'It's . . .' He lifted up his leg and wiggled his toes beneath his sock. 'I thought it was . . .' he mumbled, and looked around the floor and under the desk as though it had just jumped off his foot and hidden itself nearby.

Neil spoke from the doorway. 'Mark. A word?'

Henry was down on his hands and knees now, searching for his missing shoe. 'Sounds like you're in trouble,' he growled from the floor. 'What have you done now?'

Mark didn't reply and moved over to the doorway, his eyes not daring to leave his father so he could intercede in whichever embarrassing move Henry decided upon next.

'Della is ordering a taxi,' Neil hissed. 'What's going on?'

'I wish I knew,' Mark replied, casting an uneasy glance in Neil's direction. 'He's been like this all weekend.'

Neil grimaced. 'You're going to have to take him home.' He turned to look at Mark. 'Are you sure you're up for this workload at the moment, all things considered?'

Mark's heart sank. He wanted to be in on this case; and he didn't want to be remembered for letting them down when they needed him. 'Of course,' he said. 'It's fine – I can do what you asked, honestly, I'll work on it all night if I have to.'

'Mark, I don't think –'

'Neil,' Mark said, his voice so unintentionally aggressive he feared Neil might react and sack him on the spot. 'I can do it – I'm a good way through already – further on than it looks. I'll bring all my research in first thing tomorrow.'

Neil sighed. 'Okay then. It looks like you've got a lot to deal with today, but if you're going to do this then don't let me down, okay? We're out of time on this one.'

'I won't,' said Mark, wondering why he couldn't have just taken the easy way out.

Henry refused to leave the office, until Mark told him that he was taking him home to show him the Abbott research as he needed his advice. It was humiliating, addressing his father in such a condescending way while Neil and Chloe watched. Neil had wanted to help them outside, but Mark had assured him they were fine, and had managed to steer his father through to the entranceway fairly quickly, just grateful that Neil's office was near the main doors so there wasn't far to go or too many people to pass. With the one or two offices they couldn't avoid, Mark had looked in and waved at his colleagues, trying to keep up the appearance of normality, though since there was a secretary in on this, the episode would be travelling through the office gossip lines faster than the speed of light once they'd left, he was sure of that.

He was bundling his dad into the taxi when he heard his name being called. He turned around to see Chloe running up to him.

She looked at Henry in the car. 'Mark, I'm so . . .'

He held up his hand. 'Don't, Chloe.'

'God, Mark, I'm only saying –'

'Look, I've got to go.'

She put a hand on his arm. 'Call me, if you can't cope with the work. I'll help you. I've got nothing better to do.'

He looked at her hand and then into her face. 'I thought you had just as many problems as me at the moment.'

She stared back at him. 'My problems seem to have walked out on me,' she said, her mouth a tight line.

Mark's brow furrowed as he looked at her, slowly comprehending, then he heard a groan from inside the taxi. A look inside told him his father was going a strange colour, and the driver had turned around, eyeing him suspiciously.

'I'm sorry, I've got to go,' he said, and Chloe nodded and stepped back, then turned away and walked inside.

In the taxi Mark dialled his mother's number.

'Mark, I'm very busy,' she snapped as she picked up. 'What is it?'

'I'm with Dad,' he said. 'He's not very well.'

At that point his father leaned into his shoulder. 'Are you speaking to Emily?' he asked.

'He sounds drunk,' came his mother's waspish voice on the other end. How the hell she could tell that from just a few words overheard down a phone line, Mark had no idea. 'Is he drunk?'

'Mum, Dad isn't well,' Mark tried again.

She snorted down the line. 'I could have told you that years ago,' she said.

'MUM!' Mark's gradually eroded patience finally crumbled. 'Dad is sick. Something is very wrong. I am taking him back to my apartment, and I want you to come over and sort this out. RIGHT NOW! My boss is going to sack me if I don't keep on top of my caseloads, it's a critical time at the moment –'

'Mark, I'm at work *right now*.' His mother wasn't one

for backing out of an argument. 'I can't just drop everything because your father chooses to –'

'Dad just walked into the office wearing my suit with the trousers undone, and with only one shoe on,' Mark announced. 'From the sopping wet sock, I think he came all the way into town like that. He's been comatose in my bed for much of the week. I haven't had a straight word out of him. This is not *just* my problem, so stop being so selfish.'

He turned around to see Henry had fallen asleep, his head lolling back, his white-bristled jaw loose and his mouth hanging slackly open.

There was a long pause on the line, so long Mark thought his mother might have hung up. Then he heard her sigh. 'I'm on my way,' she said, her voice flat and defeated.

67

When Amy had first seen the reports, and Alex had explained that the police had linked this case to hers, she had seemed willing to confront the situation. But now, as Alex watched Amy, he began to worry. On one printout there had been a pixellated photo of one of the men, which had left her shaky and withdrawn. Perhaps that was playing on her mind, as Alex could tell she was having major doubts now, and he didn't know how much heed to pay them.

Besides, he was having second thoughts as well. He felt very nervous. He didn't know if he could trust either of them to act predictably or sensibly when they got there. How would Amy cope with seeing the men who had harmed her so terribly? And how would he handle it, come to that? But not going at all: that could be far worse, he knew, and he could not countenance it – that after all this time they would still be mired in the interminable decay of inaction.

Alex had the feeling that he was going to have to be the one to make plans. So once he had assured Amy he would be back later that afternoon, he headed outside.

As soon as he was in the fresh air he tried Chloe again: no answer on either her home phone or mobile. Where the hell was she? Desperate now, he rang the office again, and got Jana.

'I need to find her straight away,' he said tersely. 'It's urgent.'

'I'm sorry, Alex.' Jana sounded embarrassed. 'She left half an hour ago with a bundle of work and said she'd be working at home this afternoon. Try her mobile.'

'She never has it bloody switched on,' he snapped, then added a quick 'Sorry' before they said their goodbyes.

Quickly, he made his way towards the station and home, dialling another number as he did so.

'Lewis speaking,' a voice cut in after a few rings.

'Lewis, it's Alex.'

'Alex, don't tell me you've finished our project already! Do you work at warp-speed?'

Alex laughed, trying not to dwell on the amount of work he had waiting for him.

'No, Lewis, I'm ringing for a favour, actually; want to pick your legal brains. I'm following a trial that's going on in Australia, and wondering how long it's likely to last. I need to know the procedure for this kind of thing.'

'Well,' came the reply, 'it depends on all sorts of things – amount of witnesses and evidence – could be weeks, months . . . What's it for?'

'It's a murder case – I'll tell you what, I'll forward you the web link, just give me a sec.'

'All right, mate,' Lewis replied. They hung up, Alex fired off the message, and his phone rang a few minutes later.

'Won't run for too much longer, I wouldn't think . . .' Lewis said without preamble.

Alex felt his sense of urgency increasing. 'Okay, then; thanks, Lewis. I'll make sure I get some design considerations to you asap.'

'No problem, Alex, thanks. Although I thought you said your wife was a solicit—'

'Thanks again, Lewis, much appreciated,' Alex cut in, hanging up and praying he hadn't sounded too discourteous.

The train, as always, took its time in getting him home. As he walked up the street, his heart sank when he saw that Chloe's car wasn't parked outside. His suspicions were confirmed once he opened the front door. The place was dark and empty. Upstairs, her toiletries had gone from the bathroom. She was staying somewhere else.

He left her a brief note saying he was looking for her, then headed out again. His mind was working frantically as he walked back towards the station. Chloe was doing a great job of avoiding him, and he and Amy were running out of time. By the time he reboarded the train he had made a decision.

When Alex got back to Amy's ramshackle flat, he had news for her.

'There's a flight this evening, and I've reserved us seats,' he told her.

'What?'

'Get packing.'

'Alex, this is crazy, we can't just –'

'Amy, the longer we hang about, the harder it's going to get. Besides, the court case has been going on for a while. If we don't go soon it'll be over.'

'Alex, will you *please* call me Julia. And I just don't know if I can do it.'

He walked over to her. 'You're not Julia to me. You're Amy. And I understand that you're scared. I do. But you *know* you want to see these men behind bars. You need to see it. *I* need to see it, come to that. And this is your chance to have closure. This might set you free.'

He pushed the words at himself as much as her, desperate to believe them.

She looked down at her hands, and just nodded.

They were ready to go by teatime. They rode the tube in silence, steadying their bags against the rocking and jolting carriage, not touching one another. At the airport he tried Chloe's mobile again but it went through to voicemail. Her voice asking him to leave a message was like a snap of fingers bringing him back to reality.

He hesitated after the beep. 'Chloe, I'm sorry . . .' he began cautiously. He paused again. What could he say? There was so much that needed to be said, he didn't know where to start. 'I hope you're getting my messages. I'd really love to talk to you. I'll try you again soon.' He hung up.

Only later did he realise that it would sound fairly obvious from the background noise that he was at an airport. God only knew what she would make of that.

68

Chloe had spent the afternoon at the library, needing to escape the office but wanting to delay heading back to an empty house. As she finished up the day's paperwork, she knew she wasn't doing very well. She had started to wander around like a zombie, even simple tasks taking a lifetime, doing everything on automatic pilot. Sometimes, when she'd sat in front of Mikaela's TV, nibbling on a cracker or sipping tepid tea, she had tried to make herself laugh at the incredulity of the situation.

She would never have suspected that her marriage could be rocked by scandal – it was the kind of thing you read about in the cheap women's magazines that cluttered the surfaces of waiting rooms: 'My husband ran off with a stranger'; 'My husband is a bigamist'; 'My husband had a secret life'. Pictures of normal-looking, scruffy, smiling men held up by pale, sad-faced women in tracksuit pants. Wedding photos showing people wearing out-of-fashion clothes, and brides with too much makeup, the happy couple separated by a superimposed tear down the middle. Yes, sometimes she could almost laugh about the absurdity of it all, before reality came flooding back.

She had still told no one except Mikaela that Alex had gone. She barely understood herself what had happened, and couldn't think how to begin to explain it to everyone else. There had just been another message from Alex flashing up on her mobile, and her finger didn't hesitate on the delete button. She was far too angry and upset to talk to him.

As she gathered up her things ready to go home, her thoughts turned briefly to Mark's father. No wonder Mark was so ashamed. He didn't say much when people talked about his dad, but he didn't have to – she could almost see the hairs on the back of his neck bristle with pride when someone recognised him as Henry Jameson's son. However, she knew it wasn't always easy for him – there was a lot to live up to in having the Jameson name, and there seemed to be plenty of disadvantages in going into the same field of work as your parents. Not that Chloe had had any chance of that – her mother was a full-time homemaker, and she hadn't got a clue what her real father did.

She felt a familial pull towards her brother. She really should call Anthony. He used to be such a large part of her life. They had the same sense of humour and she'd always felt they would be close friends as grown-ups, but since he had moved to America, their relationship had drifted into the territory of polite pleasantries during intermittent phone calls. They'd been to each other's weddings, but weddings

were such huge occasions that you didn't get time for intimacy unless you were the bride and groom – well, barely
even then – and Chloe had felt very strange at Anthony's,
meeting all his Yankee friends and hardly even knowing his
bride. Her mother had refused to come, saying she was too
ill at the time to travel all that way; but Chloe had thought
it was really because she was worried their father might be
there. She had wondered the same thing herself, but had
stopped looking when Anthony whispered a curt 'He's not
here' in her ear as he saw her casting her gaze around. Thank
god Alex had been there to hold her hand and make it feel
okay.

And so her thoughts were round full circle, back to Alex
again.

She stopped off at McDonald's on the way home. It was
her third takeaway in as many days, but cooking for one
felt too depressing. As she exited the restaurant, she briefly
imagined Alex coming home to find she'd gained a couple
of stone and laughed bitterly at the irony. If he took too
long she really would have gained that much in baby weight.
As she walked, she took a bite of her hamburger and envi-
sioned the baby coming out of her with a spotty face and
bad breath. She threw the meal into the next bin she passed.

Once at home, she unpacked the bag she'd taken to
Mikaela's, then put on her tracksuit bottoms and a T-shirt
and headed into the lounge room for a quick blast of mind-
numbing TV. On the way she caught sight of a blurry figure
stumbling past the hall mirror. She stopped in shock. Edging
towards it for a closer look she took in her wild hair and
red-rimmed eyes and gasped in surprise. She looked like a

ghost, her face so pale that it almost blended into the white wall behind her.

She glanced at the answer phone in the hall. No messages on there today. She didn't know if that felt better or worse. Then, as she glanced down, she saw Alex's scrawly handwriting on the memo pad next to the phone and felt herself start. He'd been home? The note said little except that he was looking for her, and he'd signed it with love and kisses. She felt her anger subside a little. She missed him, and wondered where he was.

Perhaps she should take a day off tomorrow, she thought, and phone the hospital to rearrange the ultrasound. She couldn't face going there alone. She should be going with Alex; it was just too much to contemplate in the glare of his absence. Besides, the Abbott case wouldn't wait – in fact, she really should fish out the paperwork now and get on with it. She decided the TV viewing would have to come later, and walked into the kitchen to find her briefcase, while idly flicking through the post, just bills and statements, hieroglyphics of numbers marching straight into a black vortex in her brain without even pausing for her to consider them.

All at once she was tired of being cross and miserable. She wanted to break through this impasse with Alex, but she didn't know how. She thought about the messages he'd left on her mobile and began hunting for her phone in case there was another one.

There was a knock at the door.

It could be Alex, she thought, looking down in dismay at what she was wearing. But then, why would he knock?

All the lights were on, so there was no pretending she

wasn't home. Another knock and she was scurrying down the hall.

When she opened the door she thought at first glance it *was* Alex, but then the vision coalesced into someone similar but not quite her husband.

'Jamie? What are you doing here?'

Jamie came in without waiting to be invited. 'I've been trying to ring Alex all weekend. He's not answering,' he said, injecting his strange flat speech with a touch of indignation. 'Where is he?'

'He's out,' Chloe replied, heart sinking. Jamie wasn't easy to talk to at the best of times. In theory she felt sympathetic towards Jamie and his problems, but when actually confronted with this bewildered, erratic man, she usually felt more awkward than anything else.

'When's he back?'

'I don't know.'

'You must know.'

'I don't, I'm sorry.'

Jamie looked at her as though trying to figure out if she were teasing him. 'So where is he?' he repeated.

'Jamie,' she said, exasperated now, 'I *really* don't know.' She walked back through to the kitchen with Jamie following her. 'Do you want a drink?' she asked politely.

Jamie was looking round the room as though Alex might leap out from a hiding place at any moment saying, 'Boo' and grinning. 'Just water,' he said, going over to the tap and pouring himself a glass.

'So,' he turned around and leaned against the sink while sipping his drink, 'how come you don't know where he is?'

Chloe closed her eyes, steadied her thoughts, and sighed. 'He's gone to help a friend,' she said.

'Which friend?'

'Julia.'

'Julia? I don't know any Julia.'

I'm sure you don't know *all* Alex's friends, Chloe felt like saying.

And then she realised. Jamie might actually be a source of information here.

'Old girlfriend, dark hair, turned up out of the blue. Seems to be having some problems.'

'Old girlfriend? Well, that's got to be Amy – he's only really had two of you that lasted beyond a month!' Jamie grinned.

'Amy?'

'Yeah, Amy Duvalis, they went out at university and afterwards went on a long holiday together, but then she disappeared. Something happened to her.'

'What? What happened?' She was eager to see if Jamie's version of events matched Alex's.

'I think she got attacked.'

'Oh,' Chloe said, her mind whirring. 'I see.'

'Yeah,' Jamie said, pouring himself another glass of water. 'Alex was a mess. He was gutted.'

'Oh,' she said again, unable to think of anything else. It was the same story Alex had told her. But why the hell did the woman have two names? And how could Chloe compete with tragedy? And was it awful that it was this thought playing on her mind rather than any sympathy for the woman?

There was another knock at the door.

'I'll get it, maybe it's Alex,' Jamie said, completely incurious as to why Alex might knock at his own front door.

Chloe closed her eyes. She didn't want anyone else here. When she heard Mark's voice, her heart sank.

And then the phone rang.

She rushed to pick it up. The line was faintly crackling, but she could hear Alex's voice saying hello.

'Alex, where are you?'

'Chloe, don't freak out, okay. Did you get any of my messages?'

'I haven't had a chance to check,' she lied, not wanting to admit that she'd deleted them. 'What did you say?'

'Oh god; well, listen to them, please. It's just – look, I'm on a plane. I'm going with Amy to –'

'Amy? So it is Amy? Hang on – a PLANE?'

'Yes, it's Amy. And yes, a plane. I can't talk much now, but, Chloe, please, you have to –'

And then the phone was snatched out of her hand. 'Alex, where the hell are you?' Jamie blurted down the phone. 'You promised me a trip to the pub last night, I waited for you.'

Chloe had the urge to grab the phone back off him and hit him over the head with it. But she was far too polite for that – which was something that, seconds later, she would regret immensely.

'I came to find out where you were,' Jamie replied in answer to the questions Alex was obviously asking. 'Yeah, she's fine. Why? Thingy's here. You know, the lawyer bloke,' he said, lowering his voice a notch or two even though Mark was by now only a few feet away.

There was a pause while Jamie listened. Then he held out the phone to Chloe. 'He wants to speak to you again,' he said, looking cross.

'Alex,' Chloe began, hating herself for feeling guilty.

'Why is Mark there?'

'I don't even know myself yet,' she said, trying to keep her tone light. 'He's only just got here.'

Even though it was the truth, she felt like she was telling a lie. She looked at Mark, who rolled his eyes and lifted his briefcase pointedly. 'Work,' she added. 'Remember that case, the Abbott one? It came to a head this morning, so we're panicking a bit.'

'I see.' Alex's voice had a new, cold edge to it. Chloe felt completely on the back foot, and desperate, as though she were the one entirely in the wrong.

'Look, I've got to go, Chloe,' Alex said, as Jamie leaned forward next to her and said, 'When's he coming back?' Alex seemed to have heard him. 'Tell Jamie I'll ring him at home.'

'Al, at least tell me where you're going?' Chloe asked.

But he'd already gone.

Chloe felt tears welling again but the company she was in kept them at bay.

Jamie looked warily at Mark. 'Chloe, I'm going to go, okay?' he said.

'Okay,' she nodded, and followed him along the hall.

At the door, Jamie turned around. 'I don't think Alex likes him being here,' he said, nodding his head towards the kitchen.

'It's okay, Jamie,' Chloe told him, knowing without a doubt that he was right, 'he won't be here long.'

'Right,' Jamie replied, and then disappeared into the darkness of the evening without another word.

Chloe turned and headed back to the kitchen, where Mark was waiting with an annoyingly condescending look on his face.

'What are you doing here?' she asked, more aggressively than she intended.

Mark held his hands up, which, along with his briefcase, contained two bottles of wine in a plastic bag. 'I need a partner to drown my sorrows with.'

'Oh, Mark, I . . .' Chloe's hand rubbed her stomach as she thought of all the excuses she could use as to why she wasn't drinking. 'I've got a full day at work tomorrow, I don't know if I . . .'

'You can have a couple of glasses, Chlo, you're not a complete lightweight,' Mark said presumptuously. His eyes flickered over the items around the room – including a big picture showing a smiling Alex and Chloe peering out from a shiny wedding car and holding champagne flutes.

'Everything okay?' he asked.

'Fine,' she said. She felt slightly appalled at how easily the untruth tripped off her tongue, and Mark, lightning-quick predator of lies in the courtroom, merely nodded as his eyes lingered on the picture for a second, before he grabbed a bottle out of the bag he was holding and unscrewed the cap. There was a determined, slightly manic glint to his eye that made Chloe feel uncomfortable.

'How's your dad?'

'Awful. Let's not talk about it,' he said, brandishing the open bottle as he turned towards the kitchen cabinets.

'Now, where do you keep your glasses?' He began searching through cupboards, energetically pulling doors open and letting them swing shut with a bang.

'Are you okay, Mark?' she asked nervously.

'Of course,' he said dismissively, then exclaimed, 'A-ha!' as he found what he was looking for and pulled two glasses from the shelf. He brought them over to the table, and Chloe sat down hesitantly, unsure of what to say.

He poured their wine, pausing to lift his glass to hers, looking directly into her eyes and saying, 'Cheers.'

His piercing gaze was disconcerting. 'Cheers,' she replied uncomfortably, clinking glasses and watching as Mark raised his to his lips.

69

Amy had begun to doze while Alex was in the toilet, but when he came back he woke her up, flinging himself into his seat.

'What?' she said, surprised.

His eyes were two bullets of frustration as he looked at her.

'Nothing,' he answered crossly.

'Al.' She put a hand on his leg and he brought his own hand across as though to move hers off, but then paused and patted it instead. He leaned back in his chair and exhaled a long sigh.

'I have no fucking idea what I'm doing,' he said loudly.

The woman across the aisle from him, a toddler on her lap, turned to glare at them for a moment.

Under her breath, Amy said, 'Great, thanks,' feeling tearful.

Alex was still staring at the ceiling of the plane. 'Oh, for god's sake, don't jump to conclusions about what I mean.'

Her tearfulness turned to anger. 'Well, if you don't want to be here . . .' she hissed.

Alex turned to her, looking irritated. 'What? What, Amy? What should I do? Just parachute out of the plane, and set my course back to England? I think I'm pretty well committed to being here, don't you?'

Now the woman in the aisle was openly staring at them, alarmed. Amy turned away and leaned against the window. 'Just get some sleep, Alex,' she said over her shoulder.

He looked at her sadly but didn't reply.

70

'Mark, are you sure you don't want to talk about your dad?'

Mark's lips formed a sudden dam against the wine that sloshed back into his glass. 'No, he's fine,' he said irritably, putting his glass down, rocking back on the chair and looking at Chloe, sensing there was more to come.

'He didn't look very good earlier on,' she said tentatively. 'Do you think you should have left him?'

'Chloe, this afternoon it's been one long marriage-guidance session at my place. My parents are just pathetic. Their relationship is more like that of business partners than a married couple – I realised on the way here that they don't communicate, they transact. Neither of them will talk properly to the other, they're just locking horns like a pair of fighting stags. Mum left in a huff an hour or so before I did, then I watched Dad count out four sleeping tablets and wash them down with whisky, which he had to go and buy himself since I've hidden the small stash of my booze he hasn't got through already. I don't think he'll be going anywhere for a while, and I fancied chatting with someone who's a bit more than semi-conscious tonight.'

Chloe looked riled at his supercilious tone. 'Charming – I'm so glad you picked me,' she said as sarcastically as she could muster.

'You're welcome,' he replied, lifting his glass to his mouth and tipping his head back while he took an enormous slug of wine.

'So, what's going on with Alex?' he asked, eyeing her carefully. 'When's he coming back?'

'Soon,' she said. But she had paused a fraction too long before answering.

'Soon?' He raised a prosecutorial eyebrow. Like a fox at a rabbit hole, he was scenting just how close he was to trapping her.

'Mark, don't,' she began, her voice cracking slightly as she said it.

Various sarcastic comments ran through Mark's mind, but then he leaned forward, took her hand, and said, 'What's going on, Chlo?'

She looked startled by the sudden intimacy of his gesture. His hand held hers, steadily, and he waited. Her mouth twitched a few times before she eventually answered with a bleak, 'I don't know.'

'I presume it's all to do with Julia?' he asked, leaning in to her.

'Yes,' she whispered. 'Have you seen her?' Mark could

hear the begging note in her voice, the desperation for any information he might impart.

'Not since I saw her here last week,' he said grimly.

Chloe cracked. 'Well, it appears her real name might be Amy. Jamie just told me. What the hell is all that about? Apparently, she was attacked while they were together.' Chloe had been toying with the stem of her wineglass, but now picked it up quickly and took a large gulp. 'I just don't know what to think,' she said. 'It was only a week ago, that awful night at the restaurant. *Just a week*. Some beautiful ex-girlfriend turns up out of the blue and my husband is immediately doing her bidding.'

'I don't think you've got that quite right, Chloe,' Mark said, wondering why the hell he was allowing Alex any leeway.

'Go on then,' she demanded. 'How does it appear to you?'

'Like there's a lot we don't know,' he suggested. 'But any fool can see Alex loves you.'

'Really?' Chloe asked pathetically.

Mark tried to hide his grimace. 'Really.'

'God, but why couldn't she be twenty-five stone and covered in boils? Why did she have to be so stunning?'

'You're stunning.' The words were out before Mark thought about them. He tensed. But Chloe didn't take it quite the way he thought she might. She laughed.

'Yeah, right.'

Mark didn't want to repeat himself but nor did he want to let it drop. So he said, 'Of course you are. In fact, I was just looking at that photo,' he gestured to their wedding picture, 'and thinking that you look quite a lot like Julia there . . . when your hair was longer . . .' He trailed off.

Chloe's face had blanched.

'What?' Mark asked warily. 'What did I say?'

71

Chloe stared at Mark, dumbfounded. She was remembering all too clearly.

He thought I was her. At the station. When we first met.

She could picture his face quite clearly: tentative, hopeful recognition quickly replaced with politeness.

He thought I was her.

Oh my god. What was she, really, to Alex? Just a second-string replacement in the absence of his one true love?

Mark had rushed round to her chair. 'Chloe, what is it?'

She pushed him away blindly. 'Nothing.'

'Jesus, I thought you were going to faint. Here –' He ran over to the tap and got her a glass of water, came back and placed it in front of her. Meanwhile, Chloe stared at the wedding photograph on the shelf, her favourite photo becoming an image of the two of them smiling like imbeciles while stupidly clinking glasses.

Was he thinking of her on our wedding day? When I walked down the aisle, did he pretend it was her until I came into sharp focus?

Was nothing real?

'Chloe, please talk to me,' Mark was saying, squatting down beside her chair. 'You're freaking me out.'

'I think I just need to have some more wine,' Chloe said, pouring herself a generous top-up, putting the baby right to the back of her mind.

This obviously signalled to Mark that she was coming out of her reverie, and he went and sat down again on the chair opposite.

'I'm sure Alex will get whatever it is out of his system pretty quickly,' he continued, oblivious to her thoughts. 'There is something really wrong with that woman. She's gorgeous, but . . . complicated . . . a bit, well, weird.'

Out of his system? Who did Mark think he was talking about Alex to?

Chloe clenched her fists under the table. She had no idea why she had ever dated Mark when he was like this. Now was one of those moments when she could see clearly what Alex saw – a smug, condescending, arrogant man. She sifted through her memories, recalling how he had made her laugh, how he had seemed confident yet, at times, uncertain when they'd first met. Every now and then he would show his vulnerability, and because of those times she had hung in there, but finding it was like hunting through heavy law books for the one small paragraph that might turn a case – both exasperating and exhausting.

'How can you be so . . . so cold about it?' Chloe asked

sharply, ignoring the twinge of conscience she felt thinking of law books and the fact that they should both be going through the Abbott case notes right now. How could Mark dismiss someone he'd sounded so excited about just a week or so ago in a couple of swift sentences? 'Doesn't anyone ever get under your skin?'

Mark looked into his lap and gave a short bark of laughter. 'You think I'm shallow?' he said, looking up at her.

'No,' Chloe began, and then a surge of impatience overtook her. Why shouldn't she say what she thought? 'Well, yes, actually – at times.'

'Now we're getting to it,' he said, staring at her, a malevolent glint in his eye. 'You expect too much of men, Chloe. We're not given to excesses of emotion. To women, things might be myriad shades of grey – but to men, it's pretty much just black and white.'

'Not all men.'

As soon as she said it, she knew she'd made a mistake.

Mark snorted loudly and derisively. 'I presume by that you mean Alex? Really, Chloe, I thought you'd be the last person to defend him at the moment, since he's proved to be so flighty.'

Chloe stood up abruptly, her wine glass wobbling dangerously as she did so. She was so enraged that she didn't notice Mark reaching out quickly to catch the glass before it toppled. She had lost all efforts at control now. She came at him, her fists flailing, ready to inflict what damage she could. 'How *dare* you!' she cried. 'How fucking dare you!'

She tried to connect, but Mark caught her wrists tightly with a strength that surprised her. She struggled with him but he held on firmly, and the small bolts of pain that shot through her arms stopped her in her tracks. Her face was contorted with anger as she spat at him, 'Why do you have to be so bloody horrible, Mark? Why do you have to be such an arrogant, condescending bastard? You're always so bloody rude. And you've always hated Alex. What has he ever done to you except be civil?'

'He has you,' Mark murmured fiercely, holding her wrists tight.

'What?' Shocked, she was suddenly still. 'What do you mean?'

'You know full well what I mean, Chloe,' he said, his voice full and deep. His grip on her wrists slackened and he leaned forward as though to kiss her. But she quickly stepped backwards.

'You're outrageous!' she said, her voice high-pitched and shrill. 'What on earth are you doing? You HAD me, Mark. A long time ago, you HAD me. And you blew it. You ruined it completely with your selfishness, your complete lack of . . . of . . .' She felt agitated, breathless, and sat down suddenly, putting her head in her hands, trying to resist the urge to sob. What the hell was going on with her life?

She heard the scrape of a chair as Mark drew his closer to hers. She could feel his breath on her face, even though she wouldn't look at him. He was quiet for a moment, and she waited, every nerve primed for what might come next.

'Chloe.' His voice was a sigh. He wrapped his arms around her, and she held herself stiff but didn't push him away. 'I know I ruined it. I know. I just didn't realise . . . what I had, how important it was, until it wasn't there any more.'

She could feel his chin resting on the top of her head. It felt so nice to be held. She closed her eyes and imagined they were Alex's arms wrapped around her, then wondered if that was what Alex did when he held her – imagined she was Julia – or if, at this exact moment, her husband's arms were wrapped around a stunning brunette. For a second, hatred for Alex pulsed through her, and she gasped at the strength of it.

The noise made Mark move. He pulled back from her and looked into her face. 'What are you thinking, Chloe?' he asked.

She stared at Mark. She saw him every day. She thought she knew his every expression, but here, just at this moment, it seemed there was more kindness and concern in his features than she'd ever seen before.

He leaned towards her.

I don't know where Alex is, she thought blearily. Or who he is any more. Or even if he cares. And Mark is here. He's here for me, right now.

Mark saw how she was looking at him, and immediately pulled her close. As his lips pressed against hers, she blanked all other thoughts from her mind, just let herself feel his warm touch against her skin. As though brought back to life by it, heat was transmitted to her through that small, soft connection, and she felt herself stir, her own mouth beginning to respond in kind.

72

The plane journey was bringing back uncomfortable memories for Alex, of his journey from Australia ten years ago. Now he'd made another choice, and once again he was questioning the wisdom of it. Meanwhile, he was going through the motions, sitting as though in a cramped theatre, watching movies, sipping wine, eating questionable food, while they hurtled through the air in a reinforced metal rocket. He kept trying to focus on Amy and what she needed from him, but his thoughts reverted back to Chloe at every opportunity. Plus, now Mark was in their house, and he was helpless to do anything about that. And Chloe was vulnerable, and he had seen the way Mark looked at her – predatory – wolfish, almost, at times. Alex wasn't blind to the truth, even if he didn't always choose the best course of action in dealing with it.

He remembered the first time he had seen Chloe. It had

been Amy he was looking for, but through the brief cloud of disappointment he had focused enough to see the possibility of something else – the emergence of a new fork in his path. And so he had taken it, and never regretted it. Even after the past week he had never once wished himself back to a time before Chloe; he had only wished away the pain of it all. How on earth had he got into this, and how was he going to get out?

The lights were dimmed so they could get some sleep. There were so many forms of entertainment to choose from on the LCD screen in front of him that he couldn't seem to make a decision, but he knew he wouldn't rest. Amy appeared to be sleeping, though he thought he knew better. She was a little too still. Her head had fallen towards his shoulder, but the only thing connecting them was a few fine wisps of her hair. A little earlier, as he glanced towards her, he'd thought he saw the damp course of tears on her cheeks, but had feigned ignorance. They were sitting too close to others to be able to talk.

He leaned his head back, closed his eyes and tried to concentrate on the drone of the engines. He wanted the practicalities of the court case to take precedence in his mind, for he had the feeling that getting Amy and himself through the next few days was going to be quite a task. But one thing kept coming back to him: that this wasn't over – and although he didn't know exactly what would happen during the next few days and weeks, he was starting to dread it. If only this aeroplane could have flown him further away from the inevitable, but, like everything else in life, it was moving inexorably forward.

73

Chloe woke up with a start, a shiver of trepidation running through her before she even had time to think. She looked down to find herself sprawled among a heap of bedclothes that barely covered her. It was cold. She still had her bra on underneath her half-buttoned shirt, and her knickers. But that was all. And she could hear the radio playing downstairs. She shivered, swung her legs over the side of the bed, and sat up. Her head was pounding, though she didn't remember drinking that much, and her eyes felt swollen.

A wave of queasiness washed over her as she thought about the previous night. Mark had kissed her, and she'd kissed him back. What a mistake that had been. After they'd broken apart she remembered bursting into guilty, hysterical tears, and ranting and crying while the expression on Mark's face varied from sympathetic to shocked – mostly the latter.

She recalled him helping her upstairs and cuddling her on the bed when she had finally calmed down, and then he'd started to undress her . . .

Shit! She jumped up and headed for the bathroom, confirmed briefly that yes, her eyes were red and half-shut, and grabbed her dressing gown, pulling it on in a rush as she ran down the stairs.

Mark sat at the kitchen table, reading a newspaper. He was wearing the shirt and jeans he'd been in the night before, but the shirt looked rumpled and creased now.

'Morning,' he said, looking up.

Chloe was suddenly overwhelmed by the urge to be sick. She put her hand over her mouth with a squeak and ran to the kitchen sink, where she promptly threw up a watery mess. Acutely embarrassed, she avoided turning around as she ran water and rinsed the basin.

'What a delightful effect I have on you, Chloe,' Mark's voice drifted over to her.

'You stayed,' she said uncomfortably, splashing her face with water and then turning around. She was remembering more pieces of last night and trying to block them out. She felt as though she'd had gallons of alcohol to drink, but knew she couldn't have.

'I couldn't leave you, could I,' he said, half-exasperated. 'But I really should get going now. God knows what state my dad will be in after a night with just the whisky bottle for company. Hopefully not dead, is all I ask.' He jumped up and came over to kiss her cheek. 'I feel like a bloody nursemaid at the moment. I'll call you later.'

'There's no need,' she began, but she didn't have time to

add anything before she was overwhelmed by the urge to be sick again. She turned back to the sink and felt Mark's hands pull her hair back as she bent over double.

He reached across her to turn the tap on.

'I'm so sorry,' she said, feeling wretched and humiliated.

'Don't be,' he answered. 'Pregnancy looks like a blast,' he added sarcastically.

She swung around, almost knocking him off-balance. 'You know?' she gasped.

'Jesus!' Mark held his hands up, a smile curving his lips although his eyes were solemn. 'Chloe, how stupid do you think I am? You're throwing up in the mornings, and you mumbled the word "baby" quite a bit last night – though it was hard to make out what you were saying at times – at first I thought it was an endearment.' He mock-rolled his eyes at himself.

She could feel her cheeks burning. 'You undressed me . . .' she began.

He looked at her, and she saw his expression change to indignation as he realised what she was implying. 'Last night . . .' he began, then obviously decided to change tack. 'I didn't take advantage of you while you were sleeping, if that's what you think.' He snorted derisively. 'I prefer my lovers conscious, and preferably not pregnant. Besides, I tried to help you but you wouldn't let me near you – you took your own trousers off and then ordered me out.'

Chloe felt absurdly insulted and deflated by his words. '*You* kissed *me*,' she added petulantly, berating herself as she did so. She sounded like a twelve-year-old in the playground.

'Okay, Chloe, whatever.' He held his hands up. 'I really

do have to go, you know. I'll speak to you later.' He came across and pecked her on the cheek, and she tried to avoid his gaze, feeling the intensity of it beating down on her, and leaving her more confused than ever.

74

By the time they reached Perth it was too late to do much except find their hotel and grab a meal. Alex had pre-booked a twin room over the internet, but there was an embarrassing farce when they were shown to a double and he had to go back and request two single beds. The young man on reception kept his face a mask of politeness as he sorted it out.

Alex wasn't even sure if sharing a room was the right thing to do, but he considered Amy a flight risk, with good precedent, so felt he needed to keep her close. She hadn't said much for the whole journey, and after dinner immediately took herself off to bed. Alex's mind was tired, but he still couldn't sleep, so he set up his laptop and began checking things out online.

It wasn't hard to find details of the trial. The local media had been reporting it faithfully, even if just a paragraph on dull days of legal procrastination. The evidence against the three men seemed substantial. He couldn't see there was any way they'd be set free.

He had been so quick to get them here that it was only now, when they had flown halfway around the world, that he realised their plan was somewhat absurd. What if, somehow, these weren't the three men they thought they were? What if this was the worst decision they could have made? What if, against all the odds, these men were found innocent? They would have to stand by and watch them walk free. Jesus, Amy couldn't do that; it would break her all over again.

Plus there were smaller problems. He had presumed they could get into the public gallery, but what if they couldn't? It was a high-profile case; why had they just assumed they would be able to do what they wanted, when they needed to?

He looked away from the lamp-lit desk to the sleeping bundle that was Amy, in the shadowy corner of the room. He wanted to wake her and tell her that he was hopelessly out of his depth, that every decision he had made since this nightmare began so long ago became flawed in hindsight, even if it seemed right at the time. He didn't trust himself any more. She would be better off with Chloe, he thought, who would have some idea of how to get into a courtroom, how to follow legal proceedings. He had a pang of desire to reach out to his wife and appeal for help, but he felt that would be asking too much of her. And what if Mark were still with her? Could he bear to know that, as he sat here thousands of miles away? No, he decided – he would wait until tomorrow, when he could tell her more about the trial, before he called again. Although, in the future, would this be another regrettable choice of his – yet one more thing that he'd long to undo?

75

On the way home to find out if his dad was still alive, Mark couldn't stop thinking about Chloe.

What a liar he was, cajoling her into thinking that friendship was all he wanted, when the more he thought about it, the more he felt she was right for him, always had been. He could see that Chloe was worried she was second fiddle to Alex's affections for Julia; how ironic that the roles of the two women were reversed in Mark's mind.

And now she was pregnant! Mark couldn't get his head around what that meant for him. He tried to block out uncomfortable thoughts, but they kept sneaking back in again.

Bloody Alex. He hated that man.

When he got back to the apartment, to his surprise his father was actually awake and drinking coffee.

'Didn't come home last night?' he said gruffly as Mark

banged his briefcase down onto the table and headed for the bathroom.

'Obviously,' Mark replied.

'Good night?' his dad asked, still studying the paper.

'Fine. Did you get anything sorted with Mum?'

'That woman is a liability – haven't heard from her since she stormed out. Too bloody emotional and hypersensitive, that's her problem. She thinks the world revolves around her.'

Finally, Mark had had enough. He came back and threw himself down into the chair opposite his father. 'You both need to grow up,' he said bluntly.

His father looked up in surprise, mug poised against his mouth. He put his drink down slowly, his hand trembling momentarily so that the mug rattled against the table. 'I beg your pardon?'

'You heard me. Whatever is going on with you, sort it out. Mum might be like a bulldozer, but you're just as bad. Otherwise, why have you run away from home, Dad?'

Henry's face had reddened. Mark waited for the outburst, but instead, his father leaned back and sighed.

'It's complicated,' he said, like a petulant child.

Mark leaned further forward. Now he had his dad on the ropes, he dared not let go – it might never happen again.

'Try me.'

'Getting older isn't easy, you know,' Henry said belligerently.

'Don't tell me this is your mid-life crisis!' Mark snorted. 'Bit late, isn't it?'

Henry's next verbal blast pushed Mark back with such

force that their roles were instantaneously reversed. 'You little shit!' he shouted. 'You think you're so clever, sneering at your father because he's *old*. Relative youth doesn't give you any advantage, you idiot, except a false sense of security that is soon enough undone.'

'Dad, I . . .'

'DON'T YOU DARE,' Henry growled, leaping up and heading for Mark's bedroom.

Mark's hands were balled into tight fists, but he kept them on his lap. He ceded this argument for now, and changed tack as he called after Henry.

'Dad, I need to get ready for work.'

'I'll be out of this place as soon as possible, don't you doubt it,' Henry raged, slamming the bedroom door behind him.

Mark leaned back into his chair, looked down at his shoes, and sighed.

76

To get to the Supreme Court you had to walk through glorious lush gardens, where lemon gums and umbrella trees sheltered you from the fierce midday sun, and brightly coloured flowers lined your way. For Amy, it was like walking through the Garden of Eden to get to the Gates of Hell. She wondered if the gardens made it worse for all those who knew they walked this way in their last moments of freedom – a stark reminder of what they had forfeited their right to.

The court building itself was one of a cluster of historical buildings incongruously sandwiched between modern skyscrapers and laissez-faire pubs and sailing clubs by the river. Thick white pillars supported the porticoed entrance. It was at these pillars that Amy's step faltered, and she would have stumbled if Alex's hand hadn't been there, grasping her elbow.

She hadn't slept much over the past few days, but her brain seemed to have decided that now was a good time to shut down. Her mind was foggy, her eyes bleary, and all she really wanted was to go back to bed.

A couple of security guards turned suspicious gazes on her. She smiled feebly and righted her stride, allowing them to check her bag as she heard Alex asking in hushed tones for Court Number Two. The entrance hall was full of people, a babble of noise. The guard asked why they were there, and Alex quickly told him they were related to the victim. She supposed it wasn't even much of a lie. They received instructions on general court etiquette, such as bowing to the judge, which her sluggish brain did its best to remember.

There was an extravagant staircase ahead of them, which, while more suited to the frippery of a stately home than the practical environment of a court of law, made the place seem all the more foreboding. Amy grasped the thick wooden rail tightly as they climbed. She felt as though she were hyperventilating. Her heart was beating erratically – strong beats staccatoing against her chest. She desperately sucked in air. The surroundings swam before her eyes and she thought she was going to faint, but the twisting molasses inside her head continued. Alex's arm was firmly around her waist, and he was marching them on. There was no way he would let her back out.

When they got through the doors to the upper gallery, there were people already seated in the public viewing area: a middle-aged woman with tired, sad eyes; a quartet of girls in their early twenties; three police officers; and two court security officials. Amy was surprised. She'd thought there would be more people here. The press must be somewhere else.

Alex took her hand and guided her to seats at the front. She held on tight, feeling a small pulse throbbing through his fingertips and connecting with her own.

From where they sat they could clearly see the front of the courtroom. She took a tentative look down at the lawyers' desks, vertigo like a slow spinning top in her head, but was then distracted as the jury filed in. They were followed by the judge, who strode confidently to his chair as they all stood for him. As he sat down, his expression was unreadable and Amy marvelled at how this could be. He reminded her of her dad – she'd be embarrassed to use a mild swearword in front of this man and yet he'd just spent days digesting the most obscene details of this case.

Before she sat down she automatically glanced over the railing again. And saw three men, besuited, standing in a line. As she watched, one of them turned briefly to look up at the gallery and she quickly strangled the squeak of shock that escaped her. The judge glanced up, and people nearby turned to stare at her. Alex's grip on her hand tightened, but she sat down quickly, outwardly quiet, even though her heart was thundering.

It was overwhelming to see them in the flesh, she thought, trembling. They might be evil cloaked in skin and bone, but they were just three men. So ordinary, yet she had recognised the one who looked up as the man who had pinned her in the back of the van – Dregs, she'd never forget that name. He was a lot thinner now, and his hair was shorter, but his features were more memorable. She stared at her feet, trying to shake off the thought that they were so close to her.

Nevertheless, she didn't last long after the first defence witness of the day was called. The man described seeing the victim, Vanessa, smiling at the men as they chatted to her in the bar where she had last been seen alive. He recalled that she didn't look too worried. But under cross-examination, the man admitted that he played football with the brother of one of the defendants.

Amy was shocked. Surely no one would choose to defend these animals because of such a tenuous link with them.

And then she realised with a start that there might have been a trial like this for her own murder, but for their botched attempt at killing. If the knife had cut her throat as deeply as they had meant it to, then Alex would be here alone, her mum at his side, maybe her dad, watching on as people who had never known her talked about her. Or maybe her body would still be lying under the trees somewhere, like Vanessa's had been for six weeks, decomposed, half-eaten by bush animals.

Her first retch was dry, because she hadn't eaten anything that morning, but on the second she disgorged thick white sputum into her hands. She got up hastily, even remembering to make a weird attempt at a bow to the judge, who, she half-noticed, was looking up again, before hurrying towards the door, which a security guard opened for her. Although she had said nothing to Alex, she was certain he was behind her, and, sure enough, as soon as they were outside, his arm came around her shoulder, and she shrugged it off.

'Amy!'

It wasn't Alex who had just spoken. She was frozen like a hunted animal, fearing to look behind her, but her body responded like a reflex to her name and turned anyway.

Alex was turning too. And she was still registering the man's face as he said, looking pale with shock, 'I thought it was you.'

77

As she stared at the man, who was looking at her intently, it seemed she was destined to become Amy again. Everyone around her was forcing her back into her weak, tremulous body. It really was too much.

She recognised this man, but didn't know from where, until Alex said, 'Detective Thompson?'

The man turned to Alex. 'Yes,' he said, his features opening as he smiled, as though he were mightily pleased to see them. He looked from one to the other. 'I didn't expect to see you two here. Amy, the last time I spoke to your mother, you were still missing. Does she know you're okay?'

Amy's mouth opened and closed but nothing came out. She and Alex exchanged glances, each of them willing the other to talk, to tell the detective of their harebrained plan for her to find 'closure'. It was ridiculous, Amy thought now – she would never find closure. She had done better in the last ten years through denial than she ever would by raking over the past again and again.

The detective looked at them and seemed to decide that they really shouldn't have this conversation in an open space. They were quickly led down a labyrinth of corridors to a small, featureless room, with chairs around a meeting table and a water dispenser in one corner. Alex went over and filled two white plastic cups, returning to the table with them. Amy sat down and drank greedily, her throat objecting to the sudden coldness sweeping across it. Alex silently took her empty cup, got up again and refilled it for her.

The detective closed the door, and came to sit opposite them. 'How are you, Amy?' he asked. The concern on his face seemed genuine. 'I've often thought about you, you know.'

She tried out a smile. It didn't work. 'I'm okay,' she said quietly.

'You're here to see these men get put away,' he said, a statement, not a question.

'We thought it would be a good idea,' she replied, putting her head in her hands. It felt far from a good idea right now.

She looked up again and the detective was nodding, but he didn't say anything.

'Will they?' Alex asked, urgency in his tone. 'Do you think they'll be found guilty?'

They both watched Detective Thompson intently. He nodded. 'They will,' he said, no trace of doubt showing on his face. 'Of course, the law can be strange . . . unpredictable at times. But unless something happens that we haven't anticipated, and I can't for the life of me think what, then this case is cut and dried. They'll be in prison till they're old men, if not until they die. Amy . . .' he reached across and put his hand over hers, and she concentrated on not snatching it away, '. . . I think you were right to come,' he said.

'I don't think I can stay, though,' she replied, still staring at his hand on top of hers. 'I thought it would be good seeing them there, but . . . the details . . . I can't . . .' She took her hand from under his and smoothed her hair down over her ears.

'Amy –' Alex began, but the detective held up his hand.

'I can understand that, Amy.' He paused and appeared to be thinking. 'But the case is nearly over. The defence has almost finished, closing arguments won't take long. Why don't you stay in Perth, rest a while, and when the verdict is announced I'll make sure you're here for it.'

This sounded like something she might manage. She nodded. 'Okay. Thank you.'

'Of course.' Detective Thompson got up. 'Just give me your number.'

Alex pulled out a business card. 'My mobile works here,' he said, handing it over. 'And we're staying at the Crowne Plaza.'

The detective nodded. They shook hands.

'Thank you,' Alex said.

'No problem. I'll be in touch. It's good to see you.' Detective Thompson put a hand on Amy's shoulder briefly as he left. He turned at the door. 'If you haven't already, Amy,' he said, 'phone your mum, love.'

Then he was gone.

***

By the time they got back to the hotel it was early afternoon, and jetlag was catching up with them.

'What do we do now?' Amy asked.

Alex looked embarrassed. 'I might sleep for a few hours, then see if I can reach Chloe – if I leave it till teatime here, it'll be early morning there.'

Amy nodded, then watched him lie on his bed and fall asleep. She was tired too, but she knew she'd never drift off, not after today. She couldn't stop thinking about the court. The horrible details. That stupid witness. Those men . . . their blank, unrepentant faces . . .

Before she knew it, the bottles in the minibar were all empty.

She was sitting on the floor beside her bed, unsure how she had ended up there. She reached to try to get up, and sent an object crashing to the ground. She put her hand back down on the floor and felt a sliver of glass biting into it. As she watched, a red stream began to course along one of the lines in her palm.

In no time, it seemed, there were arms around her, pulling her up. Alex's hair was ruffled, his eyeballs pink with tiredness. She watched as he looked down at the shards of glass on the floor, and then he picked her up and carried her the short distance to the tiny cubicle of a bathroom.

'Thank you,' she said wearily, over and over.

'It's okay,' he shushed her. He sat her on the toilet and pulled her arm towards the sink tap, within easy reach. He washed the blood off and took a good look at her hand. 'It's not so bad,' he said. 'I'll wrap it up.'

Once he had wrapped it in a flannel belonging to the

hotel, he carried her back to the bed. She noticed a smear of blood on his neck.

'Rest, Amy,' he told her.

She tried to sit up, but her head had drums inside that began a frantic banging in response to the movement. She quickly lay down again. The fog in her brain was welcome; she much preferred it to clarity right now.

'Sssh, Amy.' Alex was stroking her hair. His voice became sludgy as she began to drift towards unconsciousness.

And then she told him. Why at that moment, she didn't know. But she just couldn't continue holding on to it alone any longer.

'I had a baby, Alex,' she whispered, pausing. 'And then I did a terrible, terrible thing,' she added, just before the world went black.

78

Chloe was at the office and finally getting down to some work, grateful that when she'd woken that morning she had felt a little better. She started to believe that if she didn't think too far back or too far ahead, she could do this, she could ride out this period of uncertainty without completely falling apart. In fact, she began to feel strangely empowered. The situation with Alex couldn't turn her into a wreck. Work couldn't break her. The baby was too important for her to come undone. No, when Alex returned, he'd be surprised to find her more confident, more self-assured, and more composed. No more doubting, no more worrying. She was done with that. She had found a way through.

And then the phone rang.

'Chloe?'

It took Chloe a couple of seconds to place the voice. 'June?'

'Yes, Chloe.' June's voice sounded nervous.

'Is it Mum?'

'Yes, I'm afraid so. She's in hospital.'

'Oh my god,' Chloe cried. 'What's happened?'

'I'm not sure, they think it might be a heart attack,' June whispered. 'I'm so sorry, Chloe. We're on our way there now.'

Chloe was already standing up, throwing things into her bag. 'I'm on my way too,' she said, ascertained exactly which hospital they were heading for, and hung up.

Even in the face of something so urgent Chloe baulked at telling Neil she was leaving the office again. The whole sorry mess of her life felt like it was crashing down on top of her once more. She fired off a brief email to Neil before she switched her computer off, then hurried out of the building after a quick word with Jana, praying she wouldn't bump into anybody else, and grateful at least for that small mercy when she got outside unchallenged.

It took forty-five anxious minutes on the stop-start tube for her to reach home. At least once she was in her car and driving she felt more in control, with something practical to keep her occupied, although all road sense seemed to have deserted her and she had about half a dozen near misses. She was surprised there weren't any blue flashing lights behind her yet, as she had taken no notice of any speed limits, going as fast as the traffic allowed. So much so, that now she had nearly reached Kendal, where the hospital was located, in what must have been record time from London.

Her phone began to ring as she negotiated a roundabout,

and she pulled it out of her bag, her eyes darting back to the road and adjusting her steering as she veered towards the kerb, but not wanting to stop.

She snapped it open without looking at the caller. 'Hi.'

'Chloe, it's June. Your mum's been discharged. We've brought her home. Don't go to the hospital, come to the house instead.'

'Discharged? After a heart attack? That doesn't sound right.'

'Just come to the house, love – where are you now?'

'Kendal.'

'Great; well, we'll see you soon.'

Chloe hung up, grimaced, and, without indicating, at the next roundabout went all the way round to go back in the direction she'd just come, causing an irritated motorist to honk his horn at her. She resisted the temptation to give him the finger.

It took her another forty minutes to reach the laneways near her mother's house, and as she did so, the phone rang again.

'Hi,' she said, holding the mobile sandwiched between ear and neck to allow her hands to remain on the steering wheel.

'Chloe, it's Mark. What's going on? Jana said your mum is ill.'

'Yes, heart attack,' Chloe replied, frantically turning the steering wheel at a tight bend. 'I'm nearly there now.'

'Where?'

'Lake District.'

'Christ. Chloe, I'm so sorry . . .'

Chloe felt tears welling again. God, she was so *sick* of crying. 'Thanks, Mark. Look, I'm driving, I can't really talk.'

'Okay, but ring me later, won't you? Let me know you're okay.'

'Thanks, I will.'

She hung up, gritting her teeth, and threw the phone onto the passenger seat. The conversation she'd just had should have been with Alex, not Mark.

June came out of the front door of Chloe's mother's house before Chloe had even stopped the engine. As soon as she got out of the car she was enfolded in a hug, and Chloe responded for a moment, before pulling back and looking at June's face, reassured to see only concern there.

'Where's Mum?' Chloe asked.

'Right this way,' June said, leading her towards the front door, when George appeared.

'June –' he said.

'Just let her see Margaret,' June replied, not looking at him, trying to usher Chloe inside.

Chloe stopped for a moment. This was a little odd. The two of them seemed tense, and terse with one another.

'What's going on?' she asked.

'Nothing,' June demurred in an overly bright voice, as George said, 'Chloe, a word,' and motioned her back towards the driveway.

'George –' June began, but he raised his hand to quieten her.

'We'll be there in a minute,' he said.

June shook her head but went inside.

Chloe was alarmed by all the subterfuge. 'What's going on, George?'

He looked solemnly at her over his half-moon specs. 'Your mother called from hospital this morning, saying she'd had a heart attack. So, June called you and we went down there, and waited while they did some tests . . . But, apparently, it wasn't a heart attack after all, it was an anxiety attack.'

Chloe stared at him, dumbfounded. She was aching and tired from racing up to see her mother, thinking she was critically ill, to find out she had had *an anxiety attack*?

'She seems fine now,' George continued. 'I just thought I should warn you, as I think June might have misled you on the phone this morning – unintentionally, of course. She was very worried at the time.'

Chloe nodded, still at a loss for words. She followed George into the house, and they walked through looking for her mother, who was eventually located in the kitchen.

Ironing.

'Chloe, darling!' her mother trilled as she broke off from flattening the sleeve of a blouse and came around the ironing board to embrace her. 'You're such a sweetheart to come. Silly me, thinking it was a heart attack, but I couldn't breathe all of a sudden, and then I felt so terribly dizzy, it was like I was getting sucked into a big black hole, and so I called the ambulance. And they were ever so nice, in the ambulance, they figured out it was nothing pretty quickly, but they took me in and did all the tests anyway, and said that, actually, I've got a first-class ticker, how about that?' She began to set about the sleeve with gusto. 'June and George have been marvellous, of course,' she said, finally pulling the blouse off the board and searching a nearby laundry basket for a hanger. She smiled across at June as she said this, and June, who was filling the kettle, smiled back.

There was silence as they all waited for Chloe to say something. George still looked sombre, while June was engrossed in finding tea bags, and Margaret was smiling beatifically at Chloe.

When Chloe finally spoke, it didn't sound much like herself, but the words were definitely coming from her mouth in a stream of bilious abuse.

'You selfish, selfish woman,' she spat, watching the two women's expressions become startled, and noticing somewhere in her subconscious that George was registering absolutely no surprise at her words. 'I have driven *five hours* to come and see you; I have broken speed limits all the way here; I have come, despite being incredibly tired and nauseous, all the time desperately worried about you . . . to find you *ironing*, drinking tea, perfectly well, and completely oblivious to the effect you have had on me – to the kind of stress you've caused me today – when I'm, I'm *pregnant* –' the secret was out of her mouth once again, and she registered the lack of shock on George's and June's faces with no real surprise – of course her mother had told them, her mouth was bigger than the Channel tunnel – 'and when my husband is *god knows where*' – at this, they did all look surprised '– but that's okay, Mum, my life is going down the toilet, but as long as *you're* fine . . .'

Margaret's face was a picture of shock. Having returned to the iron, she put it down absent-mindedly, not noticing as June discreetly righted it so it wouldn't burn a hole in the cover. 'Chloe –' she began.

'Save it,' Chloe said, holding up her hand. 'I don't want to hear it. Just stay away from me. Just leave me alone from now on.'

And she ran out of the room, down the hallway, and through the front door.

She was clutching her car keys, trying to find the right key on the fob, when she heard steps behind her. She swung round ready to launch into another tirade, to find George there.

'George, don't –' she said.

He put his arm around her. 'I'm not,' he replied. 'Just . . . don't drive all the way back tonight,' he said, pressing something into her hand. She looked down to see two fifty-pound notes there, and reacted by trying to give them back to him.

'Chloe,' he said, ignoring her and holding her shoulders gently. 'I'm your uncle, or as good as. I'm paying for you to find a hotel for the night. Humour me. Okay?'

She nodded, looked quickly into his eyes and then down at the gravel drive.

He kissed her on the forehead. 'We'll call you,' he said, walking back towards the front door as she got into the car, and stopping the two women, who had come behind him, from going any further.

'Chloe,' Margaret called, and her voice was high and unnerved. 'Please.' But Chloe was in her vehicle now, and she drove away without looking back.

79

As the sun cast the dusky pinks and mellow oranges of dawn onto the river, the first boats were already making their leisurely way along. The city was lazily yawning and stretching, preparing for another busy day. By contrast, as he stood on the hotel room balcony, Alex's mind was frantic. He had given up all thought of rest some hours ago.

He was out of his depth here. How had it come to this? How come it always felt like he was on the back foot, desperately parrying what everyone else could throw at him?

In his hand was his plane ticket. He had been thinking all night of heading to the airport, catching a plane back to Chloe. He'd been intent on calling her yesterday evening, but Amy's revelation had thrown him completely off-kilter again. He didn't know how much more he could take; the whole thing was becoming a bigger and bigger mess. He tried to imagine how he would be feeling in Chloe's position. He felt he had let her down, and for what? A girl from his past he thought he owed something to; a girl who this morning he didn't feel he knew at all any more.

He was so angry with Amy.

But then, as always, his thoughts came back to the fact that nothing was her fault. She, more than anyone else, was the victim in this.

He was not that far away from the street where she'd been snatched. He wondered if it would be cathartic to go back there, or whether he would be torturing himself by retracing the steps of a journey that was immeasurably painful the first time around. He had no fucking idea. No clue about the rights and wrongs of any of this.

He leaned against the balcony railing and breathed in the fresh morning air, trying to think of the way forward. Maybe the problem was that he was letting things happen; the empathy he had for everyone else was colouring every action he thought about taking, converting them to inaction. In fact, his decision-making abilities seemed so far to have been paralysed.

But not any more.

He stood back from the railing, stretched, and headed inside.

Amy was asleep, a mound under the sheets, her face buried in the pillow. Alex grabbed his phone and went down to the lobby.

Chloe's mobile rang until her voicemail cut in. He had forgotten it was late at night there; she might well be asleep.

The soft, cheerful sound of her voice made him unbearably homesick. After the beep, he tried to leave a message.

'Chloe, I'm so sorry about all of this. I —' He paused, trying to think of what to say. 'I want to explain, please give me that chance —' He didn't know what else to add, so in desperation he hung up and tried the number again, not expecting an answer, but then heard a click as it connected.

'Alex?' Chloe's voice came on the line, low and cautious; for him it was like water on parched skin.

'Thank god. Chloe, I'm so sorry. Are you okay?' There was a pause. 'No, of course not. Stupid question. Did you get any of the messages I left? I've wanted to talk to you so much; to explain. I shouldn't have left like that —'

'I deleted a lot of the messages, Alex. I was too upset to listen to them.' She sounded weary and reserved. Not like her usual self at all. He cringed at having done this to her. To them.

'Okay, then I need to tell you — we're in Australia because there's a trial — for the murder of another girl. It's the same people, Chloe . . . Amy wanted to come back . . . she's completely alone; I felt I owed her this. And it was now or never. Last time I let her down . . . this time I wanted to do something . . . These monsters need to get put away.'

'And what do you think you're doing to me now? For god's sake, Alex — *Australia*?'

He didn't know what to say to that.

'Just how long are you planning to be in *Australia*? Why haven't you called before?' she said, still sounding tired.

'I know, I'm sorry,' he began. 'It's just, it's hard to get a moment alone . . .'

He trailed off, but she didn't miss a beat. 'Please don't tell me you're sharing a room with her, Alex.' There was an edge to her voice, and his mind was shouting, *Lie, lie, don't let her think this of you*, but the words wouldn't reach his mouth, so, stupidly, he paused for too long, until saying anything would have been worthless.

There was an almighty silence. Then he heard her voice again, and it was cracked with rage. 'And what about a *bed*, Alex, are you sharing a bed too?'

'NO! Chloe, don't . . .' he said, but the line was already dead.

He remained frozen for a moment with the phone dangling uselessly from his hand. Then a wave of weariness crashed over him, and he headed back to the hotel room, lay on his bed, and tried to rein in his rising emotions.

After what seemed like hours, sleep finally descended on him.

When he woke up, Amy was dressed and sitting by the window.

'What time is it?' he asked, trying to clear the fug from his head; remembering with a pang that his conversation with Chloe hadn't been a dream.

'Half-past twelve,' she replied.

'Bloody hell.' He ran his hand over his face, slowly coming to. 'How long have you been awake?'

'A while.' She wouldn't look at him.

'Amy?'

She remained stone-still.

'Amy, look at me.'

Slowly, she turned her head. His heart sank. Her face was stricken and tear-stained.

He got up and dressed in silence, while Amy continued to stare out of the window. Then he put his hand on her shoulder.

'Let's go and get something to eat.'

She shook her head.

'Amy.' His tone lowered as he barked at her, his patience thinning. 'It wasn't a question. Come on, let's go.'

When she lifted her head, she looked taken aback. But she did as he said, getting up and slipping her shoes on, and they headed out the door. This time, Alex was determined to excavate right to the bottom of all their secrets, and uncover some answers.

80

They bought sandwiches and drinks and headed down to the river, finding a spot on the foreshore away from people, listening to the raucous cockatoos flapping from tree to tree. They were alone, except for the occasional walker or cyclist briskly crossing their path.

'Last night –' Alex began.

Amy held up her hand. 'I'm sorry, I was drunk.'

'Yes, well, for a start that isn't like you –'

She bit back, indignance hammering against her throbbing hangover. 'Alex, really, how would you know what's like me? You haven't seen me for ten years! You're now a married graphic designer; how the hell do you know what I've become?'

What on earth have I become, she thought as she finished, momentarily quaking inside.

'Okay, point taken.' He paused, took a deep breath. They

both knew what was coming. 'But, Amy, you said – you had a *baby*?'

She nodded, staring out across the flat water of the river.

'So it's true?' Alex said softly.

She nodded again.

Another long, weighty pause. Then, 'Was it mine?'

She shook her head. She wouldn't look at him; she didn't want to see his expression. She couldn't believe there were more tears left in her, but here they were again, falling silently down her cheeks.

'Amy,' he said, and before he could ask any more, she was compelled to start talking.

'You don't understand at all,' she said quietly. 'Being . . . attacked like that . . . it causes scars that can't ever fully heal. But it's more than just a few marks on your body or in your head. In that one day, I lost everything. My self-confidence was gone. My trust in people was gone. I lost my parents, who didn't see me as their innocent girl any more, but as their daughter "the victim". I lost my friends, as I couldn't face any of them. I felt like what had happened was written all over me, that people knew how disgusting and violated I was as soon as they looked at me. I felt worlds apart from everyone; I couldn't even understand what I'd ever had in common with anyone.'

Her voice was unnaturally high, breaking as she spoke. Her throat felt heavy with the truth of what came next as she looked at Alex. 'And I lost you.'

Alex tried to meet her eyes, but he could see too deeply into them. He flinched and bowed his head.

'We lost each other,' he said to the grass. 'And I know that there's nothing I can say to put that right.'

But she was not ready to be silent and listen to him.

'When something so utterly vile happens to you, it feels like a new person has taken over your body – like you've been possessed by this stranger. And you're forced to live with them and get to know them, and respond to their wants and needs and desires, because they are you . . . and yet, they are not you. And while this walking ghost takes over your life, you are desperately trying to find ways to exorcise it – but you never can, because a living, breathing memory has given birth to it, and unless you can get rid of every second of that memory, you can never regain full control of yourself. So I've been wandering like a lost soul within the confines of my own body, hoping beyond all reason that one day I might come back and be myself again. And I'm still waiting, Alex. I'm waiting and hoping and praying . . . I don't know how much longer I –'

Her voice rose and was absorbed into the wind. She couldn't go on.

Alex's arms wrapped around her, and he pulled her close. She clung on to him desperately, crying, not noticing until her tears began to subside that his body was heaving too.

'I'm so sorry, Amy,' he whispered into her hair.

After what seemed like a long time, they were both calm and quiet again, staring out across the water. Something had shifted in Amy, and, remarkably, it felt a little like a brief snatched moment of peace.

'Are you going to get in touch with your mum?' Alex asked.

'I don't know.'

'I think you should.'

She looked at Alex. He was still watching the water. 'I'm not sure she'll want to talk to me after what happened with Dad.'

'Amy, your dad was an old man –'

She interrupted, 'Who had a heart attack because of stress. I'm sure of it. If I hadn't – if it hadn't happened, he wouldn't have died.'

'You don't know that.'

'No, I don't, not for sure, but I'm pretty certain. I ran away because I was desperate, but I was so selfish – I didn't think about the effect it might have on my poor dad. I just knew that people love to gossip, and when you're the victim everyone looks at you and feels so sorry and sad for you, and then they go home and curl up on the sofa and feel so grateful and smug that they're so lucky. I used to do it – I didn't know that what I was doing was so hurtful, but I did it. And I didn't want the sadness of my life to be the prop in someone else's self-esteem, for people to be looking at me and thinking, *Well, it could be worse, I could be Amy Duvalis.*'

She was expecting Alex to object to this, but he didn't say anything for a while. The silence between them was heavy, but not uncomfortable. Finally, he said, 'Amy?'

'Hmm.' She didn't look at him.

'Please tell me about the baby.'

She knew that there was no going back after she told him. She knew he might well judge her. But she also knew it had to be said.

'I didn't know for ages,' she began. 'My head was so messed up, I didn't notice I'd barely had a period for months – I presumed it was all part of the trauma. There was no reason for me to think that . . . they had done a test in the hospital, and given me the morning-after pill. Twice, if I remember rightly, because I kept being sick and they were worried I was throwing it back up. Obviously, they were right. When I finally twigged, it was just from seeing myself in a full-length mirror one day – big boobs, rounded tummy. It suddenly dawned on me – it's crazy, I know.

'At first I wanted to get rid of it. I was in Thailand at the time, and I went to a doctor . . .'

Telling it also meant reliving it. *The dirty waiting room. The wrinkled doctor touching her stomach, nodding, gesturing for her to take off her underwear. His impatience when she refused, grabbing her arm, causing her to run out of the place without even paying, the sounds of his unintelligible shouting chasing her down the street.*

'I was in denial till I was about six months gone. I was checking in with Mum and Dad most weeks, telling them I was okay, not mentioning it to them at all. I was bracing myself to come home, but also putting it off.'

She closed her eyes, remembering how her dad would plead every time for her to come back, or at least tell him where she was. How she wished now that she hadn't refused him.

'After I began to accept what was happening, I wanted the baby to be yours,' she said, not daring to look at him. 'I dreamed of presenting you with your child, and your over-joyed face when you saw us, and the dream sustained me. In fact, I was convinced it was yours – although I still wouldn't come home. Looking back, I'm sure that somewhere in my subconscious I knew that if I did, I couldn't keep alive the spell I'd woven around myself – there would be too many questions.

'Then, when I was eight months pregnant, I called home . . .'

Another raw, crippling memory. *Her mother, the calm, practical one, had been hysterical. Her dad had already been dead three days from the heart attack. Her mum was alone. She had begged Amy to come back.*

'In the emotion of it all I promised I would come home, but I knew I couldn't. Even if I'd wanted to, no airline would have let me on a plane – I was enormous. I was in a state of terrible grief, I was inconsolable. And alone. I don't remember much about the week after that phone call.'

Bangkok, a dirty, bare-walled room with a faint smell of sewage. A bed with a grey sheet, on which she had lain all week. The concerned owners – an old, hunched Thai couple – whispering whenever they saw her . . .

'My waters broke one morning about a week after I heard about Dad, and the hostel owners took me to hospital. The wife even stayed with me, and held my hand, and gave me instructions in faltering English when I didn't understand what was going on, and calmed me down when I tried to push doctors away from me.'

And cooed over the baby when it was born, and looked quite upset when Amy wouldn't really look at the child.

'The birth itself was horrific. But that night, after I had her, I couldn't help myself. I *looked* at her, and, beyond my expectations, the whole mother-love thing happened. She was beautiful. Actually, I was enraptured for five whole days while I was in hospital . . .' She paused; took a slow, deep breath.

'Then, when we were leaving, they gave me her medical records.'

She had taken them so readily, just a form listing a few details. Her eyes had scanned once . . . and then again, more slowly, everything inside her shattering in a blast of grief as the truth had torn through her.

'Do you remember my dad making us find out our blood groups before we went on our trip, just in case?'

Alex nodded. He knew what was coming, and closed his eyes as he listened.

'She was A negative. We were both O. She wasn't yours.'

Alex's eyelids flicked open after she'd said it and he stared at her. She held his gaze.

'I took her away anyway, but I was in terrible, terrible shock. I couldn't live in denial any more – I couldn't ignore such concrete evidence, I couldn't un-tell myself the truth.

'That night I tried to persuade myself I could keep loving her, but something had changed and I couldn't turn it back. God, it was awful; in a way I loved her beyond anything I'd imagined, but I was in turmoil and I knew – I just knew – I couldn't keep her. What if she looked like one of *them*? What if she asked about her father when she got older? It's hard even to describe what was going on – it was like my head was full of demons whispering relentlessly, and I was just fighting to breathe. I was insane at the time, crazy with choices that all appeared to lead to terrible consequences.

'I had a bath in my room. I hadn't had a proper wash in the hospital. I filled it with water . . .'

Her voice was cold and almost alien to him.

'Amy –' Alex began, eyes widening in alarm. 'Don't. Please stop. I don't want to hear any more.'

'I thought about it,' she said, ignoring him. 'She was sleeping, and I thought about gently putting her in the water and letting her sink to the bottom. Only for a fraction of a second, but I was horrified at myself nevertheless. After that, I knew what I had to do. I couldn't be trusted around her. And this beautiful little thing deserved a chance. But she couldn't stay with me. I couldn't even take her home to my mum and ask for help, not with every millimetre of that space screaming out the absence of my father.

'So I did the only thing I thought of at the time.'

Trembling, the scissors on her penknife moving towards her soft, vulnerable head, taking a small lock of downy hair, a tiny keepsake.

Alex braced himself, tensed, waiting.

'I wrapped her in a shawl, then put her in a cardboard box. And I left her on the doorstep of a nearby Buddhist monastery.'

The spot behind the wall where she had stood for what felt like hours – though it was probably only minutes – watching that box until the door opened. Stray dogs sniffing at it, chickens running next to it, her heart thundering.

'So many times I nearly ran back. In fact, I was about to, when the door opened and a monk stood there . . .'

He had been blinking in the early light, as though he couldn't quite believe what he was seeing. Wrapped in orange robes with his alms bowl under his arm. Middle-aged, bald, bespectacled. Kind-looking.

'He just peered into that box, picked it up and carried it inside and closed the door, like he was collecting the post, no emotion showing on his face at all.

'And then she was gone. And I left.' Amy released all the breath in her lungs with a huge sigh, then covered her eyes with her palms and mumbled towards the ground.

'And that was that.'

81

Alex had no idea what to say. Amy looked at his face and could see that he was stunned.

'Amy,' he breathed eventually, still incredulous about what he had heard.

She had been so calm as she told him all this, but now her voice cracked. 'I know,' she said. 'It's awful. There have been so many times I've wanted to go back and ask about her, but I don't dare. I abandoned my baby girl – the only way I can get through it is that in my daydreams she's living a happy and secure life with people who love her. Otherwise . . .'

'What did you do after that?' he asked quickly to distract her.

'I left Thailand. I went to Europe. I pretended it had never happened. It wasn't too hard, in a way – my whole life became surreal very quickly. The baby began to feel like a strange dream. My nomadic existence became normal. And the years slipped by. I did lots of different things, went to lots of different places – hell, once or twice I was surprised to find I was beginning to enjoy something. Many times I thought about ending it, often just after an unexpected high, when the low that inevitably came next was all the more crushing. But I had made a promise to Mum and it stuck – something in me felt I owed it to her, I guess.'

'Or maybe you just didn't really want to die,' he added.

Amy looked taken aback. 'I wanted to die,' she said.

'Maybe you just wanted the pain to go away,' he continued. 'And it was the only way out of it you could think of. But it's not the same thing.'

He could see she had never thought of it like that before. 'Well,' she said, after a pause, 'now you know just how evil I am.'

Alex moved closer to her, and put his arm around her shoulders. 'Nothing you've told me has been evil,' he told her. 'Tragic, yes. But that's all.'

'I abandoned my baby, Alex,' she said.

'I know.' He kissed her hair. 'God, Amy, what you've gone through – it's unimaginable. And I let you down, right from the start. I should have kept you close, helped you to –'

'I don't feel like that,' Amy interrupted. 'I've been angry at you, sure – when you walked out of the hospital, I felt I hated you for a while. But I've had a lot of thinking time since, and I understand. It wasn't your fault either, we were both caught up by circumstance. If it hadn't been for the baby, I'm sure I would have come back a lot sooner.'

Alex's heart surged with affection for her as he took in her softly spoken words. 'Well, everything is changing now,' he told her. 'It's going to be okay. I already have a plan for what we should do.'

Amy rested her head on his shoulder as he talked, and together they watched the boats bobbing on the river.

82

Mark hesitated as he checked the screen on his mobile. He hadn't seen his father since Henry had stormed out of the apartment. Yes, it was pricking at his conscience, but he easily put it to the back of his mind because, first of all, he was getting heaps of work done, and secondly, he'd been spending a lot of time with Chloe.

Finally, they were getting on top of the Abbott research. On Friday, Mark had been intrigued to see Chloe, dressed in jeans and a T-shirt, walking hastily into her office and had followed her inside, closing the door behind him.

'What's going on?' he'd asked, gesturing to her unorthodox officewear.

'Don't ask,' Chloe had said, shaking her head, but then, as he sat in the chair usually reserved for her clients, she proceeded to tell him what her mother had done the day before.

When she finished, by saying 'Can you believe her?', Mark had shaken his head.

'What's wrong with our parents?' he'd asked.

'God knows,' Chloe said, her own head shaking again in echo of his. 'I'm worried Mum is losing it, and I can't expect June and George to be responsible for her. But I also can't race up there every time her heart skips a beat and she panics and phones an ambulance.'

'It could be worse,' Mark said. 'She could be coming into your office wearing your clothes and trying to take over your cases.'

They'd looked at each other for a long moment, and Mark had laughed first. Chloe quickly followed, and for a moment they revelled in the release of it.

'God,' Chloe said, reaching for a tissue and blowing her nose. 'I keep trying to think back over what I've done to have attracted such incredibly bad karma.'

'Don't waste your time,' Mark said, sobering. 'None of this is your fault. Sometimes life is just shite, I reckon.'

Chloe looked at him and sighed. 'Yes, I know you're right. To be honest, I'm fed up with going over and over everything. I just want to forget about it all for a while and get on with this.' She gestured to her paper-strewn desk.

'Fancy a working weekend?' Mark suggested. 'I'm thinking we surprise Neil by actually displaying a certain degree of competency about the Abbott case by Monday morning.'

Chloe had smiled, then nodded. 'Definitely.'

So they had worked on Friday night, over a Thai takeaway; then all yesterday, stopping only for a deli lunch break, and a fish and chip supper. Mark had slept on Chloe's couch, and they'd resumed again in the morning. They hadn't talked about anything awkward – certainly not the pregnancy, which Mark was doing his best to pretend didn't exist – it was either the case, or irrelevancies like politics, TV or which films they'd seen recently. By lunchtime there had been an efficient pile of notes, and nothing much left for them to do, so Mark had decided to head back to his apartment, but not before telling Chloe he was taking her out for a meal later.

They were growing closer, he could feel it, and he was revelling in it. He'd never expected to have time alone with her like this again, but in the past week they had established a cajoling, easy banter that he didn't even remember them having the first time around. His chest swelled with happiness whenever he made her smile. He was also boosted by the knowledge that each smile was a small victory over her undeserving husband, proving that Chloe might still be happy without him.

But now the phone was ringing, distracting him from these welcome thoughts, and when he saw who the caller was, it was with the greatest reluctance that he decided he had to take the call.

'Hi, sis,' he said.

'Mark,' came his sister's no-nonsense voice down the line. 'I'm calling a family summit.'

Mark rolled his eyes at her words. 'Okay, Diane. Still the drama queen, I see.'

'Well, *you* could try and wait for at least sixty seconds before acting like an arse, Mark,' his sister said in reply.

They'd always been this way. Mark was fairly sure there was a mutual affection hidden under the surface somewhere, but he'd yet to locate it conclusively. He found his sister curt and condescending, and knew without a doubt that she had exactly the same opinion of him.

'Go on then, let's hear it,' he said.

'Well, obviously, it's about Dad,' she replied. 'And since I know he's been staying with you a lot recently, I'm surprised you haven't been in touch.'

Mark tried not to be riled, but it was a losing battle. 'What for?'

'What for?! Well, perhaps because it's bloody obvious from where I'm standing that Dad is having some kind of breakdown, and needs our help.'

'He's not having a breakdown, he's just – he's just having a rough time.'

'It's more than that, Mark.'

'I know, Di,' he said, allowing his exasperation to become evident. 'He's been lying comatose on my couch for a fair amount of time over the past week.'

'Exactly. And yet, you didn't think this was a problem.'

'Jeez, Di, don't play the doting daughter with me. It's not you who's had to put up with him.'

'Er, actually, he's been in my spare room since Thursday. Not to mention the fact that Mum is on the phone all the time, either pouring her heart out or ranting about divorcing him.'

Mark's heart sank. So that's where he'd gone. He felt pretty awful that he hadn't checked – his father could have been lying dead in a gutter for all Mark knew – but he just didn't want to deal with this. He wasn't even sure why, but recently every time he thought of his dad's troubled, decrepit face, it made him want to find something solid to hide behind.

'Di, I don't know. Mum and Dad have never exactly been open to us giving our opinion on things . . .'

'Well, it's about time they were, then. They're both being daft. They are completely unsentimental, egotistical idiots, but I can't believe they don't care about each other. It's up to us to bang their heads together.'

Mark snorted. 'Okay. That's a sight I'm curious to see, if nothing else. What's the plan?'

'Dad's not going anywhere, he's hardly left the spare room since he got here, and I'm doing far too good a job of waiting on him. Can you bring Mum down one night this week?'

Mark sighed. 'I guess.' The thought of travelling to southern Kent after work didn't enthral him, but at least now he had confidence that he was back on his game as far as Abbott was concerned. 'I can't do tomorrow or Tuesday, but maybe Wednesday.'

'Okay. Your job is getting Mum here. Then we'll stage an intervention.'

'A what?'

'A family crisis meeting – we'll force them to confront what's going on.'

'I can't wait.'

'Just call me back when you know for sure about Wednesday,' Di said, hanging up.

Mark sighed again as he snapped his phone shut.

83

Amy ran out of the sea, smiling, water cascading off her smooth skin, and pushed her sodden hair out of her eyes, blinking the salt away. As she walked towards Alex, a wave rose up behind her, only just above the height of her knee, but with enough strength to knock her off balance. She staggered forward, arms in front of her, but righted herself before she hit the sand, and as she did she was laughing. Alex was laughing too as she caught his eye. And there she was again.

His Amy. The one he had fallen in love with all those years ago. The one he saw returning a little more each day.

They were only three or so hours' drive from Perth, but it was as if they had been transported to another world. It seemed to Alex this might be one decision he hadn't got wrong. Although, his plan hadn't started so well – the drive down in the hire car, in the fading afternoon light, had been through deserted bushland most of the way, and Amy had been so pale he had worried he'd have to turn off course at any moment and find her a doctor.

They had arrived late. To a quiet, darkened resort, an empty reception area, then a girl handing them keys for a villa he had prebooked on the internet only hours earlier, which they had to walk down a pitch-black path to get to. By the time they had unlocked the front door and Alex had turned on the lights, Amy had been white-faced, silent, shaking, her chest rising and falling rapidly, and she'd gone and locked herself in the bathroom for over an hour, while Alex contemplated whether he was really up to this new, proactive approach.

However, the next morning, when they had woken up to the sounds of the sea and the excited squawking of children and gulls, and headed out for breakfast to find themselves in a beautiful, bustling resort, he knew for sure that his idea had been a good one. Waiting it out here would be a completely different proposition to their small, claustrophobic hotel room in the city. In fact, as the days had gone by, they both seemed almost to have forgotten that they were waiting for anything at all. They had swum, and eaten, and read, and taken walks along the beach. Last night, on one such expedition at sunset, Amy grabbed hold of his hand and held it for just a moment, while Alex thought uneasily of his wife.

When they had first got there, he had used the hotel internet and sent a long email to Chloe. He'd tried to be honest about everything, but had realised as he was typing that there were things he would never be able to explain fully. How could he tell her about his confused feelings for Amy and ask her to understand? Plus, he couldn't tell her about Amy's revelation regarding the baby; that one really wasn't his secret to divulge. So, even as he pressed Send, he'd felt it was a futile gesture; another way of disconnecting them while trying to bring them closer again. The only way he could really begin to make amends, he had come to realise, was to abandon Amy and go home. The thought nagged at him every time he checked his email. It had been five days and she hadn't replied.

He hadn't had any heart-to-hearts with Amy this week – it had been an unspoken agreement between them. They had talked a lot of baloney, really, about current affairs and other guests in the hotel. Of course, a lot of subjects veered towards uncomfortable territory, but they had both become adept at steering the conversation back on course. And they had been laughing, and teasing one another, and sometimes it had felt like they'd never stopped, and that was killing him.

This time together had made Alex realise how much he and Amy had been robbed by circumstance. Whenever he thought about it, his blood heated up with anger and injustice. He thought about his time with Chloe: Chloe laughing, dancing, cooking at home, heading off to work. He thought about Chloe in her wedding dress. Amy should have had that. If not for the twists and turns of fate, then Amy would have had it all – probably with him. How he wished he could make it up to her.

The sun had begun its descent as he watched Amy lean over him in her bikini, reaching for her towel while dripping water onto him. She had just begun rubbing her hair when Alex's mobile phone began to trill. The noise stilled her hand.

'You need to come back,' Detective Thompson said, without preamble, when Alex answered the call. 'The defence has closed. The jury are about to retire. I don't think they'll be out for long.'

Alex met Amy's eyes. She didn't need him to do anything further for them both to know that this halcyon period was over.

84

Chloe had woken up with the feeling that something was wrong. Given that everything seemed wrong these days, it felt strange to think that way, but this was different. More nagging. More troubling.

It wasn't that she was trying to block out the thought of her husband sharing a room – and a bed? – with another woman, because she had been doing that 24/7 for the past few days. Nor was it the email that was sitting patiently in her inbox, full as it was of pleading and excuses and guilt, which she still couldn't begin to think how to reply to – although that wasn't exactly helping her in her endless quest for an uninterrupted night's sleep.

Nevertheless, despite her fresh misgivings, she went to work. The Abbott countdown was now days rather than weeks. The atmosphere in the office was tense. Even the solicitors who had nothing to do with the case knew that the way it played out could have a dramatic impact on the fortunes of them all.

There was now a small scrummage of media to contend with outside the office, wanting the first sound bites, any insider knowledge. When they'd initially appeared, a couple of days earlier, Mark had described being harangued by them as he tried to walk inside; yet they'd left Chloe alone, seeming largely uninterested in her. They probably assumed she was a secretary. If so, it appeared that sexist assumptions weren't completely dead, she thought, though media savvy possibly was – the secretaries knew far more than anyone else around here.

In the office, she munched her way through a packet of crisps as she read over what seemed like dozens of emails, mostly irrelevant, paying careful attention to all those marked Abbott. Her stomach was aching at the thought of their first trip to court – another time she might have found it exciting, but she wasn't in the mood.

The morning dragged by. She didn't stop for lunch as she didn't have much of an appetite, and she couldn't wait for the day to be over. Mid-afternoon, she made her way around the desk and headed for the toilets to splash water on her face. Her body felt sluggish, out of sorts, her feet a little unsteady.

In the bathroom she stared at her face in the mirror, eyeing the girl who stared back with the same suspicious eyes. She had just turned the tap on and leaned over when the first spasm rocked her, making her almost double up. She instinctively curled into herself, going to her knees on the hard floor, trying to steady her breathing, failing before the second wave of pain rolled in. She gasped, just as the door to the toilets opened, and there was Jana, her expression moving into shock, staring at Chloe on the floor.

'Call an ambulance,' was all Chloe could murmur, before the floor quivered like the shimmer of a heat haze, and she keeled forward.

85

'You still have a life, you know,' Alex said. 'I think you're just choosing not to live it.'

They were back in Perth, sitting in a bar near their hotel, and they had both had a couple of whisky chasers. That was probably why he felt emboldened to say such a thing, Amy thought.

She had just told him she had nothing. No direction. No purpose. No attachments. Nothing. She had just said she didn't know what she would do if the verdict was not what they wanted it to be. And it had made him unaccountably angry.

However, his reply riled her.

Alex looked her in the eye and continued, 'It's beyond terrible what you've gone through. I know that. But . . .' he paused, glanced down, then back at Amy, and there was a fierce glow in his eye as he stated firmly, 'You have a life,

Amy. You are *choosing* not to live it. And every day you do that from now on is another day you let them win.'

Her mouth fell open. The tears gathered in readiness. 'That's not fair, Alex. I can't . . .' she said, voice breaking. 'I don't know how . . .'

'No,' Alex replied, the lines of his tanned face softening as he reached for her hand. 'It isn't fair. And you couldn't . . . and you didn't . . . But think about why we're here. Now, Amy, I think you can.'

Maybe he was right, she thought, seeing past her emotion for a second. It was why she had felt compelled to come this far – she needed to see them get what they deserved. She had to see them punished, because if she did, then another small chink of her ethereal life might crack and reveal something solid underneath that she had been missing. Something she could hold on to and tease out until it grew bigger.

86

Chloe braced herself as the doctor walked towards her, notes in hand, and reached her bedside. She'd been groggy ever since the ambulance ride a few hours earlier.

'Good news, Mrs Markham,' he said, looking down and flicking through a few sheets of white paper. 'There's no sign of any problems on the ultrasound and your bloodwork is as it should be. Your gall bladder looks fine too. However, since we're not sure what this pain was, I'm recommending at least a good couple of weeks' rest. We can discharge you when you're ready, and you should come straight back if you have any more problems.'

Chloe nodded mutely, trying to be thankful that the baby was okay. But she wanted to cling to his coat and cry like a child, tell him how much she missed Alex and how she wished he were here to take her home.

He wasn't. He still didn't even know she was pregnant,

for god's sake. And she realised there was only one other person she wanted to phone.

After the doctor had gone, she used her mobile to make a call. She got an answering machine, so dialled Jana instead. The secretary picked up straight away with a practised 'Lewis and Marchant'. Chloe tried to imagine the everyday happenings in the office going on as normal. It seemed so remote from where she was at present, even though she'd been a part of it a few hours before.

'Hi, Jana,' she began.

'Chloe? Chloe, I'm so sorry, are you okay?'

'I'm fine,' she said. 'Can you put me through to Mark?'

'Mark? Mark's not here. I haven't seen him all morning. Isn't David still with you? He took a taxi and followed the ambulance.'

'David?' Chloe looked up in surprise and, sure enough, she could see her boss through a small window, standing outside the door talking to the doctor, his face grim. He glanced at Chloe as they spoke.

'Yes, sorry, Jana, I've just seen him,' she said.

'Get well, Chloe,' Jana replied. 'Just let me know if you need anything.'

'Thanks,' Chloe said, hanging up and leaning back onto her pillow, not wanting to look in David's direction. How embarrassing. Things were getting weirder by the minute.

David finished his conversation with the doctor, and then opened the door.

'The doctor says you're fine to go home, Chloe. I'll take you there in a cab. Unless there's someone else – ?'

Absurdly, with Alex absent, it was Mark's face that

sprang again into her mind, but she could imagine David's eyebrows never returning from his hairline if she told him that. So she shook her head and said, 'Taxi's fine.'

David disappeared, and Chloe nestled into the pillows, staring at the ceiling. Her womb still ached; the poor baby must be very uncomfortable. What had she done to cause everything that was happening to her? First Alex, and now this.

She thought back to Alex's email. She wasn't going to write back; what was there to say, as, while things were like this, the ball had to be in his court. She couldn't beg – even if she felt like it, which she wasn't sure she did – because if anything changed as a result, she'd always wonder if it had really been because he wanted it to, or if it were just because she had made him feel guilty.

And why did she want *Mark* right now? Heaven forbid, she wasn't somehow, in some unbelievably stupid way, rekindling feelings for him? No, she reassured herself, it was because, even though Mark was completely annoying, he knew her. He could rile her, but he also understood how to comfort her. And he knew about the baby. And he was dependable. The thought surprised her. Yes, Mark was, for all his faults, dependable, if you really needed him. And, right now, he was pretty much the only person she felt that way about.

'Chloe?' A nurse's head popped around the door. 'The taxi your dad ordered is here.'

'What?' Chloe was taken aback. 'He's not my dad.'

The nurse shrugged, uninterested. 'Well, whoever he is, he's come to collect you. You ready to go?'

Chloe nodded. The nurse came in with a wheelchair, then

helped Chloe off the bed and into it. 'Remember, straight into bed when you get home, okay?' she said. 'Now, here are your ultrasound pictures.'

Chloe took the proffered envelope as though it might explode in her hand. Then, gingerly, she pulled out the contents, and stared at the black and white outlines of her baby. She could make out a nose, a spine, even fingers. She laughed in wonder as her eyes moistened. It was the first time she had felt anything like happiness in weeks. 'Hello, little one,' she said, stroking her tummy while staring at the irrefutable evidence that there was another life inside her to think about now.

She pushed the pictures back into the envelope as David came in and spoke to the nurses, then was given her belongings. He looked smaller somehow in the hospital, and his crisp pinstriped suit stood out incongruously against the white jackets. It was as if he'd lost the ability to frighten her here, like she suddenly saw through the whole charade of power that was behind labels such as 'boss' and 'mum' and 'dad' and 'doctor'. It reminded her of the first time she'd seen her mother in this way, stripped of the thin façade of parenthood that maintained the proper distance between mother and daughter, realising she was fallible after all. The image was disconcertingly incomplete, and Chloe shrugged it away quickly.

David took the handles of her chair, and she let him wheel her to the entranceway, feeling mortified, the silence between them not helping. At the taxi's door she got up, swayed slightly, and he put a steady hand underneath her elbow to help her rebalance. She was aware of the hand and held that side of her body stiff, wanting to pull away but keen not to appear rude.

The silence continued on the journey, until they drew up at the house. All Chloe wanted was to exit the car as quickly as possible and run inside, locking the world out. But as she made to get out, so did David.

He followed her wordlessly up to the front door. Her hands trembled as she twisted the key, and she left the door open, aware of his presence behind her as she made her way up the hall.

Once in the kitchen, she tried to appear normal. 'Tea?' she enquired breezily.

'Sit,' David commanded, pointing to a chair. 'I'll do it. You're meant to go to bed.'

He moved deftly to the sink and filled the pot. Chloe watched him, marvelling at his ease in an unfamiliar kitchen. She always felt awkward when in someone else's territory, never sure of the correct mix of etiquette between unobtrusive and helpful.

'I'm sorry, David,' she said. 'This is a terrible time for you to be out of the office.'

He held up a hand, turning to face her. 'Here's what I know. We are expecting great things from you and Mark Jameson, and over the past ten years you have never let us down . . .'

Chloe thought back to the law ball dance floor and the look on David's face as he'd chastised them in his office afterwards, but didn't remind him.

'. . . and yet in the past few weeks you have both become creatures of scarcity, shall we say. You each have a look in your eyes akin to battery-farm chickens trapped in cages waiting for the electric current to reach them, and now I pick you up from hospital, where your husband is conspicuously absent, and I am told that the baby you are carrying is absolutely fine!'

He paused and shook his head in incredulity as Chloe stared at him. 'Chloe, they said you are over four months pregnant – when were you going to tell us?' Despite the admonition, David's tone was surprisingly gentle.

He paused, taking a breath as if what was coming next would be the crux of it all. 'Chloe, is this Mark's child?'

Chloe stared aghast at David, remembering Mikaela asking the very same question, then Mark's lips on hers, then Alex's tight, distant expression. Her husband was in another country with a woman she'd only set eyes on twice; and she remembered again the looks on their faces when they'd first seen one another.

Her mind swam. It was all too much.

She burst into unstoppable, uncontrollable tears. She bent double, her arms wrapped around her stomach, frightened that this outburst would be the last straw for the fragile being trying to cling on inside her, but unable to control the great well of emotion that suddenly breached the walls she had been building and fortifying for the past few weeks. She was so tired of being angry. So tired of feeling out of control. So tired of spending each day on the very tip of a knife edge.

So tired.

She had even forgotten that she wasn't alone, until strong arms came around her and pulled her in. At first she resisted, but then gradually she let herself fall against him, allowing her weight to lean on these arms that held her, until, after an age, she subsided into smaller snuffling sobs, entirely spent.

'Chloe, Chloe . . .' As she grew quieter, David pushed her back so he could see her face. She didn't want to look up, the first trickles of embarrassment now finding a route through her emotions, and kept her eyes on the buttons of his shirt.

'Chloe, you must talk to us. Of course we would be concerned, perhaps annoyed, and yes, we do have the business very much at heart as well, but we are just like you at the end of the day – just as capable as you are of screwing up every damn thing.' She looked up and he gave her a smile and raised an eyebrow, and appeared pleased when she couldn't help but give a small smile back.

'Besides,' David's jaw clenched, 'Mark is just as accountable for this as you are, and, from what I can see, he's not giving you much support.'

'No, no,' Chloe said immediately. 'It's not that.' All at once she wanted to laugh. 'Thank god it's not that! My husband is, in fact, the father of my child!'

David looked uncomfortable. 'I'm sorry, that was most presumptuous –'

Chloe cut him off, waving his apology away. 'Don't worry about it. But as for Mark, did Neil not tell you about Henry?' she asked.

David sat back and sighed. 'Oh, so that's it, is it? Do you know what's going on with Henry?' He sounded weary.

Chloe shrugged. 'No, and I'm not even sure that Mark does.'

David nodded and looked at his watch. 'I might try to

find Mark, then, when I head back, and see what's what. I seem to be spending the day ensconced in the mysterious subterranean world of my staff, so I may as well carry on.

'Now,' he continued, looking at Chloe. 'I'm going to have to go, but I don't want you to be on your own. I want you to call someone.'

'I will,' she said, with no such intention.

'Now, Chloe, while I'm here.'

'I'll call someone, I promise.' She looked up at him indignantly. 'Don't you trust me?'

'No,' David replied. She waited for a smile to appear, but he just stared at her expectantly. She could already feel his role changing from that of her confidant back to her superior, and she got up and went to the side table, where both the phone and her address book lay.

She paused over the address book, mentally riffling through lists of names without even opening it. Who could she call? She discounted friends with small babies, friends with work commitments, friends who lived too far away. She didn't want to go to someone else's house; she wanted to stay right here and rest among her own things.

In the back of her mind, despite everything, there was just one name. She picked up the phone and dialled. A voice answered after only a couple of rings.

'Mum?' Chloe said.

87

By the time Mark got onto the train, it had already been a long day – the court session had dragged on interminably with convoluted legal argument, then as the barrister had summed up the jury had looked at him like he'd just stepped out of a shiny silver spaceship and tried to talk to them in Martian. They had screw-all chance of winning this one. The only consolation was that, deep down, Mark knew his client was a wanker, and deserved what was coming; still, he hated defeat.

His mother was waiting in her car at the station.

'Ready?' she asked as he got in and leaned across to kiss her cheek.

'Yep. What about you?'

'I don't know why I let your sister talk me into this,' she said, pulling out into the heavy traffic.

They undertook most of the hour's journey in silence.

It was after seven when they finally pulled up, and Mark thought his mother looked as tired as he felt. He wasn't sure exhaustion was the ideal prerequisite for a family show-down, but there was not a lot they could do about that.

No sooner had the engine gone silent than Di's front door flew open, as though she'd been watching for them. She rushed out and hugged her mother, then Mark, though less enthusiastically.

Di looked nervous. Her face turned from one to the other as she said, 'He doesn't know you're coming.'

Mark couldn't hide his frustration at such pettiness. 'Jesus, Di,' he said, rolling his eyes.

'Well, I didn't think he'd hang around if I told him,' Di shot back, annoyed.

Their mother looked at them both. 'Stop bickering, you two. Come on, let's go and get this over with.'

They trooped inside, following Diane down a narrow corridor to the sitting room. Mark briefly glanced at the magnolia walls and the worn beige carpet – he hadn't been here for over eighteen months, but nothing had changed. It was still as drab and depressing as ever.

They all rounded the doorway to see Henry, dressed casu-ally in cord slacks and a jumper over a buttoned-up checked shirt, watching the news on TV, with Diane's husband, Sol.

'What the – ?' Henry said, half-rising out of his chair upon seeing them.

'We're here to talk to you,' Mark's mother said snippily.

Henry sank back into his chair with a noticeable thump and a muttered 'Christ', defeated now he was cornered. Mean-while, Sol took his cue and left the room without a word.

Diane strolled over to the remote and flicked the TV onto standby. The silence suddenly became apparent, like a fifth person in the room.

Mark and his mother were still standing in the doorway, neither of them making a move. Diane looked at them, shook her head, went over to sit on the sofa near to her dad's chair and took his hand.

'Dad, please don't feel got at,' she said, trying to look him in the eyes, though he couldn't hold her gaze. 'We're really worried about you. What's going on?'

Mark watched as Henry struggled between his soft spot for his daughter, which Mark had always found contemptible, and his rage at being outmanoeuvred like this. Diane was looking at Mark and her mother, her eyes imploring them to do their bit. His mother seemed frozen to the spot, so, reluctantly, Mark went and sat down on the sofa next to his sister, noticing the lack of support in it as he was swallowed up by the sagging cushions.

'We just want to help, Dad,' he said quietly.

Emily was still statue-like by the door, everyone watching her now. She had folded her arms and pursed her lips, and Mark was trying to quell his rising irritation. They'd driven all this way; she could at least try.

Then Emily began talking and Mark wished she hadn't. 'Look at you, Henry, your children fawning over you like you're an infant. What's all this nonsense about? Is it retirement, is that the problem? Because no one asked you to retire, you can head back to work if that's what's making you behave like a fool.'

Now Henry was riled. He sprang to his feet. 'I didn't

ask you to come. You can sod off if this is how much you care.'

'Dad!' Di interjected, shocked, but now their father was on a roll.

'So you want to know what's wrong, eh?' he said, marching across to his wife and spitting the words right into her face. 'Well, all right then, I'll tell you. I've got bloody Parkinson's, that's what's wrong. Instead of living a full life of retirement on the golf courses and with my friends, I'm going to be turning into a stuttering, shaking fool. That's what's bloody wrong,' he roared. 'That and the fact that I'm married to a woman with not a scrap of compassion in her body.'

Emily stood her ground, their faces only inches apart. 'The compassion drained out of me somewhat after you went out whoring,' she replied.

Henry threw his hands up. 'One time, woman,' he barked, 'one little dalliance, years ago, and you can't bloody let it go.'

'One time I actually caught you with your trousers down, don't you mean,' Emily retorted, arms folded, lips pursed.

Mark was gaping at them, lost for words, and a quick glance at Di's stunned expression told him he wasn't the only one. The sagging sofa didn't seem so bad now; in fact, he wondered if he leaned back a little further, whether it might swallow him whole. If they weren't blocking the doorway, he'd have made a dash for it rather than have to listen to any more of this.

Di recovered first. 'Mum, Dad, stop it,' she said firmly, going over and tugging on their arms as they glared at one another. 'Sit down, both of you, and keep it down, you'll wake the kids.' She pushed them in the direction of vacant seats, and then went and shut the living-room door before sitting again.

Now there were three of them in a squashed row on the sofa, like a jury appraising Henry in the adjacent armchair.

'Parkinson's, Dad,' Di said softly, reaching for his hand again, though this time Henry was quicker and moved it out of the way.

'Well, Claire's husband has had Parkinson's for years,' Emily put in after a pause, though her voice was less strident, 'and he's not too bad.'

Mark was still assessing this turn of events, and trying to ignore the revelations he'd just been privy to. Alzheimer's had been his diagnosis, he realised, surprised that his sub-conscious had thought this way all along but he hadn't really acknowledged it. 'Dad, what's with all the drinking, and the weird behaviour then?' he said, before he could stop himself.

Both his father and Di glared at him.

'I may have been on the sauce rather heavily of late,' his dad replied huffily, 'but I have been coming to terms with things.'

'I see,' Mark said, not knowing how to follow this up.

'Typical,' Emily snorted, still with no apparent sympathy in her voice. 'Always thinking of yourself – *oh, what does it mean for me* – never mind what it means for the rest of the family. We're the ones who'll end up nursing you and putting up with your moods.'

'It's hard to tell that you even care, Emily,' Henry said sarcastically.

'Of course I care,' Emily snapped, sounding anything but sympathetic. 'Although you make it mighty hard at times. But if you want my support, you have to earn it – if you want to have a little self-pity party, then you're on your own.'

Henry opened his mouth to reply, then seemed lost for words. This shocked Mark as much as any of the other revelations of the night. He was also reeling from the dawning comprehension that his mother and father didn't really seem to like one another much. Why hadn't this registered with him before? Thinking back on it, he'd never seen them being loving. They were merely civil – in fact, the times they seemed most together were when they held court in front of others at dinner parties, or at family gatherings. Then there was a united front, but he hadn't thought that behind it they were actually miserable. However, judging by what he'd seen tonight, a front was all it really was. Was this the end for them, now things were out in the open? Divorcing parents, at his age. How embarrassing.

'What do the doctors say?' Di asked.

'A lot,' Henry said, turning to her. 'I've got a specialist. I'm only in the early stages, and they've got various medications they can try nowadays, apparently.' He sounded disgusted at the thought.

'Dad,' Di said, sounding upset now. 'That's good. You know, you're not in this alone.' She reached across and stroked his arm, since Henry had kept his hand tucked away.

'I'd be better off in a home out of everyone's sight,' Henry mumbled. 'Less embarrassment all round.' He looked pointedly at his wife.

'Don't be ridiculous,' Emily said. 'Come home, Henry. Go to the doctor's. Get on with your life. Stop all this silliness. You said yourself that it's been caught early. It's not the end of the world.'

Henry flared up again, but the spark of it was diminished now. 'Easy for you to say,' he said wearily. 'Wait until you get a diagnosis like this.'

Emily looked like she was about to snap back, but then Mark's phone began beeping. He pulled it out of his pocket. Neil's name was flashing on the screen.

'I've got to take this,' he told them, pushing himself up off the sofa with an effort, and hurrying out of the living room. 'Neil,' he said, while going outside, not wanting to be accused of waking Di's boys.

'Mark,' Neil sounded weary and tense, 'have you heard about Chloe?'

Mark felt his heart do a quick, painful tremble in his chest. 'No? What's happened?'

'She collapsed at work, and was taken to hospital. Turns out, she was pregnant. Now she's been consigned to bed rest for two bloody weeks! Mark, I need you to help me handle everything she's dropped, this is the worst possible time –'

Neil sounded almost frantic now, which temporarily turned Mark's mind from worrying about Chloe.

'Of course,' Mark said. 'Surely the family law can wait for her, or one of the legal officers can help out there? It's only really Abbott that's urgent . . .'

'*Only* Abbott!' Neil replied, his voice rising. 'I could have the whole firm working on this case and still not feel prepared – it's a nightmare.'

Mark was surprised to hear Neil sounding out of his depth. 'No problem, Neil,' he said. 'I'll get in touch with Chloe and get everything we need from her, and liaise with you tomorrow on what else we need to do. Okay?'

'Fine.' Neil still sounded somewhat panicked. 'Thank you. Good night.'

Mark snapped his phone shut and walked back towards the house in the dark, his feet sinking on the dewy grass. He felt he was missing something. He'd never heard Neil this stressed. Then he stopped in his tracks by the door. He'd said Chloe *was* pregnant. Did that mean . . . ?

Surprisingly, he didn't feel the relief he had expected upon thinking the baby might not have survived. He had thought of the baby as an encumbrance he would have to take on if he were to have a chance with Chloe, but he realised now that, deep down, he had imagined being part of a family, the three of them, and it had felt all right. Better than all right, even. Much better.

Di met him at the door and interrupted his reverie. 'I've just left them for a minute,' she told him, looking worried, as though they might hear a scuffle break out at any second.

'Okay,' Mark said. 'Look, I can't stay too much longer.'

Di nodded. 'I'll take Dad back home tomorrow. Let him pack his stuff and get himself organised.'

'Right.' Mark was still distracted by the tone he had heard in Neil's voice.

'You should come more often,' Di continued quietly. 'The boys would love to see their uncle a bit more.'

'Hmmm,' Mark replied, then registered what she'd said and looked around. 'Yes, I –'

But Diane had turned away and was heading for the kitchen. 'Tea?' she called over her shoulder.

'Please,' Mark said in reply. He walked towards the living room. He would have a quick drink, then get away. He wanted to sit in silence for a while and process everything he'd heard tonight. His Dad. Parkinson's. Neil. Abbott. And he wanted to call Chloe.

There was just a chink in the living-room door where it hadn't quite been pulled to. Mark headed to open it, then stopped as he saw his mother and father. His mother had moved to the end of the sofa nearest Henry and taken hold of his hand. They were whispering to one another, and the conversation still looked animated and not totally friendly, but their hands were firmly linked, and gripping on tightly.

Mark moved away from the door and headed to the kitchen to have tea with his sister.

88

Something was banging but Chloe didn't want to acknowledge it. She pulled a pillow over her head, but it wouldn't stop. Sighing, she flung the pillow away and then listened again. Silence.

She lifted herself on to her elbows and looked at the clock. Two thirty a.m. It must have been neighbours coming home late, banging doors. She collapsed back onto the bed again, closing her eyes.

A sharp crack against her windowpane startled her.

Chloe threw back the bedclothes, padded quickly to the window and opened the curtain.

She hadn't dreamed it. There was a crack in the glass. Heart thudding, she looked down to the pavement, and saw a familiar face with a hand pressed to her mouth; whether suppressing shock or a smile, it was impossible to tell in the dark.

'I'm so sorry, darling,' her mother said when Chloe got downstairs and opened the door. 'I'll get it fixed for you in the morning. You should really get a bell, you know.' She began to move bags from the doorstep into the hall. Chloe counted one, two suitcases, and some smaller luggage. How long was her mother planning on staying? she thought with alarm.

'What are you doing here?' she said.

Her mother looked up at her sternly, as if she were stupid. 'You called me, Chloe, don't you remember?'

'Yes, but,' Chloe stammered, 'I didn't mean you had to come immediately.'

'Well, I didn't come "immediately", did I – I tried to get a train but I couldn't get one until tomorrow morning, and I didn't want to wait that long. So then I called June, because I was worried about my car lasting the distance, and so I've swapped and they've got mine and I've got George's . . .' she gestured behind her at a pristine BMW standing proudly against the kerb, '. . . it was lovely to drive. And I have to say that – no, don't lift that, dear, I don't want you lifting anything for now, I'll do it myself in a minute – yes, I have to say that even without much traffic, it seemed to take forever. I hadn't realised just how long you would be spending in the car, because although the train takes a long time, well, that's just because it's the train, isn't it –'

'Mum, stop!' Chloe was feeling giddy from the torrent of words rushing from her mother's mouth so quickly there was barely time to digest them. 'But you never drive on strange roads?'

'My daughter needed me,' Margaret said, reaching

forward to kiss Chloe's cheek as they stood crowded against the cases in the hallway. 'And so I've come.'

Margaret was still wired from the drive, and Chloe was wide awake, so she let her mother make them some tea.

'I can't believe you didn't tell me that Alex has gone,' her mother said. 'You should have told me, Chloe.' She looked reprovingly at Chloe over her glasses.

'I didn't want to make it real by telling anyone,' Chloe replied, her voice soft. 'I thought if I kept it to myself . . .'

'He might come back and you could pretend it never happened?'

'Well . . . yes,' Chloe said, thinking it now sounded a bit daft. 'But things have changed – I've made a decision after today – it's me and this baby first, and everything else second.'

'Why do you have to do that?' Margaret moved across the room and sat down on a chair.

'What?'

'Come to a momentous, entirely narrow-minded decision, and close the door to all other possibilities. I swear, it must be a lawyer thing.'

'How can it be narrow-minded? I just can't continue letting him rule my life, Mum, my emotions, everything.' Chloe gestured manically as she spoke, almost spilling her tea. She was unnerved – she'd felt much better since making that decision, and didn't want to change it.

'He doesn't have to, Chloe.' Her mum moved the mug a little further from the table edge, and sighed. 'Why do you try to see things in black and white when there's a whole kaleidoscope of colour in between?'

'What are you saying?'

'That people do things for all sorts of reasons – whether good or bad, right or wrong, misguided or not – and that to have any hope of understanding what's going on, you need to find those reasons. You don't have to agree with them, or accept them, but you need to know what they are. There's no difference between living a life based on lies that other people have told you and living one that's based on a lie you've told yourself.'

Chloe had to stop herself from laughing at her mother's brief turn as a sage. 'Okay, Mum,' she sighed. 'Well, if he ever gets back, I'll hear him out.' She took a sip of tea and slammed the mug back onto the table.

Her mother put a hand on her arm. 'Calm down, Chloe love.'

'It's just . . .' Chloe rubbed her neck. 'I've finally decided to move forwards. I don't want anything to get in the way – to make me feel like I've felt for this past month.'

'Chloe, you're not moving forwards. You're running around closing doors as fast as they open until you've only got one direction to go in. But you're still frightened of what's behind all those other doors. If you're not prepared to take a look through them all, and accept what's there, then you'll never be able to move on. You'll always be scared of what's chasing you.'

'How do you know all this?' Chloe was startled. Her mother never talked this way.

'Because I think I do it myself, every day, with you,'

Margaret admitted, holding her daughter's gaze. 'It's why I prattle on at times. If I leave too much of a silence, I worry what that might mean – what you might say to fill it that I don't want to hear.'

Chloe just stared at her mother, open-mouthed. 'What could I possibly –' she began, then stopped herself. She was realising that her mother hadn't always been so twittery and fretful; that when she thought back to being a little girl, her mother had always seemed so strong and self-assured. She'd noticed the change in her teenage years, and it had become more obvious since then, but she had decided her mother had always been like that and as a child she had just been too young to notice it properly. But maybe this wasn't the case.

'Look what happened with Anthony.' Her mother gave a sad smile. 'I feel . . . oh, Chloe, now is the last time I should be talking to you like this. You should be up in bed, and I should be looking after you, not bringing up all this baggage.'

'No,' Chloe said, 'it's okay. Go on.'

'Well . . .' her mother began softly. 'I feel like I failed Anthony, but I look back and I can't see where I made the wrong turn. Of course, I could have never married your father – but then neither of you would have been brought into the world, and I wouldn't like that at all either.'

Chloe was beginning to feel uncomfortable. 'I don't think you failed Anthony,' she said.

'We're in an awful deadlock now,' Margaret replied. 'I don't even know my own grandchildren.'

'Well, America's a long way away.'

'It's not that,' Margaret said. 'It's that for Anthony to understand, I have to be honest with him about his father. And I can't do that.'

There it was. Margaret had laid the subject on the table. Chloe knew she was meant to ask about her father, but she didn't want to.

'Mum, surely honesty is the best policy. This is *exactly* the problem I'm having with Alex. Why can't people just be honest with one another?' Her voice began to rise.

'Chloe,' Margaret said, looking alarmed. 'Don't get yourself worked up, love.'

'Why not?' Chloe banged a hand on the table, and tea slopped over the edges of both their mugs. 'Why the hell not, Mum? Why couldn't he have just told me the truth from the beginning?'

'Chloe,' Margaret said, leaning forward. 'What if he felt that the truth might be the most painful thing you could hear? Yes, Alex is being quite unfair on you now, but does he want to be? Probably not. Even I know Alex well enough to say that. He may not be making good decisions, but you don't know what his motivations are. And yes, it's difficult for you, I'm not denying that, but maybe Alex is trying to protect you, had you ever thought of that?'

Chloe was taken aback. 'From what?'

'From his past? From the parts of himself that might make you doubt him, or make you love him less? From pain? From involvement in something that will only cause you grief?'

'By going off with another woman? More likely, he's trying to protect himself from the consequences. Running away is never the right thing to do.'

Margaret shook her head sadly. 'Don't you remember, Chloe?'

'What?' Chloe said, unease beginning to stir within her.

'We ran away once. We had to. And I think that, somewhere inside you, you remember everything. That's why you can't bear to speak with me about your father. It's so much easier to pretend you don't know.'

89

'How do you find?' the Judge's Associate asked the foreman after reading out the first charge of murder. 'Guilty or not guilty?'

The pause seemed to last forever. How could there be so much time between a question and a reply? Alex glanced at Amy, who was hunched over, trying to hide her face, staring at her knees. He couldn't begin to imagine her torment. The whole court was silent, expectant, the ordinary-looking man in a dark grey suit about to utter the response that would have a great bearing on the lives of so many in the room.

'Guilty.'

Chaos erupted. There was a babble of chatter in the general arena, and at the front of the gallery a woman screamed, then began sobbing, held in the arms of a younger couple.

Alex had jumped up before he realised it, punching the air

with a loud 'Yes'. His reaction was so reflexive he couldn't stop himself, causing quite a few at the front to turn and stare at him, their expressions ranging from sympathetic to angry, but all looking curious as he sat down again.

The judge restored order and the associate continued reading out the charges against the men. To each one, the response was 'guilty'. To Alex's right, Amy was breathing hard, still staring at the floor. He put his arms around her, unable to remain still, anger coursing through him, causing him to shake. He whispered into her hair, 'It's over, it's over, Amy,' and felt a hand on his shoulder, looking up to see the detective beside them, his face sombre but his hand giving Alex a squeeze, trying to convey what scrap of comfort he could.

The jury was dismissed and then the judge began to speak again, setting the date for sentencing. Amy remained huddled within Alex's arms, leaning into his chest, breathing heavily. They stayed that way until people began getting to their feet, then stood up to watch the judge leave the courtroom.

'Let's go, Alex,' Amy whispered to him. 'I just want to get away from this now.'

Alex kept his arm around her as they made their way downstairs. 'I just need to nip to the bathroom,' Alex said, when they reached the ground floor.

'Me too,' Amy replied. 'I'll meet you back here in a moment.' She gave him a long look, as though she were trying to tell him something, and let go of his hand.

Alex pushed through a door into the bathroom to find it surprisingly empty. He made his way over to a urinal, relieved himself, and turned to go, heading towards the door as another man entered, wearing a dapper navy pinstriped suit and a bright yellow tie. His face was stricken, his dark eyes tormented, and Alex asked instinctively, 'You okay?'

The man nodded, at first unable or unwilling to speak. He murmured what sounded like 'A terrible day.'

Alex grimaced. 'I know, mate,' he said, as he made his way back outside.

At first Alex didn't panic when he couldn't see Amy. But when after a few minutes she still didn't appear, a small, insidious roiling began in his gut. He walked up and down the corridor, looking for her familiar dark head.

Ten minutes went by, then another five. He was biting down the urge to shout her name, walking frantically back and forth.

Of course she had gone. The court case was over, the verdict announced. In Amy's head, all that was left now was to watch him walk away, back to his old life, leaving her to try to pick up some semblance of the pieces of her own. Of course she would have decided to leave first, sometime when he wouldn't be expecting it; of course she wouldn't want to go through such a painful goodbye.

He felt desperate. He didn't want it to end like this. How could he have been so stupid as to let her slip out of his grasp again?

90

When Chloe woke up, it was all there in front of her as though she had never pushed it away; as clear as the daylight pouring through the crack in her curtains. She choked and spluttered at the intensity of it all, unable to believe she had kept this thing buried in her subconscious for so long.

As she tried to calm herself, she could hear her mother humming in the kitchen. She couldn't make out the tune.

Fractured images paraded past her like a police-station line-up. First, there were the three of them, Mummy, Daddy and little Chloe; a storybook setting, the trees green, the sky blue, the sun yellow, and life rosy. Then came the baby, Anthony, and nothing changed, it all just glowed that little bit brighter. They lived in America. There were fourth of July parties, with shrieking fireworks and dancing. Chloe could remember her mother in beautiful dresses, kissing her shyly in the early evening, and hugging her tightly later at night when it wouldn't matter what stains Chloe could transfer onto the silken material. Her father, ruffling her hair, kissing her forehead, swinging her up onto his shoulders. He was godlike, the world bending to his will. Chloe and her brother watching their parents in awe as one shimmered and the other commanded.

Then, during the night after one such party, Chloe had been disturbed by a noise. It had scared her too much for her to stay in her room so she went looking for comfort.

And, eventually, she had found her father wrapped around her brother, his face turned away, but small movements shaking his body.

Too much flesh. Anthony's eyes vacant. Chloe peeping in, her small fingers clutching the door.

Running to her mother, asleep in a chair downstairs, putting a tiny finger to her lips, and her mother, thinking it was some kind of child's game, unfurling in easy delight like a cat, and letting Chloe lead her to Anthony's room.

Standing together at the doorway. Margaret dropping Chloe's hand.

Tears streamed onto Chloe's pillow, helpless from gravity's push. The humming from downstairs sounded like a child's, and it was ceaseless. She wanted to turn it off, or tune it out, while she gathered together the broken threads of her memories and turned them over, trying to repair them to become something she could use.

* * *

That was how she had last seen her father. Through a crack in a doorway. His face turned away from her. Her mother had also turned away then, in silence, and Chloe had watched her begin to walk off, sliding along the floor, her whole body stiff, ghostlike. Then Margaret had remembered her small daughter. Had padded back, scooped her up. Chloe had been laid on her bed, then, a while later, Anthony was brought into her room and put into the bed with her, and her mother lay down next to them in the long, cramped space, and put her arm across them both.

In the morning, Chloe had woken of her own accord, which was unusual. Her mother was normally already in her room and flinging back curtains, chattering merrily. That morning there had been nothing; Anthony and her mother were no longer with her. She had arisen in her nightie, and wandered around the house looking for Margaret. In her parents' room she had found her, frantically packing, shoving everything into cavernous suitcases. 'We're going on holiday, to England,' her mother had said in a strange singsong voice. 'It's an adventure, honey.'

Chloe knew England – it was where her grandparents lived. They came to visit now and again, and Chloe had seen pictures of herself there when she had been a baby. So she had packed for a holiday, leaving behind the doll's house; her special light that, when switched on, showed small furry rabbits living inside; her collection of seashells. And all the rest that she wouldn't need for a holiday.

Anthony had been quiet all the way to England. He sat on his mother's knee and stared resolutely ahead. Her mother sat in perfect imitation of her son, her eyes fixed forward, responding to Chloe when she felt a pull on her sleeve, but otherwise letting her be, even when she drew in crayon all over the pull-down table in front of her.

Chloe had been five years old when they'd stepped off the plane onto English soil. She remembered her grandparents' delighted, surprised faces when they opened their cottage door to find their daughter and her children waiting, and how their smiles had faltered slightly as they'd looked at Margaret and then been pinned back in place as they turned to Chloe and Anthony. The children had been told to go into the garden to play, and they moved off holding hands. Chloe looked back as her grandparents turned inwards, a carapace for their daughter, and saw her mother's head go down and her shoulders sag as she made it to the doorway, then slid down it to become a shaking, wailing heap, Chloe's grandmother quickly going to her side.

In the garden, Anthony had let go of Chloe's hand. The trees were bare and brown, and thick white cloud blotted out most of the leaden-grey sky.

Chloe raced downstairs as though the hounds of hell were chasing her, and burst into the kitchen, where her mother seemed to be in the process of emptying a cabinet of glassware, washing it all and putting it back again.

Margaret turned around in surprise at the sudden sound, and took one look at Chloe's face, then said, 'So, you do remember.'

'Mum!' Chloe was forcing herself to stay still, to keep her hands at her sides, though she felt like moving across the room and throttling her mother. 'How *could* you –' She registered her mother's shocked face as she said the words. 'How could you let Anthony go to America like that? You *should* have told him. You *should* have. What if . . .' Now she was registering her mother's expression becoming one of relief, and then Margaret said:

'Chloe, you underestimate me. I've known where your father was all along. Anthony was never in danger, you needn't worry about that.'

91

In the bathroom, Amy splashed water on her face, bracing herself for everything that must come next.

Guilty. They were going to prison.

She was so relieved. But what this meant for her life, she really didn't know.

As she turned to grab a paper towel, two women came through the door; one her mother's age, the other probably a little younger than Amy. She didn't recognise them, but was all too familiar with the hollow look in their eyes.

She threw her paper towel in the bin, keen to leave, when the older woman began speaking to her.

'Excuse me . . . Did you know my daughter? Did you know my Vanessa?'

Amy was so shocked that she began speaking without even thinking about it.

'No, I'm sorry, I didn't. But I'm so, so sorry.'

The woman came over and took Amy's hand. 'Then what happened to you?' she asked softly.

The woman's gaze was boring right through her. Amy felt almost transparent, like the woman could see into her brain and out the back of her head. Slowly, she unwound the scarf around her neck to show both women the scar that sliced across her skin.

'I'm pretty sure I was meant to die too,' she said.

The younger woman gasped. The older one took a long, appraising look at Amy's neck, the rest of her body completely still.

Amy didn't know what she was expecting the woman to say, but she felt immeasurably guilty, as though she could have done something; perhaps stayed and hunted down these men before they had preyed on someone else. She was expecting harsh words, a slap to the face, and was waiting for but not shirking from them; in fact her mind was inviting them to confirm everything that she knew she was.

So, the words that finally came shocked her more than anything she had imagined. The woman leaned forward, her arm stretching out towards Amy's face. Amy instinctively recoiled, but there was something gentle in the movement that slowed her backwards arc, and the woman's hand connected with Amy's face to stroke her cheek, just once, with the lightest of touches. Like Amy's mother used to do.

'I am so very glad that *you* didn't die,' she said, with both sadness and kindness in her eyes.

Amy let out a sob and then collapsed into the woman's arms, as a torrent of emotion gushed from her. The younger woman came and joined the embrace, and the three of them were locked together for what might have been seconds or hours, Amy couldn't tell, though she vaguely registered the bathroom door opening and closing more than once without anyone coming inside.

When the woman stepped back, she said, 'I'm Vanessa's mother, Jean, and this is her sister, Natalie.'

Amy took her hand.

'I'm Amy,' she said, first of all. And then, 'Thank you.' They smiled at one another, but there was nothing else to be said.

'Look after yourself, Amy,' Jean added, as Amy turned to go.

'You too,' she replied, without looking back.

The peacefulness that had temporarily overcome Amy was blown away by Alex's anger when he saw her.

'Where have you been?' He wiped his brow and agitatedly ran his fingers through his hair. 'I've been looking everywhere.'

'I met Vanessa's mother and sister in the bathroom,' she replied, surprised at his agitation.

Alex looked bewildered for a moment, and then understanding crossed his face. 'Oh, I see,' he said, his shoulders slumping, the fight leaving him.

Amy was confused until he added, 'I thought you'd gone.'

Another time, she might have been affronted, but now she wasn't. Instead, she gave him a small smile. 'Well, I didn't,' she replied.

'No.' He looked at her, his face relaxing, and then said, 'Okay then, let's go.'

As they headed for the door, Detective Thompson approached. 'Just what we hoped for,' he said, shaking Amy's hand and then Alex's, but Alex's attention was caught elsewhere for a moment, and she followed his gaze.

The detective's words faded away.

Time drifted, then slowed, then fractured.

A navy pinstriped suit teamed with a trendy yellow tie. Dark hair, a thin face, a vertical scar slicing his cheek just beneath his right eye.

Two black eyes were staring back at her. Spittle on her cheek. A body bearing down, violently crushing air from her lungs.

And then she was screaming as loudly as she could, because this time she didn't have a petrol-soaked rag blocking her throat.

92

Chloe was frustrated. She had thought that last night she and her mother had broken through some kind of communication barrier, but today it seemed as if it had only been temporary, as her mother was back to fussing at every opportunity. Margaret had refused to enlighten Chloe further on the subject of her father, saying that first and foremost she needed some rest. She had insisted Chloe go back to bed, had brought up breakfast on a tray, and, unbelievably, chattered on about her journey and the latest gardening club gossip. When Chloe remained morose and uncommunicative, Margaret eventually left her alone to 'rest'.

Chloe tried to settle down with her book, staring unseeingly at the pages. She dozed every now and then, intermittently hearing her mother banging around downstairs, presumably checking out where different things were kept.

She tried not to think about what was getting rearranged or thrown out, or silently noted as inferior.

She had intended to get up and cajole her mother into explaining things properly, but after a while found that tiredness descended upon her like a thick blanket.

At lunchtime, hungry, Chloe wandered downstairs but couldn't seem to stand up for long. Margaret made her some sandwiches, and urged her to lie down and not fight the tiredness. Chloe lay on the sofa this time, flicking through TV channels and then dozing off again.

When she came to properly, the curtains were closed and a small table lamp was the only light in the room. Margaret sat next to it, leafing through a magazine. She looked up and saw that Chloe was awake.

'How are you feeling, darling?' Margaret immediately enquired.

'Tired!' Chloe said, amazed that she could still feel so weary after sleeping all day.

'You've got a fair bit of rest to catch up on, I would imagine. Can I get you a drink?'

'Just a glass of water would be lovely.'

Margaret hurried out of the room and Chloe heard the gentle tinkling of glasses and a trickling of liquid before she returned, one hand bearing a glass of water and the other holding a glass of white wine.

'I didn't know I had any wine,' Chloe said.

'You didn't. I went and got some,' Margaret replied.

'I must have slept more deeply than I thought.'

'You were out like a light. Cheers.'

They clinked their glasses together and both took a gulp.

Chloe settled back against the soft sofa cushions, and pulled the blanket up to her chin. They sat in silence for a while in the soft light; then Margaret spoke while looking down into her glass.

'I was surprised it took so long to drive here. It must be awful on a Friday night, never mind having to do it all again two days later. Thank you for coming to see me so often.'

'That's okay.' Chloe immediately felt guilty at the amount of times she and Alex had moaned about the trip.

'I think I might come down a bit more from now on.'

'Of course,' Chloe replied.

'Besides,' her mother continued, smiling, 'you'll need help when the baby arrives.'

Chloe felt a pang of discomfort. She took a breath and bit the bullet. 'I will, Mum. But I might also need some space.' She looked across at her mother, waiting to see her reaction.

'Oh, I see,' Margaret replied, leaning around and plumping the cushion behind her. 'Well, if you don't want me, I –'

'Mum! Will you listen properly. I'm not saying I don't want you, I just want you to respect my right to a little space – surely that's not too much to ask.'

'Okay, calm down, Chloe,' Margaret said snippily. 'I'm just saying that when – if – you need me, I'll be here. It's just . . . I'd like to be useful to somebody, at least.'

'I'm really not saying –' Chloe began immediately, but her mother raised a hand to stop her.

'It's okay, Chloe. I know just what you're saying.'

Chloe gave up; whatever she said seemed to be wrong. There was an awkward silence, before Margaret finally sighed and said sadly, 'I envy you, you know.'

'You do?' Chloe asked, surprised.

'You have it all ahead of you.' Margaret nodded her head towards Chloe's stomach. 'So much joy, so many surprises . . .'

'Is that how you felt?'

Margaret looked taken aback at the question. 'Of course. Well, actually, I was scared rotten during my whole pregnancy with you, desperately praying you would be okay. But seeing you for the first time was the happiest moment of my entire life, even though I'd just been through fifteen hours of hell!'

'Don't tell Anthony that!' Chloe laughed.

'I don't think Anthony would care,' Margaret said sadly. 'He's always been so independent-minded – so determined. Whereas you, you were my little girl, and you would look at me so openly, so trusting. In fact,' her voice cracked, 'sometimes I would give anything to see you look like that again.'

'Mum, I'm . . .'

Margaret shook her head. 'Don't, Chloe. Life moves on.'

Chloe felt tears smarting. 'Mum,' she said softly, 'I'm so sorry about what happened . . . if I hadn't – with Dad – then . . .'

'Don't you *ever* say that. Do you realise how silly that is? Thank god you did take me up there. You saved Anthony, Chloe. You saved us all, I think.'

Chloe mulled that over for a while. 'Mum, did you really think you were having a heart attack?'

Margaret nodded, and cast her a quick, embarrassed glance. 'Yes, for a little while – you have no idea how silly I felt when the doctors told me that it was just my nerves!'

She shook her head. 'But Charlie . . . his began innocuously enough, so we didn't ring the ambulance straight away, and by the time we did, then got to the hospital, well, it was too late. So I think I panicked, presuming it was going to be the same with me. I know it sounds silly *now*, though. I am embarrassed about it, if that makes any difference.'

'Mum, I don't want you to be embarrassed – it's just that – well, it feels like, although we talk a lot, we don't really *talk*, do we? I'm sorry I blew my top when I got up to see you; it's just I was so worried, and I've been so stressed out about –'

'I shouldn't have made light of it,' Margaret interrupted. 'But I felt silly and I didn't want you to worry and start fussing. It was a genuine mistake, Chloe, and I was pleased to see you – I'm very lucky to have a daughter who will drop everything for me in times of need, I realise that, especially with what you've had to contend with recently. I know it might have looked a bit selfish . . .'

Chloe was about to accept the invitation of the ensuing silence to tell her mother, no, of course it wasn't selfish, when she stopped. From now on, she was going to be honest. From now on, she wasn't going to accept excuses from anyone, including herself. From now on, she was going to do exactly what she thought was right, without being trapped by indecision because of worry that she might make a mistake. If she did veer off course, she'd just have to sort it out as she went along.

The weight that lifted from her as she had these thoughts was so enormous she felt almost faint from the release. She smiled, and her mother looked bemused.

'What are you thinking?' she said.

'It doesn't matter,' Chloe replied. 'But I want you to tell me about my dad.'

Margaret looked worried, but she didn't try to hedge. 'Okay, Chloe,' she said. 'But I'm afraid it won't be nice to hear.'

Chloe pursed her lips. She was determined to know everything. Margaret saw the gleam of her eyes and said, 'Right. Well. After we left, there was quite a bit of contact with your father – my dad took most of the calls, it was pretty nasty. We threatened to go to the police if he didn't leave us alone, but since he was in the police force over in America, things were a bit tricky. But I felt terribly guilty about just leaving – I couldn't see a way out, I thought we'd have to inform the authorities because I couldn't let him get away with that – I mean, what if he . . . there were plenty of children around. But then . . . things were taken out of our hands. He went out on patrol one night a few weeks after we left and caught two youngsters stealing from a garage. He chased and caught one of them, beat the boy in a rage, even though it was basically food they were stealing . . . beat him so hard that the boy later died in hospital.'

Chloe's hand flew to her mouth. 'Oh my god.'

Margaret nodded. 'His defence tried to get the charge down to manslaughter – irony of ironies, part of their argument was that his wife had just left him and taken his kids, and he wasn't of rational mind – but he still got convicted in the end. Which was a real relief. I knew which jail he was in to start with, but then I lost track of him. When Anthony went over, I tried to do some digging. It turned out he'd been released, and searching for him took about a year, and a fair bit of money – but I found him.' Margaret moved across to the sofa, then reached out and put a hand on Chloe's knee. 'He died, love. Around the time Anthony left for America. He had a stroke.'

Chloe's hand was still covering her mouth. She didn't know what to think. It seemed – surreal. She didn't really feel anything on hearing he was dead, which, in itself, felt wrong. She thought that perhaps she'd known all along the story went something like this, and she'd just put off having to hear it spoken aloud.

'Poor Anthony,' she said eventually. 'When did he find out?'

'A few months after he got married,' Margaret replied sadly. 'He rang one night, sounding like he'd had a few to drink, and told me I'd denied him the chance of ever knowing his father. He knew about the prison sentence before that, I think, but he said he still wanted the opportunity, that I should have let him make up his own mind before it was too late.'

'And you didn't tell him anything,' Chloe said; a statement rather than a question.

Margaret shook her head, biting her lip, her eyes dewy. 'I've always been so grateful that he was little when it . . . when we left America. It gave him a chance to forget. I don't want to take that away from him, ever, even though he's a man now.'

'Oh, Mum.' Chloe put her hand on top of her mother's. 'This must all have been so hard for you.' She paused, thinking; then, curious, asked, 'Did you love our dad?'

Margaret nodded. 'I did – well, I thought I did, but I think

I was also hypnotised by him. He was a powerful man, with a cruel streak, and it took what happened with Anthony to bring me to my senses. I have always felt guilty about putting both of you through that. Yes, you too, Chloe. You should never have had to experience that. You were a *child*. I was your *mother*. It was down to me.'

'Mum, you didn't –' Chloe said automatically.

Margaret moved even closer to Chloe on the sofa, and began to stroke her daughter's hair, pushing loose strands back behind her ear. 'Thank you for saying that,' she whispered. 'However, although I may come across as a silly old fool at times, when I think of you and Anthony, in my heart I am a lioness, and you will always be my cubs. I want to roar at anyone who threatens you and tear the heart out of anyone who hurts you.'

There was silence for a moment, and then Chloe looked up at her mum, a soft smile on her face. 'Poor Alex,' she said.

'Quite,' Margaret replied, and smiled back.

93

The last twenty-four hours had been crazy.

When Amy had begun to scream, the man had bolted out the main doors of the courthouse. Alex had been transfixed by both things, but Detective Thompson had set off in pursuit like a cheetah after prey, as did half a dozen court security guards.

They hauled him back in moments later; Detective Thompson coming first, wiping his brow, shirt half-untucked and tie askew. He straightened his clothing and flattened his hair as he walked towards Alex and Amy.

As Amy saw the security men bringing the man back in, she moved closer to Alex and buried her head in his chest, and he put his arms around her.

The detective moved around so Amy could see him without having to move her head.

'Is that one of them?' he asked her gently.

Amy nodded.

'I'm sorry, Amy, but I need you to look at him quickly and make a positive ID,' the detective said softly.

Slowly, Amy turned her head. The man stared right back at her, remorseless; sneering, almost.

Alex watched Amy as she nodded.

Before he could think, Alex had thrust Amy out of his arms towards the detective. He heard himself screaming obscenities at the cocky monster in front of them, determined to rip him apart. He had almost reached him when one of the guards grabbed Alex's arms. He writhed to be free and more guards came over. He was bundled outside as he fought back, and they pinned him on the ground.

'Pull him up,' a voice said.

As they hauled him to his feet, Alex could feel his face still distorted with the rage that consumed him. When he was upright, Detective Thompson stepped forward until he was so close their noses were almost touching.

'I know you want to,' he said, his eyes boring into Alex's. 'We all want to. But it won't help. So calm down. You need to look after Amy.'

As soon as he said her name, Alex spotted her, standing behind them, her face tear-streaked, her expression distressed, and the fight began to drain out of him. He held his hands up in acquiescence, and muttered 'Sorry, sorry' as the officers gradually stood back. They didn't go far, in case, he guessed, he ran indoors again to find the bastard and kill him. Instead he went over to Amy, and put his arms around her once more.

'It's all right,' he said, pulling her close and stroking her hair, whispering against it. 'It's all right.'

She pulled back. 'I thought I didn't recognise all of them,' she said, alternately looking at the detective and Alex, her voice shaky and high. 'But it's been ten years and I –'

'The man we just arrested was the brother of one of the men convicted today,' Detective Thompson informed them. 'We had some issues with whether the third man belonged to your case as well, as he had an alibi, but it was only a wobbly one; and his brother would have been only eighteen when they attacked you, so we weren't sure. Without you we had no way of checking.'

'Why didn't you tell me this before?' Amy asked, horrified that one of her attackers had been wandering freely so close to her.

'I'm sorry.' The detective looked ashamed. 'I didn't want to frighten you, as you were already so distressed when I last saw you. I thought that when today was out of the way, we could talk properly.'

Amy looked astounded for a moment. 'Did you just set that up, so I would see him?'

'No, of course not.' Detective Thompson seemed affronted. 'I've never seen him at court before; if I had, I wouldn't have let him near you. He must have just come in for the verdict, and I'm surprised at that, as, unless they're in the dock, his family usually stay well away from anything involving the law.'

'Oh.' Amy looked at her feet.

'So what now?' Alex asked, suddenly aware that this was a very public conversation. People were passing them on the way to and from court, many eyeing them curiously, probably having just witnessed the scenes inside.

'For now, we detain him for questioning,' the detective said. 'You two head back to your hotel, and I'll come and see you later.'

They returned to their hotel in silence.

'I'm sorry, Amy,' Alex said at one point.

'Don't be,' she replied. 'I wish they'd let you kill him. I would have watched.'

They didn't say much after that and spent the next few hours feeling restless. The hotel had an outdoor swimming pool so they swam for a while, then came back to their room. Alex was just wondering how long they'd be climbing the walls for, when the phone rang and the receptionist informed them that Detective Thompson was in the lobby.

They headed downstairs and sat with him in the large open-plan reception area.

'He's practically confessed,' the detective said. 'We'll be able to charge him, I'm sure. I'll take a statement from you both about what happened today, and then, further down the line, we might need you back again, Amy.' He looked at her seriously. 'Is that okay? Without you, if he decided to try to get off, we wouldn't have much of a case. I'm hopeful he might spare us all and go with guilty, but we just don't know what will happen once the lawyers have had their hands on him for a while.'

They all knew he was asking Amy if she was a flight risk.

'I can do what you need me to,' she answered, meeting his eyes. Alex believed her. From the look of it, the detective did too. In fact, Alex thought, it looked as though Amy believed herself as well.

'Well, let's go down to the station now, and do the statements, and then you're free to go,' Detective Thompson said. 'No point in keeping you here longer than needed.'

The next morning, Alex woke up before Amy, and lay staring at the patch of blue sky he could see through the window. He heard her stirring sometime later, and turned around and smiled at her. She smiled briefly back, then got up, headed for the bathroom and got dressed. When they were both ready, they went down for breakfast.

'What do you want to do today?' Alex asked, munching on a mouthful of toast.

Amy looked at her plate, thinking.

'I want to leave,' she said, looking up. 'To find a flight and go – back to England, or anywhere else, I guess; just away, for starters. Is that okay?'

Alex nodded. He knew there was no point remaining there any longer, but leaving meant taking the next step. It meant he had choices to make. And he didn't feel ready. He didn't think he would ever feel ready.

94

Early on Friday morning, Mark was on his way to see Chloe with two things on his mind. He had to make sure he collected all her Abbott notes and picked her brains. And he was also going to tell her how he felt about her.

He'd been going over and over the family meeting in his head. A number of things had unnerved him.

First, of course, his dad had Parkinson's. He'd spent the past twenty-four hours swotting up on it when he could grab a spare moment, and none of it had made pleasant reading. He kept trying to imagine how his dad would cope when the symptoms became obvious. So far, Mark hadn't even noticed him have a tremor; he wasn't looking forward to the first time he did, sure that he wouldn't know how to react.

He was discomfited by the relationships in his family. He knew Henry had always had a soft spot for Di – different things were expected and hoped for from a Jameson daughter. But he had been touched by the rough affection he had seen between his mother and father when they had thought no one was looking. And he was also surprised at how strong and unshakeable his mother was – while Henry was barking out commands, it was easy to believe he was the linchpin of the family, but, perhaps, all the time his mother had been stealthily doing that job herself.

So where did he, Mark, fit in to all this? He was an absent brother and a pretty crap son, with little idea what to say to any of them, and even less notion of how he could take charge. Out of everyone who had been involved in the family counselling session, he had been the limp lettuce. It made unpleasant thinking.

But here was one thing he could do something about. Chloe meant a lot to him, and he had to tell her before her husband came back. Alex had been gone for a while now – really, how would those two ever get back on track after this? Whereas he and Chloe might just be able to . . . The last time, they'd been young, inexperienced, ambitious. This time Mark felt more confident that he could settle down, and that his career wouldn't suffer unduly.

And if she'd lost the child, as Neil had implied, he could tell her now without there being anything in the way. There could be other children for Chloe. Mark had no objections to starting a family sooner rather than later. It might be better if Chloe left the firm, anyway; there could be problems if the two of them continued to work together.

* * *

Chloe's mother opened the door.

'Mark, it's been a while,' she said, civilly holding out a hand.

'Hello, Margaret,' he replied, shaking it. 'Is Chloe up and about?'

'She's in the sitting room.'

Mark went on ahead and rounded the doorway into the lounge. He stopped in shock. Chloe's face was pale, her eyes had dark circles underneath them, and she was nestled under a duvet surrounded by pillows.

'Bloody hell!' he said.

Chloe smiled. 'Did you just think I was skiving?' she asked. 'Nope, I am actually not feeling so great.'

'I can see.' Mark sat down opposite her. It wasn't quite how he'd imagined pouring out his heart – he'd have preferred her well and seated opposite him in a restaurant somewhere so that it felt more romantic – but she didn't look like she'd be going out any time soon, and this couldn't wait.

'I've put all the Abbott papers over there.' She indicated a pile on the table nearby. 'Do we need to go through anything?'

'No, it's fine. I'll call you if I have any questions.' Mark paused. 'I also came to find out how you are.' He moved closer and took her hand. 'I've been really worried about you.'

'I'm fine,' she said. 'Just got to take it easy.'

'So,' he began, nervous of the answer to the question he was about to pose. 'Did you . . . are you . . . ?'

Chloe looked puzzled.

'I got the impression, from Neil, that you might have lost the baby,' Mark blurted.

Chloe looked surprised. 'No! And thank god! I don't know where he got that from.'

As he watched her rubbing her belly, Mark tried to take in this information, and what it meant for them. What should he do now?

'It gave me a scare, but I've just got to rest up a little and it should all be fine. I'm really sorry about the Abbott case, though, leaving you in the lurch,' she said.

Mark's mind had wandered. 'What? . . . Oh, don't worry. I can handle it.'

'I've no doubt about that,' Chloe laughed. She paused, and looked at Mark curiously as he sat awkwardly opposite her. 'Is there something on your mind, Mark?'

Mark looked down. He still had hold of her hand. She was watching him, meekly, sweetly. She was waiting. Could it work with a baby that wasn't his? Should he speak? He had an innate feeling that this was his one opportunity, right here and now.

'Chloe, I've been thinking . . .' he began. He cleared his throat. 'About us.' He cleared his throat again and patted his chest. *Get a grip, man.*

Chloe was looking a little uncomfortable, he noticed, but it was too late to back out now. He ploughed on desperately. 'These last few weeks I've come to realise –'

'Mark, don't.' Chloe put a hand on his arm and shook her head as she looked at him. He fell silent, appalled at how this seemed to be unfolding.

'I have really enjoyed spending time with you recently.

You have been such a good friend –' she paused, seemingly lost for words, while Mark stared down at the slick lines ironed into his trousers.

'Mark,' she tried again, 'I'm so –'

He knew for sure that he didn't want her pity. 'Forget it,' he cut in, more abruptly than he intended, and waved his hand dismissively. Chloe reached across to touch his arm again, but he moved away. 'No need to feel sorry for me, Chlo,' he said, a slight coldness to his tone. 'It's not like anything has changed. Friends?'

He held out his hand formally, and ignored her amused expression.

'Friends,' she smiled, taking his hand and giving it an agreeable shake.

'And perhaps not so much criticism of my husband in future?' she added.

'Actually, he really does deserve it at the moment,' Mark retorted.

Chloe opened her mouth and then closed it again. Because, unfortunately, Mark was right.

There seemed to be little else they could find to say. Mark was about to make his excuses when Margaret came in with tea, so he was forced to sit in excruciating awkwardness and try to sip it down quickly while it was still scalding hot. He was relieved to be finally given a reprieve from this torture by his ringing phone. 'Excuse me,' he said, rummaging in his pocket. He flicked open the lid without even registering who was on the other end; he was just grateful to them for buying him some thinking time.

The voice that began speaking was frazzled with worry. Mark listened, his eyes widening.

'Oh, Jesus,' he eventually spluttered.

Chloe's eyes were saucer-wide as she watched his expression change. 'What?' she asked. 'What is it, Mark?'

95

The flight home had taken Amy and Alex into a kind of limbo-land. They hadn't talked much during it. There was either too much or too little to say, and neither of them knew where to begin.

Amy had spent a lot of the time remembering the idyllic few days at the beach – just them, together again, something she'd had only in her dreams for ten years. They were still good together, she could tell. So right for each other. If only . . .

When they had cleared customs at Heathrow, neither of them knew what to do next.

'Shall we go for a coffee?' Amy asked eventually.

Alex nodded, his face weary.

They collected watery coffee from a kiosk and found a table free of debris. Alex stared into his cup, brooding, as though looking for answers in the brown murk.

'Al,' Amy tried, gently.

Alex just shook his head. When he looked up, there were tears in his eyes.

'What am I meant to do now, Amy?' he asked. His voice was an entreaty, a plea for an answer she couldn't give him.

She reached over and grabbed his hand. 'Al,' she took a deep breath, 'I still love you. I can't change that. But I understand the situation you're in. And I won't hold your decisions against you.'

Alex shook his head, his eyes growing tearful. 'Fuck,' he growled, banging his fist on the table and looking down at his steaming coffee as it slopped over the edge of his mug.

'Look,' Amy said, wondering where she was summoning her words from. 'Just listen to yourself. That's all you can do. You and I – we'll –' she had to fight through her own emotions to say it '– we'll never be history, it's not possible.'

Alex looked up, his face wretched, listening to her intently.

'You and I,' she continued, 'we share something, something that I don't think can be broken. But it's not just about us any more, and there's not a damn thing we can do about that.'

'Amy, I don't know what you're saying.'

She tried out a quick laugh, but there was no merriment in it. 'Neither do I, really. But, Al, if you can take your guilt out of the equation for just one moment, if you can bring yourself into the here and now, don't you know what you want, really – don't you know, deep down, what you're going to do next? Aren't you holding yourself back because of the pain you might cause, or experience, not because you don't know?'

She could see in his eyes that he knew exactly what she was saying. She held her breath, because this was it: she had pushed him to this point, and couldn't undo it, but she was also terrified of what would come next.

Suddenly he got up, came around, pulled her out of her chair and cupped her face in his hands, and his mouth met hers in a passionate kiss that she melted into, heart and soul.

96

'*We stand before you today on behalf of a young girl who was unable to defend herself. A young girl whose life ended just when she should have been reaching her prime, because of the cruel, callous, unendurable acts of a few, and because of the wilful negligence of the school to provide crucial, fundamental support to her – support which, as one of the bastions of our education system, this institution was morally and socially and legally obliged to provide . . .*'

Mark ran through the victory speech in his head, the one he would give to the press outside court on behalf of his client when the case was over. He wouldn't be delivering it for a while, but he was confident that, in the end, he'd get a chance to do so. He could already see himself standing on the steps, surrounded by cameras and tape recorders, all eyes on him as they devoured his every word. His time had come – the legal world wouldn't be able to stop talking about him when this case was finished.

They couldn't lose – they had Carl Blaine, the best barrister in the business, on their side; it was only day one and already the defence looked rattled. Mark had watched in admiration as Blaine railed at poor Kara's fate and the blocked avenues of support that had led her to such drastic action – vowing that such a tragedy should never happen again, and so it was critical to make those responsible accountable for their role in events. Now, walking alongside Mark as they faced the media ruckus, Kip Abbott was holding his head high, looking far less nervous than when he'd arrived at court.

'I should never have asked Neil to do this,' Kip had said when they'd shaken hands earlier in the day. 'He's been so hyped up about it. It's been far too personal for him.'

Yes, it had been, Mark had thought grimly. But a good lawyer, a Jameson lawyer, could put aside emotions, knew that doing so was critical, in fact. Not that they didn't ever emote, sometimes it was called for – but it was all scripted to perfection.

Mark still couldn't believe that Neil, so strong and fit on the squash court, had had a heart attack, and he did feel a little guilty that it was his boss's illness that had provided him with such a huge opportunity.

Henry had been sticking to Mark closer than his own shadow in recent days, going through the papers, supporting him, moulding him, encouraging him. Mark had had a thrill running through him the whole time. This was what he'd been waiting for – his big chance. There was no way this one was slipping away from him; he would grab it with both hands, make his father proud, people would pay thousands to have him working on their cases.

Neil was still critically ill in hospital, wired up to machines. He'd had to have a triple bypass over the weekend, and the recovery time was predicted to be months. David was already in the middle of another important case; and while there were other partners and senior solicitors at Lewis & Marchant, no one knew the Abbott case like Mark did. Henry had lobbied for his son to take charge even before Mark had found out about Neil, and so, by the time he'd picked up the phone at Chloe's, he was on the biggest fast-track ever heard of in Lewis & Marchant, or probably any other London firm. This case would see his name well and truly made.

As Mark neared the car, he remembered that he'd seen Henry today, standing at the back of the public gallery, his legs casually crossed as he leaned on a wall. After the close of the afternoon session, Mark had looked at him and Henry had given him a brief nod. Mark's chest swelled at the memory of his father's acknowledgement; of his respect.

They had reached their vehicle. He opened a passenger door for Kip, then went around to the other side, ignoring the shouted questions from the media, shut the door and felt the adrenalin buzz still coursing through his veins in the sudden silence of the car's interior. As they pulled away, he rested his hands across his stomach, a studied pose of concentration, but in the lull his mind didn't hesitate to drift back to Chloe's small, vulnerable face. Instantly, he simply felt tired. He sighed. This case could be a welcome distraction, if only he could stop thinking about her. He was trying to tell himself that it would never have worked, but he could only hope that his career was about to go stratospheric, and the whole thing would be some kind of blessing in disguise. He studied his short fingernails and tried not to think of Chloe and Alex together – the way Chloe's face softened and brightened as she looked at Alex – a look Mark had only witnessed, never received. Surely Alex couldn't be so stupid as to give that up?

He leaned back in his seat and stared sombrely out at the traffic as they edged their way forward. He knew it was nothing to do with him now. Finally, after all these years, it was time to let her go.

97

Chloe was fed up. She wished her heart would stop pounding every time there was a knock on the door or the phone rang. She felt pensive, uncomfortable. The day seemed somehow pivotal, and she wasn't sure why. After a weekend resting, she felt more alert, and was having to force herself into inaction. Her mother wasn't helping. She was mostly back to her twittering self and was beginning to get on Chloe's nerves with her constant fussing.

Her first surprise visitor of the day had been Jana. Chloe had felt uncomfortable being caught by her secretary makeup-free and wearing a grubby old tracksuit, but Jana hadn't shown any sign of noticing, and simply said she'd taken a long lunch hour to come and offer her support.

'My sister almost miscarried,' Jana announced, 'and the whole family was a wreck. I just wanted to encourage you to rest and to let you know that she now has a healthy baby – a girl – and so will you.'

'How can you be so sure?' Chloe asked quietly. 'I feel I hardly dare move in case I dislodge the baby inside me.'

'After what you've been through – if that baby wasn't determined to be born, it wouldn't be here now,' Jana said firmly.

It turned out that David's secretary had taken less than twenty-four hours to spread Chloe's problems around the office. Chloe had sunk back into the pillows once Jana had gone. How was she capable of scandalising the office on a regular basis when she thought of herself as a very uninteresting person? Still, it had been lovely of Jana to pop around, she thought. She should probably give her an easier ride at work; she realised that she'd unwittingly been treating the new secretary as suspiciously as she had Charlotte, whereas she had a feeling that Jana might make a very good confidante and ally.

Barely an hour had passed before there was another rap at the door. Chloe's heart began to thump as she heard Margaret pad down the hallway, but then sank as she heard Mikaela's horrified-sounding voice saying, 'Auntie Margaret, I didn't realise you were here.'

'I'm sure you didn't, Mikaela,' she heard her mother retort primly. 'But come on in.'

Mikaela had appeared in the lounge doorway brandishing flowers. Chloe had told her about the baby scare via text, but she hadn't expected her cousin to make an unannounced visit.

'How are you, Chlo?' she asked.

'Getting there, thanks,' Chloe replied.

Margaret had come in behind her niece, and there was an awkward silence before Mikaela looked between them and said, 'Look, I'm going to go. Sorry.'

'Oh, sit down, Mikaela,' Margaret had replied, irritated, from behind her. 'I'll go and get you a drink.'

Mikaela had sat obediently, and pulled a face at Chloe as they waited for Margaret to return. When she did, to the other women's surprise, she was carrying two large white wines on a tray as well as a water for Chloe.

Mikaela mutely took the wine, and Margaret sat down. Then Margaret looked intently at Mikaela, and Mikaela reddened. She was about to speak when Margaret said, 'For god's sake, Mikaela, just phone your mother.'

Mikaela looked down. 'I can't. She told me never to contact her again.'

'Oh, don't be silly,' Margaret snapped. 'She's always been a drama queen, your mother, you know that.' Chloe bit back the temptation to point out that it obviously ran in the family, as Margaret continued, 'but she loves you, Mikaela, and she misses you.'

'I'll only put my foot in it again,' Mikaela argued. 'And pee them all off. Really, what's the point?'

'Look –' Margaret put her wine down with some force so that liquid sloshed over the top of the glass and ran down the sides – 'I can't bear it any longer. Where do you think you get it from, Mikaela? Your mother is no saint; nor am I, for that matter. I ran off to America when I was barely eighteen, and your mother was barred from St Michael's Church for life when she was still a schoolgirl, after she was caught doing something obscene with one of her boyfriends in the church hall toilets. Our mother despaired of us, I can tell you.'

Both Mikaela's and Chloe's mouths had dropped open.

'Honestly,' Margaret said, grabbing some tissue and wiping her glass, then picking it up and heading out of the room. 'You lot imagine you are pioneers of being young and reckless. Well, think again.'

Chloe and Mikaela had watched Margaret leave, still dumbstruck. Then Mikaela turned to Chloe and wrinkled her brow. 'That is one image of Mum that I really don't want to hold on to,' she said, then cracked one of her trademark grins.

Mikaela had stayed for what seemed like hours, a captive audience for Chloe's mother, who wittered away, filling her niece in on every tiny development in the extended family over the last few years, while Chloe closed her eyes, tried to tune out the relentless voice and pretended to doze, beginning to think of ways that she might get her mother to leave, now she seemed to be getting her strength back. She definitely appreciated her mother the most in small, albeit regular, doses.

However, there was one thing she really wanted to do for her, and sooner rather than later. As evening fell, she had begun working on a letter to her brother. It wasn't easy, but she wanted Anthony back in her life, and for him to understand their mother better too. She tried to explain everything as best she could, and, as she sealed the envelope, she hoped that was enough.

She smiled grimly as she thought of her closing line. '*And in a few months you'll have a new niece or nephew to meet,*' she'd written, while thinking that Alex would soon be the last person in her life to know he was going to be a father; but, when all was said and done, he only had himself to blame for that.

98

Before Alex's lips even left hers, Amy knew he was saying goodbye. She pushed every ounce of herself into that kiss, wanting it to last forever, holding on to him, feeling the heat of him. Knowing it was for the final time.

Even though both their eyes were moist by the time they pulled away, Amy noticed that Alex's face had lost a little of the haunted look. He was making the right choice. And, really, they both knew it. It was time for each of them to move on.

But actually walking away was never going to be easy. They were stuck now, staring at one another, drinking in their last few moments together, knowing there was so much still to say; so much to be left unsaid.

'Thank you,' was all Amy could manage.

Alex shook his head, his eyes still fixed on hers, unwavering. 'There's no need.'

Amy shrugged; then they were back to standing in excruciating silence. Before long she couldn't bear it.

'Make it quick, if you're going,' she said, trying to smile.

Alex nodded. He didn't seem able to speak.

'Go on,' Amy persisted, the smile pinned to her face, betrayed by her eyes.

'I still want to help,' he said finally, his voice choked with emotion. 'There will be another court case now, and you might decide you want to . . . you still need support . . .' His voice trailed off.

Amy knew what he was referring to. In the darkness of the plane, he had asked her whether she would go looking for her little girl, and she had told him that at some point she probably would.

'Al,' she put a hand on his arm, 'you can't be all things to all people. Besides, I think that's something I need to do on my own.'

He looked momentarily hurt at this, but nodded, went back to his chair, picked up his bag, and slung it over his shoulder. Then he came across to her again, and brushed his palm against her cheek, their eyes drinking one another in.

'You'll be okay?' he asked in the same wracked voice.

'I will.'

'I think you will, too,' he agreed, nodding, looking at her with such intensity that she had trouble holding his gaze.

He began to walk backwards a few steps, still watching her. She held her breath as she registered his every movement, praying for him either to come back or turn around. His last look was so passionate and lingering that she wondered if he were about to change his mind, but then he turned quickly and almost jogged away.

She sat down and stared at Alex's half-drunk cup of coffee, the only sign now that he had been there. She had thought she would collapse at this point. But she didn't. Her body felt surprisingly light.

She picked up her own bag, turned away from the table, and set off in the opposite direction.

She knew exactly where she was going next.

99

As soon as Alex was away from the airport concourse, he took out his mobile phone and speed-dialled the familiar number. He was relieved when the call was answered, but that quickly turned to alarm when he registered the voice that had just said hello.

'Margaret?' he began, his concern increasing by the second, knowing that her visits to the south were extremely rare. 'What are you doing there? Where's Chloe?'

'Chloe hasn't been well,' she replied curtly. 'I've been looking after her.'

'Well . . . thank you,' Alex said, embarrassed. 'What's happened? Is she okay?'

'What do you think has happened, Alex?' Margaret answered, then continued snootily, 'Do you want something?'

There was no point, Alex thought, in letting his hackles rise at her tone, for her anger was completely justified. She had been looking after Chloe when that was his job.

'Can you tell Chloe I called? Please ask her to call me on my mobile.'

'Okay,' she said, as if she were going to hang up, before he cut in.

'Margaret, please tell her . . . tell her I love her.'

'I'll pass the message on, Alex,' she replied neutrally, and then the line went dead.

After checking into a hotel, Alex spent two days trying to steer around Margaret before Chloe came on the phone, and it was another twenty-four hours before she agreed to see him. In one way he found it agony, having her so close and yet being so far apart, but it was also a relief to be able to focus all his energy on putting this right. Why, at the start of all this, had he shut out the person who had brought him back to life; who, since they'd met, he had never doubted was the future he wanted?

They arranged to meet at a café not too far from home, but far enough that they were unlikely to bump into their neighbours. Alex was there three-quarters of an hour early, and soon realised that it was a mistake to sit and wait for so long, as his nervousness quadrupled every minute that went by.

Then Chloe arrived. She looked thin, and tired, and beautiful. They stared at each other, Alex trying to transmit all his apologies and love to her; while she looked like she wasn't sure whether to leave or sit down.

When she finally pulled out a chair, she said in a monotone, 'So, you're back.'

His heart sank. Her voice had no relief in it; the tone was more like resignation.

He nodded. 'It's over.'

She picked up a menu. 'Great,' she said as she looked at the food on offer, nonplussed.

He took a deep breath. Although he'd had a wild day-dream that she might fall into his arms, he was sadly aware that this cold reception was no more than he deserved.

'Have you been ill?' he asked.

'Just a bit under the weather,' she replied, waving her hand as though to dismiss his concern, but she wouldn't meet his eyes.

'Chloe,' he said, touching her arm to try to get her to look at him. 'I'm so sorry about everything I've put you through. I really am.'

Her eyes locked with his, and they were angry. 'It's too late, Alex. You should have explained yourself from the start – if not years ago.'

Upon hearing her say those three little words – *it's too late* – he felt more wretched than he ever had in his life. He bowed his head and quickly wiped his eyes.

'So why didn't you tell me any of this at the beginning?' she asked, her voice softening slightly.

'I should have. But one of the biggest regrets of my life is that I abandoned Amy when she needed me most. I was too ashamed to tell you. And when she turned up, I felt she needed me again; and that this time I owed it to her to put things right. And it meant a lot to me, too, to see those men get caught. I thought I'd laid it to rest, but once Amy came back and we found out about the trial, it was like it had never gone away. I needed to see them convicted almost as much as Amy did, I think.'

'But I'm your wife, Alex. I needed you too.'

'Yes. I'm sorry.'

'You know one of the things that hurts the most?' Chloe said. 'What makes you think that if you'd told me everything to begin with, I wouldn't have understood? Why did you think that the only way through this was shutting me out, treating me like I was invisible, as though I couldn't help you at all?'

He was dumbstruck. She was right. And he was just beginning to understand how big a fool he had been.

'. . . Unless you still love her?' she finished, still watching him closely. 'And this trip, for you, has been about making a choice?'

He paused. The moment was pivotal, he knew; the answer critical. How could he be sure of getting it right?

He couldn't, he realised. So he went for honesty, fervently hoping that this would fill rather than deepen the rift between them. He started from the beginning, explaining everything to her: the events that had taken place; the choices he had made; and the reasons behind them.

Chloe listened to it all, nodding now and again, emotions passing over her face like heavy clouds, intermittently closing down her features before they opened again a little as Alex continued.

She took her time when he had finished, letting everything he'd told her sink in.

'Was I ever a replacement?' she asked finally.

'Never.' He looked into her eyes, unflinching as she held his gaze.

'When we met . . . at the station . . . you thought I was her . . .'

'Yes,' he agreed. 'I thought you were Amy at first. Until you lifted your head. And then I saw *you*. And, Chloe, I haven't stopped seeing you since, not for a second. You are the best thing that has ever happened to me. Amy was my first love. She and I were caught up in a disaster; and it didn't work out for us. But *you* are the love of my life. *You* are my future. I'm so sorry I didn't tell you right at the beginning what was going on. It was selfish – I was worried that if I told you what happened back then, the mistakes I made, then you would see me differently, and I would see myself differently too – and I love our life, I love *us*.'

'This is . . . a lot to take in . . .' Chloe said eventually. 'But I'm sorry about what happened back then – to both of you – I just wish you hadn't shut me out.'

'I'm hoping you can forgive me for that,' he told her, 'and giving you a promise, here and now, that it won't ever happen again.'

Chloe nodded. Smiled at him for a moment, then seemed to think better of it. But still, there was a light in her eyes, a fire and energy that Alex wasn't sure he had seen before. Just having her in front of him and not being able to hold her was torture.

'It's going to take time, Alex,' she said eventually. 'If we're going to try to get back to normal. We need to take it slowly and see what happens.'

'Okay,' he agreed. His whole focus from now on would be to spend every minute of every day putting this right. He was going to try to make Chloe happier than she had dared dream she could be. 'Where do you want to start?'

She looked at him as if coming to a decision, then took a deep breath and said, 'Right here, I think.' To his surprise, she took his hand and pulled it forward, placing it over her stomach. She looked at him intently, conveying a knowledge that made his skin prickle as he realised there had been far more going on back home than he had ever imagined.

'Alex, I have something to tell you,' she began, and, in astonishment, he watched her lips moving, before there was a quick, shy flash of that lovely smile of hers, in answer to his own.

100

When Tess Duvalis opened the door, her expression was a blank of shock. She briefly put a hand out against the doorframe to steady herself, and then her face filled with joy and she moved swiftly towards her daughter, whispering, 'You're alive, you're alive, thank god, thank god'. She caught Amy in a hug so fierce that it crushed the breath from her, leaving her gasping for air, as they sobbed their relief into one another's shoulders.

Eventually, Tess let her go, and they moved into the house. Amy felt light-headed, floating.

There was so much that was unfamiliar, but the totality of the place was achingly like home. Although everything Amy was seeing was answering her questions, it was not until she made her way over to the mantelpiece that it sank in. There were old pictures of her on the wall – various school photos showing her metamorphosis from child to adult.

And on the mantelpiece, another photo – Amy, and yet not Amy.

A single photo. But it answered the one big question she hadn't dared face for all these years.

Tess came up behind her. 'She's at school,' she said.

Amy turned around and saw everything in her mother's eyes – frustration, sadness, understanding, concern, love.

Amy's voice was a sob. 'I'm so sorry.'

Tess came and held her. 'What for, my darling?'

'I left her. I just left her.'

'Yes, you left her. But you left her with a way home.'

A letter in the blanket. A number scrawled on her tummy in eyeliner, just in case the letter got lost. Such precarious links, but at the time it was all she had been capable of.

'Listen,' Amy's mother said as she held her. 'As soon as I got that call, I understood. I'm so sorry, Amy.' She stroked her daughter's hair.

Amy could barely get the words out through her grief, but gradually stuttered, 'I'm the one who should be sorry.'

'What for?' Tess asked. She moved Amy away from her, holding her by the shoulders. 'She was never a burden, Amy. She was a gift. I have been able to do things for her even if I couldn't do them for you. It has been a precious, precious link between us while you've been gone.'

'What's she like?'

Her mother smiled. 'Cheeky. Moody. Funny. Actually, she's pretty much like you.'

Suddenly Amy forgot how to breathe again. 'I need some air,' she gasped, and rushed for the back door. She flung it open and sat on the steps, her eyes closed, concentrating on the in and out of her tired, aching lungs.

Her mother sat down beside her, putting her arm around Amy, staring into the distance. When Amy looked over, she saw Tess was crying silently. She rested her head on her mother's shoulder as they sat there and let their feelings flood out of them.

After a while, in a small voice, Amy asked another question she hardly dared hear the answer to. 'Mum, did Dad die because of me?'

Tess took a deep breath and let it out in a sigh. 'Amy, of course your dad was very upset by what happened to you. But any number of things could have triggered the heart attack. He never ate very well, he drank, he'd only given up smoking a few years before. And although he was sad when you left, and wished he could have supported you more, he was always optimistic when he spoke of you. He knew you loved him; he understood why you left, even though he didn't like it, and he was sure you would come back.'

'That's the crazy thing, Mum. I was on the verge of it all the time until he died. And then I just couldn't.'

Her mother rubbed her back in reply.

As Amy looked down the garden, her gaze caught on something at the end. She jumped up and ran, until there it was.

Her garden. Their garden – in a tatty wicker basket, with new patches of moss and a few tiny flowers.

Tess came and stood behind her. 'Beth thinks she looks after it,' she said, a wry smile on her face.

Amy smiled back, overwhelmed just by hearing that name. *Beth. Her daughter.*

She fished around in the inside pocket of her jacket until she found what she was looking for, and then placed the wishing well back in the centre of the tiny garden. It settled snugly into the space it had been taken from nearly ten years ago. It looked like it had never left. She glanced briefly to the sky, then both she and her mother stared silently at the wishing well.

'I'm scared to meet her,' Amy whispered eventually.

'I know, you're bound to be,' Tess replied. 'Although, to be honest, she's like a mini-whirlwind most of the time, full of questions and energy and activity – I'm sure she'll suck you up into the madness straight away.'

Amy managed a small smile, then asked another of her endless awkward questions. 'What does Beth know about me?'

'That you're her mother. That you had to go away and you will be coming home as soon as you can. That you love her.'

'And what about . . . her father?'

Her mother sighed, tears shimmering at the edges of her eyes. 'I'm afraid I've told her he's in heaven. I didn't know what to do – I thought that might be best.'

Amy nodded. 'I think it was, at least for now,' she said.

Tess continued quietly, 'I prayed every day that you would call, so I could tell you I had got her. So you didn't have to worry.'

Amy shook her head. 'I should have, Mum, I know. But I didn't dare. I always wanted her to be here, with you, but when I let myself think about it – that letter; the phone number – they were such tenuous links to you. What if the letter was lost, or not read properly – it was a foreign country, after all. What if the number was smudged, or they didn't understand what it was? I knew if I contacted you and you didn't have her, she would probably be lost forever. And if that had been the case, it would have truly, finally broken me; I would never have found my way back from it. So it was better to be in the dark and to hope. I've only really stopped blanking things out in the past few weeks, because I've been forced to confront them.'

Then she told her mother about meeting Alex again, and the court case. Tess just listened, her eyes conveying the emotions she felt about everything Amy had been through.

When Amy had finished, they stood there in silence again, looking at the miniature garden. Then Amy asked, 'Wasn't it risky to tell her anything about me when I might not have come back? You could have told her I was dead too. Or pretended she was your own.'

Her mother's gentle hand was resting against Amy's back, as though she needed the touch to confirm all this was real. It felt heavy, but Amy didn't mind the weight.

'I never lost hope, Amy,' Tess said.

Amy looked into her mother's steadfast eyes, and saw, without the tiniest thread of doubt, someone who had never stopped knowing her or loving her or having faith in her. And, instead of drowning in each and every moment, she felt propelled at speed towards a glassy surface, gasping as she broke through. Drawing in huge lungfuls of fresh, clean oxygen. And finding, at last, that it no longer hurt to breathe.

acknowledgements

Many people have contributed to this book being published, both personally and professionally. My thanks go to: Paul Binney, for being an inspirational English teacher and helping to start the ball rolling; Nick Sayers and Patricia Parkin, for giving me my first job in publishing, which inspired me to rekindle my writing dreams; Jane Barringer, for teaching me such a lot about editing; Georgina Hawtrey-Woore, who did so much more for me than she realises; Jessica Adams, for reading some early writing and being very kind and encouraging; Tara Wynne, a fantastic agent with a super eye; Stephanie Thwaites and Alice Lutyens, for all their early help; Shuba Krishnan, for the short-lived pseudonym (RIP Eva Miller!); Sylvia Lewis, Justine McLeod and Stuart Moss-crop, for letting me quiz them; My much-loved mentor Larissa Edwards and the team at Simon & Schuster Australia; and Sophie Ambrose, who made this a much better book than it was originally. I couldn't have wished for a more delightful editor to work with.

To my circle of family and friends who make up my world, whose love and support I truly value, and who have all been very patient while waiting for this book I kept talking about to come to fruition, thanks for all the love and encouragement along the way.

There are a few special people who have gone above and beyond. First of all, my mother, Marian Agombar, who has read countless drafts of my writing and has the grace to look interested when I ask her for yet another piece of advice. You have been wonderful in so many ways. Raymond Agombar, who has known the struggles and loved me through it. Jose-phine Foster, who can really champion a girl. Karen Elgar, for always being there and making me laugh like no one else can. And my husband, Matt – you are the most amazing gift that I've ever been given, and your strength and support con-tinually replenish me. And finally, thank you Hannah and Isabelle, for lighting up our lives with your smiles and giggles. You make everything worth it.

Sara Foster

If you enjoyed *Come Back to Me*,
you'll love Sara Foster's hotly anticipated fifth novel
The Hidden Hours, available now.
Read on for a sneak peek at the first two chapters.

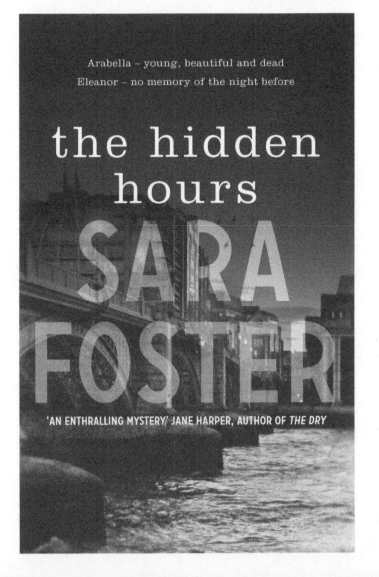

Arabella – young, beautiful and dead
Eleanor – no memory of the night before

the hidden
hours

SARA
FOSTER

'AN ENTHRALLING MYSTERY' JANE HARPER, AUTHOR OF *THE DRY*

prologue

April 2010

Tim Willis collects the manila folder and sees his last client of the day is Eleanor Brennan. Fifteen years old, with two overdoses and some self-harm under her belt already. His notes convey the weeks he's spent sitting patiently with her, getting nowhere. Her determination to shut the conversation down had proved a match for anything he could offer. She'd told him, more than once, that she was only here because her mother had begged her to come.

Until last week. They had been going through the same motions when he had pressed her for a happy memory. To his surprise, she'd suddenly started to talk. She'd told him a sweet story about her family, how her father had a party trick he'd learned as a kid. A Japanese friend had taught him how to make paper cranes, and he often used to fold them while Eleanor slept, leaving them on her pillow. She had vague memories of them in her cot; clearer recollections of them appearing next to her in her first big bed.

However, her father had stopped doing this when he lost his job, she'd explained quietly. Although by then her older brother Aiden had learned to copy him. For a while, scruffier cranes would sometimes land next to her while she slept, the white paper blotched with thumb prints. Then Aiden had stopped too, when they moved.

'Did you ever feel that these birds were their way of telling you they loved you?' Tim had asked gently.

Eleanor had gone rigid at the question. Her face paled; her hazel eyes widened. She had stared at him wordlessly for a moment, before letting out a guttural groan as she folded into herself and sobbed with her forehead on her knees. *Hallelujah*, Tim had thought as he watched her fragile body quivering, *finally we're getting somewhere.*

His step is light today, as he clutches the folder and heads towards the waiting room. He rounds the doorway and sees Eleanor and her mother sitting next to one another. 'Hello,' he says in his friendliest tone.

Gillian Brennan responds, but her smile is forced. Eleanor ignores him. As soon as Tim sees her stiff posture and averted gaze he knows they have somehow gone backwards.

'Ready, Eleanor?' he asks brightly.

She still won't meet his eye as she gets up to follow him. *Damn*, he thinks, as he closes his office door and they take their seats. He tries not to show his disappointment, readjusting his focus towards this traumatised girl in front of him, who still desperately needs his help.

'All right then,' he says, his mind busily searching for new ways to reach her. 'It's good to see you, Eleanor. How are you today?'

1

an announcement

December 2016

*T*he body bobs lightly against the grey stone wall, ensnared by something unseen, resisting the current. A police diver slowly untangles it, and gently pushes it towards the waiting boat. People watch from the footbridge, transfixed. Some cover their mouths with gloved hands, pointing, gasping, retching. Others clutch their phones in a chokehold. One woman takes furtive pictures. They are all relieved it hangs face down in the cold, murky river. No one wants to see the person to whom that long blonde hair once belonged.

The body floats towards waiting hands. A tiny crab scuttles down the slim line of one of those ghostly white legs and disappears into the gloom.

Three hours later

Eleanor joins the back of the crowd and waits. She is shivering, desperate to sit down; her head pounds and her legs ache. The air is rife with murmurs and confusion. No one wants to be here. Only a handful of people are already aware of the chain reaction of events that began at dawn.

The message had pinged up on screen five minutes ago, summoning the entire workforce to the courtyard *immediately*. Eleanor had grabbed her bag then followed the group from her office, eavesdropping, with no one to talk to. She had prayed this wouldn't take long, because she couldn't shake the nausea that had been there since she woke up.

The last of the morning's frost still glitters on the ledges of doors and windows. Bulging grey clouds obscure the sky, and the cobblestones are slippery from overnight rain. Eleanor hugs herself, wrapping her cardigan tightly around her, in part to keep her warm but also to hide her unironed cheap white blouse, as she shifts apprehensively from foot to foot. She is still getting used to the eviscerating coldness of London in December.

The courtyard is surrounded by red-brick office blocks, hidden from the street, connected to the main road by one narrow, high-walled passageway with security gates at either end. The open space is lined with huge trees set in man-size pots, silver tinsel winding down each trunk, and on the northern side a wide flight of stairs marks the entrance to Parker & Lane, one of the book industry's darlings, already crowned Children's Publisher of the Year for the third year running.

There must be well over a hundred people now, and more keep arriving as the minutes tick by. They are a jittery bunch, huddling together, waiting for someone to tell them what is going on. It's a far cry from the pictures of this courtyard that line the foyer walls just inside the entrance to Parker & Lane – famous authors holding wine glasses, a blur of smiling faces just out of focus, and the backdrop of tall trees festooned with multicoloured lights.

Eleanor's gaze drifts over the crowd, but she doesn't recognise anyone. She's only been working here for three weeks, there has not been much time to form friendships, but from what she can gather, this company-wide summons is unheard of. Snippets of speculation swirl through the air. An emergency drill? A company collapse? A takeover, maybe? Immediate redundancies just weeks before Christmas? Surely not.

Each conversation begins to float away, one after another, until the only sound is of someone clearing their throat. Eleanor follows the collective gaze and looks upwards. The black-and-white sign for PARKER & LANE stands proudly above the triplet revolving doors, and just above that, on a small balcony, is Caroline Cressman from HR, wringing her hands as though she has forgotten her lines. Eleanor has a horrible urge to shout, *Deny thy father and refuse thy name!* as she had once needed prompting herself in high school. She stays quiet, but her heart is restless – every few seconds she feels it stall and tenses, willing the next beat. Everybody is hushed, waiting.

'I will only keep you a moment – this is the one place we could gather you all together at once.' There's a discernible tremor to Caroline's voice. She takes a deep, shaky breath. 'I am so very sorry to tell you all . . .'

Eleanor's thoughts tip, beginning to gain speed. Something big is coming.

'. . . that Arabella Lane has passed away.'

Shock steals the air from Eleanor's lungs. The scene before her disintegrates; she is powerless to stop it. *This cannot be true*, she thinks. *It cannot be true.*

She waits for the collective gasp, but there is nothing, absolutely nothing. Perhaps it doesn't seem real to anyone else. Perhaps they are thinking, as she is, that only a few hours ago their Director of Marketing and Publicity had been very much alive at the Christmas party – drinking and dancing, working the crowd, her face animated, her body in constant, seamless motion.

A few images strobe through Eleanor's mind. Arabella is dead, and Eleanor knows what a dead body looks like. Parched in places and purple in others. A waxen effigy of a real person. Nothing like Arabella.

A distant memory rises swiftly, like a vulture startled from carrion. It draws closer, and closer, until Eleanor can feel its black wings beating against her neck and she ducks away, terrified, her legs buckling from under her. Coins tumble from her pocket as she hits the cobblestones.

For a moment she is no longer twenty-one. Instead she is nine years old again, standing in a small room in the middle of the Australian outback. A body swings in front of her, his face obscured by flies, and the tips of his toes skim-kiss the floor, as though he were almost through a jump when that rope twisted and caught him, slicing across the bulge of his neck.

Without realising, she flings her arms over her head, trying to protect herself from the memory, before the vision can fully claim her. Nevertheless, she begins to dry-retch.

'Eleanor,' someone is close by, talking to her. 'You okay, Eleanor?'

She remembers where she is.

Arabella is dead.

Elegant, graceful Arabella, who plays with her hair while she talks, whose bangles jangle when she moves, whose laugh can make you smile even when you haven't heard the conversation.

Arabella is dead.

She opens her eyes. It's Will Clayton, the art director, leaning over her. His thick eyebrows frame his concerned expression. She's got to know him a little over the past few weeks, has enjoyed their flirtatious banter, particularly in contrast to the disinterested glances of others. However, now his face is grim and pale as he offers her a hand and sets her on her feet. He picks up the loose change and hands it to her, his fingers cold but his touch a reassuring link to reality.

She's alert enough to nod, although she's not okay at all. She feels for her bag, pats the strap looped over her shoulder, and clutches it close. Those in the vicinity have all turned to watch them. She wants them to stop looking at her – she wants to go back to being invisible.

Luckily, Caroline helps out. 'There will be an investigation,' she wails above them, hiccupping her words, seemingly ignorant of what's happening below. 'Her body was found near Waterloo Bridge at dawn.'

There are sobs. Someone cries out. It's real now.

'The police will be here shortly to take statements about Arabella's last few hours, and we ask you all to cooperate fully. There will be rooms made available for the process, and we will also have places set aside for those who need somewhere to take a breather.' She takes a big breath herself. 'Or if you would like to pray. Please come and see us, or talk to your manager and tell them what you need.' She pauses. 'Our hearts go out to Nathan ...' Her voice breaks. 'And to all of Arabella's family and friends. There will be further announcements shortly as to how we might best support them in the terrible days ahead.'

Nathan. Eleanor feels a stab of horror at the mention of Arabella's husband. It's been hard enough temping for him these past few weeks, but she has no idea what the duties of a PA might involve for a grieving man. She tries to soften the antipathy she has felt for him, reminding herself of what he must be going through, but all she feels is numb.

Will hovers beside her, until a colleague leans forward and whispers in his ear. He nods, gives Eleanor a brief pat on the arm. 'Are you all right now?' As soon as she nods, he turns to leave.

Quickly, Eleanor turns her focus to the day that looms ahead of her, and is overcome with dread. Instinctively, she searches the melee for Susan. She will help, won't she? But Eleanor can't see her anywhere among the crowd, or on the balcony. Surely, as the company CEO, Susan Mortimer should be here?

Caroline has gone as suddenly as she appeared, and people begin to disperse. Most walk in stunned silence – a few have their arms around one another, holding on tight. Some go towards the main entrance, while others head around the side of the building for the fire exit that leads to an internal set of stairs. Eleanor decides to follow the latter group. She needs to drag out every second she can while she tries to wrap her thoughts around what this means. She feels feverish, gripping the banister tightly as she makes her way to the second floor. Her bag bangs against her side with its new weight of guilt, as though she were concealing a murder weapon.

She attempts to recall the previous evening from start to finish, but there are hot knives in her brain, pressing against half-formed memories that fail to trigger. She knows she talked to Arabella for a while, but her last recollections of the party are hazy, recalled through a blur of dry ice and spinning faces.

In a daze, she interrupts a small group that has congregated in the stairwell, two women leaning together, crying heavily, while another woman clasps a tissue in a shaky hand and pats one of her pals on the back. '*She was planning her thirtieth birthday just last night,*' one sobs. '*She said she wanted to go to Paris.*' Eleanor almost apologises for the intrusion, then realises they are absorbed in their grief. She passes by them unnoticed, a will-o'-the-wisp lost in daylight.

As she makes her way through the office, some people are already back at their desks, frowning at their screens, looking for answers, or just an escape. Or perhaps they have no choice but to carry on. In the brief time she's been here, Eleanor has come to understand that daily deadlines and crazy hours are part of most people's work ethic.

She passes the closed doors of management, aware of stricken voices and low murmurs. She glances past the hanging Christmas decorations – oversized baubles gently twirling as the heat from the radiators rises – and instead keeps her gaze fixed on Nathan's door at the far end of the office. Just to the left of it, behind a partition, is her own desk. She hurries past giant cardboard cut-outs of *Smoky the Cat* and *The Pig That Could Fly* – two of Parker & Lane's recent acquisitions. Their strong lines, clear colours and gaping smiles don't seem to belong here anymore. Her legs feel weightless and hardly under her control as she staggers towards refuge. She needs to hide awhile and try to compose herself.

Relief washes over her as she reaches the partition. Until she sees the CEO of Parker & Lane sitting in her chair.

Susan's right elbow rests on the files that Eleanor was meant to stow back in the cabinet yesterday, while her left hand has crept across to open Eleanor's sketchbook, and she is flicking through the pictures, her head down.

Eleanor is furious at this breach of privacy. 'That's private,' she says, before she can help herself.

Susan looks up, her eyes red and weary. She stands up, fingertips smoothing the sides of her sleek black hair, which is pulled tight into a bun. She closes the book without a word, straightening her Chanel suit jacket, while Eleanor's throat burns with the abruptness of her words. She swallows, trying to absorb her anger into something more palatable. She knows that Susan holds virtually all the cards to her life right now. She's not only her boss, but also her landlord. And her aunt.

They have had an uneasy relationship from day one. When Eleanor's uncle had invited her to stay in their Notting Hill home when she arrived in London, she hadn't expected such a frosty reception from his wife. They had known of one another for over ten years, but had never met until three weeks ago, and Susan was not at all what Eleanor had expected. She suspects the feeling might be mutual.

Susan is scrutinising her, making no attempt to smile. Eleanor can't think of the right thing to say, but she tries. 'I'm so sorry about Arabella.'

Susan sighs and looks away for a brief moment. Then she fixes Eleanor with a stare. 'You look dreadful. Do you want to go home? I can get Priscilla to take over here today, there will no doubt be phone calls from the press, and from authors. I don't expect you to have to deal with all that. We'll figure out something else for you to do on Monday.'

She doesn't know, Eleanor thinks. *She doesn't know I spoke to Arabella last night, or she'd tell me to talk to the police.*

And yet, unintentionally or not, Susan is throwing her a lifeline. This is her chance to escape, to gain time, to think over what to do before she has to tell anybody what she's concealing. Instinctively she pats the cloth of her bag, wondering if she has made this up. Can it really be happening?

'Thank you, Susan.' She reaches over and grabs her sketchbook, slipping it into her bag. She's about to turn to go when Susan says, 'Oh, and Eleanor . . .'

Before she can reply she hears heels clacking quickly down the corridor. She turns at the noise and finds Caroline hurrying towards them, faint streaks of mascara on her cheeks.

'Susan, Sky News are setting up outside the building,' Caroline says breathlessly, eyes shining like a startled animal.

Whatever Susan was going to say to Eleanor is forgotten. She smooths her hands over her knitted jacket, then says softly, 'And here we go.'

Eleanor watches them leave, before collecting up the paperwork on her desk and pushing it back into her in-tray. Then she grabs her coat and hurries towards the stairwell, anxious to be gone before any more news crews arrive. Her temporary status requires her to sign in and out at reception, and once downstairs she heads quickly across to the logbook, which is left permanently open at the front desk. Two of the receptionists are deep in discussion.

'I just cannot believe she would jump off a bridge,' one of them is saying.

'Me neither,' the other replies. 'She was always such a happy person.'

For a moment, Eleanor cannot move the pen in her hand. *Not last night, she wasn't.*

Before they can engage her in the gossip, she turns towards the doors. She sees a cameraman screwing something on to the front of his camera. The reporter clutches his microphone to his chest like he has just caught a bridal bouquet. Two lackeys have been tasked with holding umbrellas over the men, to protect them from the persistent rain.

They all look at Eleanor as she exits the building, but before they can decide if she is important enough to accost, she has hurried down the passageway, waved her key card at the exit gate and continued towards the main road beyond. She pauses a moment, her head spinning in this shining world where the shops twinkle with Christmas lights and an accordionist plays 'Jingle Bells' and the cars are adorned with reindeer antlers and all is merry and bright. She takes a few gulps of air to steady herself, and then she sets off for the tube, for Uncle Ian, for some semblance of safety.